CHALLENGE

Books by George Foy

Asia Rip

Coaster

Challenge

George Foy

CHAL

LENGE

VIKING

SEP 1 2 1988

VIKING
Published by the Penguin Group
Viking Penguin Inc., 40 West 23rd Street,
New York, New York 10010, U.S.A.
Penguin Books Ltd, 27 Wrights Lane, London W8 5TZ
(Publishing & Editorial) and Harmondsworth, Middlesex,
England (Distribution & Warehouse)
Penguin Books Australia Ltd, Ringwood,
Victoria, Australia
Penguin Books Canada Limited, 2801 John Street,
Markham, Ontario, Canada L3R 1B4
Penguin Books (N.Z.) Ltd, 182–190 Wairau Road,
Auckland 10 New Zealand

Penguin Books Ltd, Registered Offices:
Harmondsworth, Middlesex, England

First published in 1988 by Viking Penguin Inc.
Published simultaneously in Canada

Illustration on title page courtesy of
the Bettmann Archive.

LIBRARY OF CONGRESS CATALOGING IN PUBLICATION DATA
Foy, George.
  Challenge.
  I. Title.
PS3556.099C4   1988   813'.54   87-40464
ISBN 0-670-81727-9

Printed in the United States of America by
Arcata Graphics, Fairfield, Pennsylvania
Set in Caslon 540
Design by Kathryn Parise

For my parents

Many people helped in the research and production of this book, among them Gerry Brown, Sterling Lord, Elizabeth Kaplan, Gerry Howard, Roger Marshall, Captain Fred McKnight, C. A. Crosby Jr., John Marshall, John Airison, Jim Herman, F. M. Schaefer, George Day, Ned Goetchius and family, Arthur Brountas, John Bigwood, Erik Palin, Hali Jones, David Runnion, Dr. Louise Godine, and Pam Hepburn.

CHALLENGE

C H A P T E R 1

Suzanne came back to Paul Briggs that night, in her usual way, full of guilt and promises whose ruin was part of their attraction.

The details were very strong: she perched cross-legged on the counter, drank thin yogurt with both hands, hummed on the toilet.

He sucked it all down like an alcoholic, aware of his addiction and its consequences, unable to live without: and when she left, as he'd always known she would, the agony was a friend, and in any case more welcome than waiting for it.

The end came familiar: a car, skidding out of control, down a darkness so complete speed had no meaning—till the shock, the unbelievable noise, the instant flood of flames, their fierce heat curling skin from flesh that could not move to save itself. . . .

Paul woke up as he often did, both arms wrapped around his face, screaming without a sound.

Even after he'd got some of his bearings back he remained in this position.

Their bedroom, his house. The blend of wood smoke and mildew was unmistakable. The smells brought their own freight of memories, but these belonged to waking dreams, relatively easy to blank out, or at least control. He opened his eyes.

The ceiling stretched above his head, familiar in broad white planks.

The moon poured silver in squares through his windows.

His sheets were soaked in sweat.

The crackle of fire faded, was eaten by the greater silence.

Paul groaned and rolled over to look at his clock. 3:07 A.M., it declared, in brash digital bars.

He shifted to the other, dryer side of the double bed and sought sleep again, but the dream had set his adrenaline flowing, turned the night behind his eyelids into a place filled with heartburn. His mind rang with voices he could not quite identify, tempting, pleading, touting the fast luxuries of despair. Like winter rain the voices whispered and spoke of pain that never ends.

After a while he stopped trying to force what could only come with letting go. Switching on the light, he picked up a book from his bedside table.

Suzanne, his vanished wife, watched him from a Lucite frame beside the dormer window. The photo of Nicole, his lost child, hung by the bookcase. Lamplight quenched the moon, turning the windows black. Electricity had driven out the voices as well, but now, perversely, it was the silence that pounded at his ears, loud with absence.

Paul got out of bed, put on his clothes and went downstairs, kicking laundry from underfoot, collecting dirty coffee mugs.

There was no sound from his younger daughter's door, but Nat was in the living room.

Nat rented a downstairs bed, along with couch space and kitchen privileges in exchange for a hundred dollars a month and occasional baby-sitting.

It was hard to tell whether Nat was awake or asleep because in either state he kept the TV on and looked exactly the same, lying prone on the sofa under three sleeping bags. In this case you could tell he was conscious because he held a glass of milk in one hand and the remote control in the other as he flipped through channels on satellite TV, looking for reruns of "M*A*S*H."

"Sit down, chief," Nat said, taking off his earphones and turning up the volume. "This is a good one. This is the one where Radar sneaks a nurse into Charles's bed."

"Narr," growled Paul; he had trouble at the best of times escaping the hangover of sleep, and sleep taken over by the fire-dream could stay with him for hours.

In the window he could see the moon lurk fat and full behind maple skeletons, igniting dead leaves wherever it touched. Shadows stretched that much darker across the glowing hills. The dream was always strongest at the full moon, he remembered. He went into the kitchen to brew coffee.

If the rest of the house looked like a war zone, the kitchen was the business end of a car bombing. Half-empty plates occupied every horizontal space. Someone had taken out the stove in bursts of red, meat-flavored spaghetti sauce. The floor was thick with "Diet-dinner" trays. It took Paul five minutes to find the espresso filter. The coffee was in the bread box, for some reason, behind a Mason Jar filled with sprouting beans for Jessica's natural science project. He really should clean the house, Paul thought vaguely, if only for Jessica's sake. This was no environment for a six-year-old to grow up in. When Nicole was her age the house had been tidy as an engineer's fantasy.

Nicole's dimple, Suzanne's grin. They played in his brain, behind his eyes, a private screening even caffeine could not stop. He added rum and brought the mixture to the alcove but did not drink it at once, let it steam before him instead, his own private hearth against the dark. Suzanne's avocado plants cried soundlessly for water beside the alcove windows. They had been dying, on and off, for three years.

When the spell of first coffee began to fade he put a cassette of Beethoven's Second Symphony on the tape player. Turning to the bookshelf, he yanked out a volume of Nathanael Herreshoff boat designs and flipped through them without plan.

There were only two designers represented in the book: Paul's father and Nathanael Herreshoff.

John Briggs's drawings were rough, drawn with heavy pencil on cheap paper that had yellowed and stiffened with age.

The Herreshoff designs were smooth, finished, clipped from books made of good vellum.

Out of habit, the scrapbook fell open at the *Maria*, the racing schooner that made his father famous along the Maine coast a long time ago.

Paul kept going, stroking the pages over so as not to loose the inserts. Past Herreshoff's *Istalena*. Past the *Maria*. Looking for lines that meshed with his mood. Until he came to the *Persephone*.

The *Persephone* was a fifty-foot Herreshoff ketch with a long stern, a spoon-shaped bow. The curve to her hull struck an almost perfect balance between fullness and length. The lines seemed to flow and come together with a harmony only Beethoven could match. You could almost feel how that boat would slip through the water before the sea even knew it was there.

Before his family fell apart he'd believed such lines were within his grasp, believed he might perhaps improve on them, if it were possible, using new techniques he would bring in at the yard: reduce the draft a touch, add a small skeg keel, gently fair in the buttock line, come up with a design for glass-and-epoxy laminate that would have the looks of the Herreshoff boat but would be faster and cheaper to build. . . . Paul looked around for a pencil. He dumped three half-full bags of cheese-flavored potato chips off the table. Two coloring books, on dogs and colonial costumes, and a month's worth of sports pages followed, to no avail. There were no pencils by the phone. The kid had to eat pencils, he thought, the way they disappeared.

"Nat," he yelled, and went into the living room.

"Wait—this is where Charles says, 'My blood may be blue but I'm as red-blooded as the next American,' " Nat recited, invisible from under the sleeping bags. "Jesus, Winchester."

"Is there a pencil in this house?"

"Pencil? What you want a pencil for?"

Paul adjusted the thermostat, looked for his jacket. "You going out tomorrow?" he asked, "I mean, today."

"Dunno." Nat beeped the TV off for a commercial. "Squidlips hasn't called. Don't think so."

"I wanna go down the boatyard. Work on something. You think you'll be here till six maybe, keep an eye on Jessica, case she wakes up?"

"Work on something, chief? With a pencil? Since when you use a pencil? I thought you only use computers now."

One intelligent eye peered from under a fold of nylon down. It took in six feet worth of Paul—bony frame, even features, gaze level as a draftsman's rule. The thick black hair held a natural cowlick that he was always trying to brush back. With ease of practice Nat's eye skipped the blotch of scar tissue on his chin and neck. "I'll stay here till six," he offered. "It's too damn cold to go lobstering, anyway."

"But Squidlips—"

"Screw Squidlips."

"He'll fire you."

"So he fires me."

"So how you gonna pay the rent?"

"I'll make the rent, chief. Besides, you won't kick me out. I mean, who's gonna keep this place neat if I'm not around?"

Paul laughed, despite himself. Nat stuck out a bare ankle and scratched it. At the foot of the couch a mass of fat and fur heaved, raised an arthritic paw, and clawed hard at an area five inches from the point it was aiming for, to flatter its master with imitation. Paul gave the dog a pat and half a bologna-cheese sandwich from under the couch before climbing the stairs to Jessica's room.

In the glow of night-light he could see her mouth half-open, drooling onto a flowered pillow. He envied her this oblivion. One small hand throttled a gingham dog. She slept as hard as she played. A minute of hearing her breathe and the dissonant rhythms that had intruded on his night were already smoothing out. Maybe this time he could draw something clean, Paul thought, and touched his younger daughter's hair, very softly, as if innocence rubbed off on fingers.

Outside, the temperature was already dipping below twenty, though it was not yet Halloween. Paul put on felt boots and ski gloves. He let the car warm up, then drove off.

The village was asleep. Only the Diner and the cubicle where Sam Gilbert's kid dozed in a nest of yellow light, waiting to raise the drawbridge for shrimp boats, lower it for ice trucks, kept watch against the sea.

When he took the turn to the boatyard, hard frost groaned beneath his radials. In the frozen mud of the drive, straight tire tracks crossed more complex spoor of deer, rabbit, and coon. The headlights froze a possum beside Number Five Quonset. Then again, why fool with perfection? Paul asked himself. He could turn around, make more coffee, add rum, clean the kitchen. Comfortable, familiar. No one was about to match the boats Herreshoff had drawn. Not even Jack. Not even Jack's Twelve-Meter.

He was almost there. Strange shapes loomed on either side. A stem here, a rudder, a prop somewhere else betrayed where boats, hauled for the winter, hunched unhappy under blankets of dead leaves and plastic. Behind them the crazed shingles of Briggs and Sons' Boatyard measured the blackness of Eel Pond.

He parked the wagon by the chandlery and walked around the glare of yard lights to the door of the woodworking shop, expecting Old George to bumble out of the shadows, hiding pint bottles in deep pockets, feigning alertness. George or Bobby, the new guard from the security company in Portland. Bobby, who watched over the Twelve-Meter shed.

No one stirred. Old George would be snoring in the paint store. From this angle Paul could see a wide square of neon reflected against the tar-paper peak of the sail loft. The lights to the drafting room. Jack must have left them on last night, he thought, groping in his coat for the keys.

The cold made his scars ache. Frost crystals sneaked down his exposed neck as a breeze dusted the shed's roof. The door to the shop swung open an inch, two inches, and back. It hadn't been locked to begin with.

For the first time a sense of unease touched at Paul's mind. Even George, simple as he was, always remembered to lock the door. Paul pushed it open, stepped inside, and felt for the switch.

To the uninitiated a boat shop looked like hell's backyard, a frozen storm of sawdust, planks, pipes, band saws, chisels, strange "knees" and augers and paintbrushes; all scattered in mad disarray, impossible to find anything in.

A boat builder, however, saw in the same boat shop a finely controlled ballet where a thousand different bits of bronze, lead, resin, wood, pigment, nylon, and canvas all came together and separated and came together again in a choreography as precise as Balanchine's.

There was absolutely nothing out of place in Number One shed. Saws hung by their felt-tipped outlines on the wall; the wood stove glowed, gently banked against the cold; vapor seeped thin from the steam box, softening white oak for the sloop curving on timber props before him. The cadence of boat building vibrated in every scarred stud and rafter, in every length of mast or boom stored by his father or his father's father and left to be forgotten until the right job came by for son or grandson to finish; it hung in the taste of manila and varnish and paint, ready to pick up where the beat had stopped, yesterday, at four in the afternoon, closing time.

Paul walked through the shed and checked the ways. The Thomsons' dragger sat huge and uncomfortable, waiting for a rebuilt engine. Its deep hull smelled of bait and salt and dead sailors. Its wheelhouse windows reminded him of eyes tuned to far horizons, blinded by walls, desperate to find sky again.

To his right stood sliding doors leading to the new shed where the test-tank models for the Twelve-Meter lay in a sleek loneliness of glass-fiber; but the electronic locks had not been touched, the door had not been tampered with, and there was no other way into the workshop, not even windows, for security reasons.

Beside the door, the panel of alarms protecting the Twelve-Meter shed winked cheerful green dots at him. If anyone moved in there he was as cold as the plastic he looked for and displaced no air to set off the delicate gauges.

Anyway, Paul was out of that project; from now on it was Jack's baby, his concern. In fact, the light in the drafting room might even indicate his cousin was still here, working all night on details for the "damn Twelve," as some of the carpenters in the yard referred to the *Challenge*.

The syndicate Jack worked for wanted the boat finished by summer. They wanted a good ten months to test it before the first races of the America's Cup, nineteen months away. That kind of deadline made late nights the rule rather than the exception.

Yet Jack, more than anyone, would make sure the doors were locked behind him. Paul found his feet hurrying, forced himself to slow down. Where in hell was the new guard?

The drafting loft hung off the sides of the main shed, twenty feet over the system of tracks and carriages leading through huge doors to the harbor outside. The indoor windows were on a level with the Thomsons' radar scanner. It was close to high tide, and as he climbed the stairs water lay black as oil, creeping up as if to reclaim boats hauled in the shadows beneath Paul's feet.

There was no one in the outer office; gloom reigned where the accounts were done. Paul approached the light. He opened the glass door to the main room and stopped dead.

A natural disaster was his first impression, closely followed by the clicking updates of logic: nothing wrong with the rest of the shop;

no winds, no tornadoes to make such a mess in one room only; it had to be men, thieves, who had left the front door unlocked in fleeing. He pushed the door—it moved reluctantly against some obstruction—took a step into the room.

Ordinarily this was a cheerful, open place, an old countinghouse arrangement whose high desks had been replaced by long architect's tables. Wide, double-glazed windows and a new skylight let in natural illumination. Green-painted barn boards, shelves of drafting equipment. Sheaves of sketches, precisely stacked. The ancient safe in one corner, a modern computer system in another.

Remembered neatness made the room's present state that much more obscene. Two of the four design tables had been turned over. Blueprints were scattered everywhere. Computer printouts spiraled in purple streamers, back and forth across the room.

Drawers lay upended: erasers, pens, pencils, compasses, slide rules, splines, curves, dividers, quills, planimeters, thumbtacks, and triangles—all the tools, the hoarded angles of the naval architect's trade lay scattered where they had been flung.

"What the—" Paul whispered, breath catching in his throat. He pushed harder at the door, for space to swing his torso. A shoe swiveled at the base of his vision.

A man lay twisted in the corner, next to the baseboard, one leg blocking the doorway's arc.

The shoe was a Maine hunting boot, the hair was dirty blond except for a small patch the size of a half-dollar where blood had flowed briefly, and crusted over. Corduroys, fashionably cut, enclosed the leg. The hand was big, familiar—familiar, and so still—

"Jack!" someone yelled. Paul jumped over the body and dropped to his knees. "Jack." It was his voice doing the shouting, Paul realized. He made himself go slow, grab the shoulder, shake him gently, what the hell good would that do, what in God's name was wrong with him? "Jack," he repeated desperately, "it's me, wake up."

Neck wounds, head wounds, be careful how you move him. Stop hyperventilating, for chrissake. His pulse, feel his pulse. The throat was warm, but not warm enough, his blood pressure must be down, shock, can't be anything else. Carotid artery, left-hand side, have to pull him over a little, sorry Jack, oh Christ his eyes are half-open, he used to sleep that way sometimes when he was a kid, overnights giggling at knock-knock jokes. There was blood on the floor where his right ear had lain, and nothing, no pulse at all, where Paul's fingers touched, at the depression between windpipe and neck tendons, not higher up or lower down or sideways.

A draftsman's "duck"—a heavy, whale-shaped piece of lead used to hold curves on a blueprint—lay on the floor beside him.

"Jack," Paul whispered, and turned his cousin all the way over. He shook him hard, harder. His glasses fell off. Jack's left eye was bruised. The panic rose in Paul's throat, paralyzing his thoughts, making him want to vomit, faint, sleep, go back in time, escape in any way possible. He closed his eyes briefly to clear perception.

When he reopened them he saw, with a brief surge of hope like April in his chest, that maybe it was not Jack after all. The features were different, unfamiliar, weighted in odd ways; but that was only because he had lost his glasses, because a face was a medley of little springs and catches that worked against the life force and there was no life force here and Jack was dead.

Paul grabbed his cousin's body around the shoulders. Slowly, with great difficulty—he seemed impossibly heavy now—he pulled him to a sitting position.

A floppy disc Jack was lying on lost its purchase on his sweater and slipped to the floor.

Paul braced the lolling head and held him in a posture only living forms could take, seeking, at a level far below thought, the grace of sympathetic magic.

C H A P T E R 2

When the phone rang, fracturing the night into a million pieces, Paul did not flinch, but lowered his cousin's body with great care to the boards and got up, steadily, to answer it.

"Jack?" A woman's voice, husky, intimate. It broke into the void around Paul's stomach. "Jack, what in God's name are you doing?"

"Ashley."

"It's—it's four o'clock in the morning."

"Ashley, it's Paul."

"Paul?" Her voice took on wariness whenever they talked. So did his own. "But—I'm sorry. I'm looking for Jack. He—I didn't—I mean, he's not here. He's not there?" she finished, lamely.

Paul had to sit down all of a sudden. He propped himself on Sally's desk.

"Ashley, something really serious, I—" His courage collapsed. "We—I need you to come down here. Right away."

"What's going on? Paul, what's wrong?"

"Please, Ashley. Don't ask any questions. Just come. Now."

Paul hung up, or tried to. The phone bounced off its hook. His fingers were trembling. He changed his mind, picked up the receiver, dialed the emergency number, dutifully filled in blanks offered by an officious voice at the other end—location, name of victim, name of caller. Type of emergency: death. Murder, in fact. Some thieving son of a bitch had killed his cousin Jack, but Paul would find the man and kill him. She told him to get off the phone.

He went to kneel by Jack's side again, his mind drifting behind the shock. What would he tell Ashley when he saw her. She and Jack had been married only a couple of years. He would not think about last Labor Day; that was so out of joint it was part of a different world altogether. In any case, Jack had never found out.

He didn't want to think about that. He didn't want to think about Suzanne either. She had been very fond of Jack. He wondered once again if his wife kept any channel open when she left, if someone would tell her of this, a week or a month from now, third- or fourth-hand. . . .

The last time he'd talked to his cousin they had argued over diverting more of the yard's resources to the America's Cup effort. How corny, he thought, and punched the wall. With the blow something cracked in his glaze of shock and tears seeped through to his eyes. Warm, treacherous, the tears melted his chest, allowing spasms he had to fight to control.

The sirens came first, bouncing red light through the windows. Shouts from downstairs. An emergency medical technician from the fire department, Red Burke from the town police.

Paul went to the stairs to call them up; they spoke short phrases to emphasize their control over random events.

"You called in?"

"What's the problem."

"Where's the victim."

"In there." Paul gestured at the door.

They walked fast, equipment squeaking. The paramedic put his tool kit down in the corner next to Jack's head, felt his pulse, put a mirror at his mouth, touched his face. Paul, for some reason, kept seeing Jack fixing his plastic battleships, biting his tongue in concentration, the fumes from model cement pricking their nostrils. The *Yamato* had been his favorite.

"He's been dead for some time," the paramedic said, and zipped away his stethoscope. "An hour at least. You didn't give him mouth-to-mouth, did you?" Paul shook his head.

Red Burke looked at the corpse briefly, then kept his eyes averted as he quizzed the paramedic. Finally the deputy took Paul back into Sally's room and made him sit down.

"Did you see anybody? I mean, anybody else."

"No."

"I've called the state police," Burke went on. "You know it looks like he was killed. I mean, on purpose."

Paul stared at him. Burke's face was very white, he noticed.

"He was murdered," Paul agreed quietly. "It's not fair."

The mask of authority slipped for a moment. "I know you guys were close," Burke began.

Paul nodded. The policeman turned, found his eyes seeking the door to the drafting room, dragged them hastily back.

"I have to ask you this," he added, pulling out a book full of tickets. "What time you found him, when you last seen him?"

Paul responded mechanically but felt his mind start to slide away from the proceedings again, back into the past, sidelong into irrelevance. A lot of this grief stemmed from fear; fear came from the weakness inherent in losing a partner. A buddy. Loneliness was fear. Together they might have built some wonderful boats, if Jack had not gone overboard on Twelves and all their sham and glory.

Burke sucked at his pen in concentration, wrote the facts on speeding summonses. "It's unbelievable," he muttered after every notation, or else, "Holy Jee-zus."

More feet stomped up the stairs, men's feet.

Two Maine state troopers walked in, boots gleaming, badges polished. A sergeant and a patrol officer. Paul did not recognize either of them but the sight of their Smokey hats brought the old frustration back in full force.

The staties flashed Polaroids of the scene and dropped the lead "duck" in a plastic bag. One of them had a constant half-smile on his face. They both chewed gum. They repeated Burke's questions and asked some of their own. Paul found it impossible to talk to the one who smirked. In the middle of a question Paul heard the sound he'd been dreading. He held up a hand and even the troopers fell silent.

A high, female voice cut through the ambulance driver's bass. A frantic tripping sounded on the stairs. Ashley burst into the office. Her face was rigid but her makeup was perfect. Platinum hair, tied back in a ponytail; square chin, nice lips, straight nose. She and Jack made a handsome couple. Their wedding pictures looked like an ad for expensive whiskey.

"Oh, no," she said when she saw Burke. Her eyes locked on Paul. "Where's Jack."

Paul took a step toward her, his hands out, open, a stupid gesture. He tried to speak but his throat was knotted tight and all he could manage was a croak past the dryness: "Ashley."

"What's happened, is he sick?" Her eyes swerved toward the door, where the paramedic was unfolding a body bag. "Oh, my God," she said, and covered her mouth with both hands.

Burke caught her before she got to the door. "No," he told her, shaking his head very forcefully; death tonight was a presence too close to name out loud.

She understood right away, but refused to believe it, it wasn't possible. She denied it to the skies, to Paul, to the strange faces in uniform. For five minutes she tried to keep his flame alive in the reality of other people's memories, resolutely avoiding the door to the drafting room, where Jack's body steadily lost warmth to the cool air. One of the troopers made quiet, nasal noises over the phone.

A half hour passed. The room grew close with people. Dr. Knowles showed up, fussy as a crow in his black coat. Ashley ignored him as well. Finally she began to cry.

Paul hugged her, very loosely, and stroked her back. He was always amazed at the width of her shoulders. A swimmer's build. Hyperventilating together spread the sorrow. Her Madison Avenue clothes and bright colors seemed like clown's apparel when set beside her grief.

The smiling statie came back with Old George, and the outer office took on the smell of rye.

"He was in the next shed," the state policeman announced, "in a paint room. He said Mr. Briggs—Paul Briggs—told him not to patrol this shed."

Old George avoided looking at Paul. His thick fingers wrestled with each other. The filthy captain's cap he always wore sat askew on his head.

Paul nodded.

"There been some radios stolen from the other sheds, from commercial boats," Burke volunteered.

"There's usually a guard downstairs, to keep an eye on the models. It should be enough. But he's not around," Paul added, remembering. "Shouldn't you be looking for him, maybe? 'Stead of asking questions."

The statie's smile vanished for an instant. The sergeant—his name was Murdoch—nodded. "Why does he always smile?" Paul asked over Ashley's shoulder.

Murdoch shrugged.

Knowles straightened up. The ambulance men lifted a stretcher full of meaningless curves strapped under a blanket and maneuvered for the door.

"But we had it all planned out," Ashley protested, working at her cheek with a knuckle. "We had it *all* planned out."

Paul remembered that Ashley had lobbied hard for the Twelve-Meter job. In fact it was her godfather who recommended Jack to the Challenge people.

"We're taking him to the hospital, Mrs. Briggs," Knowles said, "Mr. Briggs. You can come in my car, if you want."

"Dang it!" George burst out suddenly, and blew his fat, wet nose.

Ashley shook her head without lifting it. "I can't see him yet. Don't you understand, not yet. I want to keep it good."

Knowles nodded. He was Jack's physician; he was everyone's physician. He buckled his bag and followed the rescue squad out. Paul's chest seemed to cave in on itself for a moment when the blanket disappeared from sight.

Red Burke cleared his throat. "I guess we should go, too," he began, but Murdoch held up a restraining hand.

"We still have questions," he told Paul. "We'd like to get them over with."

Burke moved easier now the body was gone. "Don't you think," he waved toward Ashley, "this can wait?"

The staties glanced at each other. Murdoch said, "Based on what you're telling me, Red, I think we should get a statement now, what his movements were last night."

Paul stared at Murdoch, until the sergeant dropped his eyes.

"You gotta be outta your mind."

"You say you came here," the smiling statie pointed out, and gave his gum a couple of extra chews for effect, "at four in the morning? To work?"

"Tell him to stop smiling."

"He was at Pleiku," Murdoch said indulgently. "He's used to this stuff. Homicide, I mean."

"That's ludicrous," Ashley stated, very quietly, and raised her head for the first time. "My husband's dead." From the corner, George made a noise like a goat.

"Could you," Paul cleared his throat, "take Ashley to my car, George? I'll drive them home," he told Burke, not looking at the troopers. "Then, if you want, we can all go to the station."

"But I can't go home," Ashley said, very firmly, and dug her nose into Old George's chest.

"She can't go home," George agreed, putting his arms awkwardly around her shoulders and wiping his nose on her tweed.

"Then stay at my house," Paul said, avoiding Ashley's eyes, but it was Burke who looked up at his words and held his gaze longer than seemed necessary.

Murdoch told the smiling statie to remain in the drafting office. They filed slowly out of the room, down the stairs. On their way out the shop door the sergeant held Paul back with one hand and pointed at a lever that normally tripped an old-fashioned alarm when the door was opened. The lever, a three-inch strip of steel with a plastic roller at the lower end, was hooked to a wire that in turn pulled an electronic switch to trigger a bell. Paul saw the wire had been cut and tied back with a length of tarred line, sabotaging the process—an unnecessary precaution, since the alarm had burned out months ago and not been fixed.

"Weird knot," the statie said, stroking it with a leather glove and watching Paul's eyes.

Paul examined the marline, dully, then took a closer look. The discovery seemed to turn inside him, uncovering a pocket of anger lying hidden beneath the loss, behind the shock, bitter and filling, in the dark.

"Recognize it?" the trooper asked.

Paul nodded. It was an unlikely knot, three half-hitches around a nail and another slip-knotted around the tense part of the line itself. He had seen that before, though he could not quite place where. He felt like a dog getting its first scent of danger on the wind, the hackles on the back of his neck prickling up in response to the oldest of instincts: stranger here, enemy about. The knot was like a signature.

Murdoch sniffed. Paul said nothing. He noticed the sky was trying on blues, across the harbor, toward the east.

A gull screamed from the roof outside, bringing an end to the night's quiet.

They went out into the morning.

C H A P T E R 3

The town of French Harbor, where Paul Briggs lived, was best approached from the sea. This perspective offered its most elegant profile—and, to give the approach some historical symmetry, it was from this direction it was colonized, in 1755, by a boatful of French refugees from the sack of Acadia, some miles to the east.

Closing in from the southeast as the Acadians had done, with your sails full of the prevailing wind, you first spotted a pair of rounded hills rising over a forked peninsula.

On your right and left as you entered the deep channel stood the poles of French Harbor's existence—the remains of old Jesuit breastworks on Fort Island and the Gothic gingerbread of a more recent summer colony on the point.

The town opened between, in growth rings that accurately marked the fast summers and long winters of its fortunes. Stone piers, once used to load granite, lay on one side; schooner wharves rotted on the other. Halfway up one of the hills rose the steepled tower of the Union Church (Congregational), built in times of plenty. Nearby stood the unadorned peaks of the Baptists and Methodists, erected when money was scarce. A level lower, a stretch of pretentious brick mansions built by clipper captains and stone merchants dominated the half-Capes and trailers of lesser folk.

Perspective as well as deeper water led the eye to focus on the middle of this panorama, a group of white-frame warehouses perched on pilings sunk around the channel leading to Eel Pond and the Briggs boatyard beyond. This was the epicenter of town: the fishing cooperative, the town dock, the drawbridge.

Dead center of all this stood the Bridge Diner and General Store.

The Diner, as it was known, included a gas station, a shack selling tourist souvenirs, and a warehouse full of fishing gear and spares for marine diesels; but its nub was a prefabricated building beside the warehouse where a long chrome counter linked tight wooden booths and green-checked curtains under plastic signs advertising beer. It was here that anything worth happening in French Harbor was discussed, if it hadn't occurred at the Diner to begin with.

☙

A day since Jack Briggs's death and the Diner was filled to capacity, which was normal; but Abbie, the waitress, already had twice run out of half-and-half and had to fetch more from the reefer out back.

Outside the windows, the fog stitched together black water and the remains of night. Inside, smoke from grease and cigarettes turned the neon light green, bringing out B-movie angles in the face of "Squidlips" Coggeshall, owner of the *Betty-Ann*, a thirty-five-foot Jonesport lobster boat moored in Eel Pond.

"Tune it to WTOZ," Coggeshall suggested. "See if they have anything new, down to Bangor."

"Gawd," Abbie replied, flipping her long gray-blonde hair, but turning the dial anyway.

"Here come Freddy Farren," announced Little George from his booth by the door.

Cold air stirred the room like a spoon, mixing smoke with the smells of last night's beer and rotten pogie—lobster bait—from Coggeshall's boots.

"Hiya, Freddy," Abbie said brightly, with a significant look at the Prouty brothers, down the counter.

The new arrival straddled a stool, pulled a baseball cap tighter over his eyes, and pointed at a fresh pot of coffee.

"So what they sayin' down to Portland, Freddy," Ed Prouty said, smiling at Abbie, but not too broadly, given the atmosphere of almost pleasurable melancholy that hung thicker than the fog, thicker than the butt smoke even, around the Diner.

"Coffee," Farren stated in a tone of tight-leashed rage.

"About Jacky Briggs," Prouty went on, his smile fading because he'd gone to elementary school with Jack and this gave him a right to be sensitive.

The baseball cap shifted. "USA: Champs," it read, in red, white, and blue letters.

"What about him."

WTOZ filled the room with warm praise for snowblowers.

"Why, you know." Ed was taken aback. "What they think. 'Bout the killing, I guess."

Farren turned his head. His little eyes narrowed against the smoke and his jaw jutted as he replied.

"I got stopped for speedin' outside Thomaston. When I got to Portland, they run out of ice and I had to wait. I had other things on my mind than askin' damn fool questions."

Abbie noted the response. A single phrase from Freddy Farren was evidence of lurid interest. Three sentences was further proof of the astonishment that gripped the town yesterday, upon learning of Jack's death. There had not been a murder in French Harbor since 1938, when "Sugar" Gilbert found Henry Sears in bed with the Snow sisters—both of whom he'd been engaged to at one time or another—and stove in Sears's head with a splitting maul.

The significance of Farren's reply was not lost on the rest of the Diner.

"He was a good guy," Little George agreed, for the seventh or eighth time that morning, and there was a chorus of sighs and grunts from booths up and down the room.

"He patched up Hinks's sardine carrier for a whole summer, for free," Coggeshall told his beard, "when Will Hinks broke his neck picking apples."

"That were Paul."

"No it wasn't either." Pulling his beard aside with one hand, the fisherman added, "Paul Briggs was in Tahiti or the South Pacific or some such place, bumming around on windjammers. It was Jack."

"Seem to remember he fixed your boat pretty cheap, too, huh Squidlips?"

The big lobsterman shrugged.

A disc jockey on WTOZ cheerily predicted morning fog for coastal Maine, followed by rising winds and gale warnings as a low-pressure front moved in from the west.

A splash of headlights came through the window, diffused by fog.

"Here come—" Little George rubbed a circle into the condensation to see better—"Here come Bud."

The background of slurps, burps, and clinking mugs faded a little as Bud Fossett came in. Fossett ran the carpentry crew at Briggs yard and could be counted on to talk.

"What you hear at the yard," Ed Prouty asked down the length of the counter, after enough time had passed for the carpenter to down his first cup of coffee.

Bud shrugged.

"Cops?"

Bud nodded and dunked a doughnut in his second cup.

"Staties," he said.

"Staties," Fred Farren said, like spitting out a bad piece of food. "All the way from Searsport."

"Awful decent of 'em to come all that way, don't you think, Ed?"

"Hate to think they had to drive all of forty miles, though, only makin' twenty-five dollar an hour an' everything."

"They hear anything more about that night watchman?" Abbie asked, to keep the gossip on track.

Bud shrugged his shoulders.

"He din' see anything," a voice from down back ventured. "Never even made it to the yard. Somebody snuck right up on him in the motel, where he was stayin'. He's from Portland," the voice finished, as if this were explanation enough.

"They got the payroll," someone else suggested, "when they broke into that office, at the yard."

More words of agreement from the far booth, but Bud shook his head.

"Din' keep money in that office anymore," Bud insisted. "Just computer programs for those damn Twelves. Wicked secret," he went on, looking around the room for effect. "You steal those, you steal the boat. Maybe it's why they killed him?"

"Who's 'they'?"

"Who knows," the carpenter replied, and held his coffee mug for Abbie to fill.

"So they could stop the *Challenge?*" Abbie prompted him, holding back the coffee till he replied.

"I guess," Bud acknowledged, lifting his mug higher. When he realized further talk was the price of coffee he added, "Maybe 'cause it's going to be fast. The Twelve-Meter. That's what that computer said. Somebody's worried 'bout that boat, that's for sure. Somebody or other." He looked at Abbie for approval.

"If it was robbery, that's one thing," Ed Prouty mused. "If it was to wreck the plans, that's another."

"Reckon you're right, Ed," someone laughed, amid the resumption of small talk.

"Unless wasn't any of those," his brother put in, softly.

The next table heard him and cut the small talk short. The rest of the Diner soon followed suit.

"What you mean," Ed Prouty said at length, into the sudden opening of quiet.

Al Prouty leaned over nervously and played his empty mug back and forth between two palms, like a hockey puck. "Unless it was someone who knew him. Maybe someone he was, like, arguing with?"

Squidlips put his coffee down with a bang that reverberated around the hushed diner.

"Just say it, man. Don't jerk us off."

"Paul Briggs. He means Paul."

Squidlips Coggeshall shifted on his stool, lifting one massive ham an inch off the Naugahyde. A sound like ripping plywood reverberated around the Diner. Abbie screamed and rushed into the kitchen, clutching a dishcloth to her nose.

"Holy Jesus, was that the Russians?"

"Damn Guineas, dynamite fishing in Eel Pond again."

"No, that's just the Vinalhaven boat. Must be foggy out."

Fred Farren moved a seat away from Squidlips. The lobsterman had been known to eat his own bait, and his gas attacks were the stuff of legend.

"Horseshit," Squidlips stated succinctly.

"Just 'cause Paul don't like that Twelve-Meter."

"Did all the computer stuff on it," the carpenter said. "All he does, now."

"Like brothers." Abbie came back out. She began wiping the

counter where Squidlips's coffee had spilled, then paused, her hand in midmovement, a soap opera trick. " 'Course, like they say. Takes a good friend to make a good enemy."

Someone cleared his throat nervously.

"Paul been pretty strange since his wife left," a voice from the back commented.

"Never found his little girl," someone else added, clicking his tongue.

"Just disappeared, walkin' to the school bus," a third voice agreed.

"Wonder why he never remarried," Abbie remarked.

Fred Farren jutted his jaw out, pulled his cap tight over his forehead. Slowly, almost painfully, he said, "You could ask Jack Briggs's wife that question."

"What you say?" Squidlips asked, unbelieving. Swiveling around to look at Farren he repeated the question. If the Diner had been quiet before, it was dead silent now.

"You oughta be careful what you say about people, man," Ed Prouty advised. "Lotta people around here like Paul."

"All I'm saying—"

"You talk poison," the big lobsterman interrupted, and flexed his fingers as if to test the pressure they could exert around Farren's neck.

"You callin' me a liar?"

"Why, yes." Squidlips Coggeshall spoke with mild surprise. "I guess I am."

"Well, you can go straight to hell, 'cause it's the truth."

"Bullshit." Squidlips let fall a giant hand, almost gently, on Farren's left shoulder.

"You boys stop it," Abbie said. "Or I'm calling Red. Vic!" she yelled, illogically, toward the kitchen.

"Let him talk," Little George piped up from his booth. "Bet I already heard this one."

"He's said his piece, anyway."

Squidlips pulled his hand off, reluctantly.

"Ah the hell with it." Farren hunched over the counter again.

"It's too late now," Abbie told him, pouting. "You gotta say it now."

Farren took off his cap, twisted it to fit. His face was very red.

"Aw, he knows it's a lie." The lobsterman turned away.

"All right." Farren shot a twelve-gauge look at Squidlips's back. "It was on the boatyard picnic."

"Talk louder."

"Labor Day," Farren spoke up. "It was at Jack Briggs's place, but he was in New York, talkin' with America's Cup people. My cousin did the clambake. Sam finished up real late, maybe midnight. Halfway home he remembered he forgot all his tarps, and he went back."

"So," Al Prouty breathed.

"So nothing. He just saw them, that's all. Through the window. Paul and Miss Hoity-Toity. Spoonin'."

"What!"

"Kissing. Spooning. Yeah. Their tongues in each other's mouths." Farren's nose wrinkled in embarrassment.

"There goes the school bus," Little George called.

"Christ it's seven-thirty." The boat carpenter left behind a quarter for Abbie and a look of contempt for Fred Farren. He went out the door, bent with hurry.

Without a word Squidlips got up and followed him, trailed shortly thereafter by the Prouty brothers.

"Why'd you have to say that," Abbie asked Farren, a little sadly. "Christ I never hear you talk so much."

"Why not." Farren pulled his jaw back in self-defense.

" 'Cause Al's a honorary deputy," Abbie indicated the door with her thumb, "and you know he's goin' straight out to tell Red."

"You soft on Paul, too," Farren complained, and pushed his cup toward the coffee. "Everybody soft on him."

"I'm not soft on him," Abbie retorted, pouring. "I went to school with him. It just makes me angry. I mean, he had it all: the yard, the education. No one around here starts off like he did."

Farren shrugged his shoulders.

"He had a spell of lousy luck." Abbie ignored him. "And he had to let it spoil everything for him. It's just—dumb," she finished, disgustedly, and passed down the counter to stack plates.

C   H   A   P   T   E   R   4

At a quarter to eight that same morning Paul Briggs watched his
daughter disappear in the school bus's friendly yellow roar, then
walked slowly back to the house to find the day taken over by the
housekeeping of death.

Gray dishwater practicalities Jack's wife could not even address
demanded immediate attention. He spent the morning checking on
her horses, boarding her cat with neighbors, arranging services, signing mortuary release forms, sending a check to the funeral home,
getting the heat and water turned on in Jack's parents' house.

Piet Hendriks called from the testing tank in the middle of this,
complaining there was a major discrepancy between what the computer predicted and what the twelve-meter models were doing, and
John Poole, the foreman, came up from the yard, looking for a desk
where the buck finally would stop. Paul fended off their questions
to keep coping with the details.

It was amazing how many ends were left loose when someone
was ripped bodily from the fabric of his life. Somehow the very
pettiness of the details strengthened the feeling of suspended ani-

mation, as if tragedy shut down the daily illusions to bring a sudden clarity of being. Whatever the reason, it kept the absence of Jack, the implications of loneliness, to the back of Paul's mind, where his subconscious could cut it into bite-size chunks, to digest more easily.

The coping grew more difficult as the day wore on, however, for Ashley's refusal to go back to Jack's house made Paul's the headquarters for community ritual.

Friends, families from the boatyard filled the old house with demonstrations of loss. Matrons put hamburger-and-Velveeta casseroles in the oven for two hours at three-fifty and filled armchairs with their broad-hipped sympathy for equal amounts of time. Friends of Ashley's from Blue Hill brought a wicker basket full of Scottish shortbread and beluga.

Old George, cherishing his involvement in events, raked leaves around Paul's house all morning, waiting to give Ashley the comfort he thought she craved.

Ashley slept, with the help of sleeping pills provided by Dr. Knowles.

Paul soon found the demonstrations of others made him uncomfortable, almost jealous, as if grief were a commodity cheapened in proportion to the number of people partaking of it. By one in the afternoon he had had enough. He put on his coat, left the house, and headed down the studio trail.

Paul thought the trail would be completely overgrown, then remembered Jessica often asked permission to bring her school friends to the studio to play with stuffed bears, crayons, and old pots when it grew warm. The feet of children had been enough to keep a rabbit-size path open through the weeds.

The woods felt deep and alien. Fog covered the slow retreat of night. Saplings wore cloaks, bushes were mysterious strangers. Tall pines vanished in the smoke overhead.

When he reached the studio he almost stopped in surprise because it was so precisely as he remembered it, a small whitewashed clapboard cabin hidden in a clump of blueberries. Apparently the years had not marked the studio. Of course this was only fog hiding details of peeling paint, mouse turds on the porch, dead weeds in the window boxes. Yet the illusion of having strayed into some temporal DMZ, a place where time and space called a truce, stayed with him as he stepped inside.

The lights still worked—another surprise. Faces sprang out of the corners when he flicked the switch. Clay faces with gigantic noses and staring eyes. Wood faces with gouged cheeks and yawning mouths. Stone faces with chins like Mount McKinley. Thick dust and spiderwebs could not soften the astonishment in every feature—as if these men and women, only just liberated from pine or granite, suddenly had caught sight of themselves in a mirror and realized for the first time the flagrant incompetence of their creator.

Suzanne was not much of a sculptor, but catharsis, not beauty, was her objective. Paul could see her in his mind, pounding on a cold chisel with all her strength, sweating and cursing at the helpless substance.

Paul picked up old pots and teddy bears and stashed them in a corner. He walked over to the workbench to look at the snapshots she had tacked above the window.

Jack at the boatyard, in dungarees, at the launching of the *French Harbor* 38, the last boat they had designed together. Jack smiling that big "the world's my oyster" grin. Jack in his favorite Oxford shirt, drawing in the drafting office where he had died only the night before last. Jack pouring champagne on Paul's head under the *Zulu*'s elegant, haunted bow. Jack and Paul together, shingling the roof of this very cabin, with a thermos full of iced White Russians to ease the sunburn.

That had been one hot summer, Paul remembered. A long potlatch of barbecues and beach picnics. It was just before his cousin met Ashley, and he practically lived at Paul and Suzanne's house. They had fished and sailed and worked together. Jack took care of the kids. They had never been closer. It was because of that summer there were practically as many shots of Jack as of Paul on her window.

It was very cold and dank in the studio. Paul found some kindling and newspapers in a box by the wood stove and made a fire. "Mondale Blasts Reagan Budget," a headline read. Smoke leaked from joints in the stovepipe but it was better than the smell of mold. The solitude was like cool lotion after the hysteria of mourning. The wood was bone dry and the cabin warmed up quickly. Paul switched the cheap turntable to "on" and was only mildly astonished when it hummed back to life as quickly as the rest of the cabin. He found an old recording of Yehudi Menuhin playing Mozart's Concerto in G Minor. The magic violin transcended scratch and static to weave a spell across the room. Suzanne believed the music bled from her fingers to affect what she carved. Paul shifted a grotesque clay self-portrait from her workbench to the shelf. He sat down at the bench and rubbed dust from Suzanne's chisels.

Outside, the fog ignored weathermen and got thicker. She said it always reminded her of great gray elephants rubbing their backs against the windows. It made the cabin warm and yellow by comparison. Fog outside, fog in. To Paul it felt like general anesthesia, stealing hard angles from the world. It sapped his ability to recite the alphabet backward or feel anything but a vague hollowness where his gut should have been.

He put his arms on the bench and rested his head on them. He wanted very badly to sleep. He could steal some of Doc Knowles's pills but Ashley might be waking and he did not want to face the reflection of his own useless guilt in her eyes. There was only one person he wanted to see at this point but the old man had not been around all morning. . . .

≈

Paul woke up with the void still in his stomach and a sense of having been startled.

Outside the fog had lifted somewhat and Paul could see waves curl around the small cove below the studio. The record player made mad, recurrent, scraping sounds.

A large crow dropped to the window ledge before him and flapped its wings noisily, struggling to keep its balance. It scrabbled for purchase on the narrow ledge, gave a desperate croak, and fell off, without dignity.

Paul got up stiffly. He switched off the turntable and opened the door. His grandfather, who was leaning on the latch, talking to someone beside him, stumbled across the sill and tripped backward into the cabin. He would have fallen all the way had the sleeve of his coat not caught on the latch to hold him upright.

"Jesus!" he grunted hoarsely, steadying himself on the jamb. "Goddamn it to hell, I been lookin' all over for you." Paul tried to help him get level but Bull shook him away.

The old man's breath reeked of rum and cigarettes. There was a long tear in his sweater and a hint of bird droppings on the shoulder of his old frock coat. The oversize mouth and nose gave his face almost farcical overtones, like a cartoon or one of Suzanne's sculptures. White hair sprayed from scalp and eyebrows. He looked like a cut-rate prophet, or a bum with stature. The blue eyes were bright with hoarded tears. Looking at his grandfather Paul felt the way he did when the wind let go of a boat on the point of capsizing and it settled back closer to an even keel.

"I been trying to phone you," Paul said.

Bull looked away. He took out a filthy bandanna and blew his nose.

"Christ I been walkin'. Thinkin'. Lookin' for you." He belched, miserably. Paul smelled rum. "Your mother's not comin' up til tomorrow."

Paul touched his grandfather's shoulder. "Who's with you."

"He was at the house," Bull explained, still looking away. "Wanted to see you. Said it was urgent."

A figure appeared in the doorway. Murdoch nodded at Paul, looked curiously around the studio.

"No," Paul told the statie forcefully. "I haven't had time. There's a thousand things I got to do. I'll talk to you tomorrow."

"It'll only take a few minutes."

"Christ," Paul said. "I'd forgotten what you people were like." He paced to the window to slow his annoyance. This cabin had always been a haven from the world Murdoch represented, with its hard and broken edges. But he must learn there was no escaping that world. As Nicole had found out. As Jack had learned.

Paul fished a twenty out of his pocket and told his grandfather to go to the package store and come back in half an hour. The crow screeched and left the window. Murdoch came in and, with an unerring instinct for power relationships, sat down in the only chair, by Suzanne's bench. A tightly built man. Round face set on a solid neck. No chin to speak of. Cop eyes, watching, watching. He was in plain clothes, today, of brown, nondescript cut. The nylon pants were sharply creased. He could have been a liquor salesman or a franchise operator, except for the eyes.

Paul rekindled the stove and leaned against a misshapen marble torso, near its heat. How long had he been asleep, he wondered? He felt chilled through and through. From this angle Murdoch's head was surrounded by cousins of the Easter Island monoliths. On the wall above him hung a picture of Jack at the tiller of the *Ettie.*

They used to go sailing on the *Ettie* before Nicole was born, picnics down to Two Ladies Islands. Before that even, Jack and he would take her on cruises, beer in the bilge and college girls in the cockpit. They used to anchor in the Waquoit River and skinny-dip hopefully in the quarry ponds. When the night breeze came up they roasted lobsters in hot rocks and seaweed on the beach, lying about things they'd done and how it was downright impossible to sail home in the dark. Too many rocks. Fog. Ghost ships, they said, to make the girls come closer. In fact Jack and Paul often sailed all night, just the two of them, running down the western stars, to Little Bremen Island for the annual Friendship Sloop Regatta.

"Crummy weather, huh," Murdoch said, and stuck a piece of chewing gum in his mouth.

Paul nodded. The world, whose colors had come closer to normal when Bull came in, took on a tinge of nausea again.

"Why'd you kill your cousin," Murdoch asked, casually.

Paul stared at him.

"What?" he grunted, stupidly.

"Why did you kill your cousin?"

Anger spread through Paul's system. He leaned over the stove to stare at Murdoch.

"Let me see your warrant, or whatever. Otherwise, you know," the sprouting anger made him stumble over words, "you can just get the hell out of here."

Murdoch opened a plastic attaché case on Suzanne's bench.

"You're going to have to answer that question, sooner or later. If not with me, then with a judge."

"Forget it. Not till I get a lawyer."

"I'm not charging you."

Paul brushed his hair back with his fingers, roughly, a gesture of frustration.

"Then what are you doing?"

"Just trying to get at the truth."

Paul laughed, without mirth.

Murdoch took a ballpoint from his jacket, fiddled with it.

"Come on, Paul," he said. "Let's let bygones be bygones. I've read the file on your daughter. I know you had problems with that investigation. We did the best we could. Stranger-abductions are the worst."

Paul did not answer. The policeman leaned forward.

"I'm not getting heavy here." His voice was low, intimate. "No Miranda. No charges. I just need input. Hear it from my point of view."

Paul shrugged. Murdoch took the gesture as consent. He pulled a pad of yellow legal paper from his attaché case, lined it up before him.

"Listen, this isn't New York City. This is a little town on the coast of Maine that should prob'ly have been shut down a hundred years ago."

He took a piece of chewing gum out of his mouth and looked for a place to put it.

"Nine times outta ten, around here, you find the guy who did it standing right in the same room with the victim. Nice 'n' neat."

Paul's legs suddenly lost interest in the job of holding him up. He found a seat on the wood box, with his back against the torso, where he could look over the rocks and seaweed of the cove instead of Murdoch's face.

Murdoch took the opportunity to wad his old chewing gum under the bench.

"Why didn't you just say this at the station, yesterday," Paul asked.

"We found out more since then."

"Such as."

"Well, we had opportunity," Murdoch said. "No problem. But now we got a reason, too."

"Oh my God." There was more fatigue than sarcasm in the words.

Beyond the cove, Paul saw Squidlips Coggeshall's lobster boat slide through the channel between Fort Island and Cully Head, very white against the mouse-colored threads of fog still scattered on the Sound. In the stern, Nat lined up busted traps, lines coiled and buoys stacked, ready to unload. They were coming in early, before the front hit.

Nat could pick Jessica up from Gilberts'. Paul could take the rest of the day off, do anything. Sleep. Fly to Montreal. Go sailing. Take the *Ettie*, drop her lines, hoist her sails and pound straight out into the teeth of the gale.

Go sailing. The need came from the gut of him, physical, urgent as thirst. He could almost feel the mainsheet running in his hands.

"Tell me, Mr. Murdoch," Paul said, still looking at Coggeshall's boat, "why the hell I would want to kill Jack."

"Because the Briggs and Sons boatyard is held by a family corporation," Murdoch recited, looking over his notes. "Because 51 percent of the corporation's shares are held by Benjamin B. Briggs, your grandfather. The remaining 49 percent is held by Jack Briggs's parents, also Lucinda Briggs, your mother. Because, according to, uh, sources, when your grandfather dies, control of the boatyard goes to the current directors, John A. and Paul W. Briggs. And because now, with John A.'s death, you get the whole ball of wax."

"Maybe I should kill my grandfather," Paul suggested, still looking out the window.

Murdoch watched him carefully, as if thinking Paul might do just that.

"You know," Paul added, "you're not even considering the most obvious possibility. I mean, that Jack was killed because of the Twelve-Meter. It was probably someone trying to steal the plans for the *Challenge*."

Murdoch put on a polite smile.

"Sure, you think that's funny, or impossible," Paul said, feeling the anger burble back a little. "You don't know, you don't realize how much stealing and spying goes on in that scene. The America's Cup. Always has, since the beginning. Back in the eighteen hundreds, Jack told me, the Americans sent a diver to New York to sneak a look at the keel of a British challenger. The water was so filthy he couldn't see anything. There were other times," Paul continued, trying to remember what his cousin had said. "Just before the Second World War, I think, we sent a spy to England, to check out a really good new sail the English were trying to keep secret. Then there was the whole 'Keel-gate' thing: the divers, sabotaging the support boats, putting a spy with the customs. And last series, one of the Australians used a blimp to take aerial pictures of an American keel. Then someone threatened him—the Australian—and burned down his sail loft." Paul looked back at the statie. "It's getting worse, you see, because suddenly the Cup's big business, and people have tens of millions of dollars in promotion riding on it, and it could have happened like that." Paul found he was short of breath. "It could be a spy. It could have happened differently from how you see it."

"It could have happened differently," Murdoch conceded, "in

hot blood instead o' cold. See, the two directors of the boatyard argue over this new project, the Twelve-Meter—"

"Christ," Paul burst out, "you didn't listen to a word I said!"

Murdoch continued, imperturbable. "Arguments turn to blows. All of a sudden"—Murdoch snapped his fingers—"there's a guy on the floor, dead. So if you cop a plea now," he finished, brightly, "you could probably get away with a second-degree or manslaughter charge, walk in five-to-seven. Maybe less."

The D. A. would go along with it, Murdoch added, in a tone that indicated the district attorney always did what Murdoch told him in indictment proceedings.

"What about the guard," Paul heard himself reply in a reasonable, if abstract tone. "I tied him up before I went to the boatyard and—killed Jack?"

"More or less." Murdoch opened a fresh stick of gum.

Paul said the D. A. might have a little trouble buying the "hot blood" angle.

Murdoch admitted the contradiction.

"I would never have hurt Jack," Paul stated, keeping the feeling carefully out of his voice, as something too clean to be brought out for cops. "He was my best friend."

"Is that why you slept with his wife," Murdoch asked, softly.

Paul stared at Murdoch, feeling the blood drain from his face.

The sense of things private and soft being pawed by outsiders overflowed what controls he had left.

He got off the wood box, quite slowly. Turned his back to the policeman. Held himself very straight. With a deliberate motion he placed both hands flat on one side of the marble torso. Convulsively, he flung it sideways to the floor. It hit the boards with a huge noise, cracking a plank, rattling the little cabin. Suzanne's self-portrait toppled off the shelf and smashed into three pieces.

"Get out of here," he said, his back still to Murdoch.

"Why wait," Murdoch said, seductively. "Let it come. Get it off your chest."

"Get out," Paul repeated. "Get off my property." He kept his hands balled in fists at his side to hide the shaking till Murdoch had gathered up his attaché case and closed the door behind him.

Paul looked at what was left of his wife's contorted vision of herself. The anger uncoiled further inside him. Between that and the loss beneath, there would soon be no room for himself.

He waited to give the sergeant time to negotiate the trail before leaving.

He would miss his grandfather, but if he waited Paul felt something was going to snap. He ran to the garage, got in the jeep and drove straight to the boatyard.

Buildings he looked at every day of his life seemed strange, out of true, as if something very heavy had leaned on them just a little. He had not been here since finding Jack's body. He took a shortcut between two Quonsets to the rigging dock, where the boats were moored.

The wind had freshened, twenty to twenty-five, shredding the fog. Clouds scudded by like late commuters.

He could take the *FH* 38, a fast, dry, handy boat. It had sails that could be shortened, roller-reefed in seconds if the wind got too heavy. Unlike the *Ettie*, it would point into the headwinds of Fort Island Channel with no problem.

He hesitated for almost a second, and walked past the *FH* 38 to where the older, clipper-bowed sloop was moored.

"Come *on*," Bull Briggs yelled, from the *Ettie*'s cockpit. He waved a bottle of rum that was already a quarter empty. "I been waitin' for you for *hours*."

"How did you know," Paul shouted back.

"Where you always go when you get mad?"

Paul unfastened the mooring lines before climbing down into the old sloop. His grandfather started the engine. Paul took the tiller.

Within five minutes they were heading out to sea.

C H A P T E R 5

They had to take a double reef in the mainsail halfway down Fort Island Channel. The wind was gusting harder now and a Friendship sloop was not built for leaning to heavy canvas. But she tacked well under shortened sail, treading the choppy inshore water under her flared bow with great contempt.

Bull Briggs sat just aft of the cabin trunk, gleaming in black oilskins, keeping the rum bottle level while trying to light cigarettes as the sloop cut Georges Sound into cold, flat sheets of spray.

When they left the lee of Cully Head the wind began shifting easterly and increasing in strength. The waves lengthened into long swells—towering, cold, white-veined walls of gray that rolled the resentment of deep water all the way from Portugal. Bull let the mainsheet out. The cordage groaned its discomfort as they eased off downwind. He tightened up on the headsail to soften the steering for Paul. Staring above him to check how the sail filled, his nose and eyebrows wrinkling under a woolen watch cap, he looked like a seahawk, scanning the clouds for prey.

Inside the cabin Bull's pet crow shifted back and forth along the rim of a bunk, visibly uncomfortable.

Paul caught sight of water breaking white over Hen and Chickens rocks and pointed up again on a southerly course. The wind howled its pain in the standing rigging. The waves were getting bigger but the *Ettie*'s deep, fat hull took them with equal measures of respect and grace.

Paul held the tiller with both hands. His boat was a living thing that sought a perfect line through all the forces affecting her. Bracing himself against the waves, leaning back to hold her kicking rudder, his face growing numb under the windchill's lash, he felt her control surfaces carve a work of power from each plane of air and sea.

Slowly, the bad taste of Murdoch faded. The sense of unreality dwindled, whipped away by the harsher economies of navigation. The absence of Jack took up more room, but lost its tinge of betrayal. Rum made the sadness warmer, blended it with earlier grief without diluting it. Two Ladies Island disappeared in the scud to port as they left Georges Sound for the open Atlantic.

The wind freshened steadily. Fifteen minutes after losing sight of land, a particularly strong gust caught the *Ettie* as she leaned off the back of a wave. Neither of them saw it coming, and Bull could not get the mainsheet loose in time. The sloop heeled sharply, burying her lee rail. Paul pushed hard against the tiller to head upwind, but the sloop's massive rudder fought back every inch and she would not come up fast enough.

Water began creaming over the coaming, flooding the cockpit. Its weight increased the angle of heel, made it that much harder for the rudder to bite. The crow squawked in panic.

Bull struggled with the mainsheet but the wind's strength had jammed it solid in its cleat.

"Cut it!" Paul yelled.

Despite the rum—or perhaps because of it—Bull could move with astonishing speed when he chose. He whipped out a jackknife, opened it, and sliced the mainsheet in one fluid motion. The sloop righted herself immediately, sails banging in the breeze. They took a third reef, spliced the mainsheet, bailed out the cockpit, and headed south again.

An hour later Paul tacked her around to a compass heading of eighty degrees, looking for a landfall at Bass Island. Dusk was falling,

Paul's glasses were rimed with salt, visibility was only one or two miles in drizzle and they would have missed the island entirely if Bull had not caught sight of the Bass Island light buoy winking unexpectedly astern of them.

The run back north was pure luxury. Sails full on a broad reach, they surfed with swells they'd fought hand to hand the other way. The sun vanished in a pride of purples. It looked like every hue from pink through lavender to indigo was attending a carnival in the clouds out west. In the dusk their wake glowed a ghostly green from phosphorescent plankton. The moon rose and Bull could finish his cigarettes and Paul could spare a hand to keep the bottle at his side, instead of Bull's.

The lighthouse on Cully Head came into view soon after four and they entered Eel Pond before five o'clock.

Bull's crow hopped out of the cabin to perch on the tiller, blinking.

"I'm gonna miss the living hell out of him," Bull said, cleaning droppings from the cockpit deck. It was the first statement he had made since leaving harbor, except for routine acknowledgments of sailing.

"I wish we'd talked more," Paul said, carefully. The rum made tying the sail down a chore, and his tongue had to pick around the vowels.

Bull sat down abruptly, looking very old in the cabin light.

"You haven't been around to talk to, much."

Paul thought about that for a while. The wind pulled canvas out of his hands and he ended up tying the sail down in bunches. He couldn't find the sail ties so he used the mainsheet. It looked messy but it would hold until morning, and he was too loaded to give a damn, anyway.

"They think I did it."

"The cops?"

"Yeah."

"Figures." Bull gave a short bark of laughter that described better than words what he thought of police IQ.

His voice offered the same kind of trust Paul and Jack used to give each other when things got rough.

"You know what," Paul said.

The old man said nothing. He had never liked rhetorical questions.

"We gotta find out who killed him," Paul said finally, "if the cops don't."

Bull nodded. There was moisture on his cheeks and Paul felt tears welling warm around his own eyes, only partly because of the liquor.

Paul furled the jib and finished cleaning up the boat. Despite his loss of coordination, he managed the task in less than ten minutes.

꿈

Paul called Sal Vanzetti as soon as he got back from sailing.

There were multiple clicks on the line as the call was forwarded back and forth around Bangor. A man with a heavy French-Canadian accent answered. Bar talk and the canned enthusiasm of TV football filled the background. Paul asked for Sal Vanzetti and the man said, "Jiss minute."

In roughly a minute someone picked up the phone and said, "Yo."

"Sal," Paul said, "it's Paul Briggs."

"Briggs." The private investigator's voice was guarded. "I sent you that report. You got it, didn't you?"

"It's not about Nicole—"

"I located that couple, it's in the report." There was something familiar about the way Vanzetti talked. Paul realized he was enunciating with great care, picking a way around the beer in his system, just as Paul was doing with the rum in his. "In Nashua, Noo Hampshire," Vanzetti continued. "It just din' work out, man. They were in the area, right time, but they're tourists. Got a kid of their own. No funny moves that week or anything. It's in the report."

Paul originally had hired Vanzetti because of his reports. They were copious, double-spaced, full of details and written with a verve that to some extent made up for the lack of grammar, the lack of results.

The private detective had tracked down leads the cops would not touch, clues bearing only the thinnest connection with Nicole's disappearance.

The last report had come in over four months ago.

"I'm not calling about that," Paul repeated. "I'm calling about my cousin."

"Your cousin?" Vanzetti thought back carefully. "I met him once. Jim. Joe!"

"Jack."

"Yeah, Jack. So what about him?"

"He's been killed."

The detective said he was sorry, with no great feeling.

"Murdered," Paul added.

"*Murdered?*" Vanzetti's tone rose, incredulous. "In *French Harbor?*"

Briefly, Paul ran down the details of Jack's death.

"Son of a bitch," the detective commented when he had finished. There was a sound of swallowing and a suppressed belch. "And the staties think you did it. Well, that figures."

"What figures?"

"It's the way they think," Vanzetti replied. "They never worry it's too obvious. Nine times outta ten, they're right, too. 'Specially here. Potato farmers sleeping with each other's sisters, they whack each other with deer rifles. French millworkers cut up Spics want their job. Fisherman pops another guy's pullin' his traps. Obvious."

"Well, this is the 10 percent that ain't," Paul objected. "Besides which—"

"Keep your shirt on," Vanzetti interrupted. "Listen," he went on, "I gotta go. I'll call a guy I know in Augusta, see what the staties are up to. Get back to you first thing."

"So you can do this?" Paul put in hastily.

"What do you mean?"

"You can look into this? I can't trust the state police. Like you said. They haven't forgotten."

"I think," Vanzetti replied carefully, "I can find the time." A hoot of laughter came from the background. The sound of clanking beer mugs drowned out the TV as the detective hung up.

☰

Vanzetti did not get back to him, however, and in his continuing state of space-out Paul forgot all about the detective.

Ashley stayed in bed, eating nothing but strong red-and-white pills.

Jack's parents and Ashley's parents and Paul's mother arrived in a single rush the next day from Hawaii and Florida and Connecticut. Paul's uncle looked thirty years older, his aunt kept having to sit down. Ashley's mother wore a long mink coat and stared at Paul as if the whole thing had been his fault.

She took Ashley away in a rented car, and the house immediately drained of callers.

Nat reclaimed his couch and caught up on "M*A*S*H" reruns. Paul's mother began scrubbing the kitchen and spoiling Jessica with a determination that matched her own unhappiness. The funeral arrangements were finalized for Saturday—two days away. Paul suddenly discovered he had nothing left to do.

The thought of inactivity scared him. He grabbed the phone to call the yard manager when it rang in his hand, startling him so he jerked the receiver off its rest and dropped it to the floor.

There was silence on the line when Paul got the receiver to his ear, and he wondered if the phone were broken.

"Hello? Hello. Damn," Paul said to the electric buzz.

"Briggs," whispered a voice on the other end.

"Hello?"

"You're scared," the voice continued. "You should be. You're in dee-e-e-p shit."

"Vanzetti!"

"I got news. Meet me in Georgeville. Riverview Motel, Unit twelve. Half an hour," the voice finished darkly, and rang off.

Christ, Paul said to himself, refusing to acknowledge the tiny stir of excitement inside him. So many times Vanzetti had hinted at breakthrough, discoveries, new ideas that petered out to nothing but a blacker despair. Rather than follow that line of thought he drank another cup of coffee, topped up his hip flask, and went out to the Jeep.

C H A P T E R 6

You could tell when you got to the Riverview on Route 197 because what view there was of the Sancastin River disappeared completely behind thick second growth just before you reached the motel. The buildings stood in warped two-ply rectangles with one door, window, and parking space per unit, stained a uniform coffee color. They huddled under the tall pines as if ashamed of their very existence. A one-room office stuck out of the central block. A neon sign with the "RI" and "EW" letters inoperative beckoned by the side of the road, so that local kids knew it as the "Vervi." The "No" in the "No Vacancy" sign did not work; however, this did not matter since in a quarter century of serving the horny, the lost, and the suicidal, the Riverview Motel had never seen a full night.

There were no numbers on most of the units. Paul counted from the first number he found, a "4." He knocked at a door eight units to the right. It opened. He went in.

The walls of the room were covered in fake veneer, grooved to look like planking. Its floor sagged to one side under cheap green carpeting that turned everything the color of pus. A queen-size bed took up most of the room, sagging conveniently uphill. A large TV was placed at its foot, like an altar. The place was so tiny Paul's entrance seemed to crowd the other two men inside.

Bobby Leone, the guard, sat facing the television, his long frame taking up most of the bed. He was dressed in uniform pants, a T-shirt, basketball shoes. His face was pink with acne and a multitude of small scratches. It opened in relief when he saw who stood in the doorway.

Sal Vanzetti stood by the TV, leaning on a plastic chair. Even in the squalid surroundings he looked neat and condensed as Paul remembered him. His thinning hair was combed back with styling cream. The broad "paisano" face still looked like an ambush, with its bandit's moustache and bushwacker's nose lying in wait for the humor in eyes and mouth. In this context the dark, well-tailored suit was like a stage prop.

Paul said "Hi," dropped his jacket.

"Where the fuck you been," Vanzetti said.

Paul told him and looked for a place to sit. Bobby the guard started to explain, wanting to make sure the boss knew he had not talked out of turn; he'd only told Vanzetti what he told the police. The guard's Adam's apple jumped when he talked. His face was very long and sad, like a bassett hound's. Paul saw there were no other chairs in the room. Even the trash can, which he could have turned upside down to sit on, was filled, incongruously, with hardcover books.

"We been talking basketball," Vanzetti interrupted. "This guy's a Lakers fan."

"He still thinks the Celts," the guard said in disdain, and looked away. After a pause he said, "Mr. Briggs, I don't know how to say, like, I'm real sorry about the other night?"

"Skip it Bobby. It wasn't your fault."

"No. I shouldn't a let myself get jumped like that. I mean, like, I always wanted to be a cop—"

"Forget it."

Bobby shrugged unhappily.

"I don't know, Briggs." Vanzetti took out a pack of cigarettes, every movement timed. He tapped one on his watch to compress the tobacco. Then he took out a box of wooden matches and lit the cigarette. "What I don't understand is why you went back, man. You shoulda let someone else discover it."

"Vanzetti—"

The private investigator grinned. "Just checking."

"Screw you. I get that from the cops, I don't need it from you."

"Don't be like that," Vanzetti complained. "You should be nice to the guy who's gonna keep your WASP ass out of the slammer."

Paul asked him if he'd talked to the state police. Vanzetti nodded. He blew out a lungful of smoke, keeping his profile to the light so everyone could see how artfully he Frenched the smoke between nose and mouth. He told Paul a Sergeant Murdoch in Searsport thought there was enough evidence for an indictment.

"You said you got some news," Paul prompted, keeping his voice bored, deadpan. The guard started to interrupt, but Vanzetti held up both hands to command silence. He stepped into the middle of the room, literally taking what floor there was. He pulled the cigarette out of his mouth and paused for effect, standing with legs spread like a samurai. "To make a long story short," he announced, "I got this all worked out."

Paul looked at Vanzetti, then at Bobby, checking their eyes. "What," he said. "You're kidding."

"Uh-unh." Vanzetti shook his head. "I know who did it."

"He stayed here one night," Bobby cut in quickly. "The night before Mr. Briggs was killed; I mean, Jack. There was only him and me at the motel. I figured he was a tourist or something."

"So how do you know?" Paul bit down a surge of hope.

It was his car, the guard continued, glancing at Vanzetti for confirmation—a late-model sedan, probably a Plymouth, light blue with Maine tags.

"Smashed-up door, right rear, yellow fog lamps." Vanzetti broke in smoothly, waving his cigarette, the light flashing off his glasses. The private investigator had been at the town police office, talking to Red Burke. According to the town cops, two men from the boat-yard recalled seeing a similar car parked near the yard the day before Jack's murder.

So why, Paul asked, were the cops getting on his case?

It wasn't the town cops, Vanzetti said. The town cops were keeping an open mind. It was the staties who wanted Paul's ass. Besides, the detective added, watching Paul carefully, love triangles were the oldest motive in the book.

Bobby looked up quickly, and flushed.

"It's got nothing to do with anything," Paul growled. "What did the guy in the motel look like," he asked, to change the subject.

He was medium tall, Bobby answered, maybe Paul's height.

The private detective looked at Paul, speculatively.

Bobby stretched his long legs, a little self-consciously, and finished the description. Obviously he'd talked long enough with Vanzetti to see through the bluster. Strong, he continued (checking Paul's chest), probably lifted weights, or did Nautilus. Very large chest muscles. There was something else.

The hairy ears, Sal Vanzetti finished. One of the boat builders had stopped to ask him if he needed help. He didn't remember much about him, except for one detail; he had tufts of hair sticking out of his ears like parsley.

Both Bobby and Vanzetti slid their eyes toward Paul's head. Paul forced himself not to check; he knew he had no more strands of hair poking out of his ears than most men.

He would ask the staties to do an artist's rendition, Vanzetti added in a tone that implied hell would freeze over first.

Paul picked one of the books out of the trash can beside him, his thoughts racing. The textbook was *Applied Criminology*, by Milton Cook.

"Do you think it was the same guy that held you up," he asked the guard.

Bobby was noncommittal. Whoever it was had been very professional, never letting him catch more than a glimpse of silhouette. He had a mask on his face and rubber dishwashing gloves on his hands. His voice was high, gravelly. The gun was a .38, police special variety, snubnosed with a large black silencer attached. He had held the gun on Bobby, thrown six sleeping tablets on the bed, saying he would shoot his knees if he refused to eat the tablets. Then he tied the night guard's hands behind his back and led him outside.

How did he tie the hands, Paul asked, taking a second book out of the trash can. This one read: *Criminal Law: A Handbook for Police Cadets*.

The man had used a rope. He forced Bobby to walk in front, in the pitch dark, through the woods, which was how come he got all those scratches on his face. Finally, the man tied him to a tree, next to the river, and left him. The noise of rushing water drowned his calls for help. It got very cold overnight. If a fisherman hadn't come by the next morning—Bobby shook his head, in awe at possibilities his youth did not really believe in.

"How did he tie you to the tree?" Paul insisted.

"With the same rope."

"What kind of rope."

"White rope, pretty thick," Bobby said. "Like you tie up the boats with. He used wicked good knots," the guard added. "I tried all night to like get my hands loose but they just tightened more; the more I pulled, the tighter they got."

Bobby thought the rope was still down by the river. The police claimed they couldn't lift fingerprints off it. He could find where he'd been tied up, if they wanted, Bobby added.

They put on their coats and walked directly into the woods behind the motel, Bobby leading. The ground, rough with rotten branches, rusted beer cans, and scrub growth, soon angled downward toward the river. Vanzetti grabbed at branches and slipped down the soft pine needles in his city shoes. He cursed as his city clothes picked up pine resin. The stream spoke senseless sounds, louder and louder. They reached the river bank, then followed it northward, skirting patches of swamp and mud. Bobby stopped a hundred yards farther up and started casting around uphill.

"It's opposite that big rock, on the other bank," he shouted, against the noise. "There's a wicked big pine—here it is." He started coiling a length of white rope, yanking it out of the bushes, un-kinking it as it came.

"Don't untie that knot," Paul yelled. He took the rope and looked closely at the ends—and got it immediately. A flash of hands un-looping a line from bollards, three hitches yanked out fast to free the barge or whatever before it pulled the tug off course. The small heat of anger he'd first known at the boatyard glowed, then burst into flame. He finished coiling the rope and put it around his shoulder. There was nothing else to see and they made their way back to the motel.

The anger was thinned by the clean breath of woodland by the time they got to the guard's room. Paul dumped the trash can over, picked out the textbooks and tossed them at Bobby.

"Don't give it up," he told the kid. "Not if it's what you want."

"You're gonna make a good cop." Vanzetti patted Bobby's shoulder condescendingly. "You got the feel. Take it from a pro. I was a good cop for nine years; you see where I am now."

Bobby, politely, said nothing.

Vanzetti lit another cigarette and went outside.

Paul found him resting against his sports car. The car was cherry-red and Italian. Paul raised one eyebrow at him.

Vanzetti flicked ash.

"So it's a start," he said finally. "Where we go from here—" He shrugged his shoulders, an untypically modest gesture.

Paul leaned on the car beside him.

"You mean you don't have any idea?"

"Sure I got ideas," the PI snarled. "There's lotsa possibilities." He sucked at the butt. "But you gotta remember, it could be anybody. Other boatyards around here. Don't smile—it happens. Or the other America's Cup boats, like you said. It could even be the Wise Guys—the Mob. You don't believe me?" Vanzetti shook his head, a pitying smile on his lips. "You think their bookies aren't already raking in thousands of bucks on the next cup? I *know* those guys."

"Not so fast," Paul held up a soothing hand. "You're missing something."

"I'm missing something, he says. Another fuggin' expert, like that kid. What am I missing?"

"The knots," Paul said. "The knots."

"The knots, the knots. What about the knots."

"He's a tugboat man," Paul said urgently, "the guy who killed Jack. He tied the alarm in the shed. Left the same knot he used on Bobby. I just figured out where I've seen it before. It's an inshore towing hitch. That's a tow-boat knot."

"So?"

"So I know where we can find him," Paul said, and took a step toward his Jeep. "At least, I know where to start looking."

"Where?"

"In New York. We could drive down. I know a guy on the tugs in New York. Walshie, Jeff Walsh. I worked with him on a tug for a summer. He'd help us out.

"See," Paul continued excitedly, "we know what the guy looks like. We know he has something to do with tugs. And tugboating's a real small world. Walshie used to talk about it. There's not too many boats left, and the crews know each other. It's worth a shot."

"Also"—Paul was thinking aloud—"New York's good for another reason."

Vanzetti played with cigarette smoke again, refusing to ask the question, so Paul answered anyway.

"That's where the big East Coast Twelve-Meter people hang out in the winter. Maybe I'll hear something. If one of them was especially worried about the *Challenge*, or something."

"You really think that's why he was killed? 'Cause of the Twelve-Meter stuff?"

Paul shrugged. "Why else?"

"Why else," Vanzetti agreed thoughtfully.

They talked for a few minutes more. Paul wrote Vanzetti a check. The PI stood aside and watched Paul drive off. He looked around him, at the woods, the empty road, the dingy motel surrounding him, and sighed heavily. Then he got in his own car and revved the motor. Tires squealing, he made a three-quarter skid in the middle of 197 and sped off, in the opposite direction, toward Bangor.

C   H   A   P   T   E   R   7

Jessica refused to change out of her Halloween costume the morning of Jack's funeral.

Faced with this rebellion, Lucinda sent her looking for her father. Jessica found Paul in his room, sitting on the edge of the bed, staring at his one dark suit, waiting for the smell of mothballs to fade.

She came in wearing a blue skirt with yellow felt stars sewn on. The large stitches were Lucinda's handiwork. She had a rainbow-striped blouse and a shawl of the same material. Burnt cork on her cheeks did not entirely conceal the freckles beneath, or dim the cornflower shade of her eyes.

"Hey, gypsy woman," Paul said to her, "look in your crystal ball and tell me where my daughter Jessica is."

Her mouth twitched a little. She said, "You know it's me. Jessica."

He feigned surprise. The smile grew, then faded. With a twinge of guilt Paul remembered she was like her mother—eyes like calm water, and large sea creatures roiling around beneath.

He patted the bed and she climbed up next to him, losing half the shawl. He complimented her on her costume automatically. She asked if he was still taking her trick-or-treating. He told her yes.

"Lucinda says you don't want to change out of your costume?" Paul ventured, after a pause.

The girl shook her head.

"Even gypsies wear normal clothes when they're not doing gypsy stuff."

It didn't work. She stared at the floor.

"Is it," he ventured gently, "because you don't want to go to church—to the funeral?"

A very round tear rolled over the arc of her cheek, leaving a trail of white in the cork behind.

Paul put an arm around her.

"Does it scare you? The idea of funerals, people dying?"

Jessica shrugged. Snot hung off her nose. Paul found an old bandanna for her to blow into.

"When I was real young, my grandmother died," Paul said. "She died right in granpa's house, in her bed, and my pa made me go look at her."

"She was dead?" Incredulity in Jessica's tone. The cornflower blue turned in his direction, bright with water.

"Dead as a doornail," Paul agreed. "But I didn't want to see her. I was about your age. I screamed and dug in my heels and my pa yelled at me. But Lucinda came and sat on my bed, just like we're doing now. And you know what she said?"

Jessica shook her head.

"She said, 'Aren't you curious?' And of course I was, though I said I wasn't. I'd never seen a dead body. And Lucinda said you had to see somebody dead to realize that being dead didn't mean anything. She said that when you died your life didn't disappear, it just went into the living things around you, like air and heat and grass—"

"She already told me that," Jessica said.

"Oh." Paul felt slightly foolish. "Well, you think it's true?"

His daughter shrugged, one shoulder only this time. Paul said, "I won't make you come. It's just a way to remember Uncle Jack when he was alive."

She thought about that for a while.

"What did she look like?"

"Granma? She didn't look like my granma at all. She was like those fiddler crab shells you collect on the beach in summer, but the fiddler crab was gone. You won't see Uncle Jack, anyway," Paul added, hastily. "He'll be in a coffin."

Jessica thought about it some more.

"Can I go in my costume?" she asked finally.

Paul sighed, and compromised. "As long as you wear a coat over it. And you can't tell fortunes in church."

Jessica giggled, and they left it at that. Paul had the strong impression he had not got to the bottom of what was bothering his daughter. He put it out of his mind in the confusion of getting ready and out the door by nine-thirty.

Jack arrived at the meetinghouse, on time as always, in a long black limousine. The box he lay in looked like an earlier version of the limo, all round shapes and plated fixtures. It was very heavy. Paul, his grandfather, and four men from the boatyard carried him into the church with some difficulty.

A great number of people sat crowded in box-pews as tiny and rectangular as Puritan thinking. Paul recognized people from the boatyard, the village. Warren Hillman, the manager of the Challenge syndicate, had come up from their training base in Newport. He sat in one of the more prominent pews with a large, sandy-haired man Paul had never seen before. Immediate family occupied a box directly under the pulpit.

Jack lay on sawhorses below the altar.

A strong wind blew from the southeast that day, and it came off Georges Sound and shook the building with Old Testament enthusiasm.

The preacher was tall and fiftyish and had a fine head of snowy hair that he liked to fling back dramatically. He did not know Jack but made up for it with long adjectives. "A glowing inspiration, a diligent employer," the preacher intoned, gripping the pulpit rail. He showed expensive teeth. "A loving husband." Then he went into an endless metaphor comparing the sea to life and boats to people, liberally grinding up clichés and throwing them in with half-remembered quotes from Masefield, Tennyson, Herodotus.

"Jack was a sailor," the preacher thundered, getting into the rhythm, "a man who did not fear storm or collision from ships passing in the snow or rain or dark of night. And if he crosses the bar, and we see his running lights beyond that distant shore, we must remember that here was a man who asked for nothing but a tall ship, and a star to steer her by. . . ."

Ashley pushed her nose deep in a black veil. Paul looked at the coffin and thought, this isn't Jack.

When the service was over they filed out the side door to the cemetery. Paul's daughter hung back, dragging harder and harder as they approached the grave.

Paul bent down and whispered to her. She didn't answer and he repeated his question. Her eyes would not meet his.

"Is my mother here?" she muttered at length, still not looking at him.

Paul kicked himself inwardly, called himself names.

"I told you, Jess," he said. "Mummy's alive. She's OK. She sent me a postcard, remember?" Almost two years ago, the last postcard had been.

"But if Uncle Jack can just go, maybe my mother can just go, too."

She was absolutely right, Paul thought, but what he said was, "Your mom's very sad. She got sad when Nicole disappeared and she went to be alone, by herself. She's not dead, though."

"How do you know?" Jessica insisted.

Paul looked at his daughter. Her face bore a curiously familiar look, as if all the world's useless quests had been congealed into a single emotion. He bent down, a little, to her level.

"I don't know," he told her seriously. "I don't think she's dead, though. I think she's gone somewhere warm." Wondering what the hell was the difference, to those she left behind.

They stood at the edge of the crowd, behind a yellow backhoe that lurked, its shovel folded scorpionlike, waiting for the fragile human ceremonies to end so it could get on with the earth's real business of clay and rock. The wind was very cold; it ripped through the ancient tombstones like bad breath through rotten teeth. "Captain Jedediah Poole, Hsbd. of Amelia, born 1802, died nr. Funchal Madeira Oct. 9, 1837." Many French Harbor men had died and been buried at sea over the years. The churchyard, like Paul's mind, was full of headstones with no bones underneath. Ashley came over and took Jessica's hand. They stood and froze together while Paul and five other men lowered Jack into the grave with ropes.

Afterward everyone got into their cars—turning the headlights on to ward away any lingering ghosts—and drove to Bull's house on Cully Head.

Bull's was in fact three houses. It consisted of a gloomy Victorian pile with gables, tall chimneys, and a cupola, nailed onto an older saltbox which in turn was hooked up to a barn. It was surrounded by rotting gazebos, wild raspberry bushes, fallen stone walls, and tall pines in which friends of Bull's crow would sit and crack dirty crow jokes, day in, day out.

The reception was warm and noisome as the cemetery had been cold and empty of human sound. Birch logs cracked sparks into the dark drawing room so that someone was always busy tap-dancing to crush out cinders near the fireplace. Nat and Squidlips Coggeshall guzzled beer with grim dedication in a corner. A naval architect from Boothbay said Jack was the best damn boat designer Maine had ever produced. Old George fed cookies to the crow. Bull, who had already sunk most of a bottle of cognac, stood on a couch and informed the crowd that this was a party, this had nothing to do with his grandchild, it was all to reassure the mourners that when they died they wouldn't disappear as if they'd never existed. By remembering Jack existed, they could all fool themselves into believing their own lives meant something in the scheme of things, he finished. Then he started sniffling, honking his large nose, turned maudlin by the brandy.

Paul put a couple of bottles of beer in his jacket pockets. He left Jessica with his mother and a plateful of gingerbread cookies, and went up to the cupola.

The cupola had served many purposes in its time: pirate quarterdecks, castle towers, bomber cockpits. From here you commanded sea approaches all the way to Two Ladies Island. If Jack was usually pilot, admiral, seneschal, then Paul was content to be mate, navigator, your common-or-garden knight. The sound of shoes unused to the cupola's steep stairs came as an intrusion on boyhood.

Warren Hillman came through the hatch. It did not take him long because he was all of five foot two. The tall man he'd been sitting with in church followed him up. They stood awkwardly around the windows, blocking the horizon.

"I'm really sorry, Paul," Hillman began. "We've got to get back to New York tonight. Wanted to tell you how sorry I am about Jack. We all are."

Hillman's square, English face was taut with sympathy, all the considerable energy in his compact frame directed at sharing Paul's loss. The likelihood this energy would be diverted within five minutes to a totally different purpose did not change the fact that now, this second, he believed what he said. He was a born salesman. As manager of a modern Twelve-Meter syndicate, he had to be.

The big man cleared his throat.

"This is Cy Shoop," Hillman said.

Paul recognized the name. Cornelius Shoop was one of the two principal backers of the Challenge group. He owned a clutch of defense research companies that sometimes made the financial pages, even in Bangor.

The other backer was a high-tech mail-order firm called CBM Technologies. The company sold totally useless computerized gadgetry all over the country through slick and colorful catalogs. One of their latest gimmicks was a noise suppressor, a high-tech box that was supposed to eliminate any sound you wanted by making a noise of equal amplitude but opposing wavelength.

"I have to tell you," Shoop said, "I barely knew your cousin. I came here mostly to talk to you? I know it's a bad time."

Paul looked harder at the man, noticing discrepancies he had missed before, details that did not jibe: the lazy assurance of a big man and the way his hands were never still; the shaggy hair and bifocals against eyes that betrayed nothing; the worn tweeds and the Caribbean tan.

"It doesn't matter," Paul said. "As a matter of fact I agree with my grandfather. Have a seat." He gestured magnanimously with an empty beer can.

"Good." Shoop sat on the bench that ran around the cupola. "We've got a problem here," he continued. "Warren says Jack only completed maybe sixty, seventy percent of the *Challenge*'s design when he was killed?"

Paul nodded.

"There were some major issues still to be resolved." Shoop looked hard over the reading glasses into Paul's eyes. A pronounced hook to his nose gave him a piratical air well in keeping with the cupola's history. "For example, the latest set of tank tests on the model did not square with what your computer predicted?"

"It's a process," Paul explained, wondering vaguely as he did so what Shoop was getting at, and why he always ended statements with a question mark. "There's always some discrepancies between the computer run and the model tests. I'll ask Piet Hendriks to check the calibration at the towing tank. Then I'll go through the numbers again. Then—"

"The specifics," Shoop waved a hand, "are not important. The main issue is, can you finish this boat, on time and on budget—or do we have to go somewhere else?"

Paul stared at the financier. Hillman made gentling noises, about how this was a big issue that would take weeks to resolve and in any case there was room for compromise. Paul ignored him. So did Shoop. Outside, the wind toyed with brown leaves, chased them in spirals through the air.

"Are you talking," Paul asked at length, "about the design or the construction."

"Both." Shoop steepled his fingers and kissed the tips. "The whole point of going with Briggs and Sons was you could cut costs, integrate the whole process, change things at the last minute, work with the Lloyds people. Otherwise, we would have gone the traditional route, separate designers, an aluminum boat instead of glass, the usual. Even though it's more expensive."

Paul levered himself straight from his slouched position on the bench. He pushed his glasses back up his nose, combed his forelock with one hand. He felt like a man who, using all his strength to prop up a cliff and keep it from tumbling on his head, suddenly feels the earth open beneath his feet.

Jack had remortgaged the yard to build the Twelve-Meter. If Briggs and Sons lost the contract, they would default on the mortgage. Paul's mind rebelled, refusing to face the enormity of the situation. The loss of Jack seemed to have preempted most of the disaster circuits. Something still functioned, however, for he heard himself say, "I can finish the design. The issue doesn't arise."

"Paul," Warren put in, "we know you're a good naval architect. The FH was a good series. But you've never worked on a Twelve, like Jack did."

"I worked on this one," Paul said, looking from Hillman to Shoop and back again. He knew his face was shut but underneath he now felt panic start to form and seep and short-circuit. He could not lose the yard. It had been in the family for four generations. Without it, French Harbor would starve. The herring were gone, lobsters grew scarcer every year, the tourists left in September. There was nothing else to do in this part of Maine.

It was all they had left.

"Mr. Briggs." Shoop spread his hands, clasped them shut very tight. "To be perfectly honest, what I hear about you is this? You were once an excellent designer of cruising boats. Then three years ago, your daughter disappeared. Your wife left you after that. Since then you have not designed even a rowboat. I'm sorry." Shoop's tone was sincere, but his face remained impassive, as always. The hands opened again. "Let me ask you this—would you hire yourself to design a boat for the most sophisticated, the most expensive, the most competitive sailboat race in the world?"

"I worked with Jack," Paul dodged the question. "I'm familiar with the software. I have great draftsmen here. Piet Hendriks is one of the best model engineers in the world. I tell you," he continued urgently, "we can finish that design."

Shoop frowned at Hillman. "Hendriks," he said, "there's some reason he can't take over?"

Hillman nodded. "He's a Danish national. According to the rules, an American Twelve-Meter has to be designed by an American. Like a Danish Twelve would have to be designed by a Dane."

"Well." Shoop looked at his watch, got to his feet. He told Hillman his pilot was going to run out of flying time if they didn't get back to the plane. "You can make your case, of course," he said to Paul. "But you'll have to convince the CBM people as well as me. 'Money by fair means . . . but by any means, money.' "

"What?"

"Nothing." Shoop waved away explanations. "What I'm saying is, we've already got four million bucks riding on this race, and we're not going to blow it just because you can't finish what your cousin started?"

That really hit. It cut through the panic. Paul rose slowly to look Shoop in the eye. He seemed to have no breath left, or subtlety to deal with this man and his hard words. All that he could muster, from some primitive green-scaled corner of the brain that specialized in fighting claims on territory, harem, brood, was a gauntlet flung in return.

"Give me five days," Paul whispered, "and I'll prove, not only I can finish your goddamn Twelve, but I can make it better into the bargain. I'll come to New York. I'll lay it out for you. Just five days is all I need."

Shoop kept his gaze but said nothing. Even Hillman could not come up with a reply to that one. After fifteen or twenty seconds had passed, the big man nodded and went down the stairs.

When Hillman had followed, Paul sat back down on the bench. He looked out to where the sea drooled over distant rocks and promontories they once ruled in the absolute monarchy of boyhood.

"Jack," he whispered to himself, "what in the name of all that's holy do I do now?"

No answer came. The crows laughed at him from nearby trees. Hillman was right, he had no idea whether he could finish the Twelve-Meter design right, let alone make it perform better than Jack would have done.

Paul reached for his second beer, then paused as he heard footsteps coming back up the stairs, but faster, something female in their lightness and resolve. Ashley came into view in four stages of blond hair, coral lipstick, coal silk dress, black pumps. Paul groaned inwardly.

"I was looking for you," she said, a little out of breath, and put a huge gin and tonic on the windowsill with exaggerated care.

Paul hesitated, pinched between the hangover from his last encounter and automatic sympathy for the widow. Deeper still lay a great distrust of her emotions toward himself and his own toward her and how they could react when confined in proximity. He asked if she was OK, but Ashley deflected the question with a glancing jerk of the chin to interrupt, "I heard all that."

Paul looked at her in surprise. Her eyes were very wide and she was pale, whiter even than she'd been in the boneyard.

"I heard your voice. I was going to come up, then I heard Warren and Cy. My hearing's really good, you know. I listened from under the stairs. Paul—" she leaned forward, a little unsteadily, from the waist. Paul noticed thankfully that she kept her arms folded well into the pivot line of her thighs—"you can't let them take the *Challenge* away."

He nodded, more to pull rationalizations from her than out of agreement. She was quite drunk, he thought, but she hid it well.

"You have to finish what Jack started."

Paul nodded again, wondering, behind the echoes of panic left ringing in his mind, at the raw urgency in her tone. Ashley came from a background that thought of Twelve-Meter racing the way other social groups thought of going to the high school diamond for a Saturday afternoon round of softball, but he'd never believed she'd really cared much about the yard or Maine or many of the other things her husband loved. It was her boredom and unhappiness, he thought, that had pushed her into his bed last summer—as if betrayal and guilt were any less boring in the long run.

"Paul," Ashley added with final emphasis, "I'm coming with you to New York."

He stared at her.

She gazed back at him with all the resolve of gin and the assurance of six generations of rich and educated men who believed, rightly, there was nothing they could not do once they set their mind to it. Paul looked away and told her to forget it, it did not make sense.

Why, Ashley demanded.

The real work, Paul told her, had to be done right here, before leaving; stacks of printouts to go through from the velocity-prediction program, from the test-tank computer.

Ashley could help out there, Paul continued, but she could not go to New York with him; the idea was ridiculous.

"It's not ridiculous," Ashley countered, eyes narrowed, swaying back and forth over her folded arms.

"What you don't understand," Ashley went on, "what Jack understood, is this. Selling a Twelve-Meter design is marketing and politics. As much as talent and skill. Maybe more. Hillman and Shoop and the rest of the syndicate—I mean, what do they know about sailing boats or hull design? But they're experts in the rest of it. You know, the packaging. The CYA, Covering Your Ass if the shareholders call you to account. You have to be able to say that the deal *looked* great and it's not your fault if what lay under the bright ribbons and party paper simply did not work. . . ."

If Ashley went to New York she could do what she was good at, which was the people side. Work up some slick graphics and coach Paul on his presentation. Rope in people she knew at the yacht club for political support and tax-deductible contributions. Paul was no good at that side of things, as Jack had been. She would bet—really putting him on the spot now—Paul did not even belong to the yacht club.

Paul yanked out his second beer, opened it. Foam gushed cold from the can, spilled over his fingers. Ashley took a plastic bottle from her purse, shook out two pills, and used them as an excuse to finish off the gin and tonic.

"You're scared of going down with me, aren't you," she said.

Paul took a sip. The beer tasted sharp, bitter, full of bubbles that stung his taste buds. He said, "You bet your ass I'm scared."

"Isn't that sort of cowardly?" Ashley asked, in her sweetest tone, but she couldn't quite keep the slur out of the *s*.

"Cowardly? When the staties are convinced I killed Jack because someone told them about us, about you and me," he forced himself to name it, "sleeping together? Then, a week after Jack dies, off we go to New York together? That's real cute, Ashley."

She shook her head.

"That's not what I meant," she said. "You're not like that. You wouldn't care. It's us you're afraid of. You and me. Not other people or what they think."

Paul took another long swig, then another, until he had emptied the can. By affinity the cold liquid accented the other cool feelings blending inside him. He put down the empty and rose, straightening his jacket. Ashley's blue gaze followed him up.

"I have other things to do in New York. I know people in towboats, I want to ask around if anybody knows the guy in the Riverview. You'd just get in the way."

She said nothing. The eyes tracked him as he moved. Blue for freezing, Paul thought. Black for pain. The pupils were very dilated. He wondered what was in those pills.

"OK," Paul admitted. "As a matter of fact, I don't want to give the state police any more ammunition than they already have. But if you need another reason, listen.

"Jack's been dead only three days." Paul spoke to the horizon. "I can't screw him over again, but I can keep from cheating on his memory, for my own peace of mind." He stood over the stairs, fell forward, a prisoner of habit, until his hands caught on the beam at the top of the stairwell.

"You don't understand," Ashley protested, and now her hands unlocked to reach for his jacket, not quite touching, "You're not listening to me—" but Paul grasped the top of the beam and swung himself downstairs, like a pirate boarding a ship-of-war, drawing a mental cutlass, leaning bravely into the swarming well-armed king's men and the darkness of the stairs, away from the woman and the surf of emotions still breaking above his head.

C H A P T E R 8

The phone booth stood by itself in a desert of broken brick and crushed glass. The food warehouses and leather bars it once served had been pulverized a week before by bulldozers and a wrecking crane. The booth was spared because no one touched NYNEX equipment without permission. It stayed because it turned out to be convenient; construction workers could call their girls, their bookies; city inspectors and union stewards could call the bank and proceed with work if their savings had swelled by an agreed amount.

In two or three weeks blasting would start in the vacant lot. Fences, portable toilets, and trailer offices would sprout like mushrooms after rain. Then would come the concrete and rods and the great steel I-beams and the rows of utility lights climbing higher and higher into the sky. When the building was finished they would plant little flower beds and terraces in the fresh cement and the phone booth would eventually be unhooked and hauled away.

For now, however, for this night, it was the only structure on ten thousand square feet of smashed bricks. The way it stood by itself, brightly lit, geometric on a piece of ground where no geometry was called for made it seem like a machine from another planet, dropped on terrain that would seem hospitable only to an alien mind.

The man hurried across the vacant lot toward the booth's white light, clutching his coat around him. He had spent all day in an overheated office and the breeze coming off the river was very cold. He got to the phone just as it started ringing.

"Hello," he said, and cursed under his breath. As if it could be anyone other than the caller he expected.

"It's you," said the voice on the other end.

They were all slaves to ritual greeting, the man thought. "Who did you think?" he said. "You saw the papers?"

"Yes," the voice replied, "I saw them. There won't be any problem."

"No problem!" The man laughed, a short, dry sound. "That's a funny way to put it. It was supposed to be a crummy little B-and-E, and now it's murder."

"We've already been through that."

The man repressed his annoyance. It was like dealing with a child. A spoiled, thirty-five-year-old kid.

"Anyway," the voice complained, "you told me to call you. We could have had this conversation at the meeting."

The man grimaced, an automatic reflex, a sign of strain and in this case, worry. You picked your friends, he reflected, but in this day and age you could not pick and choose people who were willing to take decisive action. That quality had been greased out of the genes by years of complacency and soft living. He would have to explain slowly.

"There may still be a problem," he said. "Apparently the cousin is saying he wants to take over. And though we may have killed the bastard—"

"Brecht, by God! I don't believe it. You're quoting Bertolt Brecht at me."

The man hesitated, equally surprised at his reference being picked up. There was a decent education there, under the bluster. Dartmouth, he thought. He would have to bear that in mind.

"It's unlikely," he continued, "that the cousin will be retained by the Challenge syndicate. He's never done anything but cruising boats, and the design is not finished. But if for some reason they finish this boat—and if it turns out as fast as they say—" He let the implication hang heavy in the phone lines.

"A little defensive blocking?" the voice suggested.

"More like constructive fouls."

"I guess."

"Only this time—"

"What?" The voice sounded nervous all of a sudden.

"I want a professional."

"I used a pro last time," the voice protested. "It wasn't my fault there was a hitch."

"Real professionals don't have hitches," the man said. "They're paid not to. I'll take care of the next one."

There was silence on the other end.

"Just from the point of view of efficiency," the voice said, cautiously. "There's police in this now. I know they're only Maine police, but still. It could get tricky."

"Are you getting cold feet already?" The man's tone was sarcastic. "One little problem, and you want to give up? I thought you were as committed to this as I am."

"I don't want to give up. But I wouldn't call it a little problem."

The man smiled. It was so easy to manipulate people. He'd turned the argument completely around. "You just said there was no problem at all." He paused, to let the contradiction sink in. "In any case, big or little, it was bungled. But don't worry," the man went on, confidently. "The cousin's nothing, a has-been. A human wreck. It won't take much to stop him."

"And if it does?"

"You'll see. All it will take is a little pressure. And if that doesn't work, we lean harder. Break his boat, or something. He'll fold like wet cardboard."

"Yes. And if he doesn't?" the voice insisted.

"Listen," the man shot back. "There are two kinds of people. There are people who win, and there's the others. We do what we have to. And you're in too deep to quit, even if you wanted to."

The man hung up, his heart beating hard.

For some reason, he felt a sudden craving for a cigarette, though he had not smoked in years.

He thought there had been just the right touch of menace in that last statement, nicely underlined by breaking off the connection. There would be no quitting now, for either of them.

He opened the folding doors, conscious now of how exposed he was in the lighted booth in the middle of a vacant lot on the edge of a polder between the great city and its river.

But if he was exposed, so was anybody watching. He laid his plans well, the man told himself, in satisfaction. Wrapping his coat once more around him, he went back out into the darkness.

C H A P T E R 9

Below the central span of the Triboro Bridge a small harbor tanker had lost its steering at a crucial moment, banged into a bridge piling, and was now burning fiercely, even as it sank into the pulsing tides of Hell's Gate. Two fireboats, a police craft, and a harbor tug fussed around, spewing foam onto the glowing wreck. TV helicopters hovered like dragonflies. The fire-circus drifted lazily with the current toward Manhattan. It blended with the last reds and yellows of sunset and chemical fumes to the north and west, staging a free show that touched the secret fantasies of a thousand car-bound rubberneckers on the bridge above.

Paul looked at his watch, checked the map for the tenth time in as many minutes.

The cat, Jacob, sensed something in the air. He climbed from the rear seat onto Paul's shoulder to poke his doggy Maine-coon snout out the sliver of space at the top of the driver's window, blinking and sniffing into a wind that came straight off the river. "Ro-o-ow," he commented in a throaty, public-radio kind of voice.

"I hope this clears up," Ashley said, looking at the stalled traffic and the cherry-top flashers of cops trying to clear cars past the spectacle. "We're going to be late for sure."

There was a new strength to her voice, Paul noticed. They had been driving steadily for eleven-and-a-half hours, but over the last two hundred or one hundred miles she seemed to be picking up energy, not losing it. Healthier creams, even pinks drove out some of the gray in her cheeks and the smudge in her eyesockets. This was a new shine that came from underneath the mascara, a glow that owed nothing to expensive French cosmetics. It was as if every mile closer to the insane brown dynamo power of New York, away from the clean pastel shadings of the country, brought more and more circuits back to life inside her. To Paul, who disliked the city, it didn't make sense. He glanced at the woman where she sprawled in the passenger's seat, legs tangled in tantric angles, her eyes on the lights that were winking on in thousands to protect the jagged skyline from the dark.

She had worn at him for three days. Sorrow seemed to alter into a determination as mica-flecked and solid as the granite underpinning those sparkling distant buildings, and he was no match for her obsessive arguments.

She'd vowed, first of all, there would be no emotional nonsense between them. They would go as business partners first, friends a long way last. Second, she would act as manager, public relations specialist, political adviser all rolled into one for his meetings with the syndicate people. Lastly, they could stay with Bradley Winton, her godfather, at his house in Chelsea—in separate bedrooms, it went without saying.

Bradley Winton chaired the America's Cup committee at the New York Yacht Club. This, too, was part of Ashley's plan.

Murdoch was still looking for an indictment, but the town cops at long last were pushing for a search focused on the stranger from the motel. Traveling together might no longer be viewed with such suspicion. . . .

Paul had given in.

He gave in partly because he was spending eighteen hours a day trying to understand exactly where in the process of feedback and correction Jack's design stood and had no energy left to argue with Jack's widow. He gave in because Jessica's birthday was coming up and he would need all the help he could get to make it home in time. And he gave in because he clearly saw the skull-face of despair behind her determination. He even agreed to bring her cat along for the ride.

Now, watching her look at the city like a lover, he wondered whether Ashley's desperation stemmed as much from Jack's loss as from the prospect of being stuck in French Harbor, when the excuse for her isolation was buried six feet deep in a hillside churchyard with a breeze coming off Georges Sound as harsh as the one now buffeting their Jeep on the Triboro Bridge.

"God, it's good to be back," she muttered to the window, as if catching the scend of his thoughts. She opened her purse for cigarettes.

Up over the crown of the bridge a van that had stalled in its driver's excitement was pulled toward Randall's Island by a pair of yellow blinkers. Cars jerked and spaced and moved out. Paul found Brahms playing on the radio station of the *New York Times*. When they got off the bridge ramp he took the first exit south, down the FDR Drive.

It was just past rush hour and the streets were clear. By the time they reached the remodeled SROs and meat-packing houses of Hell's Kitchen they had cut their delay to twelve minutes. He parked the car in an underground garage. Ashley examined him critically, touched his tie in a wifely gesture before lining her own features with different colored powders. "It's more important to look good, up there," she remarked, "than to be on time to the minute."

"Up there" was a mass of mirrored triangles, twenty stories high, built on three triangular legs over a trapezoid atrium full of potted trees and croissant stands.

The top of the building was shaped like a wedge. Its tinted glass blazed in the beam of spotlights set on nearby structures. The letters "CBM" glowed pinkish on all four sides.

They entered the atrium, signed a register, and were shown by security guards to an elevator that played synthesized rock 'n' roll tunes as it carried them to the top floor.

☷

The Challenge syndicate waited for them in the great isosceles boardroom of CBM Technologies, lined up along two sides of a conference table of gleaming steel.

The table was large and, naturally, triangular. Hillman stood on tiptoe at one apex, waiting to make introductions. Shoop lounged tweedily at the other. Between them sat three men dressed in similar blue blazers and widely divergent tie styles. Ashley stepped forward with charming phrases and automatic assurance, but it was her earlier words Paul heard in his head as she had laid out the dynamics of the Challenge syndicate during two hours of straight-line driving down the Maine Turnpike.

The main investor behind the Challenge syndicate was CBM, and CBM was these three—J. Harmon Canaday II, Robert D. Baldwin, and Douglas Munoz, Jr.

They had started the company to take advantage of the high-tech slump caused by overinvestment in the early days of personal computers. They were the first to buy out lines of high-tech products from busted companies and sell them cheap by mail order—everything from Taiwanese word processors to sonic mosquito zappers to microchip popcorn cookers. They bought good mailing lists, figured the right prices, and delivered fast. In seven years they grew to dominate the high-tech mail-order field, with sales worth over twenty million last quarter.

Canaday, Baldwin, and Munoz. All three were from the Boston area, all came from comfortable backgrounds, all had met at Wareham Latin, a prep school for whites who were not Anglo or Protestant.

Ashley's cousin Christopher knew of these men. Chris had dated a girl from Wareham Latin. She claimed the three monopolized Latin's marijuana trade, mass-marketed term papers, and rigged a basketball game with Choate, among other accomplishments. It was a true symbiosis, Chris's girlfriend added, where Munoz provided the organizing ability, and Baldwin, whose family was in politics, the contacts. J. Harmon Canaday was the brains in the equation—truly brilliant, it was said, at sensing what people would buy next, where to acquire it low, when to sell it high. It was Canaday who came up with the idea of building a bold tower in a rotting neighborhood to publicize the company name. The investment paid for itself as real-estate sharks jacked up prices and bought out the area in CBM's wake.

And it was Canaday who pushed the idea of sponsoring an America's Cup effort to publicize a new line of mail-order hardware. Five cents out of every dollar you spent on buying CBM's new "Challenge" microcomputer went toward winning the cup for the greater glory of America and CBM Technologies, Inc.

Where was Shoop in all of this, Paul had asked, somewhere around Waterville. Did Cousin Christopher know his school record as well?

Shoop had not gone to Milton, Ashley said, in the kind of tone one would use to discuss childhood polio. Shoop wanted to be known as an America's Cup sponsor so he would be invited to the chic parties, accepted in the right clubs, seated in the fanciest box when the Met season opened.

Shoop's interests in research companies that mostly worked for the Pentagon were probably worth three CBMs put together, but he was not in it for material return. The man, Ashley summed up with deadly contempt, was a social climber.

Ignore Shoop, she'd reminded him, as they left the turnpike at York. The one he had to convince was Canaday; the one to watch was Munoz.

Now Paul followed Ashley down the endless blue-green carpet. They walked past a large, backlit display case decorated with the syndicate's racing symbol—a sail surrounded by CBM's triangle logo. The case featured a selection of products CBM would market alongside the America's Cup effort. There was a science-fiction gun labeled the Official America's Cup Laser Bug-Zapper. Beside that, a portable noise suppressor and a "modem" that allowed you to control all your household appliances over the telephone. There were two versions of the "Challenge" computer.

A three-foot-high figure took pride of place. It was vaguely humanoid, with antennae for ears, padded clamps for arms, caterpillar treads for legs. Three inches of thick synthetic fur covered its frame. "Frobie," the label read, "the furry robot, Official Mascot of the Challenge America's Cup Team."

Paul had to bite his tongue to avoid nervous laughter as he passed the display case. Only Shoop got up to shake hands with Paul and brush Ashley's cheek with his lips.

On closer inspection Paul could see that despite the similar jacket styles the three CBM men were as unmatched as they could be. Baldwin was tall and thin. He parted his hair in the middle, and wore a tie that shrieked yellow flowers. Canaday was short. His bald head was much too big for its body. He had a face like a sea turtle, a thin moustache, a crimson tie.

Munoz wore a yellow tie with green whales. He was tall and blond. A bony Castilian nose dominated his face. As Paul and Ashley approached they could see that Baldwin was talking on a phone that looked like a toothbrush and had no cord. Canaday was tapping figures on a solar-powered keyboard, while Munoz watched the table in front of him and scratched under his chin. When Paul sat down he noted that each place had a video terminal recessed into the green marble and thick teak; on the screen was a graph and a jumping list of figures, headed by the words "Challenge Syndicate—Cost/Benefit Projections" in clear lime letters.

Munoz was the first to grant them his complete attention. He looked at Paul and stated, "You're Jack Briggs's cousin." He made no move to get up or shake hands. "We're all very sorry about Jack," he continued. "It's sick that something like that could happen. Sick." He scratched his chin again and glanced at the others. "At the same time," he went on after a pause, "we hope you understand this board has made no decisions regarding the Twelve-Meter; also we are in no way obligated by any efforts you may have undertaken on our behalf." Legal counsel shone like braided steel beneath the tissue of his words.

Shoop yawned. Baldwin clicked a microswitch on his cordless and folded his hands. They all waited expectantly. Paul deduced he was supposed to give the presentation now and stood up. "Lee Chow says moo goo duck's fresh and ready," Baldwin announced suddenly into the now silent boardroom. "Any offers?" Munoz held up two fingers. Canaday said, "Duck sauce." Baldwin raised his eyebrows at Ashley.

Ashley shook her head, opened her briefcase, took out folders containing worksheets of the *Challenge* design and passed them around the group. The graphics were her idea. They were attractive and glossy. Canaday pushed a button, fed his copy onto a clear plastic screen next to the computer recess. Across the room a panel whirred down from the ceiling. The image of the *Challenge* appeared instantly across its surface, bright with colors, six feet in length.

"Uh—thank you," Paul said, in surprise. He walked over to draw inspiration from the lines themselves.

A fairly standard Twelve-Meter hull. In profile she was long, smooth as a fashion model, and full of gentle curves underneath. Seen from above, she looked like a stretched teardrop, with a sharp bow and a gentle slope of transom rounding out her after shape. Her mast was taller than the boat was long. The tip of the bow was snubbed vertically to take advantage of the Twelve-Meter rule. She was stretched and bound and stuffed with tense machinery, like the rest of the Twelve-Meters.

Where Jack's design parted company with more conventional plans was most obviously in the keels. While a conventional Twelve had one keel hanging from its bottom, this boat had two. They were set parallel, like the down-beating wings of a bird, one on each side of the hull roughly halfway between the deepest part of the boat and the waterline. They carried fat lead rings, bulging like jet intakes on the ends. The less obvious differences included exaggerated trim tabs, like airplane flaps on the trailing edge of the keel and a narrow forward section designed to slice through the long rollers off La Rochelle, France. The next major event in Twelve-Meter racing—the Doyen-Kruyff Champagne Cup—would take place in La Rochelle and immediately after that, the America's Cup series.

Christ, she's funny-looking, Paul thought, but what he said was. "I've spent the last few days catching up on all the work Jack had to do when he was killed"—words still came hard against that memory—"and what I can tell you now is this design is closer to completion than I thought. There's just not that much left to do. Another month, six weeks at most, and we can lay the—keels."

Paul looked back at the table, hoping for encouragement, and picked up only Ashley's frown of worry. He was stumbling too much. He pressed on, regardless, pointing out the changes and compromises Jack had arrived at over the very last stage of the project, explaining how they made for better speed. It's yourself you're selling, as much as the boat, Ashley'd told him. Paul made an effort to marshal his thoughts, to be clear and concise. He tried to forget this was not the kind of boat he cared for, not the kind of boat he would have designed, if he'd had the gall to design anything after three years of not even picking up a pencil. But none of that was relevant, Paul thought. He injected drive and determination into his voice and body language as he wound up the summary. The only thing that mattered now was the yard.

No one spoke for a second or two after Paul finished. Sirens mourned in the streets below. In the thousands of windows visible through the boardroom's plate glass, people changed diapers, ended affairs, drew water, opened cans of dog food, oblivious to the tiny drama being played over their heads.

"It was supposed to be revolutionary," Canaday broke the silence, looking at his video terminal for support. "It was supposed to run circles round the other boats, with those twin keels. Jack said they would cut wave resistance, but his last report didn't deliver. We tried to give him a free hand," Canaday complained, and chopped his sentence short by way of interrogation.

Paul paused to plan his words.

"From what I've seen," he explained, carefully, "the problem comes when the model is tested at over fifteen degrees of heel, like when the boat is working upwind, leaning away from the wind. As you know," (he was not sure they knew, but a little flattery could not hurt) "a boat creates waves when it moves through the water. These waves slow the boat down. Now our computer model predicted that the windward keel, because of the way it sticks out sideways, would come up and create an underwater swell; kind of like when you move your hand just under the surface of water in your bathtub." Paul pointed at the screen to show the area in question. "The swell would show up here, just ahead of the quarter-wave, where you get the most disturbance at racing speeds. It would work exactly like the noise suppressor your company markets, it would create a wave of equal amplitude, but opposite wavelength, so that the two waves just cancel each other out, and there's nothing but smoothness left.

"Well," he continued, "you cancel out the quarter-wave, you get rid of one of the major sources of hull resistance; but what we're seeing in the tank tests is this: the wave friction is being cut on the side the keel comes *up*—but there's a vortex on the other side of the hull that is hurting performance. We didn't expect that. What we have to do is measure the vortex in the tank, plug that into the program, and play around with the position of the keels till overall performance improves."

Not bad, Paul thought to himself; fairly clear. Ashley's frown had shallowed out a little. It was easy to be cool and clear and dispassionate, he thought, when you had not been emotionally involved in a project.

"Uh, if you don't mind my asking," Munoz leaned back in his chair and swung tasseled loafers onto the table, one after the other, "how do you know how to do this? Warren here tells us you haven't done much in the way of design work, these last few years, and this is all, uh, fairly modern stuff, you know—models, tank tests, and so on?" He smiled, too boyishly, and picked at his chin again.

First of all, Paul answered, the principles were not modern, they were the essence of yacht design. People like L. Francis Herreshoff and Colin Archer had laid them out at the turn of the century, and no one had come up with anything better. What had changed were the techniques used to test different hull concepts, and that was where computers and towing tanks came in. These techniques were also the focus of Paul's work in the Challenge project. Jack designed the hull, but Paul had the specific task of running the "velocity prediction" programs, feeding in the data, tabulating the results.

The Velocity Prediction Program, or "VPP," Paul added, was a piece of computer software that took the basic forces acting on a boat—on its sails, keel, hull, and rigging—balanced them against each other, and then threw that balance against a whole history of benchmark tests.

These tests, done in real life on many different boats, enabled the program to predict, through equations full of variables and extrapolations, how a change in design would translate into a change in performance. Known as "curve fitting," the process called for a great deal of computer time and much sorting through columns of figures.

"Warren says—" Baldwin nodded at Hillman, "it's no secret you don't like Twelve-Meters much, you have zero experience working on them. So why," he shrugged his shoulders to emphasize the question, "why get involved at all?"

Paul made himself pause before he replied. He took off his glasses, cleaned them on his shirt. "Twelve-Meters are no different from other boats," he began, at length. The questioning was beginning to wear at him but he made an effort to keep his voice calm, patient. "Twelves are simply drawn to a specific, rudimentary formula—the Twelve-Meter rule. That imposes certain limits on what you can and cannot do. The formula's basically an equation that balances factors making the boat go fast, like length and sail area, against elements that slow it down, like weight. You see, it's not hard to design a boat within those limits. What is hard—really hard—is to create the good compromise between stability, keel forces, sail forces, and wave resistance so you get maximum speed, like with any other form of sailing hull. So to answer your question, I got involved in the Challenge like I'd get involved in any other boat project—because it's what I do." Or what I used to do, he thought to himself.

"What Baldwin means is," Munoz drawled, "why shouldn't we just cut our losses and switch to a real Twelve-Meter designer?"

"Because the design's almost finished," Paul countered, trying to ignore the sudden feeling of unreality that came with fatigue, a brief flash that he was standing in one of those myriad windows out there, looking up at the wedge of light where he himself stood, talking to four skeptical financiers, looking out at the window where he watched himself watching. He rubbed his hair and continued. "Because with our contract you also get a first-class boatyard that can make last minute corrections on the spot. Piet Hendriks, Jack's assistant, is just doing the late model tests, which will probably call for changes. That's normal. The Lloyds inspector will almost certainly want changes, and without his approval we don't race, according to the cup rules. So if he says, put another layer of glass on the ribs, to stiffen the hull, we simply plug it into the design and do it, then and there. We can do it that fast," Paul continued, "because we're the only boatyard in America that's done the job of correlating the stress loads on Twelve-Meters to a fiberglass hull. And we can do it cheap.

"Finally," Paul added, almost as an afterthought, "I've got the experience, the talent to finish Jack's design, and finish it right." He had to jail his own doubt as he said the words but they came out brazen enough.

A thin Chinese man in a blue, serge suit came in at that point and started laying out paper plates and covering them with gluey slop that smelled of chicken. No one offered around any food when the Chinese man had disappeared. Munoz broke a pack of chemical heat rods and stuck them in the food to keep it warm. Canaday opened a drawer, took out a bunch of plastic chopsticks that were joined at the middle. He held his pair at the joint and they opened and closed by themselves. Still playing with the motorized chopsticks he pointed out that Paul's reputation, such as it was, rested on one line of production cruising boats, the FH series. He had also designed a large sailing schooner, the *Zulu*, for the Maritime Trust. The schooner was very fast, despite her traditional lines. She had gone down in bad weather four years ago.

Paul refused to rise to the bait. Nor did he allow the naming of

Zulu to bother him. He told himself that men like these always poked and prodded, hoping for a reaction that would reveal the truth behind the sales patter.

"The discipline is the same, no matter what kind of boat you build," Paul insisted, reasonably. "Naval architecture's like politics. It's the art of compromise. Take the FH series. That was a compromise between comfort and speed. The schooner, the *Zulu*, was a compromise between traditional lines and speed. The *Challenge* is a compromise between the Twelve-Meter rule and speed. It's almost as simple as that."

No one said anything for a minute or so. Munoz nibbled at a spring roll and used a chopstick to poke at his chin itch. Finally Baldwin put his phone down. "I talked to a guy," he drawled, "he went to BC with my brother. He's a naval architect as well. He said hiring you would be, how'd he put it, like getting a vet to fix a Ferrari. He said you were all washed up."

That cut through the out-of-body feeling. Paul turned to the plate glass, stilling the surge of fury, looking for the tiny window of impartiality where he could watch himself perform—but the alienation had died, melted into stronger currents where he could no longer stand apart from himself.

"That's baloney."

Paul took a deep breath, but it did nothing to plug the leak in his control. The fury surged again, pushed him closer to the big table. He pointed at Baldwin with an aggressive finger.

"Baloney," he repeated. "One thing you have to remember about this Twelve-Meter scene, it's built on hype. It's nothing but a game, you understand? Played with some of the most expensive toys in the world, but still a game. The rule book for that game is some simplistic rule made up by a lot of stuffed-shirt Edwardians in Newport, in Cowes. The people who've kept the rule alive are a bunch of trust-fund yachtsmen who're the grandchildren of the same old farts who made up the rule in the first place."

"So what you end up with is the worst of both worlds. You don't have the fairness of a one-design class, but also you don't have the excitement of really fast boats, like the Maxis—or like the Jumbo-boat the New Zealanders challenged with in '87. They should have kept the rules loose, they should have *kept* racing big boats, 'stead of going back to Twelve-Meters, because what Twelve-Meter racing is, it's like getting Team Ferrari to build cars that look like Model-T Fords. And the result is hideously expensive, inefficient, unseaworthy monstrosities." Paul thought of a better analogy. "Or like Spanish galleons built by NASA. Because of the rule they barely squeak over nine knots, and they can only do that in a limited range of wind and wave conditions on one specific 24.3-mile stretch of ocean, out of the whole world of ocean they can perform only on one little course, and they're not even very fast—"

Paul stopped, out of breath. Ashley chopped a hand at her throat, a tiny gesture that said "Shut up." She wouldn't have appreciated hearing her grandfather called an "old fart." Next to her, Shoop seemed to wake up for the first time. "I suppose you could do better?" he asked sarcastically.

Anger would not help, but being cool and bland did not seem to work either. Paul was sick of the charade, sick of pretending, sick of trying to wear another man's clothes. Ashley had been wrong; these people did not worry about covering their asses. They were a law unto themselves, and already had made up their minds, slick graphics or no slick graphics.

He threw caution to the wolves, heard himself retort, "If you must know, I *could* do better. I could design a fast Twelve-Meter because I think, I mean, I know what makes them tick. You see—" he looked to Shoop's steepled fingers now, ignoring the rest, and suddenly felt all the locked little bubbles of creativity, the fettered ideas, the frozen free associations that had nowhere to go while he was trapped in his distaste for the project, all of these burst a block in his head, crowded into his mouth, and jostled for verbs to ride out on.

He let them run.

"Listen. Building a fast Twelve-Meter nowadays relies on doing two things right. First you've got to make a good all-around hull. This hull," he gestured at the screen, "is OK, but it doesn't feel right. I think we could make it a foot longer because it's too small for high winds, and they get a lot of those in La Rochelle. Rumor has it the *Bretagne*, the one Morgat is designing, is going to be long, and he knows those waters better than anyone. I wouldn't fool with twin keels either, or the ringed tips; they haven't been tested enough. More importantly, they're not pretty, quarter-wave or no quarter-wave, and I've never seen an ugly boat that was fast. You see"—

Paul spread his hands on equal planes, "a boat is more than the sum of its compromises, it's a balance beyond the balance, it's a harmonic, it has the beat, it has the pace of the sea built into its very structure, it's"—he brushed his hair back roughly with one hand, frustrated at his inability to find the right words—"it's something you *feel* when you look at it, like any work of art.

"So, anyway," he turned back to the plan, "I'd put in a graceful, high-aspect ratio keel, maybe small fins on the bottom. I'd make her finer forward, like I said, and a bit wider aft; leave her shallow at the buttocks." He swept in the curves he wanted on the screen.

"The second thing you need, to get the edge against all the other three-million-dollar boats,"—Paul paced back and forth, the audience forgotten, everything forgotten but the rhythm of his thoughts—"you need better gimmicks. Unfortunately naval architects are pretty conservative, they like to run with the herd as much as anyone else, and since *Australia II* all the herd can think of is different kinds of wings. Wings, for chrissake! Wings are fine, for more stability, for less tip vortex—but if you want a really fast boat, what you should do is work on a keel that can change shape without changing volume, putting a curve into it so the keel can work more like an airplane wing, lifting the boat out of the water, like this. It would be legal, since it basically does what a trim tab does, only better. Obviously it would cost a lot—"

Someone coughed. All of a sudden Paul remembered there were other people in the room. He realized that, with the possible exception of Shoop, no one was listening.

Ashley had her head cupped in her hands. Munoz was kneeling beside her, whispering in her ear. Canaday was wolfing moo goo duck with great predatory scoops of his chopsticks. Baldwin talked on the phone. Paul said "Anyway" in an uncertain voice.

"We should tell you," Canaday announced, with his mouth full, not even bothering to look up, "this syndicate is talking to another naval architect. He has a lot of experience with Twelve-Meters, he worked with—who was that guy?"

"Bruce Archibald," Hillman said.

Ashley looked up abruptly.

"He's the main threat, apart from the French," Hillman went on.

Munoz took up the flow smoothly, adding that at this stage it would not be too expensive to change designers, and Briggs and

Sons would get their cancellation fee, should the syndicate decide to go that route.

He put in a few phrases about how the decision was not yet final, words expressing gratitude for previous work; but all Paul could think about over the sinking in his gut was Bull's face when he had to tell him the yard was forfeit. All he could see was the salt-worn, rickety maze of pilings and tracks and sheds that had been the work of art his family had labored to build and preserve because of a certain idea they all shared about building to suit the sea instead of the other way around; an idea of harmony, when all was said and done, that was more than just a basis for boats.

They all stood up and shook hands this time. Ashley smiled and smiled and asked them to consider carefully the benefits of Briggs, as if it were a better aspirin, one doctors recommended most. She knew everyone in New York, she could rope in a lot of extra sponsors for the *Challenge*, if they decided to stay with Briggs and Sons. No one could do it better or cheaper. Her bright tone rang false in Paul's ears.

He let her talk, said nothing, dry of words, washed by fatigue and the flushing sense of defeat.

When the elevator doors finally closed behind them they did not look at each other. Massed synthesizers played "Stairway to Heaven" as they rode down to the underground parking lot and the waiting Jeep, where Jacob the cat waited for them, smoothing his whiskers against the steering wheel.

C H A P T E R   1 0

Paul woke up from dreams of chasing and disquiet to find a thin Japanese in a black bumfreezer pouring tea into a cup on his bedside table.

The Japanese unfolded a *New York Times* and placed it next to the tea before leaving on sandaled feet, as quietly as he had come.

Paul glanced through the paper but even these headlines of war in Iraq and pestilence in Somalia could not compete with the sense of doom filling him. Some of the feeling came from the dreams. More came from impressions of last night slowly clustering into an aching whole in his mind.

They had lost the *Challenge* contract. There were formalities to go through yet but the writing was on the wall. He felt some relief because now he would not have to bust his balls for months working on a boat he did not, could not like. But underneath that relief lay a deep and weighty sadness, of absence piled on defeat piled on loss—a dread that expressed itself in a slow turning in his stomach, as if he had eaten something bad.

After a while he made himself get out of bed. It took an almost physical effort. He had not fallen asleep until three or four. He got dressed automatically and went downstairs.

Bradley Winton's house was old, built in post-Federal style where the skewed streets of Greenwich Village gave way to the midtown grid, leaving room for big gardens in the process.

The downstairs shone with Irish crystal and Queen Anne chairs. Lace and china graced narrow tables at every corner. Paul found himself looking for a seat where he could stretch out without breaking anything. He went from room to room in this way until he found the library.

Compared to the rest of the house, the library exuded solidity. It had deep leather armchairs and massive bookshelves. Meaty artwork lined the walls: Winslow Homer, Thomas Hart Benton, a portrait of an earlier Winton by Reginald Marsh. The paintings in the room would buy five boatyards.

Paul sat down in one of the armchairs. He took out a twenty-pound tome on painters of the Italian Renaissance and a double-spread Caravaggio hit him right in the mouth with its hard light.

For fifteen minutes he flipped smooth pages in the quiet room. The strong colors of the artists diluted his gut-ache.

Jason came in. He circled the room twice, made choking noises, and threw up on the rug. The cat looked at Paul to see if he'd noticed, then jumped on a chair and gave himself a long, relaxed bath.

"God, you're a disgrace," Paul told him, and lost himself in the book again.

Finally he put the book away and decided to find the phone. In today's absence of alternatives he would call the various port captains and track down Jeff Walsh.

He found the phone in the sitting room by following the sound of its ringing. He was looking for the phone book when the Japanese butler appeared at his elbow and asked if he was "in for" Cornelius Shoop.

Shoop, Paul thought. He probably wanted, once again, to say how sorry he was for the rest of them. The rest of them, once again, could not be bothered.

"Christ, no," he muttered, out loud.

The Japanese—Seiji, Ashley called him—lifted his eyebrows, carefully neutral.

Paul shook his head, and resumed looking for the directory, but this presumably was one of those households where one dialed information rather than going to all the trouble of letting your fingers do the walking.

The Japanese reappeared with a slip of paper titled "While You Were Out."

"9:25 A.M. From: Mr. Cornelius Shoop. To: Mr. Paul Briggs. Please join him at the Pharos Coffee Shop at 10:00 A.M. Urgent." There was a Second Avenue address.

"No return number?"

"I suspect he knew you were in."

The butler looked sad and left. Paul shrugged. He called information and got the numbers for McAllister, Moran, and Turecamo, as well as some of the smaller tug companies, Eklof, Red Star, Thomas Brown. He added a couple of towboat users, like the Bouchard and Hughes barge outfits.

He was prepared for a long drawn-out telephone assault, but locating Walshie's boat proved ridiculously easy. Most of the port captains tried to help once he told them what he wanted.

The "Port Director" at Red Star said, yeah, Walshie did backup work for them on occasion; you contacted him through a port agent, Michael O'Rourke.

O'Rourke said the *Linda Walsh* was due to pick up a tow at Scarlatti Brothers scrap yard in Brooklyn around 9:00 P.M. Walshie did not give a damn about insurance regulations, O'Rourke added, disapprovingly; he would probably take Paul along for the ride to Bridgeport.

Paul hung up, feeling something nudge at his bloodstream like the pull of the tide itself.

The nice thing about working with boats was that you dealt with the ocean, and the ocean was one big club whose bylaws never changed, no matter what part of the world you were in. Even in this strange city of glass towers and hoarded data, home was as close as the nearest deck. Curiously, the knowledge that he could be standing on a deck in less than sixteen hours gave Paul the energy to make one last sortie among the sharp-toothed land creatures that controlled his future.

There was a bell push near the sitting-room doorway. Paul pressed it. Seiji appeared with rubber gloves and a dustpan of cat vomit.

Paul said, "Would you tell Ashley—Mrs. Briggs—I've gone out?"
The Japanese man said, "Mrs. Briggs has already left."
"She has?" Ashley never got up before ten or eleven.
"I believe she went shopping. With Mr. Winton."
Shopping was the only thing, after fire and flood, that Ashley would get up early in the morning for. It was her favorite form of therapy, not counting sleep, Jack once told him. It was almost as expensive as conventional therapy.

Perhaps Ashley was starting to get over the shock of Jack's death. Paul brushed his hair back in a confused gesture and went to get his coat, but the butler had already taken it from the closet. He stood in the doorway, waiting for Paul, holding the coat like a matador's cape for Paul to spear with his back-angled arms.

Paul walked east on Fourteenth, then north up Second Avenue to midtown. He noticed there were two kinds of restaurants. The first kind consisted of eateries with thin waiters, long-stemmed flowers, and entrées in foreign languages.

The second were corner coffee shops with formica counters and cheeseburger specials for $4.75 and paper cups with Doric motifs.

The Pharos Coffee Shop was of the latter variety, except that the walls featured posters of Cairo rather than Athens, and papyrus scrolls instead of cheap copper discus throwers. Coptic icons framed the "Specials" board. Paul walked up and down the aisle. A short-order cook noticed his back-and-forth looks and yelled to a curtain of beads by the restrooms. The curtain parted and Shoop beckoned Paul inside.

In back it was dark and thickly carpeted. A picture of Gamal Abdel Nasser in British-style uniform hung over the single table. The dark cook came in with two tiny cups of jet black liquid and left quickly, beads clicking in his wake.

"My second office," Shoop remarked. "I'm remodeling the brownstone. Place is full of plaster dust. So I'm spending a lot of time here these days. When I'm not at the Aspen house. Ever been there? Aspen, I mean."
Paul shook his head.
"Lovely town," Shoop remarked vaguely. "Lots of creative people, you ought to go there sometime." Immediately he added, "I've had second thoughts."
Paul did not answer. He tasted the coffee. It was thick, sweet,

hot, and left a gritty feel on his tongue, like river sediment. It did not matter if Shoop had had second thoughts. Ashley said Canaday was the man to convince. With hindsight Paul knew that his wild rantings about the perfect boat had really turned Canaday off. He felt himself flush at the memory and took a big sip, scalding his tongue deliberately to kill the embarrassment.

"Dimidius factiqui coepit habet?" Shoop said suddenly, in a mannered voice.

Paul's coffee cup stalled, halfway to the saucer. Shoop's accent had not altered. It sounded as if he was muttering to himself, crazed words in broken English.

"He who has begun has already half done," Shoop translated.

The financier was wearing a blue suit today with a silver tie clasp and shirt that did not quite match. Reading glasses on a gold neck cord. No Napoleon hat. Not a madman's uniform, Paul thought.

"Latin," the big man explained. "Horace. It sort of sums up your argument last night."

"Yeah," Paul replied, wondering where all this was leading.

Shoop leaned forward. His cup disappeared between two freckled fists.

"Listen, Briggs," he said. "You know how that quotation ends?"

Paul shook his head.

"With the simplest and most difficult advice ever written. 'Sapere aude.' Have the courage to be wise."

Paul shifted in his seat.

"Horace," he commented, a little harshly, "to paraphrase what they say in Maine, Horace don't shuck no clams."

Shoop's teeth shone. They reminded Paul a little of an Alsatian's.

"Perhaps my Latin doesn't impress you, Mr. Briggs. But your fake, Down-East, homespun, country-store image don't fool me, either."

Paul felt the first flicker of interest since entering the coffee shop. It took hard words to kindle interest, as it took hard flint to make sparks. He sat up straighter in his chair. Shoop pushed the cups to one side. They looked at each other across the formica. Shoop pulled Ashley's worksheet folder from a briefcase on the seat beside him.

"A lot of what you said last night was bullshit," Shoop remarked. "But you were right about one thing." He opened the folder. "It would be cheaper to keep her."

Paul's eyes were drawn, reluctantly, to the artist's rendition of the finished Twelve-Meter. Despite himself he experienced the automatic empathy he always had for a sailing hull, the instinctive projection, the sense of how water would slide and foam, break and bubble along the sleek curve of a boat. He pulled his gaze away by main force, to find Shoop's eyes looking on him.

"It's not your kind of boat," the businessman commented, quietly, "is it?"

Paul shrugged. "I already told you."

"Tell me this." Shoop pushed the folder to one side, as if blocking out new lines of talk on the table itself. "How did you become a naval architect in the first place?"

"It was a family tradition, I suppose." Paul sagged wearily against his chair. "Boat builders always used to design the boats they built, in Maine. Some still do."

"My father," Shoop countered, "was a joiner by trade. He wanted me to be a joiner. I refused. Most kids with any gumption—" He left the sentence hanging.

"Oh, sure." Paul smiled, without rancor. After a beat or two he added, "I did two years of ocean engineering at MIT. Then I told my father he could stick his yard where the sun don't shine. I wasn't going to be a boring old boat designer. I was going to be an artiste." He paused. "I waited tables, like the rest of the artists. My creations were daring, avant-garde. I used glue and glitter and stuff from people's garbage on my canvases; see, I was portraying the social turmoil of the age. I got into one major show and an artist I actually admired—there weren't many of those—reviewed my stuff. He said, let's see how he put it, I had the talent of a baboon and all the vision of a stoned high school freshman." Paul smiled at the memory. "I decided against suicide. I went to California and got a job on a windjammer instead."

The bushy eyebrows jumped, though the rest of Shoop's face remained impassive as usual.

"The *Sheba*." Paul saw her in his mind. "A traditional ship, of course. No racing machine. But a beauty, a real beauty. You should have seen that ship, with its topsails set and roaring down those Pacific rollers. . . ."

There was something about the Pacific that dulled anger, even pain, Paul remembered. Magellan had not named it for any dearth of fury, but because of the effect it had inside a man. The sense of endless water stretching around the southern earth, and around again, if you cared to continue, touched the psyche.

"How long were you on the *Sheba?*" Shoop's voice brought Paul back.

"Two years." Paul wondered why Shoop was so interested, but he had no objection to talking about this part of his life. "We sailed all over. I got to be mate. It was the best two years of my life, I think. I really loved the Pacific. I almost settled down in Papeete." Paul's voice was gentle with memory.

"And that was where you met your wife?"

"How did you know that?" Paul took off his glasses. "I never said."

"There's a file on you."

"Sure. There's a file on me." Paul tried to get to his feet, found the table in the way. "In that case there's nothing I can tell you you don't know already, is there."

"Sit down." Shoop shook his head. "Hear me out. Please." He winced, as if the last word did not come easily, and poured more coffee in an appropriately Levantine sort of gesture. Paul sank back, more out of curiosity than acceptance. There had to be a reason for this rigmarole. The coffee was cooler now. The financier used a long, level gaze to convey his sincerity as he continued, softly, "I'm in the business of making decisions about complex stuff, technical stuff. Processes I don't pretend to understand because I am not an expert? The only way I can justify those decisions is by trusting the judgment of other people. The only way I feel comfortable doing that is by finding out something about 'em. Fair enough?"

"No," Paul said, "not really. How did you find out I met Suzanne in Tahiti?"

"We used an executive search team. They talked to people, I suppose."

"Go on." Paul helped himself to some more coffee. "What else did your spies tell you."

The big man sighed, and took another folder from his briefcase.

"Let's see." Papers rustled. "Your wife, Suzanne Hart. She is a sculptress. Here is a review of a sculpture show she had in Papeete. Not very flattering, I'm afraid. 'Ça ressemble aux monolithes de l'Île de Pacques.' Hmmm . . . Your father dies while you are in Tahiti.

You go back to the States together. You decide to finish your degree. Presumably," he looked up, "there was no one left to rebel against?"

"You tell me."

"Well, whatever the motives, your career is, shall we say, a little twisty? You and Miss Hart get married," he continued. "You graduate cum laude. Then, instead of getting a job with a real naval architect, you apprentice with an old-time builder, Pete Culler, in Hyannis, Mass., before hanging out your own shingle? Ummm . . .

"Your first design as a professional is a thirteen-foot racing dinghy, the *Flasher*. It's a fluke, a big seller. You sell the rights to the Peterson Company. You buy a house and start a family with the proceeds.

"But you throw a curveball here; maybe success went to your head?" Shoop looked up from the report, for effect. "You do nothing for a year and a half. Then you come out with a racing catamaran based on Indonesian boats. It's so radical nobody wants it.

"After that, let's see," he went down a list with a large finger, "you straighten out again. Another small sailboat, not successful, a series of cruising boats. The FH 28, 33, 38. You design those with your cousin, and they catch on. Then, suddenly, you stop doing production boats; you design the *Zulu* instead. The pattern twists once more." He took the bifocals off with a curved gesture. "Why?"

"You tell me," Paul repeated, unoriginally.

"It doesn't say here. Don't you see? That's the trouble with these reports; they only cover the outside events? They don't show what goes on inside a person."

Paul was silent.

"I need to know," Shoop encouraged him in a feathery voice.

Paul shrugged again.

"I told you. I couldn't paint."

"So this was the outlet for your creativity? Weird boats?"

"Good boats," Paul retorted. "Boats that break the rules. Designs leaned down by time. Balanced boats. I told you."

Shoop nodded. He picked up the folder and threw it in his briefcase. Took off his bifocals. Steepled his fingers and kissed them, in what Paul began to recognize was a typical gesture.

" 'His heart was mailed with oak and triple brass, who first committed a frail ship to the wild seas,' " Shoop quoted.

"Great." Paul pushed back from the table in disgust.

"Last night," Shoop continued, "after you left, I argued to keep you on. I believed you could finish the job for us? I still think so. Do you want to know why?"

Paul looked at him.

"Because of what you said last night when you got a little carried away. About balance? 'Whoever prizes the golden mean.' You see," Shoop continued, "unlike you, I rebelled by *continuing* my education. I got a Rhodes scholarship. At Oxford I studied the classics, I was doing a thesis on Hellenistic influences on Jewish heresies. I gave up the classics after absorbing two lessons. The first was, harmony and balance in all things—Aristotle, you know?

"The second lesson was this: only the 'aristos' have the leisure to fulfill the first ideal. I swore I was going to become an aristo. In this country, that means money—"

"Look," Paul interrupted. "Spare me the Greek philosophy. My cousin died because of this boat, somehow. It makes me a little impatient with all the bull people keep throwing around whenever the subject of Twelve-Meters comes up. So if you have something to say, say it. Otherwise, I got things to do."

Shoop nodded.

"Last night," he said, "Canaday and I reached a compromise, of sorts. If we can make the next payment with outside contributions, then they'll consider staying with your yard."

"But that's—that's a hundred fifty thousand dollars," Paul said.

"Peanuts," Shoop waved his hand. "To the people your cousin's wife knows, that's pocket change."

Paul's eyes hardened.

"What you're saying is, it's up to Ashley and me to scare up money that *you* owe *us?*"

The big man nodded again.

"And even if we come up with the dough, you could still go someplace else."

Shoop shrugged, suddenly distant.

"That's totally unfair."

"It's your bacon," Shoop remarked. "Between you and me and the Fellahin, CBM's got real liquidity problems. . . . There's a reception for the U.S. Yacht Racing Association three days from now," he went on. "We'll be there, at least Munoz and Hillman will." He pulled a pair of gloves from his jacket pocket. "Why don't you stop by? Let us know how you did."

"In three days? We're supposed to come up with a hundred fifty grand in *three days?*"

"It gives you time to start," Shoop remarked, in a voice quite bare of Hellenistic balance. He picked up his briefcase and left.

Paul realized he was going to have to pay for the coffees. He got the cook to change a dollar for him.

He spent a minute looking for his glasses, eventually locating them in his shirt pocket.

It was crazy, he thought. Seen outside the context of desperation, the syndicate's proposal was as insulting as it was impractical.

On the other hand, they did not have much choice.

Paul went to look for a phone. He decided he would spend the day looking for investors. Just for the heck of it.

And when it became obvious he had not a snowball's hope in hell of lining up anything close to a hundred fifty thousand dollars in three days, he would go to Brooklyn. There he would hitch a ride on a tugboat, and continue trying to find the son of a bitch who had got them into this mess to begin with.

C H A P T E R   1 1

"Seems like you got a lot to do," Jeff Walsh said.

It was two in the morning. The *Linda Walsh*, an eighty-nine-foot harbor tug, barreled down Newtown Creek with a barge full of crushed automobiles in tow.

Newtown Creek was a thin wedge of water that cracked off Brooklyn from Queens, not very neatly, along a geological fault line where Ravenswood granodiorite hit a bed of gneiss.

They were coming to the end of the waterway now. Walshie checked his tow line and pulled the throttle back, gentle and slow and not very far. He gave the helm a nudge to compensate for the East River current that would shortly be hitting the tug and her charge. He unclipped the VHF microphone from above his head.

"All traffic, this is the *Linda Walsh* coming out of Newtown Creek. . . . We're making a turn north for Hell's Gate."

The radio waves hung, thick with potential.

A round, bubbling voice broke their electric simmer.

"*Linda*, this is the *Theresa Moran*. We're coming by Corlear Hook, northbound. We're light, Walshie, so watch your tail."

"Right-o, *Theresa*," Walshie said. "We're abeam of the Chicken Market now so we'll stay to starboard all the way up Roosevelt's, out."

Jeff turned down the radio but kept one ear tuned to its crackling. "Pathetic," he said. "When I started working on the boats there'd 'a been twenty guys shouting back at us to get outta the way. Containerships, tankers, tugs, everything. Now I get the one fugging tug. Listen to it." He gestured at the radio. "The harbor's dead."

The radio stayed silent but the rest of the harbor did not seem dead to Paul. Buoys, pier lights, range markers winked confusingly from the black water. Green, yellow, orange, white. A police boat rushed down the East River, intent on its own dark business.

Water was only the lowest level of traffic. Above it, on every side, movement blurred in layers of headlights, brakelights, and taillights on the FDR Drive. A cable car slid alongside the mass of the Fifty-ninth Street Bridge. Higher still, jets and choppers wheeled slowly around the city's superstructure.

"Can't seem to keep up," Walshie continued, almost to himself. "I start out in sail. Steam took over from sail, OK. Tugs take over from freighters. Now trucks take over from tugs. Rates are soft anyway, and they nail us on the cargo transfers." Walshie paced from side to side of the wheelhouse, making stops at the radar set in between to check the channels while he started the broad turn upriver. "So then the companies freeze wages. Then Three-Three-Three strikes. You know, Teamsters, Local 333, the union. So the companies jack up wages and decommission 20 percent of the boats instead." He shook his head. "Chances are the guy you're looking for has been laid off, anyway."

"But I figure people will remember him," Paul said, "or know how to find him. Like I found you."

"It's easy to find me, 'cause everybody knows the skippers," Walshie observed. "The other guys . . ." He shook his head. "Although, you're right. No one but a tug hand would tie a knot like that."

The *Theresa Moran* overtook them by the lighthouse at the northern tip of Roosevelt's Island. The tide was fair and the combination of ship's speed and tidal movement and the passing tug and the swooping cars on the FDR gave Paul a strange feeling of living in many different dimensions at once.

The Triboro Bridge uncoiled above their heads. The pace of the river increased ferociously through the bottleneck of Hell's Gate, and Walshie used all his concentration to keep the tow line taut and the barge in line through the rips and eddies of the waterway. When they were safely through to Long Island Sound he called his mate to take over.

The mate was a tall West Indian named Manley. He nodded at Paul and called Walshie "Mastah." The skipper led Paul to a saloon just forward of the galley.

It was warm and brightly lit and lined with panels of pressed wood. The engineer sat on a settee smoking menthol cigarettes. The smell of fresh-baked pie fought the aroma of diesel and cigarettes.

"Almost got killed last month, 'cause of Manley," Walshie remarked. "We'd left the *Linda* in the Bronx to wait for a generator bearing. Needed new charts for Philly, so we took the number six subway down to Manhattan. See, Manley grew up on turtle schooners, in the Caycos, and you call the skippers of those schooners 'Master.' Makes sense. Well, here we are on the IRT, I'm the only white on the train, and Manley starts yakking and calling me 'Mastah' this, 'Mastah' that. Some of the brothers start getting upset, like they say, 'Hey man, why you callin' this white asshole 'Master'. . . ."

A very thin man with white hair and a permanent scowl poured strong coffee and cut them large hot slabs of apple pie. Walshie showed the engineer the copy of the Identikit Paul had given him, but he did not recognize the picture. The cook said there was something familiar there, but Walshie claimed he never answered a question straight anyhow. Typical sea cook, just like Jens, Walshie said. Paul smiled, remembering the cook on the windjammer. He was seventy-eight and deaf as a coot from twenty years of chipping rust from steel decks. He refused to admit his deafness; instead he answered questions with what he thought the reply should be.

"I'll never forget," Walshie said, "when Irving asked him to ream out the stovepipe again, and he replied, he'd already asked, but she refused."

The pie and the warmth, the easy conversation of men who shared the same codes, the same way of living, created a semblance of tranquility in Paul. He lost seventeen dollars in pickup poker and did not think about Twelve-Meter yachts for close to five hours.

᠊᠊᠊

The wind breezed up toward dawn, and the tug punched its way up Long Island Sound into a stiff chop.

Walshie asked Paul to take over for a little while, and went below to rouse Manley. Paul was pleased that his friend trusted him with the tug, but nervous about the two hundred feet of cable, the three hundred tons of barge rolling and dipping behind.

Towing was not child's play. If you let the tow line slack just a little, or changed course too abruptly, a barge could sheer off on its own momentum. In no time flat the angle between tug and tow would become too great to correct, and you had the choice of cutting the tow line or watching the tug get pulled sideways, and finally capsized, by its runaway charge.

Repeatedly Paul checked the barge, the autopilot, the lights of other ships coming in and out of Long Island Sound. He looked up the tidal currents, laid out the next course from Bridgeport light tower. He watched the sun rise through the wheelhouse windows. Its light stained the wake pink, and made the scrapped automobiles shine as they once must have done in the showroom. Manley came up just before the light tower and said, "Friday dawn clear as a bell—rain on Saturday sure as hell. It will be a wet weekend." Walshie took over the helm to make the Bridgeport jetty. They brought the barge in slowly, under two bridges, to a pier north of the power plant. Walshie slacked the tow line, turned the tug around, and nudged the barge in with his bow while a shore crew got lines aboard. The dock master told them to lay by while they got two empty Hughes barges ready to haul back and Walshie smiled—he had not counted on a pay-tow home.

They docked upriver of a Turecamo tug. Paul watched a crane pick up the smashed automobiles to load into a Greek freighter and thought idly of all the dreams and pretensions that once were loaded on their shiny chrome and paint, only to be crushed and sold for scrap.

Walshie walked over to show the Turecamo crew Paul's Identikit, but came back shaking his head.

"You're going to have to cover all the harbors," he remarked. "Jacksonville, Norfolk, Baltimore, Philly, Boston. Not just New York. Portland, Providence, New Bedford, Fall River even. There's less tugs than there used to be, but it's still a lot of ground."

"I gotta do it," Paul said stubbornly.

Walshie shook his head. "You haven't changed," he said.

He walked Paul to the gates of the scrap yard. He promised to keep showing the picture around, and pointed out the way to the Metro-North station.

"Take care of yourself."

"You, too."

"No," Walshie said. "I mean it." He frowned to emphasize the words. "There's weird people in the unions now, since things went downhill. Switchblade artists. Kneecap boys. If you gotta ask questions, be real careful."

Paul nodded. They shook hands.

When Paul looked out the steamy windows of the 8:05 he saw the *Linda Walsh* pulling away from the pier, her skipper a tiny shadow in the wheelhouse. Commuters glanced at the tug with negative curiosity, then buried their noses in the *Wall Street Journal*. The train was so full Paul could not find a seat, and he wished he were back on the tug, with no more on his mind than getting two barges to New Jersey before the sun went down.

☷

Paul went straight back to Winton's. He found the list of potential sponsors he and Ashley had compiled yesterday. He began dialing the numbers that were left.

People Ashley grew up with. Men and women from New York, New Canaan, Newport. People she'd known at dancing school, who'd since become commodities brokers, lawyers, heirs-to. Plutocrats with summer houses on the Point, in French Harbor. Anybody they could think of with spare cash.

Ashley woke up early and joined in. They worked well into the night, fueled by take-out pizza and large pots of coffee.

By noon the next day—the day of Shoop's deadline—they had contacted a total of eighty-three blue-chip prospects. Of these, four were dead, eleven were out of town, eight were too busy to come to the phone, ten would not discuss anything, and thirty-two refused point-blank to contribute.

From the remaining twenty-three they elicited $34,230 in pledges, most of that coming from an old wire manufacturer from Ithaca who'd played tennis with Ashley's grandfather, and whose primary motive in contributing seemed to be further conversation with Ashley.

It was an impressive effort, at that, but in Paul's opinion the syndicate was acting like one of Shoop's classic gods, setting tasks to fulfill clauses in their Heroes contract, in the absolute certainty the task was impossible.

At twelve-thirty Ashley went out to meet the wire manufacturer. Shortly thereafter, Paul decided he'd had enough. With a great slash of pencil he crossed off the last names on the list. There was no point in butting your head against a brick wall, he thought.

He filled the rest of the afternoon in the library, calling up tug people. He typed out the resulting list on heavy stationery in Winton's office. He wrote a covering letter to Vanzetti, asking the PI to visit the various port captains and see if they recognized the description of the man who had killed Jack. He sealed the envelope, stuck on some stamps from Winton's desk, and posted the letters in the corner mailbox. Finally he called Lucinda and asked her to explain to Jessica that he had no choice but to miss her birthday. They would celebrate the minute he got back, it was a promise. Guilt made Paul go straight out to look for presents. He paid $130 for a four-foot-high stuffed brown bear he could barely fit in the taxi door. The effort drained what reserves he had left and when he got home he fell asleep in an armchair.

Seiji woke him at 5:00 P.M. There were noises from Ashley's room. Paul took a shower, shaved, and put on his suit again; it had seen more use in the past two weeks than in the previous two years.

When he got downstairs the Japanese already had changed into his chauffeur's uniform and was wiping soot off the Mercedes out front. Paul climbed in and poured himself a rum and tonic from cutglass decanters in the limousine's bar. He watched a rerun of a New York Giants game on the limo's television. Ashley blew through the doors in a rush of silk and perfume. Her hair was piled in a blond snake's nest on top of her head. "We have to hurry," she told Seiji. Then she rounded on Paul.

"Where the hell have you been?"

"I was getting a present for Jess," Paul explained defensively. "I was back by four-thirty. I told you."

"Did you call the rest of those names? I saw you just crossed them out."

"Ashley, look—"

"You'd think it was my boatyard I was trying to save. You'd think it was my job."

"What difference does it make?"

"Oh, sure." She lit a cigarette, but it did nothing to dull the red patch of anger in her cheeks. "I wish Jack was here," she burst out. "He wouldn't just say, 'Sure, OK, I give up, take my boat, take the yard, take my life, I'll just sit here and do nothing and feel sorry for myself, like I've been doing for the last three years.' "

Paul kept his mouth clamped to the rim of his drink. In front of him, the Japanese pressed a button and a glass partition slid discreetly into place.

"I'm sorry," Ashley said after a pause.

"They've made up their minds," Paul said. "There's no way."

"You think I don't know that?"

He looked at her.

"Then why."

"Because," she answered. Her mouth trembled in a way that reminded Paul, sharply, of Jessica. "Because we were doing so terribly, Jack and me. Because I was giving him such shit. We had a huge fight on—that night. That goddamn lousy night. Don't you get it? He went back to work because he couldn't stand being in the same room with me anymore." She blinked her eyes very fast. "Because of Labor Day, I guess. Oh, Jack, Jack, Jack." Ashley looked firmly out the window.

There was nothing to say. Seiji drove as neatly and smoothly as he did everything else. They reached Forty-fourth Street and pulled up in front of the New York Yacht Club building ten minutes later.

Bradley Winton stood waiting in the great marbled foyer as if he owned the yacht club.

Winton was tall and thin and dried-up like a pressed plant. His hair was blond, graying at the temples, his features bland as porridge. He'd gone out early and returned late every morning so it was the first Paul had seen of him since Jack and Ashley's wedding five years before. He took Paul's hand in cool fingers and signed them in with the quartermaster.

As they walked up the stairs he asked if Paul was comfortable in his house, and how the Twelve-Meter was progressing. He spoke in a soft and nasal tone. His accent was just this side of John O'Groats. He never mentioned Jack, and Paul wondered why. Winton's eyes seemed to watch faraway movies. A man called his name. He wore the same stripes on his tie as Winton had on his. Winton put the tips of his fingers on his goddaughter's shoulder, looked past Paul, apologized, and left them.

"Don't be fooled," Ashley said. "If he wasn't running the yacht club syndicate, we'd already have the hundred fifty thousand. It's thanks to him, and his friends, that I've got any contributions at all."

"How much did you end up with?"

"Mr. Hinks was sweet. He'd called in two of his partners—"

"How *much*?"

"Definitely forty. Maybe forty-five. Where are they, anyway?" Meaning the CBM people.

Paul gestured beyond an alabaster column.

"In there, I guess."

"In there" was a gigantic room of limestone and marble. A massive rococo fireplace took up half the west wall. An ornate minstrel's gallery of dark, carved wood ran along three sides. The ceiling was three stories high and made of Tiffany stained glass. The carpets were Persian and the casements stone, carved to resemble the stern gallery of an eighteenth-century ship of the line.

But what made the room remarkable was not so much the decorations as the contents. From one end to the other, from floor to ceiling, the room was filled with the models of ships.

It was not the first time Paul had seen the model room, but it never failed to quicken his pulse a little. People wandered in, swelling knots of conversation that thickened by the long drinks table, by the fireplace. Men in red jackets carried silver trays full of shrimp and scallops wrapped in bacon. Ashley spotted someone she knew and went over to talk to him. Paul caught snippets of their conversation as he stood in line for a drink. It wasn't someone she much cared for, by the stilted tone.

"How've you been."

"I heard about your husband."

"How's the boat?"

"That dinner offer—it's still open."

"Look."

"Call me."

"I don't think so. But thanks."

Paul got his rum drink and turned around, but Winton had cut in and the man Ashley was talking to had his back turned. Paul got a supply of shrimp, then ambled down the rows of glass cases. He toured racing yachts and luxury steamers and cruising boats until he got to the America's Cup models.

You could amble through the entire history of the America's Cup in this way, walking three years a step, space and time reduced to scale, starting off where the cup once stood, just outside and a few steps down from the model room.

It was here, in 1983, that the shattered survivors of the Cup Committee met to drink a toast of farewell to the *Auld Mug*. They poured a bottle of New York state champagne into the huge, ugly silver vessel—someone once compared it to a roadrunner bird trying to digest a dozen oranges—and realized, for the first time, that the cup had no bottom. The sweet, sticky liquid splashed straight through the cup and onto their shiny leather shoes. This was a fitting symbol, some felt, of what had happened.

The original *America*, George Steers's schooner-rigged variation on a New York pilot-boat theme, lay hard by the drinks table.

Off her long counter the Marquis of Anglesey almost fell overboard, trying to spot the secret propeller the Brits swore she possessed.

From the *America* you tracked backward to the northwestern corner of the model room, past the schooner era, to the elegant J-boats of Burgess and Herreshoff. Their miniature spars looked impossibly thin for the acres of canvas they'd carried.

Then, back to the southern end of the room, where two long parallel tables held scale models of every Twelve-Meter that ever raced in the cup series, from Olin Stephens's *Vim* through France's *Defi*.

Paul paced the changes in design and rig and deck layout, paying due respect to *Intrepid*'s fin, the first design to reduce water drag by cutting out the useless connection between rudder and keel. He looked at *Mariner*'s unsuccessful, chopped-off stern bustle; he noted *Australia II*'s winged keel.

He was shocked to find something akin to regret stirring inside him. Perhaps he would have liked to try his hand at it. Once. He raised his eyes to compare the mast heights of the more recent Twelves, to check what the trend in sail area had been—and all thought of Twelve-Meters vanished from his mind.

The *Zulu*.

There was no mistaking her. She stood straight and true amid the models of lesser craft, by the door. Her sleek sharklike keel and shallow draft complemented the hinted lines of a Baltimore clipper. The dacron sails and modified Bermuda rig sat well on the pronounced sheer. Unlike the Twelve-Meters, where compromises had been made to suit a rule, there was nothing off-key in her, no line that was not matched, no curve not reversed, no balance not adjusted.

Paul walked over to the case and looked at the small brass plaque. *Zulu*, it read. "Designer: P. Briggs. Builder: Harvey Gamage. Owner: Maritime Trust. Model donated by Samuel Lightoller."

The *Zulu*. She was built not so much of cold laminate as of strong fantasies. She had started off as a tribute to the men he admired most, the Yankee craftsmen who once built the finest sailing craft in the world. She ended up transcending the tribute, partly because of the improvements he drew into her. She was swift as a greyhound and graceful as a deer and nervous as a racehorse. With her long, narrow hull and sweet profile, the clipper bow and the white explosions of sail, she'd looked, under way, like a sculpture made of air and motion.

Taking in her shape, familiar as an old glove, he could almost feel the wind and the snapping sun of the September morning they launched her. Gamage's yard was decked with bright colors; signal flags, streamers, old bunting hung from every loft and mast and window. Jess and Nicole wore the little Italian peasant dresses their mother loved to parade them in.

When Suzanne broke the champagne over her bow his chest had ached like it could hold no more happiness.

When *Zulu* was lost he had thought, this must be what it feels like to lose a child. Time would prove him wrong. Yet *Zulu*'s sinking did mark the point when his life began its long, slow skid downward, ending here and now in a club he did not belong to, gambling his professional life on men he did not care for. Paul stood, lost in thought, in front of the display case. He was oblivious to the room and people around him until a voice broke through his reverie.

"Never had a chance," the voice said, forcing the *r*s through the speaker's sinuses instead of his mouth.

"You wouldn't think so," another voice answered.

A meditative clink of ice in a cocktail glass. Paul tried to ignore the men behind him, but their next words forced a path into his awareness.

"Good name, though. Spell it backward, it says, 'you lose.' "

Paul turned around.

Sandy MacLean towered at his elbow. With his large nose, his red hair, and the sunburned bald patch on his head, he looked like a six-foot-three-inch vulture. Next to him stood a neat, short, brown-haired man with glasses and good posture and a slightly mocking smile. Both men wore blazers with the club burgee sewn to the breast pocket.

"Hello, Sandy." Paul took an extra turn on a temper he knew was already loosened by rum.

"Well, I'll be damned." There was no surprise in MacLean's voice. He'd known it was Paul the whole time. "Never thought I'd see *you* here." The inflection was meant as an insult.

Sandy MacLean was the yachting world's preeminent chronicler, a columnist who made a good living writing about other men's boats, other men's talents.

When *Zulu* went down he wrote a column about it. He obtained statements from Paul, then altered the context. He finished the article by implying Paul was directly responsible for the deaths of two men who drowned when the schooner sank. It had been one of his more colorful pieces.

Paul had threatened to sue for libel, and the magazine printed a retraction, for which MacLean had never forgiven him. But the damage was done.

Paul thought about leaving. He did not want to argue with MacLean. He did not want to deal with the man on any level; but the writer and his companion had Paul hemmed against the model case, and there was no way to escape.

"So what's up," Paul said evenly.

The neat man smiled. It was a gentle, pleasant smile, not shared by the eyes.

"Well, I was just showing my friend Bruce here the boat that got me into so much trouble," MacLean said. "And he agrees with me. That boat had to be tender as hell. That right, Bruce?"

The neat man's smile deepened. He rolled a tightly balled cocktail napkin around one palm.

"I still think they should have brought criminal charges," MacLean added, then raised his fingers in feigned apology. "No offense, of course."

"Look, Sandy," Paul replied pleasantly. "You're not a designer.

And everyone knows you drink too much. But even you knew the Coast Guard said the design was sound. Even you knew a white squall is something no one can bargain for, especially in a ship designed for speed."

MacLean's face had darkened.

"That boat," he said forcefully, "was a death trap."

"I could have shown you the calculations," Paul replied. "I could have shown you how stable, if you'd asked. But you didn't ask."

"You knew," MacLean said loudly. For the first time Paul realized how drunk MacLean really was.

"Take it easy, Sandy," his companion warned, the smile deepening further.

"Jesus." Paul, disgusted, wanted to turn away, but MacLean stepped even closer, making retreat now a matter of aggression. He started to bluster, stabbing a finger at Paul's chest and stating, "You *knew* it was a death trap. You *knew*." Heads turned. A couple of men drifted closer to the noise, ears flapping. Paul recognized Ted Collins, who had just been named to skipper the New York Yacht Club's new Twelve. MacLean's companion remarked, "Incompetence seems to run in the family."

"What?" Paul did not think he'd heard right. "What did you say?"

"The *Challenge*." It seemed impossible, but the neat man's lip curled even further, and he turned away, as if bored. "Another 'breakthrough' Twelve-Meter." He pronounced the word "breakthrough" like a deadly insult. He turned further, to address a white-haired man behind him. "Sam, I'd steer clear of him this time, if I were you."

Paul wanted to grab the neat man's shoulder, ask him to repeat what he'd said about Jack, until he realized the vague features and white hair and clear eyes behind him belonged to Sam Lightoller.

Sam Lightoller, of the Maritime Trust. The man who had commissioned the *Zulu*.

"What do you mean?" Sam said, nodding once in Paul's direction. "I wondered, why all this commotion around my boat."

"They're looking for donations," MacLean pointed at Paul, "so he won't get fired, he's designing the Challenge syndicate's Twelve. I mean, they're crazy. He'll just make a mess of it. Like he did of the *Zulu*."

"Oh, really." The old man nodded again, to himself this time.

MacLean's voice carried and a crowd was gathering around them. Paul noticed Ashley pushing between people's elbows. Munoz followed behind, his eyes on her hips.

"But I thought," Lightoller protested mildly, "the *Zulu* was a good boat."

"That's because," MacLean countered loudly, "you're so old you'd think the ark looks good. You're so old you won't even back the Club's Twelve-Meter, because it's too high-tech. I suppose," he finished sarcastically, "you'd like us to go back to J-boats and good old Sir Thomas Lipton!"

A murmur of disapproval rose from the audience. Apparently, few there had any problems with going back to J-boats, either.

Sam Lightoller nodded a third time.

"Perhaps you're right. Perhaps it is time I made a contribution for the America's Cup," he announced in his clear, high voice.

"Hear, hear," someone said.

"You're doing a Twelve-Meter." Lightoller turned toward Paul. Paul nodded.

"Do you think it will be a good boat?" the old man asked him.

"It'll be as good as I can make it," Paul told him truthfully.

"Well, that's enough for me. Perhaps," the old man continued, "you would be so kind as to tell me where I can send a check?"

"Oh, *great*. He's trading on sentiment from soft old guys like Lightoller—" MacLean finished his drink and put the glass down with a crash on the *Zulu*'s case. He was about to continue but the neat man interrupted, putting a restraining arm on the writer's elbow.

"Leave it alone, Sandy," he said, but his smile did not go away. "Don't you see, it makes it easier for everyone else?"

MacLean shook him off.

There was a bang from the ceiling. Everyone looked up, then remembered that the homeless men in the shelter next-door to the yacht club liked to throw trash on Commodore Vanderbilt's stained glass. In the ensuing hush MacLean said clearly, "Using him, don't you see—just like his cousin used Ashley Palmer."

It took a couple of seconds for the words to register, but when they did Paul's arm seemed to act of its own accord. It twisted, canting the glass in its hand. Pulling toward his chest for the windup, it swung outward and stopped after twenty degrees of arc.

The liquid contents did not stop, however. Instead they flew directly into MacLean's face.

Silence fell on the model room of the New York Yacht Club. Under the dripping liquid, the writer's face turned the color of a radish. A strange, glottal gobble built up in his throat, then released. It sounded like the death ululation of Bedouin poultry.

Then everyone started shouting at once.

"I still don't believe it," Ashley said, shaking her head and hugging herself at the same time.

It had started to rain. As Manley predicted, Paul thought. They walked down Forty-fourth Street, picking their way around bums lying in cardboard and plastic cocoons on the sidewalk outside the yacht club. There were no taxis at the Algonquin, so they continued on to Broadway.

"We're invited to the reception by Uncle Bradley," Ashley continued, in a tone of wonder, "who just happens to chair the club's Cup Committee. We have to talk to people about raising money, meet with Munoz and company, show them we're, like, responsible, serious. Instead—you throw drinks at Sandy MacLean, not to mention the club's naval architect, you break every damn rule in the book—"

"That was their naval architect?" Paul interrupted. "For the *Old Glory?* The guy with glasses?"

"Uh-huh."

"You know him?"

"Bruce Archibald? Sure." Ashley giggled. She'd had a lot of champagne. "Didn't you see us talking, early on? I went out with him a couple of times, before Jack, till I found out what a stuck-up little nerd he was. Let's try Port Authority, there are always taxis there." She slipped her arm under his, an un-self-conscious gesture.

They headed down Times Square, waving their arms at the callous cabs. Rain smeared the ad colors into long streaks of red and gold and blue on the pavement.

"And to top it all," Ashley went on, incredulously, "you get away with it! Why didn't you *tell* me you knew Sam Lightoller?"

"It didn't cross my mind he'd be interested in Twelves," Paul muttered. "He always bad-mouthed 'em."

"You mean, MacLean was right?"

"What are you talking about?"

"He's too old-fashioned."

"Oh. No," Paul replied. "What I mean is, Sam's a special case. He's stubborn as a mule, he's old as Methuselah, and he's rich as—whatsisname."

"Croesus."

"Croesus. And he happens to love pretty boats. Not boats with fancy gadgets glued all over to make 'em go faster. So maybe it's not so weird, what happened tonight."

"What did happen," Ashley said, "after they hustled you down to the bar?"

"It's not too clear," Paul answered slowly.

"You weren't that tight."

"No. But I was still mad, I was thinking of all the things I could have said to MacLean."

"Uncle Bradley was *fur*ious."

"I know—but then Lightoller showed up again. With Munoz and Shoop. They'd been talking—"

"And Lightoller's going to guarantee the first payment," Ashley finished for him, shaking her head again. "No one can say you don't land on your feet."

Paul and Ashley were walking down Forty-second Street now. Marquees announced screenings of "NINJA BLOOD LUST," "TAKE ME DADDY," and "BLUE SLUTS (XXX)." Marijuana smoke laced through the raindrops. Thin men in army jackets whispered seductive sentences; "Sen-say. Sen-say. Crack, blow," they said. Colleagues hung around corners, looking for Blue. Very elongated and black Senegalese curved in Giacometti poses, hawking Louis Vuitton knockoffs, ironwood bracelets. Women looked at peep-show windows, watching the reflections for plainclothesmen. Steam wisped from cracks in the street as if the city were slowly building to an untenable head of pressure. A young prostitute turned away to follow her john through a doorway next to a peep-show arcade.

"Everybody'd given up trying to get Lightoller to donate to the cup fund—Paul? Paul, you're not listening." Ashley stopped and turned back to where he stood rigid in his tracks. "Paul, what's wrong? You're white as a sheet."

All it took was a shine of wheat-colored hair and a curve to her cheekbone and a certain way of holding her head when she looked at someone taller.

"*Nicole*," Paul breathed.

"Oh, no," Ashley said.

"Nicole!" He brushed her arm away, and ran diagonally across the sidewalk. "Nicole," he yelled.

A face flashed briefly and disappeared. A fat man poked his head from a booth inside the arcade. Someone whistled. He heard Ashley call, far off, "Paul, come back."

It had looked so much like his daughter.

He went through the doorway the girl had gone in.

The hallway it was smelly, half-lit; only the emergency lights worked in this building. It was also empty. An elevator stood open, unused. A door slammed somewhere upstairs. Paul took the stairs three at a time, his heart thudding.

The second floor was all small businesses, shut for the night. V. Feinberg, Attorney-at-Law. Ace Jewelry. The girl had seemed too old, but they made them up like crazy, Vanzetti claimed. She would be fourteen in March. Old enough.

The third floor was much the same as the second. J & R Entertainment, Inc. Sinbad Casting. The steps were cracked, grimy, and endless. The fourth floor was occupied by a photographer who kept a heavy iron gate locked across the stairwell. You could unlock the gate only with a key or by pulling a fire alarm. The alarm, Paul was sure, had not sounded.

He ran back downstairs, gasping for air. There was an emergency door he had not noticed on the second-floor landing. He moved the pushbar, and it swung open. Roof runoff spattered on his head. Iron steps led to a garbage-choked alleyway that angled back to Forty-second Street.

Paul ran out into the middle of the street. Cars honked at him as they hissed by, spraying him with rain and exhaust and invective.

"Crazy nut!"

"Get goddamn killed?"

Or, simply, "Asshole!"

He straddled the yellow line, oblivious to the drivers' anger. He searched the crowds on each sidewalk, shading his eyes with his hands. He took off his glasses, wiped them quickly on his tie, searched again. There was no one her size anywhere. She was wearing green, he thought, but the few greens he saw now were the wrong shades, on the wrong people. He lowered his hand from his brow, letting sweat and rain fill the hollows of his face and run down his neck. Something staled deep inside him. A cab pulled up next to him.

"Lady, I can't stop here!" the driver protested.

The door opened. Ashley reached out and pulled his sleeve.

"Paul. Get in."

He did not bend down. He did not even look at her. She yanked his arm, harder.

"Get *in*!"

He ripped away from her grasp and walked across the street. He heard Ashley call once more. Then her voice was lost in the rush of traffic unleashed by a green light on Eighth Avenue.

Paul walked up and down Forty-second Street for two hours. Feelings he had thought scarred into submission grew hot, festered, and burst venom through his system. Memories of absence flooded his brain.

Absence, like a black hole, was something you defined by what did not come back from it.

Everything had started so simply and gently. The elementary school had no procedure for checking on students. It figured the kids were too young to play hooky without their parents' consent. Kidnapping, those days, was something that happened to Them, the people on TV, the land where tourists came from.

Nicole was riding the school bus to her friend's house for the afternoon. Her friend's name was Kristen Sears.

Kristen called at three-thirty to give Nicole her homework assignment. She was sorry Nicole was sick.

Nicole wasn't sick, Suzanne said. Nicole was fine. Nicole was at Kristen's house.

She's not here, Kristen said. She wasn't at school. . . .

Suzanne had mother-powered imagination. She crossed straight into the world of upside-down and tore it to shreds looking for her daughter.

Upside-down was Suzanne's term. It meant a place where black was white, where reason and affection were handicaps. A place where only violence could match violence, madness match madness. Suzanne grew up in South Chicago and knew what she was talking about.

Suzanne called everyone she could think of but no one had seen the child since yesterday.

It took Paul a little longer to realize violence and madness could function as both crutch and tool. Then he joined his wife in total war. For five days straight they raped the woods with flashlight beams. They organized searches. They yanked people out of bed with 4:00 A.M. phone calls. They screamed at the town cops, the state police, the FBI, demanding they do something, anything, to fill the vacuum. Screamed at each other, finally, when there was no one else. Between the screams they recognized their isolation from the normal world and drew what comfort they could from each other's insanity.

They did not want to leave the upside-down world, toward the end, because the normal world contained too much memory, and each memory—how she said "OK" with a soft *k*, almost "ogay"; how she woke up; the way she added cereal to the milk and not vice versa—contained entire planets of pain. Sometimes they forgot, and saw her face in corner-movement, or went automatically to the peanut butter jar to make her school lunch. In their minds they gave away everything if she would just come back for five minutes. They would have sacrificed themselves a thousand times to see her, or know her safe.

In the absence of that option they had to live with a negative being, a not-Nicole that sat where she used to sit, spoke as she used to speak, filled space and time as their child once had done. This not-Nicole was a reality, an antimatter presence that collided with every particle of color and rest and pleasure Nicole had brought and imploded it all into nothing.

It was that nothingness Suzanne had fled. It was the nothingness that set Paul driving too fast, on roads that curved too sharply, slamming him sideways, two weeks after her flight, into an oak tree at fifty-five miles per hour.

〽

Paul got back to Winton's house at two-thirty in the morning. The lights in his room were on. Ashley sat in a lounge chair, reading fashion magazines. A flute glass of champagne stood handy. Jason the cat purred in her lap. He made his cheerful "roo" noise when he saw Paul.

Paul leaned on the door jamb, keeping the shakes to a minimum. He was soaked through from the rain, and it had got colder overnight.

"It wasn't her," Ashley said, "was it."

Paul said nothing. She was only an obstacle between him, the shower, and the eventual hope of sleep.

Ashley stood up, ejecting Jason. She had on a quilted pink dressing gown, with dogwood motifs, that buttoned primly to her throat. She walked up to Paul, picking her steps with care, and put a hand on his cheek.

"You're freezing," she said. "You should take a hot bath."

He barely heard her.

"Paul. Speak to me." Ashley put her other hand on his face, let her thumbs stroke one of the scar lines on his neck, gently. He pulled away.

She gave him a blank look, then marched across the bedroom to the fireplace. There she picked a Chinese porcelain deer off the mantel, and rubbed its antlers instead.

"How do you think I feel," she said.

Paul grunted. He no longer cared how she felt. He wanted her to leave. He did not want her to see him trembling or touch her concern. He needed to take off his sodden coat, but she might see that as a gesture of acceptance.

"It's bad enough missing Jack," she went on, almost to herself. "For a while, we really gave each other only the best parts. But on top of that, there's this totally irrational conviction. Like there's some kind of fate punishing me for hurting him. You'd think I was, like, Catholic or something. Penance for cheating on him. Not just with you, either.

"But one thing I'm not is, I'm not a coward." She put the deer back on the mantel, and lifted her chin. "I don't use it as an excuse. I don't hide behind being sad, even though it hurts so badly sometimes I feel I could break in two.

"I don't lie to myself, like you." She lowered her voice to mimic his: "Oh, I'm so broken up I can't draw boats anymore. When the real reason is," she turned back toward him, "you've lost it. You can't do the kind of boats you used to. You're not as good as Jack is—was, I mean. Maybe you never were. But all the time you pretend you're all busted up inside because of Nicole and Suzanne. Even Jack, now. You didn't really love them. It was yourself you loved, the whole time."

Paul took three long steps toward her, his arms rising. He wanted to take her and shake her and throw her out the door. She had no right using their names like that, he thought. He stopped himself with some effort, just out of reach.

"That's better," she said.

There was something wrong here. Something very like satisfaction glinted in her eyes. Paul ignored it.

"Please leave," Paul grunted. "Now."

"Paul, I—"

"I loved them in ways you never could. Even Jack."

Concern replaced the smugness.

"I'm sorry. I didn't mean—"

"I know what you're trying to do."

He could method-act, too, keep the coals flaring until she shut the door and cut off oxygen behind her.

Perversely, as soon as she'd gone, when he felt the familiar emptiness crowd back in, he found himself wishing she'd stayed.

He shucked off his clothes and took a long, steaming shower. The bed was fresh and warm. The city was so quiet it sounded almost like Maine. High emotion still washed down the canyon Forty-second Street had cut. "Goddamn bitch," he said to himself, turning his pillow to the cool side.

But in the red purity of his denunciation something green and unclean showed, stirred by Ashley's words. He'd been happy for Jack when he was picked to do the Twelve-Meter. He'd fought his own insecurities with Protestant zeal. He'd fought something else, too—an underground envy that popped up at odd moments to subvert his delight at Jack's success.

For twenty minutes he tossed and turned, then froze in the middle of a restless movement, aware of air moving the room with him, a sound with no source. He was not sure of what it was until the bed sagged and she found his neck with her arms and wiped her tears against his face.

"It's not you. It could be anybody. I just need something alive, to hold onto," Ashley said, turning her head to wipe her nose on the pillow.

"This is nuts," he muttered, but the anger drained out like someone had pulled the plug on it.

Loneliness was an enemy that united its survivors.

He put one arm around her, to dampen her crying with pressure. Two arms would be desire, but one arm was a gesture of friendship, he thought. Under the silk her body was warm and very soft. She told him he smelled of rum. She smelled of champagne and lavender conditioning cream. He rubbed her back almost unconsciously. She tightened her own hold.

The room's darkness seemed to isolate the process from the nobler hues of daylight. After a while her breathing changed, deepening from sniffles to something more outward-looking. She nuzzled the crook of his shoulder and he rubbed her hair. Like two horses, he thought. Only horses. She lifted her chin. Their lips found each other as if they had radar to see through the dark. They kissed, softly at first, then with increasing depth and strength. Their bodies followed through on what hands and tongues had started.

For a moment, when he slipped the nightgown over her head and she loosened his pajamas, he felt the shame come back, triggered in part by the power of his own response to her. But their loins had strength that went beyond questioning. He caressed her with his hands and she stirred against him. When the orgasm finally touched her, it was like a train on nearby tracks; a rush; a sequence of yellow frames, full of people you would never know, moving too fast to see; and last, a brief wail, immediately lost in the wind.

Part of Paul left New York glorying in the chance of salvation offered by the syndicate's reprieve.

This time he did not have Ashley's company, or Jason's.

She'd promised to come up in a few days, when the shopping was finished, when she'd had time to see some friends, catch a show she was "dying" to attend. . . .

Paul missed the new edge of intimacy between them. But he wasn't sorry to drive alone.

For some reason heading north always injected more adrenaline in his system than going south. It gave him a feeling of emergency, of dealings perilous but noble that would only be attenuated by company.

He detoured through Newport, over the great-humped ribbon of the Newport Bridge. He was not surprised to see two tall, feathered sails heading up the East Passage from the sea when he crested the span.

Twelve-Meters. No other boat that size had the overbred, inbred, thoroughbred look. No other boat had that ridiculously tall mast, the long, fine hull sticking out on both ends, way beyond its spread of sail.

Ant-size figures moved on the decks. As Paul watched, a pink spinnaker bloomed from each boat. The spinnakers carried the triangular logo of the CBM corporation. In the light of morning the boats looked like arrows on twin shafts of silver wake.

The *Valiant* and the *America*. They were obsolete Twelves the Challenge syndicate had bought to practice on. No one else was sailing their trial horses in Rhode Island at this time of year, Paul knew.

He wondered whether Hillman had forgotten Paul's call last night, when Paul had asked to go out on one of the test boats—but the team's relief man, a large, freckled twenty-five-year-old named Brian Duffy, was waiting for him at the great shingled pile on Bellevue Avenue that served as the syndicate's sailing headquarters.

He handed Paul a pair of boots and a set of designer rain gear made of lightweight synthetics originally created for use in outer space. The triangle logo was dashingly emblazoned on the back, for this was the leading edge of a new sportswear line, the first fashions to be featured in the CBM catalog. Paul put on the boots and pants, but kept his bomber jacket.

They drove to the dock and boarded a twenty-foot outboard. Duffy stowed a video camera. Then he opened the throttles and pounded them across East Passage. The snap of wind reddened their faces. The outboard came alongside to leeward of the *Valiant* as she beat into the southeast wind on a parallel course with her stablemate. Paul got a good hold on a stay and jumped aboard without getting more than a half-gallon of icy water in his boots. He made his way aft to the cockpit.

Everybody ignored him. The wind had freshened and the *Valiant* was working hard to cover the other boat, keep between *America* and the wind. The men on the coffee grinders drove their winches in a blur of orange gloves. The trimmers looked like snake handlers as they coiled lines spinning off the winch drums. The boat's forefoot crushed the humped water in regular explosions, the rigging thrummed with great pressure. A little pennant with a stencil of Frobie, the "official mascot," whipped from the radio antenna.

Gary Hopkins, the helmsman—also known as Queegie, after the

skipper in *The Caine Mutiny*—looked at the sky through mirrored glasses and complained ceaselessly about everything.

Paul stamped his feet and breathed into his rubber gloves and almost wished he'd stayed in New York City.

They sailed until eleven.

Back at the headquarters everyone changed and sat down for a late lunch and postmortem. Duffy played the videotape he'd made of the morning's sail. They watched it on a TV at one end of the long dining room.

"That goddamn number three genny still sucks," Hopkins said, through a mouthful of hamburger. "Freeze it—right there!"

Duffy pushed a button on the remote control. Hopkins padded over to the TV, licking catsup from his fingers.

"Bob," he yelled at the sailmaker, "pay attention. We gotta cut this sucker again. Flatten it out at the leech. Here. And here." He jabbed his high school ring at the frame of *Valiant* pointing hard into the wind. "Take maybe a quarter inch off at that seam. I hope," he said to Paul, "you're going to use a better locking system on the genoa halyard than these boats have. It's busted three times already this month, and we lose maybe a half inch of tension whenever the wind's over ten knots. Although frankly," he looked at a beefy man who was well into his third burger, "the way Dennis pays attention, I don't think he'd notice if the whole fucking sail fell down."

Paul smiled, thinking it was a joke, but Dennis stopped chewing and put his hamburger down. There was a frozen cast to his eyes. Everyone else stared hard at the video. Brian Duffy's face went red and sullen. The man on Paul's left muttered, "OK, Queegie, you got woman troubles, why take it out on us?"

The mirrored glasses turned in Paul's direction. The man on his left flushed, though the helmsman could not have heard the remark.

"I hope," Queegie said, walking back to his seat, "what we hear isn't true?"

Paul raised his eyebrows.

"They're gonna ditch the new boat? Make us sail on those two clunkers? I *told* 'em," he continued, "I told 'em not to try that double-keel design, but no-o-o-o. They had to go for a revolutionary boat, instead of a good evolving design. It's so revolutionary now nobody can finish the goddamn thing."

Paul took off his glasses and wiped them on a napkin, wondering how much he should tell them.

"Well," he began. "You don't have to worry. I've just come back from New York," he continued. "I've come to an agreement with the syndicate. We—that is, Briggs and Sons—will finish the design. So we can—"

"Who," Queegie interrupted, "is gonna do the design work?"

"I am."

"You?"

Paul nodded.

"You've never done this before," Queegie stated. "Jack was the Twelve-Meter man. You've never worked on Twelves."

"I worked on this design already," Paul answered levelly, wondering how much time he was going to spend addressing this particular point.

Queegie sat down. "Jesus," he said. He leaned back in his chair. Paul could see himself, tiny and warped, in the reflection of Queegie's sunglasses.

"I'm sorry about Jack," the helmsman continued. "We all were. But you don't understand, you people all think the same, you can just walk into Twelve-Meters, like they're just like the rest of 'em, one-tonners, Admiral's Cup, Solings, whatever. You're attracted by all the glitz, but what you don't understand, what I know, is these are specialized machines, they're unique, beautiful wind-engines. Duffy," his voice rose another notch, "this coffee is so fucking cold it freezes before it gets down my throat. Can't you even make us hot coffee, for chrissake?"

Duffy rose and went out.

Paul got up and put on his coat. He had not touched his lunch. He made some answer, calm, level, words to the effect that the job would get done properly and on time. He was sorry to rush out, but he had an appointment in Boston.

Queegie barely acknowledged him. Paul turned and left. He wasn't upset, and he wasn't annoyed. All he felt was a great fatigue.

These large, healthy white males, all dressed alike in CBM boat shoes and "Challenge" sweatshirts; these cereal-box athletes, with their hidden salaries and open ambition, seemed as remote from his idea of seamen as Twelve-Meters were from his kind of boat.

He went to the bathroom to get rid of some of the coffee he'd been swilling. On his way out, turning corners too fast, he literally ran into Brian Duffy, speaking on a pay phone in the lobby. The crewman dropped the phone, then hung it up quickly.

"You going?" Duffy asked, as Paul made to brush by him.

When Paul nodded, Duffy said, "Don't mind Queegie. I mean, he's not the whole team. Though sometimes he thinks he is."

Paul shook his head. "Queegie can say what he likes. I've got to be in Cambridge by two."

"He's worse than usual today." Duffy looked over his shoulder, toward the dining room. "He's engaged to this girl, Jenny. She keeps putting it off. Getting married, I mean. She was supposed to be here last week—"

Paul zipped up his bomber jacket, trying to convey departure, but Duffy had a story in him, and the anger to push it out.

"But he just got a letter from her. She's going to skipper a Trans-Pac boat so she can't come back for months." The kid almost smiled.

Paul thanked Duffy for his help earlier and escaped outside. He got in his car, thinking Queegie's girlfriend must be tougher than most if she could both put up with Queegie and skipper in the Trans-Pacific race.

Then he headed north, for Boston, and forgot all about Queegie Hopkins's problems.

☰

Paul ate on the road, a double-decker sandwich with special sauce from a drive-up, fast-food restaurant. He got to Boston at 2:10 in the afternoon. He did not have to think about how to get to Cambridge; instinct and memory conspired to steer him off Route 3, onto the Mass. Pike to the first exit, then over the Charles without thinking, like a homing pigeon.

Still working on memory, he drove south down Mass. Ave. to the MIT complex.

As always he found his bearings by the tit—the great stone dome with its meaningless inscription—"Charles Frederick Barton, Founder"—rearing in ugly grandeur by the Charles River. A number of featureless office buildings belonging to defense research companies now surrounded the campus, concrete succulents sprouting in the fertile muck of Pentagon dollars, but the new buildings did not throw off Paul's autopilot as he turned left down Vassar Street, past the cyclotron, past Building Twenty, to park beside the dingy yellow-brick rectangle of the hydrodynamics laboratory.

This building brought memory circuits to life. For a moment he almost believed he was twenty-two again, illusions largely intact, and Professor Tomkins was about to come striding around the corner in his Hush Puppies, six foot three and precise as a micrometer. They would go downstairs together and Paul would show him the three models he had made over the vacation and Tompkins would explain, in beautiful, classical, ruthless English, why the miniature hulls would drag like rafts when pulled through water.

Around lunchtime Suzanne would bop in, her hair thick with plaster dust. Tompkins would take one look at her tight T-shirt and lose his syntax completely.

But Paul had no Jeep in those days. Nor had he a house or kids or a great sump of worry in his mind. He shook off the reminiscences and went downstairs more or less in the present tense.

The hydrodynamics lab had gone downhill since his student days, Paul thought. Dust lay thick on every surface. Cast-off models were stacked anyhow beside the men's room. An unfinished propeller tunnel almost blocked the glass door to the tank. Paul wondered why Jack had chosen this place to submit his ideas to scaled-down reality when there were state-of-the-art tanks in Maryland and Virginia. Availability, he supposed, and money were the deciding factors.

And nostalgia, perhaps. Jack had gone to MIT as well.

But nothing much had changed inside the tank room itself. The same humid, cluttered perspective of old greeted Paul's eyes. Foreshortened water pipes and valves covered the ceiling and walls. Messy workbenches bore signs that read "Keep this area NEAT." Loose bits of instrumentation—force blocks, rheostats, accelerometers lay on all sides in precise disarray. Running water filters and pumps filled the place with low-grade noise.

The steaming five-hundred-foot length of the tank itself took up the center of the long room. Its massive towing carriage sat on twin, shining tubes of steel like a friendly robotic frog.

No matter how many times he came here Paul would never get over the feel of seeing such a long expanse of water set inside a building. There was something unnatural and sacred about it, as if by confining the most vital of natural elements you brought it within reach of human worship.

Piet Hendriks stood at the near workbench. He nodded as he saw Paul.

Hendriks was medium-sized and sleek. His features—pointed,

with a small, clipped moustache, and liquid, round eyes—always reminded Paul of a vole. He favored gray turtlenecks and gray drainpipe trousers. He smoked rum-scented pipe tobacco, ate little but cheese, and talked nothing but hydrodynamics in suitably fluid English.

Hendriks stuffed tobacco in his pipe as he walked to the far end of the tank.

"I am worried," he said, without preamble. "There is more in this discrepancy than you think." He did not sound worried. He sounded like he loved talking about problems, because in the solution lay further knowledge. He was a conscientious man.

Hendriks pointed at a row of four fiberglass Twelve-Meter hulls lined up along the wall. The models had been built very carefully and accurately to scale in the new Twelve-Meter shop at Briggs and Sons boatyard. Each was twenty-two feet long and made of four different sections that slotted together in any combination: underwater hull, hull above the waterline, keel, and rudder. Thus from four different models you could theoretically test a total of 256 different configurations.

"This was Jack's latest." Hendriks touched one end of a model labeled "37." The configuration was the same as the plan Paul had shown to the CBM people.

Paul helped him manhandle the boat onto a workbench with a small electric crane. It was extremely ponderous.

The Dane hooked up weights to the "force-block." The force-block was essentially a dynamometer, a system of strain gauges and bridge circuits in the model itself that measured exactly how much effort was required to tow a hull through water. Knowing how much it resisted movement, by process of elimination, would indicate how fast the hull would go in a given wind.

Hendriks connected the model circuitry to an electronic Sanborn amplifier on the towing carriage. The carriage was permanently hooked up to a twenty-channel analog/digital recorder in the control room. The recorder, in turn, was connected to a computer terminal. They walked back to the control room to calibrate the instruments, averaging the readings until they gave a consistent result for the weight the force-block was hooked up to. Methodically, Hendriks repeated the process five times, then averaged the averages, to make sure.

They removed the test weight, put the model in the water, shackled it directly to yet another electronic gauge on the towing carriage, and returned to the control room.

"We'll do a few calm water runs, with no heel," Hendriks said. He flicked on the instruments and hit a series of levers. There was a rising electric hum. Through the glass panel of the control room they could see the carriage start to slide in their direction, tripping a photoelectric switch to start the measurements. The model moved under it on the plane of green water, leaving a clean blister of wake to mark its passing.

Paul and Hendriks watched the computer screen, where the model's drag was translated into a series of orange curves on a graph. A video terminal above their heads reflected the physical symptoms of the forces at work.

Hendriks repeated the run three times at the same, low speed, then built up to higher velocities in small increments. He took a large chunk of Havarti cheese from a desk drawer and nibbled at it absently as he ran the tests.

Two hours passed. The curves rose and dipped as predicted. They began testing the model at different angles of heel and yaw—leaning the boat to one side for heel, skewing it in relation to its course for yaw. The control room grew thick with the fumes of rum-cured tobacco and cheese, and Paul escaped into the tank room to walk alongside the model as it moved up and down the warm expanse of liquid.

At seventeen degrees of heel Paul asked Hendriks to repeat the run, then beckoned him into the tank room to watch as he followed the miniature boat.

"Look at the wake," he said. "Just aft of the rudder. It's off a little. And there—" he pointed to a spot on the model's lower side, about three-quarters of the way toward the stern. "See how the wave peaks up, a bit, compared to the other runs? It's dirty water. I'll bet you anything it's drag from the leeward keel."

They replayed the test on the video monitor, then ran the model again. The water was smooth as glass until the mini Twelve parted it with its sharp bow. Chinese in its patience, the liquid pretended to accept the alien hull; it curled into pure, organic shapes, rolled aside in submission, but two-thirds of the way down the hull it surged back in a muscle of crystal that sucked and pulled at the boat right where the hull fined back down to let disturbed water close over the rudder.

"It could be dirty water from the lower keel," Hendriks acknowledged, sucking at his pipe. "It is amplifying the quarter-wave on this side. Ja, it's possible. Me, I listen only to the instruments."

"There's something else," Paul said, watching the waves climb, break, fall off the hull in limpid, almost sticky drops. "I can't put my finger on it, but it's there."

"Conan Doyle," a voice behind them said.

In this context the voice was so utterly familiar Paul barely reacted. Here, it was the past ten or twelve years that were illusion. Then he remembered.

"It isn't what you're seeing, it's what you're *not* seeing," the voice admonished. "Like the dog in the nighttime."

"Gosh!" Paul burst out. "I don't believe it." He turned around.

The technician's hair was all gray now, his face was tired. But the gentle smile, the tattoos, the compact assurance were still the same.

They called him Gosh because no one could pronounce his Polish name, which was Goscje, and because he never used swearwords any worse than "darn" or "phooey."

He had been running the tank for twenty years and knew more about ship models and the way they ran through water and how this passage could be measured electronically than many of the naval engineers he worked for.

Gosh went back to the control room, sent the carriage back to the "beach" at the tank's far end. He started the run again and darted back into the tank room.

"Look," he said, pointing at the wake. "What is it you don't see with this crazy two-keel boat? You get separation, disturbed water flow from the keels, yes. But what you don't look for is separation from the bottom of the hull. Just because your keels are not on the bottom, on this Twelve-Meter, does not mean there is no turbulence there. That is what you forgot to put in your darn computer program. And that is why your drag curves are up. No?"

Paul shrugged. It was possible. Gosh looked up from the model.

"I'm sorry," he added, "about Jack. He was a good man." The technician turned back to the tank. What was past was past, and you could not measure emotions with dynamometers. Gosh had always been like that. Paul felt a rush of affection for the man.

Paul knew the affection was really directed at lost peace, at a time when all directions were open.

But this time the past stayed in the background. Gosh had defined the problem, and now it twinged in Paul's mind like a bad tooth.

Suddenly he wanted nothing more than to go back to Maine, dust off his desk, sharpen his pencils, and fix whatever had gone wrong with Jack's boat.

When Paul came through the back door of his house, he found the kitchen hot with people and talk and the smell of pepperoni.

Nat and Jessica sat at the alcove table playing Scrabble. Woburn scratched under the table. Old George slumped beside them, rubbing his nose, listening to the game without great understanding.

Lucinda stood at the sink washing dishes.

"If it isn't himself," she called. "We thought you'd got a flat tire."

"I'm only an hour late," Paul protested. "Hi, Jess."

His daughter gave a shy smile but did not get up. Paul noticed balloons Scotch-taped to the alcove rafters, scrunched-up gift wrapping on the floor. They had put off her birthday party to wait for him.

"We saved the cake for you." Lucinda brushed her hair back. "Cake, ice cream." She automatically registered signs of fatigue in her son's face. She threw a critical glance at Paul's greasy bomber jacket, then looked away. Stepping to the freezer, she took out a decorated chocolate concoction with the sacerdotal gesture people always reserved for birthday cakes.

"There's lots of pizza left over. You want me to reheat some? Old George is staying in the barn," she added, in a lower tone. "Some trouble with his brothers. I said it was OK."

"How was New York, Chief," Nat called from the alcove.

Old George had snuck away, looking for bourbon while Lucinda's attention was distracted.

"Not yet," Paul said. "We're still in business, for now."

"Then we have three things to celebrate," Lucinda said over her shoulder.

"Nat," Jessica complained. "I've been waiting for you to take a turn for a million hours."

Paul went back outside to get his present for Jessica. He manhandled the huge box into the kitchen. Suddenly conscious of how blatantly he was buying forgiveness for missing her birthday he set it down to one side of the alcove, but his daughter already had caught sight of the box. Her eyes grew wide, her expression pensive.

"What's the third thing we're celebrating," Paul asked as he helped Lucinda bring bowls of ice cream to the table.

"The state police," Nat explained. "They said they're not going to arrest you because they think somebody else did it. Arrest wasn't the word," Nat went on, thoughtfully. "Indicted."

Paul felt as if he'd suddenly cleared an obstruction that had sat unnoticed in his chest for months.

"Well—," he breathed. "That's nice."

"They think it's somebody who was at that motel, somebody from up in Massachusetts," Lucinda took up, brightly. "They found his car in Mansfield, Mass. It was stolen."

The lights were doused, the cake was brought. Everyone sang and clapped and did everything possible to make Jessica cringe in embarrassment. When the lights came back on Paul slid out the box and helped her open it. Styrofoam peanuts littered the floor. She gazed at the huge stuffed animal in awe. Then she dragged it to her seat and, with Nat's help, set it on her knees. The bear effectively hid her from the rest of the table.

"What do you think, Jess?" Paul asked, when the adults had stopped talking for her.

No answer came.

"You like it?" Nat asked.

"She'd like it a lot more if her father was around more," Lucinda commented from the sink.

Paul made coffee. He was adding several hefty dollops of rum to his when the phone rang.

"Hello?" he said. "Hello."

It was a long-distance call, from Ellsworth or Rockland at least, the way phone lines were strung on this peninsula. But no one was on the other end.

"G'bye," Paul said, and started to hang up.

"Briggs?" The receiver crackled in his hand.

"Is that Vanzetti?" No one else called him Briggs with the same exaggerated truculence.

"Is this Paul Briggs?"

The voice was not Vanzetti's. It was too treble and breathy.

"Speaking. Who is this?"

"You got to quit working on the Twelve."

"Excuse me?"

"I said, you have to stop working on the Twelve-Meter."

"Who *is* this?" Paul wondered, in brief panic, if it were the syndicate people talking, if this were their idea of a brush-off, but the voice did not mesh with his memory of how they talked.

"They're going to dump you anyway. After the next payment. You know that."

The next payment reduced their debt burden somewhat, but it only rescheduled the yard's liquidity problem—Paul stopped short of giving a nameless caller the respect of attention.

"If this is some kind of joke—"

"It's no joke."

"Then who are you?"

"Stop the Twelve-Meter," the voice insisted.

"You're crazy or sick or something. I'm going to hang up now."

"Or we'll stop *you*," the voice hissed, "like we stopped your cousin."

"I don't believe this. What is this," Paul heard himself yell.

Everyone in the kitchen was staring at him. "Who is it," Nat mouthed, pointing at the phone. Paul cupped the receiver in his hands, turned toward the wall, and forced himself to talk evenly.

"I don't believe you," he whispered, thinking it almost certainly was a hoax. High school kids, the kind of scum who enjoyed running down skunks and cats in daddy's car, sometimes pulled stunts like this. But what high school kid could know about the payment schedule?

It might still be a hoax, one of the yacht club types looking for cheap thrills.

Or it could be Jack's killer. In that case, he must draw him out, obtain information, set complex verbal pitfalls.

"Get out of it," the voice offered, "and nothing happens."

"If this isn't a joke," Paul began, meaning to ask for some sort of proof, but the line went dead and he was left talking to thin air.

He hung up the phone.

A large, brown stuffed bear watched him from the alcove table. Four human faces also pointed in his direction, sharp with curiosity.

"A crank," Paul said, forcing a smile. "Joke call. People like that are really sad." He found his spiked coffee and added more rum, but from the way the bottle's neck almost missed the cup Paul knew he did not, on balance, believe what he said himself.

〜

November light was clear and hard, like crystal, or like the spray of filtered, heated water spilling off one of Jack's models in the test tank.

Paul wondered if this limpid quality had to do with a lack of humidity or a change in the direction of prevailing winds that spared them the accumulated pollution of the Northeast.

Whatever its provenance, the light took old colors and curried them in novel ways. It turned Eel Pond into a violence of blue-gray; it streamed through skylights to gild the design loft with a VSOP glow that belied the windchill outside.

Paul forced his eyes back down to the drafting table. According to the new agreement with the syndicate, he had one month to demonstrate "satisfactory progress" with Jack's design and another month to finish the plans. It was going to be tricky enough salvaging Jack's design at this stage, without letting his thoughts meander all over the shop.

But concentration did not come easy. The loft was full of the dead and their legacies, and drumbeats from the recent past only played counterpoint to softer, older rhythms.

At that rolltop desk his father had sat, weekends, while Paul lined up plastic soldiers in battle array on the floor. His dad sketched exquisite tall-masted sailboats. He built only two of them: the *Maria* and the *Lemuel Nickerson*, fast, elegant schooners that had no place in the twentieth century. In fact both were converted to coal barges during the war. When peace came, his father kept drawing, but he never built what he drew. Except for the occasional lobsterman, or the odd eccentric from Southwest Harbor, no one wanted wooden hulls anymore. Bob Briggs would die, quite literally, before he built anything in "damn plastic."

In those cracked armchairs, twenty years later, Paul and Jack made the decision to start building in fiberglass instead of repairing old wood. They couldn't afford to, and it meant breaking with the yard's only secure source of income, as well as family tradition, but they took the plunge, and Bull had let them try.

And in that corner, behind the door, a man with sickness in his heart and a piece of metal in his hand had cracked Jack's skull like a hard-boiled egg—burst a blood vessel, Doc Knowles said, between the arachnoid membrane and the bone—and left him dying on the floor.

Last night, the killer had promised to do the same to Paul.

In the clear light of day Paul had decided last night's caller was a well-informed crank. In any case, it was irrelevant. If it were Jack sitting here, faced with the same choice of priorities, he would finish this design on time, under budget, and worry about threats later.

Paul took off his glasses and cleaned them carefully on his shirttail. He got up to pour himself a cup of coffee from the automatic espresso machine.

Paul stared out the windows. He drank the coffee. His heart was pounding and he knew it had nothing to do with caffeine.

It had everything to do with fear: a fear that stemmed from the length of time he had not been working; a fear that fed on itself with every day he put off facing it; a fear that he had lost his touch, and the boats he sought to bring to life would remain forever out of reach.

⚏

The fear first came with the aftermath, three years ago. He did not notice how it grew around the foundations of his imagination, turning the supports to sponge.

Then, somewhere about a month after Suzanne's postcard, he

tried to fasten himself to the old underpinnings. He wanted to retreat to the fantasies of perfect boats and the drawings he made in their likeness. These were his strength, the castle keep of his character.

He found the fantasies still in the background. They never left. But when he tried to turn them into lines he found something had sabotaged the process. The firm takeoff he needed to push the pen into uncharted white paper had gone mushy and green. The reckless, surging reserve of guts he needed for the leap into nothing had vanished like it never existed.

In the design loft, three years later, Paul shivered at the memory. He looked away from the familiar forms of the loft where he once confronted the fear, and lost. He drew comfort from the fact that today, this job, would require no creativity, no imagination, no leaps into dark possibility or virgin paper—but only technique, logic, the process of elimination. Not originality of his own, but the adjustment of another's. Not invention, but calculation.

Paul shut off the worry. A certain confidence lay in the rituals, the techniques. He thought himself back to MIT, and Professor Tompkins and the first clean theorems he had known. He thought himself back to the basics of his trade.

ꓱ

The basics were perfect fluid.

In perfect fluid, an object angled against the flow could pass and the fluid would open before and close behind, smooth and seamless, with no imbalance or irregularities or differences in pressure to mark the object's passing.

Air was not a perfect fluid, however. Air was an imperfect gas, and when it passed over an object angled against its flow, such as a sail, it did not move cleanly but broke, concentrating its flow in some areas and fleeing others.

Typically the flow slowed where the molecules of fluid bunched up against the object's surface. As a result pressure rose on that surface, but pressure dropped around the back as molecules raced around to fill the "hole" left behind by the object's movement.

Because that drop in pressure was greater than the increase, and because the drop in pressure was concentrated on the forward, leading edge of the object, the object tended to "lift" itself out of the high-pressure zone into the low and go forward.

This was how a sail worked. This was also how a keel worked, because if you looked at the keel as an underwater sail you saw it lifted itself forward against the flow of water resulting from the boat's crabbed movement through the sea.

You could enhance this lift in both sail and keel by curving them, like the top of an airplane wing. This smoothed the flow and increased the pressure differential, as long as the fluid did not flow too fast to follow the curve.

The uneven flow of air and water was not an unmitigated blessing, however, for whenever pressure dropped too suddenly on the surface of sail or keel, the flow would turn in on itself, twist into little storms, eddies, turbulence that eroded the pressure differential powering the boat.

This was what was happening to the *Challenge*'s leeward keel. Based on what he had seen in the test tank, Paul was convinced the angle of the keels was so sharp it interfered with the flow of water whenever the keel was in the deep, leeward position—the angle where its wave-making properties were not needed to cancel out the quarter-wave.

There was no way to eliminate the turbulence entirely, Paul knew, for it was determined by quite rigid laws of physics, varying in accordance with the length of sail or keel, as a function of speed.

All you could do was try to push the "transition" point, where the clean flow of fluid began to waver, as far toward the back of the keel (or sail) as possible.

In the case of a keel, you did this by making the forward, leading, edges smooth, because roughness spawned turbulence. You tried to make the keel's shape as round, elliptical, organic as you could, because forms that reflected the mathematical curve of ocean waves seemed to make less fuss as they went through the water.

And you avoided sharp curves and angles because water flowing off the back of a harsh curve tended to lose pressure and "separate," becoming turbulent, and water flowing into a confined angle could resonate against itself with the same unwelcome results.

As in the case of the *Challenge*.

Paul got stiffly to his feet. He spread out the plans he had worked on before going to New York.

He looked carefully at the cross-section view, where the keels were rooted in the hull.

The cross section looked a little like a round champagne glass.

But while a conventional keel hung from the exact bottom of the hull, where the stem of the champagne glass would be, the *Challenge*'s twin keels were mounted, one on each side, like drooping airplane wings.

Paul looked at the design for a good ten minutes, letting his eye follow each line back and forth, allowing his mind to absorb the feel of the hull and compare it with a lifetime's knowledge of the ways of wind and seawater.

Jack's lines seemed to laugh at him, arrogant in their precision.

Three years' worth of exile from ink and paper rose like a portcullis before his brain.

Technique, Paul reminded himself. Only technique. Skills, for a naval architect, on the level of walking and toilet training.

More from defiance than because he had anything specific to draw at this stage, he took a T square and drew a short, neat line at the bottom of the paper.

꩜

Paul locked himself in the loft for an average of eighteen hours a day, wrestling with Jack's design.

The time seemed like a thinking coma, a waking, brain-beating knockout bounded by the wooden walls of the drafting loft and the scratching sounds of his own instruments. Occasional glances at the skylight overhead gave him a time-lapse view of the outside world where purple storms threatened and clotted, raged and faded; where sleet fell, sun warmed, frost formed; where the nights grew perceptibly longer.

Inside, part-time draftsmen appeared and vanished at his command. Drawings were roughed out, finished, crumpled. Ideas sprang up, blossomed, were cut down by sharp pencil points and ruler edges.

His grandfather took the demo thirty-eight-footer and sailed south for the winter.

John Poole tended to the day-to-day business of the yard better than he could. Lucinda tended to Jessica. Paul tried to spend half an hour with the child, before school, when he could.

About a third of the way into the redesign process Paul got a report from Vanzetti.

The report was twelve pages long. It described, in loose but colorful prose, the detective's visits to a number of tugboat companies in the Baltimore area. Two lines on the last page contained the gist of his investigation; no one in the tugboat world so far had recognized the man in the Identikit.

Stapled to the last page were another two pages worth of bills listing travel and entertainment, telephone and car-rental expenses. On top of the private investigator's per diem it all came to over twenty-four hundred dollars. Paul called Vanzetti's office and got the answering machine. Biting down on his doubts, he wrote out a check. He included a note about the police finding the suspect's car in Massachusetts and sent them to the detective's Bangor address.

⚏

The trouble with naval architecture was, it remained more art than science.

Over ten thousand years of building boats, men had learned, by trial and error, that some factors—greater length, smoother curves, a certain ratio of depth to width—made given hulls cut through the water faster than others.

Late-Victorian designers, flush with the triumphs of the mechanical age, tried to generalize this experience into broad theories, with only limited success. Colin Archer's idea that the proportions of a boat should follow a sinusoid-shaped curve forward, a trochoidal curve aft (a solution that, in mathematics at least, worked out to minimum resistance), was a typical example. The twentieth century sciences of air and hydrodynamics quantified many of the factors, without linking or explaining them. This was because a craft moving through the frontier between two very different elements had to deal with far more subtle, interlocking forces than a craft moving through only one. Which was why supersonic fighters were more predictable than Twelve-Meters.

In cases like the *Challenge*, what it still came down to was trial and error; altering one piece of the puzzle at a time and seeing if it worked better. It was a process speeded up, but not altered in any fundamental way, by the use of computers.

One option should have been to change the angle of the *Challenge*'s twin keels. However, this would be very difficult to do, for Jack had placed them very carefully.

He had started with the average weather conditions for La Rochelle, where the *Challenge* would race, for the time of year she would race in. From this he'd worked out the average angle the boat would heel, or lean under sail, for the upwind part of the course. Then he'd worked out the perfect angle for the windward keel to cancel out wave resistance. To change the position of the keels would compromise the entire design, and it was too late to start over from scratch.

One option was to narrow the root, or base of the keel, to reduce junction drag, that resonance in the tight angle between keel and hull. But he found this, too, was impossible. Paul himself had spent months measuring the stresses to be expected on every inch of a fiberglass Twelve-Meter, section by section, panel by panel, and putting these numbers into the computer. The results came out in a three-dimensional graphic where light stress was marked by cool colors, high stress in hot. In that graphic, the joint where keel met hull was marked in livid red. Paring the keel at that point would catastrophically weaken the boat. It would also make it very hard to steer.

Which left only one solution: to fill in the V-shaped angle where keel met hull, smooth the joint until it looked more like a shallow "U" that would not bounce water back on itself or create turbulence.

This, too, was the only possible way to deal with the disturbed water Gosh had spotted coming from the bottom of the Twelve-Meter's hull, between the two keels.

The only problem with this solution was, fairing in the curves and angles would increase the overall volume of the hull. This meant, under the Twelve-Meter rule, he would have to cut down on sail area, or length. . . .

He started playing music again while he worked; Wagner to balance the routine figures, Bach for the drafting. Once he even found himself conducting to the Third Brandenburg, waving his arms, throwing his hair back like a Georg Solti, never quite bringing the cellos in on time, acting like he did when he was transferring his ideas to paper as the fancy took him—he stopped himself, embarrassed. There was a draftsman in the room and anyway, it felt like a betrayal.

ꭩ

It took Paul ten days to finish the corrected draft. He could have done it a little quicker except that two of the computer discs with test-tank records on them were missing and he had to find the original records to check his input. Then he plugged the boat's new dimensions, reflecting the smoothed-in connections between keels and hull, into the machine.

From the very first run the revised boat showed some improvement. The figures came out in speed estimates for various weather conditions, and most of the windward figures all showed increments of 0.05, 0.1, even 0.13. Which didn't sound like much, until you worked it out for a four-hour, twenty-five-odd-mile boat race, and realized it could translate into a half-mile lead at the finish.

It still works, Paul thought, and a pleased feeling settled somewhere beneath the gray exhaustion. He could still do the nuts and bolts stuff, anyway.

Paul juggled the variables to the last minute, trying to get the fastest possible compromise from the corrections he had incorporated. He finished the offsets for a new test-tank model at three in the morning on November 17.

On November 18, one day before deadline, he sent the offsets via bonded courier to the CBM headquarters in New York City.

C H A P T E R · R   1 5

The syndicate approved his revised design and the first payment arrived on the second day of December. The day the check cleared, Paul began setting up the yard for actual construction.

Christmas came and went in a fever of purchase and bright paper. Ashley came back from New York the day after.

In its survey of the America's Cup syndicates, *Yachts* magazine listed December 29 as the date construction officially would begin on the *Challenge*.

On that date a national trucking company delivered a box, express rate, to the shiny new guardhouse at the boatyard gates.

The crate was three feet high and three feet wide and deep. It was solidly built of pine boards and three-inch nails. Red labels on its side showed flames, barred hooks, and announced the presence of chemicals. "This side up," "Flammable," "Do Not Drop," other labels read.

The freight was listed as "Thixotropic Resin (Gelcoat)" destined for the Challenge Syndicate, Briggs and Sons Boatyard, Eel Pond Road, French Harbor, Maine.

The day guard signed it in. A boat painter dollied it over to the Twelve-Meter shed.

The new shed was an echoing cavern where complex shapes and bright lights created weird shadows among the steel roof supports. It was one hundred feet long and almost forty feet high in the middle, but already it looked cramped for the amount of materials inside. Ten tables stacked with fiberglass matting stood in concentric circles. Forests of extension cords led from junction boxes to the shed's center. There two shiny molds, each seventy feet in length, lay side by side on heavy cradles, surrounded by scaffolding.

The molds were built to exactly reflect the shape of the boat they would form. The smaller, "male" plug mirrored the boat on its own outside surface. The larger, "female" mold carried the shape inside. When the two were fitted together, there would be room for a hull to grow between.

A short, thin, fifty-year-old with a dead pipe in his mouth and a worried frown on his face walked over to check the manifest.

"Gelcoat," the foreman said, "that's funny." He fetched a crowbar and levered open one of the top planks. The shiny tops of gallon cans met his eyes. "Hey, Mikey," he called.

A masked face peered from inside the hollow mold.

"We got more Gelcoat."

The masked man shrugged. "I got all I need. Save it for the next one," he suggested in a muffled voice and disappeared.

John Poole took the pipe out of his mouth and stared at it.

"Put it by the resin store," he told the painter. "You won't be able to get it inside; it's so full you couldn't fit a sardine in there."

The painter trundled off, swerving to avoid the boss as he walked a quiet stranger with a suit and briefcase across the cement floor.

"We're just cleaning up the prep work now," Paul explained to the stranger. "Right on target. Incredibly enough. I'll introduce you to our laminating expert. Hey, Mikey."

"What the hell is it now?" The masked man reappeared. "Oh, hi, Paul," he said, and pulled the mask off to reveal a giant brown handlebar moustache.

"Mikey Richman, this is Joe Cummings, the inspector from Lloyds of London. Mr. Cummings is going to be checking up on everything you do."

"You mean I can't put four coats on instead of five anymore?"

Mikey complained. "You mean I can't skimp on the resin, like you always tell me?" The moustache split on an evil grin.

Paul laughed, nervously.

The Lloyds man went to the plans table. Paul grabbed his tape measure and checked the dimensions of the female mold for the seventh time that morning.

The intercom announced a visitor. Paul stuck his security card in the slot to open the door. Ashley walked in, dressed in long, turquoise silk.

"Did I miss it?" she asked, in a tone that matched her bright hues.

"Miss what."

"The start of building. You know." She lifted a bottle of champagne. "Laying the keels, you called it, once."

John Poole came in behind her, carrying the top four feet of a spruce tree. He climbed the scaffolding and fastened it to the front of the mold, where the Twelve-Meter's bow would take shape. Mikey's electric buffer switched off.

"Ancient nautical fertility rites," Ashley smiled. "Jack always cracked up at that."

"It's the way we've always done things," Paul replied, neutrally.

The woman gave him a look.

"You and Jack were really different," she said. "But you've become more like him, all of sudden. Since you got back from New York. Now you've gotten all serious, like him. You work a million hours a week on that boat, like him. You look like you died."

Paul shrugged. Ashley went over to the wooden crate, by the resin store, and placed the bottle of champagne on top. She collected coffee mugs from around the shop. "Are we ready?" she called.

Everyone stood around self-consciously and lifted their mugs when Ashley said, "The Twelve." Even Ashley, unschooled as she was in these matters, knew better than to call the boat by her name before she was launched.

"We should make a habit of this," Mikey commented, licking the ends of his moustache.

"What is this," Paul asked, noticing the crate. "We never buy resin from E-Tex."

"I'll send it back," the foreman replied. "I thought Warren might have ordered it."

"Why isn't it in the resin store? It's a fire hazard."

"There's no room, Paul," John Poole said. "I'll send it back in the morning."

After the champagne was finished they all climbed the scaffolding over the concave half of the mold and watched as Mikey began work on the Twelve-Meter.

Mikey was a superb craftsman in his chosen medium. The mold—itself a reverse hull, built of fiberglass around a strong wooden matrix—was so beautifully made that every line of it seemed to flow with the force of good sculpture. Mikey's crew had polished and waxed the glass to perfect smoothness. It shone like a mirror and the reflected light hurt their eyes.

Mikey flicked on an electric pump. He picked up a spray nozzle and the hose connecting it to the pump. He made sure the nozzle was on the extrafine setting; then, without any further ceremony, he turned on the sprayer and passed it, sure and loving, across the bottom middle of the mold, working from the flange outward. Every stroke was short and accurate and put down exactly the right amount of Gelcoat. The first skin of what would eventually be a sixty-four-foot racing sailboat grew wetly before their eyes.

"Come over to my house for drinks, afterward?" Ashley murmured to Paul as they watched.

Paul shook his head.

"I have to get the sail schedule finished. I'm way behind as it is."

"For God's sake." She spoke louder now. "It's just a lousy little drink. What do you think I'm going to do—rape you?" The words were angry, but her tone pleaded.

John Poole pretended not to hear.

"Listen," Paul whispered, uncomfortably.

"No," she interrupted. "Don't talk down to me."

"I'm not—"

She waved her hand. "I know," she continued, "I know what it's like, I know we're both sleeping with ghosts. Still. That doesn't mean we can't be friends."

Paul thought about it.

"Tell you what," he suggested. "Why don't you come over to my house, supper time. Later. Lucinda and Nat are going to the movies in Searsport. That way, I can finish the sail sked first."

"I guess that's the best I can hope for," Ashley murmured, but the loneliness in her voice had eased a little, and Paul's guilt subsided accordingly.

≈

By 4:00 P.M. Mikey and his crew had finished applying the first Gelcoat to the inside of the female mold. There was no need, at this point, to hoist up the male mold and clamp it into place, for the Gelcoat consisted of a resin that would set, or "cure," without pressure. They hooked up power to the matrix of heating wires running through the mold. Mikey checked the heat-control panel to make sure it was set at the optimum temperature for curing.

Then he and his men picked up their tools and left, setting the alarms behind them.

Lucinda dropped Old George at the yard as night fell. He vaguely shone his flashlight at every building in the boatyard, then went into the main shed. He stoked up the wood stove by the steaming box. He shucked his coat, hauled out a pint of bourbon and set his pocket alarm for 4:00 A.M.

Bobby the night guard went straight to the Twelve-Meter shed when he came in. He disconnected the infrared sensor circuit, so his presence would not set the alarms off. He made sure the rest of the alarm circuits showed green, then locked himself inside.

Before the burglary Bobby would have joined Old George in the main shed, subsiding gratefully into one of the sagging armchairs around the steam box. He would have taken out his police textbooks and studied while Old George snored.

Now Bobby did none of these things. His textbooks sat in his motel room, reprieved but unmarked. Bobby slouched in a chair next to one of the mat-cutting tables, wondering how to salvage his fledgling career as a law-enforcement officer.

Between long, depressing thoughts he munched on cheese-flavored potato chips and read a paperback Western, making believe the sounds of air and sea outside were really sage brush and gulch water.

≈

At twenty-five minutes to midnight a box-shaped modern sedan came to a halt on the road running along the opposite side of Eel Pond from the boatyard.

The driver cracked his window open and ran out the antenna of a model-airplane remote-control transmitter.

He looked up and down the road, but French Harbor was long asleep, the last shrimp truck on its way to Rockland and points west, and there were no houses on this stretch in any case.

The man nodded to himself approvingly. He did not care for houses. He liked open stretches of country with nothing on them as far as the eye could see. No trees, no people. New Mexico, he thought, was the state for him. New Mexico, or Alaska. The man pressed a button on the transmitter. Radio waves zipped across three hundred yards of water to the Briggs boatyard.

Inside the crate, a receiver tuned to the same frequency responded to the transmission by switching the juice through a solenoid. The solenoid opened a second electric circuit. This circuit linked a twelve-volt motorcycle battery to an electric starter engine firmly bracketed to a wide metal box under the crate's false bottom.

The starter motor whined. Its rotor wound in a flexible wire looped around a long glass ampoule containing sulfuric acid. The ampoule was cushioned to withstand the shocks of travel, but not a steady lateral strain applied to its unsupported midsection. It shattered almost immediately. The end of the wire was fastened to the starter switch. When it was fully wound it automatically shut off the motor.

Bobby glanced up sharply at the noise. Picking up his flashlight he walked around the case, then opened the door to the resin store. He found nothing out of place. Probably the wind, he thought, clicking branches against the aluminum siding. That, or Kiowa braves. He went back to the book.

Inside the crate, the sulfuric acid pooled on a diaphragm consisting of several layers of plastic.

The watcher on the other side of Eel Pond started his car and drove off to the north and west.

He had tested the thermite device with great care. He knew the acid would take roughly three and a quarter hours to eat through the diaphragm.

Sometime around 3:00 A.M. things should start to happen.

The acid would finally make a hole in the sandwiched plastic. It would start to drip, then spill onto a three-inch layer of mixed kitchen sugar and sulfur chlorate. The combined chemicals would react fiercely against each other. They would smoke, then ignite, sparking off a second layer of sulfur chlorate. The chain reaction would spread to two paper bags full of mixed ferric oxide and aluminum powder, enhanced by one inch of magnesium spread around the bottom of the box.

Almost immediately the mixture would reach a temperature well in excess of two thousand degrees Fahrenheit. At that point fire would burst out of the metal box, smash the false bottom, and explode the crate, spewing molten metals and gallons of flammable resin in a ring of destruction that would light off everything it touched.

᙭

"Jake flipped the rattler over. 'Ever eaten snake?' he asked Janet. She paled, and shuddered. 'We used to eat a lot of snake, in Nez Perce country,' Jake said. 'Mah Pa—' "

Bobby yawned, checked his watch. Five to three. Jake was taking one hell of a long time to get down to business.

" 'The other night,' Janet sighed, 'when you held me feverish in your arms—' "

A fizzing sound interrupted Jake and Janet's passion.

Bobby looked up.

The wall before him flowered in white flame.

There was not much blast, and it was mostly terror that knocked Bobby off his chair. He scrambled to his feet, the luscious Janet totally forgotten. The smoke detector shrilled over his head.

"Fire!" Bobby gasped, shading his eyes against the intensity of the blaze. He ran to the door and hit the alarm button. Then he grabbed a fire extinguisher off the rack.

Luckily, because it formed part of police-academy requirements, Bobby had studied the fire-procedures manual.

He knew it was important to identify what type of fire this was, but he had never heard of flames like these and could not think what their source might be.

The blaze was ten feet wide and spreading. It consisted of a core of painful light where the crate once stood, and a ragged circle of liquid flame around the core. The smoke was thick, brown, acrid. When in doubt, use CO_2, he thought.

He took a deep breath of untainted air, pulled the fire-extinguisher handle and directed the puking white foam at the base of the core.

This had absolutely no effect; in fact it seemed to spread the fire,

if anything. He attacked the surrounding islands of fire with somewhat better success. Foam seemed to thicken the smoke, and he
could no longer avoid breathing it.

Bobby's very first lungful of smoke doubled him over. His lungs
convulsed in pain and tried to somersault through his throat. He lost
hold of the extinguisher.

The magnesium and aluminum raged, happily self-sufficient, pro-
ducing and consuming their own oxygen. The aluminum wall beside
the fire's core, sensing a common bond, sought the heat. It buckled
and began to melt.

Blinded, unable to suck in enough oxygen to keep his lungs under
control, Bobby staggered his way along the wall, away from the blaze,
until he found the fire hose. He pulled the valve and tried to wrestle
the hose from its hanger. He opened the door to the resin store and
fell inside, seeking clean air.

⚏

"Paul."

"Ummm."

"You awake?"

"What you think?"

"There's something we never talked about."

He looked toward her in the dark. She saw the movement.

"The Labor Day picnic," she answered for him.

"What about it." Warily.

"You never actually told me how you felt."

"Gawd, Ashley. It's—where's the—gaw, it's three in the morning,
for chrissake."

The scratch of phosphorus. The sharpness of menthol smoke.

"The guilt is so thick around you, sometimes, I can almost touch
it," she said.

"I can deal with it."

"Can you?" she snorted. "I meant what I said, earlier. You're
doing just what he did. You bury it deep, never talk. Is it that I'm
not worth confiding in, I wonder?" (A fierce sucking drag of smoke).
"I'm all right to sleep with but not to talk to?"

Far away, the village siren wailed.

"Of course not."

"Then why don't you talk to me?"

"But I do."

Paul put his hand out and touched her skin. It felt cool, and smooth as marble. Ashley shrugged away from him.

"I don't want sex, Paul," Ashley said. "At least, not that kind. I need another kind of intimacy from you."

The ensuing silence lasted for a long time. Paul was almost back to dozing when the phone rang on the bedside table.

His hand reacted before his head did, picking up the phone and offering it to his mouth for action.

The voice was young and eager; it gloated in the absolutism of emergency. Paul slammed the receiver back down and threw himself out of bed.

"Paul, what is it? What's the matter?" She switched on the light.

"There's a fire at the yard."

"My God. Wait. I want to come."

Paul did not stop to argue. He found his glasses, put on his bomber jacket, pants, and a pair of boots, and ran downstairs. Ashley dived into Paul's wool sweater and followed. Roused by the commotion, Lucinda opened her door and bumped into Ashley as she ran for the landing. Ashley ignored Paul's mother. She picked herself up and tried to catch Paul but the Jeep was already moving by the time she got outside.

She stood in the driveway, hopping from one bare foot to another to keep them off the ice.

"Wait," she yelled as the Jeep circled, "Wait for me!"

"Paul," she cried, as the taillights dwindled without pause, "I'm getting so sick of this *shit!*"

㼨

They were taking Bobby out on a stretcher when Paul drove into the boatyard parking lot. He had a transparent oxygen mask over his mouth and nose. An emergency medical technician kept two fingers on his throat and counted.

The sight of ambulances in his boatyard was sickeningly familiar to Paul.

Not again, he thought, sprinting toward the stretcher. Not again.

The EMTs shoved him away with the arrogance of training. They said Bobby would be "all right." Bobby's eyes were open, Paul noticed, and he was looking around him. That, at least, was different.

The long, sad face looked even longer and sadder than usual under the transparent mask.

Paul turned and ran into the open doors of the main shed.

Inside, glancing flashlights opened and shut thick curtains of brown smoke. Familiar shapes turned evil and threatening under the stage management of fire. Even this far away from the center of activity the smoke stung his eyes and stabbed his bronchial passages. He wrapped a drop cloth around his face and followed the taut canvas hoses to the Twelve-Meter shed.

The volunteer firemen looked like Japanese warriors in their thick coats and helmets and breathing apparatus. They danced slowly around a strange silver light by the north wall, spraying foam and fine water that turned immediately to steam. A man in a fire chief's hat—it had to be Seth Sproul—was trying to split his men and efforts between the main blaze in the Twelve-Meter shed and a sympathy fire that had started next door in the outboard shop. There, years' worth of spilled two-cycle oil had sparked off from heat coming through the wall. Seth told Paul to get the hell away, until he saw who it was.

"Is everybody out," Paul yelled. He had to repeat it twice to get through the chief's oxygen apparatus as well as his own improvised air filter.

"We got the guard out," Sproul answered, in between checking what his men were doing, directing traffic with sweeps of his oil-skinned arms.

"There were two of 'em," Paul yelled back. The fear coiled around his stomach, tightened like a boa constrictor. "Old George?"

"Just one." Sproul held up a gloved finger. "Where was Old George?"

Paul turned and ran back through the main shed, calling George's name. The wood box was glowing but the armchairs were empty. Then he realized even Old George could not have slumbered through the rush of men and equipment and sirens. He ran back toward the front of the fire. A distorted "Hey, you" followed him as Paul took the left fork where the fire hoses split, and plunged into the cloud of black smoke billowing out of the outboard shop.

It was one thing to face the heat of fire. It was almost as scary to blunder through a pit of smoke and not know where the fire was.

Paul shut the idea of searing flame from his mind and felt for the hoses with his feet, tripping as often as he stepped. Incongruously, it reminded him of how he used to fish for clams as a kid, digging with his toes into the squishy muck of the Sancastin estuary.

Fire crackled somewhere ahead and to the right. His eyes streamed from the smoke. He caromed suddenly off a wet, black shoulder holding a large canister of CO_2. There was a shout of warning. Paul tried to answer, but the smoke was now seeping through the cloth around his mouth. He could not get enough backpressure in his windpipe to form words.

A hole appeared in the black pall, affording him a view of clumped foam rolling in the flames or floating in the thermals. Wooden studs burned like racist crosses. A voluptuous Amazon in a girlie calendar had lost half a breast to the heat. A thirty-five-horse Evinrude outboard deep-fried in orange grease.

In the light of the burning motor Paul found the sliding door to the paint shed. He checked the latch; it was open, hot to the touch. As he slid back the door the paint on its end began to smolder.

He found Old George by stumbling over him. The old man was lying in a teak deck chair beside shelves of copper antifouling paint. Paul did not have to feel his pulse to know George was alive. His own eyes already felt cleaner, presumably because little smoke had penetrated the sliding door. The old man's snores rose above the crackle of flame, and the odor of bourbon mingled with the hot, acrid breath of the conflagration behind. Paul wondered, stupidly, if a man full of bourbon would burn quicker than a man without.

He supposed he would.

Paul shook Old George awake, violently. The guard was totally amazed at what had happened to his world. "Jay-sus Christ, you don't say," he muttered, foolishly, when he grew conscious of the lust and stench of fire behind the door, and he kept repeating this. He followed Paul without protest, gripping the tails of his coat as Paul groped his way through the outboard shop where the foam at last was accumulating deep enough to deny the flames sustenance. "Jesus Christ, you don't say. Jay-sus *Christ!* You don't say. . . ."

When he got Old George to safety Paul went back to the fire's center of effort. He asked the fire chief to make sure his men wetted down the paint shed as a precaution. Seth Sproul rushed off, rushed back. Even through his goggles Seth's eyes gleamed with an excitement he could barely conceal in professional jargon. When they were kids, when the Fourth of July rolled around, Paul remembered, Seth had always been one of the most reliable suppliers of illegal cherry bombs, M-80s, and Roman candles.

Paul checked the Twelve-Meter mold. At first glance he thought the actual mold had not warped or melted, but the Gelcoat must have absorbed a lot of smoke particles and would have to be re-applied. He looked at the square where the crate of resin had stood, shading his eyes. The silver light was so strong and bright it felt solid, a brilliant instrument to curette the inside of his retinas.

They got the fire just in time, Seth shouted. Another five minutes and both the resin store and the paint store would have gone up, probably taking the rest of the yard with them.

The only reason that didn't happen, Seth continued, was because the night guard jammed himself inside the resin store and ran water over the walls, cooling them down until he passed out from the smoke.

The kid deserved a medal, the fire chief said. Paul deserved to go to jail for allowing weird metals and chemicals in the working space.

"What do you mean, 'weird metals'?" Paul shouted even louder to carry through the hiss of high-pressure equipment.

Sproul pointed accusingly at the silver light.

"I thought it was aluminum, from the wall," he yelled back. "But it's not. It's magnesium. You need a special chemical agent to stop a magnesium fire. What the hell do you use it for, anyway?"

"We don't," Paul answered.

"Ain't it weird," the chief shouted, "how the worst fires always seem to come when there's ice on the ground?"

Paul grunted.

"That fire," the chief continued, admiration in his tone, "is gonna burn till it burns itself out, and there ain't a goddamn thing we can do about it."

Paul went outside. He noticed the cops had finally made it. They were flashing their red lights and acting cool for the neighbors who had got out of bed to watch the spectacle. Then the cold air got to him, and the smoke that had seeped through the drop cloth rebelled in his lungs. He coughed so hard he doubled up and fell to his bare knees on the ice.

But even as he coughed, the chief's words rang in his head.

There was no doubt in his mind. The fire had been set.

No one used magnesium in a boatyard.

And if the fire had been set, it was more than likely whoever set the fire had also killed Jack. There weren't so many people who hated the Briggs that one would be breaking and entering and killing, while another was plotting to burn the yard.

Paul remembered the voice on the phone. "We'll stop you," the voice warned, "like we stopped your cousin." He'd convinced himself it was a crank, at the time. But the son of a bitch had not been joking.

Paul cursed as helplessly as he coughed.

He got most of the foreign matter out of his lungs in fifteen or twenty agonizing heaves. When he got home he took an endless, hot shower to rinse the smoke from his hair and body, but the sharpness of it stayed in his nose long after all tangible traces of the fire had gone.

C H A P T E R 1 6

The New Year came on silent snow.

The first flakes landed slow and cautious as scouting UFOs, just before sundown on New Year's Eve.

The snow was still falling on January second. It bivouacked in deep clouds and mountains. It bandaged the smoke marks on the eaves of the Briggs Twelve-Meter shed in French Harbor. It fell on the town of Amesboro, where the police headquarters of Georges County stood. Paul Briggs watched it come down through the steamed windows of the police chief's office.

Behind him, Pete Fossett, the chief, reiterated the obvious to Sergeant Murdoch and a man from the state's arson "task force."

"It's not someone from 'round here," Fossett said, poking his finger at black bits of metal spread out on a card table by his desk.

"It's done with stuff you can buy at any ole hardware store," Murdoch pointed out. "Or a grocery store. Or a junkyard."

"It's how a professional does it," the task-force man replied. "You don't need a license to buy sugar. You don't need a license to buy fertilizer. *That's* an MO I've seen before."

Paul wondered if the snow had caught Lucinda before she got on her connecting flight to Orlando. She had left awfully suddenly, after the fire.

He thought that first snow appealed wonderfully to the human imagination because it worked exactly as imagination did, blurring hard edges to turn the commonplace into fantasy. He thought the Amesboro village green, for example, looked like a huge sugar Danish. The firehouse and the service station opposite were raisins in a generous layer of icing. Their eaves and porch columns groaned under thick dollops of white.

A plough passed as Paul watched, curling waves of snow to each side in its wake. A cherry-red sports coupé turned into the police-station parking lot, quite fast. The driver jerked the handbrake, trying to skid the car 180 degrees into a parking position, but the tamped snow of the parking lot was very slippery, and he slid backward and out of sight.

There was a thick bang and a tinkle of glass, muffled by the whiteness.

The chief and Murdoch ran to see what was going on. The arson man picked up a charred transistor and held it to the light with both hands. Paul followed Murdoch at a more leisurely pace.

By the time he got outside they already had issued two tickets to Vanzetti.

"It's your own fault," Vanzetti shouted. "You don't plough the goddamn driveway right." He showed everyone his private investigator's ID along with his driver's license to remind them who he was. He wore a cheap imitation leather jacket, denims, and high-heeled cowboy boots. His cheeks were rough and his hair was greasy. He did not look like everyone's idea of a detective.

"You're supposed to take conditions into account," the chief said. "Reckless endangerment, Red. Charlie-One was only three, four years old." He patted the bruised cruiser in consoling fashion. Crunched brakelights spotted the ice like blood. Already the buckled chrome was cupping snow.

"Tell 'em what happened," Vanzetti said. "I saw you at the window."

"He was driving normally," Paul stated, trying not to smile. "I'd swear to that."

"You see? You see?" Vanzetti shouted at Red Burke, who was writing up a third summons. "I'll fight this all the way."

Everyone but Paul went back inside to discuss in comfort the technicalities of fender-benders. Paul sat in the Jeep, running the engine occasionally to keep warm. Vanzetti came out fifteen minutes later and climbed into the passenger seat.

"You always have to make an entrance," Paul commented.

Vanzetti sniffed. "Hick cops," he complained, shuffling his summons. "They won't get away with this."

Paul kept himself under tight control.

"So they tried to git you again," the detective said, after a pause.

"Look," Paul said, "where the hell you been? I been trying to reach you for three weeks."

"I got your message."

"I got this unbelievable bill—"

"You know I like to work on my own—"

"—which you notice I paid, though you haven't accomplished shit—"

"These people killed your cousin, now they try to burn down your boatyard—"

"That's all I seem to get these days," Paul complained, "people telling me what I already know."

"Bet you don't know who did it."

"Neither do you."

"Sure I do."

Paul's gaze locked.

"You told me that once before, but that time you didn't know any more than the 'hick cops' did."

"I know who did it. I even know where to find—the killer." For some reason, Vanzetti underlined the last words with his voice.

Where, Paul asked.

"New Bedford. You were right. Works on a tug, belongs to a barge company."

"You're kidding." Paul smacked the steering wheel with the edge of his fist, then shook his hand with the pain. "But that's great! You're really sure?"

"Sure, I'm sure," Vanzetti replied. "That Identikit was real good, easy to recognize. Especially the ears. And I checked—the suspect took a week off 'round the dates Jack was killed. There's other things, too. It all fits."

"But that's great," Paul repeated. He knew he should repress the surge of energy that came in with Vanzetti's words, but it felt too good to sit still. He opened the car door.

Vanzetti wanted to know where Paul was going.

"See what Murdoch's going to do about it. Unless he already said?"

"Wait up," Vanzetti said, "it's not that simple."

Paul stopped his movement, one foot out the door, one foot in.

"Just hold your horses." Vanzetti lifted a finger to focus attention.

He knew how cops thought, he knew how they worked, Vanzetti continued. Did Paul have any idea what was the first thing the cops would do?

Paul did not.

First thing, Vanzetti said, they'd tell their buddies on the Massachusetts State Police. The Mass. staties would check it out. If Paul were lucky, they would find probable cause and make the collar, complete with bells, whistles, and Miranda warnings. *If* Paul were lucky, the judge would set high bail, or no bail at all. Then the State of Maine would officially petition the Commonwealth of Massachusetts to extradite the suspect for trial in Maine. In a couple of months, extradition would go through, and they would have to start the whole process over again in Amesboro. If they were lucky.

"Why do you keep saying, 'If you're lucky,' " Paul asked, bringing his foot back in and shutting the door.

"Because it ain't all cut-and-dried." Vanzetti pulled out his cigarettes, opened the window to ventilate the car. "The state cops don't exactly love you, for starters. Also, Identikits ain't too good as evidence in court; they'll want to do a lineup, before. If the killer's a pro, which is likely, it also means there's big bucks behind it, which could mean big lawyers, so you can't be certain they'll even get past the first hearing. There's just not a whole hell of a lot of evidence. And there's no personal motive I could figure." Vanzetti struck a match and kept his palm around it for warmth.

"So what do we do now," Paul asked.

Why didn't he run the engine, the PI suggested, instead of letting them both freeze to death.

Paul started the engine and turned the fan to high.

"So what can we do," he repeated, "that the cops can't."

"Trust me," Vanzetti said.

"Trust you?" Paul tried to sound tough, but the detective's words had set adrenaline coursing through his system in a way he had not felt since he recognized the tugboat knot behind the Riverview Motel several centuries ago. "You haven't even told me who he is."

"Who?" Vanzetti asked.

"The guy who killed Jack."

"Oh."

Paul looked at him suspiciously. If there was one thing the detective liked better than grand entrances, it was grand exit lines.

"It's not a guy," Vanzetti said.

"What do you mean, it's not a guy."

"The suspect. It's a woman."

"*What?*"

"A woman," Vanzetti repeated, and grinned in satisfaction. "Now do you see what I mean—who the hell's gonna believe that?"

"I'm not even sure I believe it," Paul replied, but he put the Jeep in gear anyway, and drove around the green to the filling station, where Andy Gilbert's wrecker had just pulled in, its plough raised like an elephant's trunk, its twin yellow lights turning the town square into a circus.

⚍

It stopped snowing just before they left French Harbor.

Vanzetti and Paul drove south through the longest winter palace ever devised; four hundred miles of pure white parquet, of silver fronds hung with crystal. Every square inch was dusted with diamond chips for the sun to fill with fire. It hurt Paul's eyes even through dark glasses. It made him think of Gelcoat and the threat of flames.

"The staties found the car in Mansfield," Vanzetti said, as they crossed the Piscataqua River into New Hampshire. "There's a concrete performance center there. Ugly as sin. Only open in the summer. The car was left in the parking lot. Had to be the same one. Plymouth sedan, dented right door, fog lights. Stolen in Arlington six weeks ago. Maine tags, also stolen. Fits. It was just dumb luck they found it before spring thaw."

The two clear lanes of I-95 narrowed to one. Traffic slowed, stopped, started. "You ever notice," the PI remarked, "how the places really get a lot of snow always have clear roads, and the ones that don't get a lot of snow are always screwed up?"

Vanzetti had been busy interviewing the personnel directors of tugboat companies, methodically working his way north from Baltimore at Paul's expense when he got the message about the car.

He assumed Jack's killer felt safe enough, the trail was cold enough, by now, to have ditched the automobile within striking distance of home base. He skipped the New York area and drove straight to Massachusetts.

"It's a matter of psychology," Vanzetti said, squaring his shoulders a little. "I coulda been a hunnert percent wrong."

But he had not been wrong, though he drew a blank with Boston Towing and O'Brien. Came up empty, too, in Providence and Fall River, the other big tugboat ports within an hour's drive of Mansfield.

In New Bedford he struck oil on the first hole.

"It's a funny town, New Bedford," Vanzetti said, dreamily. He smoothed his moustache as he talked. "Mostly Portuguese now. All the fishing boats are Portygees, 'cept for a couple squareheads. There's two tugboat outfits, though, and they're both old-line Yankee. The first one I went to, the operations manager looks like the Old Man of the Sea himself. Blue eyes, white beard. A real joker, always chucklin' and smilin' and noddin' his head 'cause he thinks he's so funny. You can see boats going in and out the hurricane barrier through his windows.

"So I give him my spiel, which I'm getting good at by now, how I'm looking for this guy, did my client a big favor, rescued his son from drowning on Horseneck Beach or something, but he doesn't know his name, just that he works for a tug company around here, big reward, blah blah blah. See," he explained, "no one wants to be responsible for trouble, but they all want to help, they all want to take credit for good news. So he looks at the picture."

The PI paused, for effect. He was enjoying himself.

"He looks at it for a long time. Then he says, 'None of the men here looks like this.' I stand up to go, and he shakes his head, and laughs, and says, 'Sure looks like Two-Ton Tina, though.'"

"I go, 'Two-Ton what?' and he says, 'Yeah, Two-Ton Tina, she works at Baybarge, across the river,' he says. 'Bosun on a tug hauls a dredging barge. She must have some kind of hormone problem, crossed Ys and Xs,' he says. 'She's bigger and tougher than most men, and she has all this hair sticking out her ears. They don't have no union troubles with Tina around. But be careful how you approach her,' he tells me, 'she's been known to break guys' arms just for talkin' fresh.' He's still laughing when I go out the door."

Paul said, "You remember that call I told you 'bout last fall? Right after I got back from New York, the first time."

"Yeah. You said it was a crank, right?"

"Right. But since that fire was set, I guess maybe it was serious. Anyhow, it was a man's voice. On the phone. Not a woman's."

"So?"

"So, this is a woman."

"It's obvious." The private investigator spread his palm flat to underline just how obvious it was. "Whoever paid her made the call. You don't think she did this on her own, do you? Some broad who works on a tug, who don't even know you?"

"Frankly," Paul answered bitterly, "I can't think why anyone would want to do this, whether they knew me or not. . . ."

They got to New Bedford as the sun set. Like ten thousand mismatched wooden dice the city rolled off a long hill into a longer harbor. Dead and dying industries littered the waterfront. The polluted sky turned snow and water the color of frozen peaches.

Past the Coggeshall Street exit, Vanzetti took the wheel. He ran down a road parallel to Route 18, skidding the Jeep on a mixture of sand, salt, and ice. Paul yelled at him to slow down. Vanzetti sniffed an Italian comment on road cowardice.

At a slightly slower pace they skirted mills that once produced shoes and textiles; now these rang with emptiness, or harbored discount-clothing outlets in their sturdier sections. The immigrants from warm countries who used to work in the mills lived in gawky frame houses. Virgins, saints, and fountains stuck out of the snow in postage-stamp gardens between the telephone poles. Edward Hopper, Paul thought, with a Catholic twist. Mahogany men standing in the windows of a club called "Recordacoes do Portugal" watched them as they drove by. Vanzetti switched the radio to the local station and fado music blared, rich with the mushed *s*'s and rolled *r*'s of Portuguese. "Got to get in the mood," Vanzetti explained and turned left.

The fish-processing plants looked shinier, Paul thought, but no more active than the mills they'd replaced. Steel draggers lined the wharves, four and five deep. Their mooring lines hung thick with icicles. They bore names like *Sao Tomas, Mario o Fernando, Virgen do la Luz*. A bridge loomed ahead. Vanzetti pulled over and parked next to a one-story building between two fish-freezing plants. It had four tiny windows. A sign read, "The Pier Tavern. Fine Food. Drink." There were two cars parked out front. Six or seven truck rigs stood lined up in back.

Vanzetti pointed out a late-model American sedan with a bumper sticker that read, "Tugboatmen do it pushing *and* pulling."

"She's here," he said. "She's always here when the barge is in."

"What do we do now," Paul said.

It was the first time he had asked the question. He had been deliberately avoiding it, not thinking about how to apply the power of their information, spinning out the rush of triumph Vanzetti's news had brought. But now events had caught up with him.

Vanzetti had it all figured out.

"I go in," the detective replied. "Five minutes later you follow. The bar's in the middle, it cuts the room in half. You go all the way, to the far side, pick a table, pretend you don't know me. I'll look in her direction a few times so you know who it is, in case you have any trouble recognizing her, which I doubt, 'cause she looks a lot like her picture. When I leave, you leave. In between, have a few beers."

"I like the beer part," Paul said doubtfully.

"Trust me," Vanzetti urged. He punched Paul on the shoulder and went into the bar.

Five minutes later Paul followed, as arranged. He found himself in a wide, low room whose primary shades were brown and cream and smoke. A pool table shared one corner with a Star Soccer pinball machine. Pieces of fishnet hung from the ceiling. Tacky oil paintings of fishermen hung cheek by jowl with photos of real draggers and a blackboard showing today's busted dreams in curt chalk digits—fish landings (by boat), fish prices (by species), and state-lottery "Megabucks" numbers. Only the Megabucks column was filled. By the feel of the bar, Paul guessed nobody here had even come close.

Vanzetti was seated at the counter, talking to the bartender. His plastic jacket glowed pink in the reflection of beer signs. Paul picked a table on the other side of the room. There were eight other customers. Three of them argued in dark Portuguese by the pinball. Paul picked her out immediately, at the far end of the counter from Vanzetti. She was talking to an old man in a blue watch cap. Paul's heart speeded up in reaction.

She was thick and broad as stacked plywood. Her chin was square and heavy. Her lips were fuchsia with lipstick, her face caked in makeup. The eyes were small and moved little. She looked like a cross between the Identikit portrait and a centerfold from a wrestling magazine.

Her hair was cut short. She wore two men's flannel shirts, one on top of the other, and blue jeans.

Her ear hair, Paul saw, was truly magnificent. It curled like barbed wire from her lobes. He wondered if she trimmed it.

Paul drank tap beer and watched her in a mirror.

His first conscious feeling was a numbness, a sense of alienation; here was a concept he'd raged at and focused on for months come suddenly to life, and he did not know how to deal with the inevitable shortfall between mind-view and reality.

When that wore off, he caught himself doubting.

There was nothing intrinsically evil in that face, Paul thought; a lack of learning, a lot of boredom, a pathetic eagerness to compensate, one way or another, for the chromosomes she'd missed.

Two fat women came in, sat at the next table, and ordered a pitcher of mudslides.

Paul got a second beer, a third, and a fourth. Brazen with alcohol, he called home from the pay phone in back, cupping his hand around the mouthpiece so no words escaped. Ashley, Nat, and George were all in the living room, taking care of Jessica, but his daughter was asleep.

Paul hung up, thinking of the adult way she'd looked at him when he'd told her he'd be gone a few days. He ordered a fifth beer and listened to the next table, where the pitcher was almost empty of its chilled brown liquid.

"I should go home. I gotta cook dinner for all them pool players."

"I doan give a shit."

"It's a twenty-five-pound turkey. You serve 'em an' you woof 'em. You serve 'em an' you woof 'em. You serve 'em an' you woof 'em!" The fat lady laughed.

"You serve 'em a twenty-pounder," her companion screeched, "screw 'em up!"

The two practically fell off their chairs.

Vanzetti got to his feet. Reaching for his bomber jacket Paul fished for money and stepped to the cash register to pay. He could hear Two-Ton Tina taking leave of her companion in a voice like acid washing through gravel.

"Doan go swimmin' in the harbor again," the man in the watch cap advised her.

"I will, if I wan'. I'll go jump off the bridge again." Tina's jaw jutted.

"There's PCBs in the water."

"I doan give a good goddamn."

"Yeah," her companion agreed, "if you start worryin' about everything, how you gonna survive."

The tugboat woman pushed her stool back so hard it fell over.

"Yeah," she said, "how you gonna get from here to there."

"Without swimmin'," the man in the watch cap answered.

Tina laughed.

"Come *on*," Vanzetti hissed, walking past Paul to the door. Paul told the bartender to keep the change and went out after him. When he got outside the Jeep was already moving. They took off in a scatter of snow toward the waterfront. They drove no more than a minute, to park deep under a cantilevered bridge peeling dark green paint into the harbor.

Vanzetti pulled a length of nylon rope from his bag and handed it to Paul. "Stay here," he said. "Keep your head down when she comes. Beep the horn if someone else shows up." He reached into his bag again, pulled out a cop's hat, and a truncheon. Lastly, he took out a shoulder holster with a large blue revolver inside. He strapped the gun around his chest quickly, a practiced movement.

"Hey," Paul said, "what you want that for."

"Just in case," Vanzetti replied.

"In case what? Vanzetti, I don't want any shooting, any of that stuff, I don't want anyone hurt, no matter what."

The detective leaned into the car door.

"Now don't fret, it's just for show," he whispered soothingly. He disappeared, slamming the door.

Paul had always thought it axiomatic that you never carried a gun unless you meant to use it. Still, he consoled himself, Vanzetti was an ex-cop. He knew guns. He probably slept with the damn thing.

Paul put it out of his mind and concentrated on matters at hand.

The wharf beneath the bridge was used as a parking area, Paul saw. Meager spots from a fish-packing plant shed light on the support beams and shadow on everything else. Across the dark water an ancient Eastern-rigged trawler lay awash and rusting. Ice covered her listing hull to the high-water mark. Cranes, barge fittings, lengths of pipe and cable littered the opposite bank, a hundred feet away. A pair of headlights moved off the road behind them and lanced whiteness into the parking area. Her car, Paul realized, or a similar model. It pulled right up to the concrete lip of the wharf, went dark, then light again as the interior lights switched on.

A shadow passed between Paul and the light. She got out of the car and stood up. Vanzetti walked up behind her, looking official in silhouette. The woman turned; then, apparently reassured by the familiar outline, bent to pull something from the glove compartment, and Vanzetti had to adjust his carefully aimed blow at the last second. The nightstick glanced off the back of her head and lost much of its momentum on her jacket collar.

Paul switched on the headlights. He saw Vanzetti crawl like a tick onto the woman's back. He saw the woman raise her huge buttocks to pin the short detective against the sill of her car door, as if trying to crush an insect. Then she started to bump and grind her hips in a grotesque, reverse parody of the love act, smashing Vanzetti's kidneys against the metal lip of the roof. Vanzetti screamed between smashes. He managed to get his knee against the car door and push himself further inside. He got just far enough to spare his kidneys and twist his arms around Two-Ton Tina's neck.

By the time Paul ran over, trying not to trip on the rope or slip on ice in his haste, Vanzetti had the nightstick around her throat. He was bearing down on her flannel withers like a rodeo star. Vulgar gurgling noises came from the front seat. "Let her go, man," Paul shouted, "you'll kill her." His voice rang back and forth in the cavern of the bridge. He took a quick nervous look to check they were still alone.

Vanzetti yelled back, telling him to hold her legs. Paul took a turn of the rope around the thick kicking ankles. Reaching over for a second turn he got in the way and a hard heel banged into his forehead, throwing him back on his ass in the slush. Vanzetti was roaring continuously now, a long free-lunged karate noise, effort made sound. Her movements grew more sluggish, and Paul could wrap the rest of the line around her legs like a sausage with relative ease.

"OK, now let her go," he repeated, urgently.

Vanzetti pulled himself backward off the woman.

He straightened up, breathing hard, and massaged his hip.

"Voilà," he announced, waving at the front seat.

Paul saw the woman's large hands were cuffed behind her back. She was rocking back and forth on the vinyl, making coughing noises. Her face rested on old pizza boxes. An eye bulged, her tongue stuck out. Paul thought she looked like a gargoyle.

Vanzetti checked around for witnesses, then switched off the interior light. "Throw her in the trunk," he said.

"Vanzetti."

"Give me a hand."

"I want to know what you're going to do. What's going on. You said we'd play this by ear. No pun intended. But you've got this all planned out, I can tell." The adrenaline was giving him the shakes again, Paul realized.

"Later. Not now. Open the trunk."

Paul looked at him. He knew that in situations like these the man with the plan always dominated the man without. Vanzetti would have to tell him the plan soon enough. So eventually he nodded, and complied.

They stashed Two-Ton Tina, with some difficulty, between her spare tire and a couple of cases of light beer. They locked the Jeep, got into her car, and drove it north, the way they had come.

The mill was made of brick, faced with Maine-coast granite.

It stood in Acushnet, at the head of New Bedford harbor, an eighth of a mile long, four stories high. Strange gables and tall chimneys broke its mass at regular intervals. A long pier fingered out into the Acushnet River, ending in a curious, peaked pump house.

It was built in 1891, when electricity and petroleum were slashing the demand for whale oil, ripping the bottom out of New Bedford's economy in much the same way Arctic ice crushed half its whaling fleet twenty years before.

In its prime the mill took up where whaling left off. It employed seven hundred people. Its towering halls were poorly lit and thick with linen dust. It generated good profits for its owners. It provided tuberculosis and a thin living for its workers, until cheap Asian products did to the American textile industry what electricity had done to whaling, years before.

The mill had stood abandoned for years. Now ivy covered its walls, prying apart the mortar. The access roads were a jungle and the roof was cracked. The snow hid holes and faults, making it seem the building was still intact, but this only reinforced the desolation, by contrast. Where are my humans, the mill seemed to ask, but no one cared or lived close enough to answer.

Vanzetti and Paul wrangled Two-Ton Tina out of the trunk of her car. They tried carrying her, but it was all they could do to lift her bulk, and she jackknifed her legs repeatedly, making it impossible to hold on. They ended up dragging her across the snow-covered weeds to the front of the mill, by the harborside. Her weight and the jumbled terrain made movement difficult. The river was narrow at this point and the lights of Fairhaven sparkled yellow across the water, affording just enough reflection to make their way by. Vanzetti located a loading door where the protecting length of sheet metal had been ripped and bent aside. They lifted the woman in and stood, panting with the exertion.

In the spare beam of the detective's flashlight Paul saw they were inside what used to be the cellar. The floor and walls were made of rock. Water seeped from every crevice and froze against the air. Rotted stairs and an arched doorway led to a cavernous space above their heads. There, a single, cathedral-high window, small and far across the building, let in streetlight from the western side of the mill.

The air surged damp and foul in their strained lungs. Hard, round objects rolled underfoot. Paul picked one up by feel and peered at it. The object was eight inches long, wooden, moldy. It was pointed at both ends, like a two-headed bomb.

"Old spindles," Vanzetti said, "for the looms. They used to offer rewards, when I was a kid, if you could figure out some way to make 'em useful or sell 'em."

"You had this place all scoped out." Paul blew into his gloves to keep his fingers warm.

The detective did not reply. He pulled out a small tape recorder, fumbled with its controls in the dark, and pocketed it again. Grunting mightily, he dragged their prisoner sideways, and loosened the towel he had knotted around her face. Paul started to ask if she was still OK when the woman snapped to a sitting position and butted her forehead into Vanzetti's face. He cursed, mightily, and tapped her with the nightstick. She subsided onto the stones and spindles. Her hiss rose from the floor, like a snake's.

"You dildo. You yak-fucker. Your mother was the whore for the *whole* navy."

Vanzetti told Paul to come over. He was holding his eyebrow with one hand. With the other he shone the torch directly into the woman's eyes. They were brown, Paul saw, pupils narrowed to dots against the flashlight. Two-Ton Tina licked her lips and breathed out harshly.

"What you guys want?"

Vanzetti said nothing. Paul followed his cue.

"You assholes. You're Teamsters, right?"

Silence. The blanket of damp hung around them. Their breaths made clouds in it. The combination of cold and humidity caused Paul's scars to ache. The woman worked her fingers to keep the circulation going.

"We want to know why you killed Jack Briggs," Vanzetti whispered.

Something shifted in her gaze. The movement was very brief, like a camera shutter flipping at one-two thousandth speed, and if Paul had not been watching her eyes he would never have caught it.

Like the space behind a camera shutter, there was only a matte darkness inside.

"I dunno what you're talking about," Two-Ton Tina grunted.

"Oh yes she does," Paul growled. Doubts that he did not know were there retreated to the wings. Confidence came back, as did the indignation, so curiously absent before. It was not a presence that caused people to kill, he thought, but an absence. Tina possessed absence, in spades.

"Screw you," Tina said.

"You left here October twenty-third," Vanzetti said. "The *Bay Jupiter*, your tug, was due for a week's tow to Baltimore, but you took leave."

"I was visiting a friend, schmuck. A *sick* friend."

"You went up to French Harbor, Maine."

The wrestler's face knotted in the half-dark. They were going to pay for this, she hissed. They were going to die.

"You broke into the Briggs boatyard."

"Whatsa matter, guys—," the woman leered.

"You stole plans for the *Challenge*, the Twelve-Meter."

"—you wanna do a 'Big Dan,' right? But you can't get it up? Awww, too bad, lil boys." Her lip curled in contempt.

She'd been seen. Vanzetti's tone was angry. Identified. They had her cold.

The sneer remained, but she gave a great tug with her legs to free them of their ties. Paul watched, admiring, as the large pectorals bulged under her flannels. They were solid muscle. Even her breasts seemed hard. Her stomach must be like spring steel, to jackknife the way she'd done a little earlier.

Vanzetti had had enough. He got to his feet. "OK," he said, "back outside."

They took the woman by her bindings. She cursed when the handcuffs tightened further around her wrists, but Paul's guilt had fled with his doubts.

The pier once had been used to pump saltwater from the harbor in some arcane and long-forgotten fulling process. The pump house at the end was built of stone, sheet metal, and timber. It was anchored solidly on the harbor bottom. Two large, iron pipes were hung under the dock's length. The old boards were capped with a neat thatch of white crystal.

They advanced cautiously onto the pier's surface. The snow seemed to glow against the dark water. It compacted and melted a little under their shoes and made the going treacherously smooth.

Only a quarter of the way down Paul's feet disappeared from under him and he very nearly slid into the harbor, pulling Vanzetti and Tina with him.

After that they dragged Tina on her back, one on each side, like a sled. She was only slightly easier to drag than she was to carry. Snow piled up against her neck and shoulders. The antique timbers groaned in menacing fashion. Vanzetti's left foot broke straight through a rotten board; he saved himself from falling into the water by embracing the tugboat woman like a lover.

Tina snarled.

They finished the journey on elbows and knees, their hands clasping Tina's armpits. "This is too much like work," Paul gasped, as they reached the pump house.

Inside the structure, cold water reigned. The din of crunching waves reverberated among stone corner foundations and timber pilings. Loose iron banged and mingled with the wind. Vanzetti shone the flashlight around them.

Pumping equipment that was new when Cleveland was president took up most of the small space. Levers, valves, strange gooseneck pipes rusted thoroughly around them. Mold grew thick in every crack and crevice. A set of corroded iron steps followed the intake and discharge pipes through a trap door. Ice clustered at the waterline like elephants' feet. The oily black waves sucked at the stairs' base, trying to hasten the inevitable collapse so they could clasp the sagging structure to their cold and salty bosom and feed the mutant gastropods below.

Vanzetti propped the flashlight against a rusted lube-oil barrel. He untied one end of the rope pinning the woman's legs. She kicked at him, using her legs like a fishtail, but he dug out the truncheon and held it over her nose until she quieted. He uncoiled the sausage arrangement until only two loops held her ankles together. He looped the bitter end of the line around one of the pump cylinders and handed it to Paul, telling him to take the slack when it came.

Then he removed his gloves, flicked the tape recorder in his pocket. He kneeled down and leaned close to Two-Ton Tina's face.

"Look," he said. "Let's just get this over with, OK? We can't do anything with it—evidence obtained under duress, ya know? We'll even let you go if you tell us who paid you to kill the guy in Maine."

"Wait, Sal," Paul broke in. "Who said anything 'bout—"

"Shut up," the detective snapped. "Talk to me," he entreated the woman.

"Go to hell," she muttered.

"Who paid you to break and enter Briggs' boatyard."

The woman suggested they sodomize a sick camel.

"That does it," Vanzetti said. He sat back on his heels—then, very suddenly, dug his hands under her back, rolled her over, and over again, down the sagging planks toward the open trapdoor. "Hey," Tina yelled, sticking her elbows out to slow the roll, "Hey!" Paul yelled at him to stop when he saw what Vanzetti was doing, but with a final heave the detective pushed her over the lip of the hole into the harbor. Paul threw himself back over where he thought the rope was. Just in time he felt it slither and grabbed hold of the rope's end as it smoked around the pump piston. He tried to break her fall.

Her weight was enormous. It dragged him bodily into the pump engine, jamming his hand against the piston. He let the rope run a bit, then tightened his grip again. Even through gloves his palms burned with friction. There was a groan of straining timber, then an unearthly reverberation of noise.

From deep beneath the trapdoor, Two-Ton Tina was screaming. "Assholes," she shrieked. "Oh you assholes!" Water and iron amplified the treble in her words.

"Jesus," Paul whispered, keeping a death grip on the rope. The detective grabbed the flashlight and leaned over the trapdoor. "What did you do that for?"

"Let it out about five inches."

"Why," Paul asked, though he thought he knew what Vanzetti was doing.

"Just let it out."

Paul eased out the rope until Vanzetti said, "Stop."

"Tina," Vanzetti called.

"Screw you, asshole!" came the reply.

"I thought you *liked* swimming. I thought you liked PCBs."

"Your mother has the clap!"

"You should know," Vanzetti agreed. "Now listen up. I checked the tables. It's a quarter to one. The tide's rising. It goes up three and a half feet every six hours or so, I figured it out, that's three inches every half hour. Let her out real gentle again, Paul. Another inch. There. Now tie her down." He raised his voice again.

"You can twist around for a while, Tina, but you're gonna get tired, you can't keep your head out for too long. Thirty, forty minutes it'll be at your nose. An hour, it'll be at your mouth. So you got an hour to make up your mind. If we don't hear from you by then, why, I guess we'll just be on our way. Nobody comes out here, Tina, you know that, so by the time anybody finds you, you'll be covered with mussels, and crabs too, though come to think of it, you're probably covered with those already."

"You lyin' asshole. You wouldn't dare!"

Vanzetti said nothing.

She damned them to hell. She would get them for this, she would get their families.

Vanzetti slid back toward Paul, chuckling.

Paul found his glasses and put them back on, though he could see very little in the penumbra.

"So the idea is, the water comes up and she confesses, right? Or else she drowns."

"Right."

He was bluffing, of course, Paul asked hopefully, as the threats and curses faded and were covered by the clanks and rushing and sucking echoes of the pump house.

Vanzetti did not reply.

They could not simply let her drown, Paul insisted.

"The only way," Vanzetti said, "to do something like this is to believe it yourself. Otherwise, *they* don't believe it."

"I'm not gonna let you." Paul felt his jaw jutting in indignation. "I mean, what are you, man?"

"Same as you," Vanzetti replied, "only I got it worked out."

He reached into his jacket and pulled out something shiny, metallic, and held it in the glow of flashlight. Nickel-plated. Grooved. Barreled.

"It's a .38 revolver," Vanzetti told him. "A 'Saturday night special.' She was going for it in her glove compartment when I jumped her. Now you gonna be so squeamish?"

"I'm still not gonna let you," Paul repeated, with a little less conviction.

"It's your privilege. I'm just trying to get results, for *you* as quick and easy as possible. You think I enjoy this? You think I *like* the cold? Come on! I'm Italian!"

In the flicker of flashlight Paul saw Vanzetti pocket Tina's gun. He turned off his portable tape machine, pulled out a bottle, and settled his back against the oil drum. He took a swig and offered it to Paul. The smell of apricot brandy sweetened the air.

"It *is* fucking cold," Paul agreed, to change the subject.

"Yeah." The accumulation of nerves, fatigue, and beer in both men had opened a lot of physical defenses that brandy pretended to close.

"You do a lot of this? Torture, extortion, that sort of thing?" Paul asked, curiously.

"No, not really." The PI waved a modest hand, then struck a match. In the flare of phosphorus his features were puffy, a little off. "Tell you the truth," he whispered, "I read this in a police magazine once."

The basis of the technique was disorientation, he continued. According to the magazine, reality was entirely subjective, a story people made up about themselves. That story was grounded on props—familiar faces, houses, memories of your place in the world around you. Subtract the props, and you were left with a fiction whose details were meaningless. In this context, secrecy had no value, and you ended up wanting to tell your interrogator everything because he was now the only prop left on which to build a whole new story about yourself.

"Did it work in the magazine," Paul asked.

"Like a charm," Vanzetti answered.

Twenty minutes later Paul crawled down to the edge and shone the flashlight down the trapdoor.

He saw a four-square pit of wood, iron, black water, and a broad corpse twirling upside down, very gently, to one side of the rusted pipes. Light bounced off the waves to dapple her face. Water lapped at her nose and some of the bigger wavelets licked her cheeks. Her short hair washed back and forth with the movement of the water.

"Jesus, she's dead," Paul exclaimed, thrusting backward.

"Shut up," Vanzetti hissed back, but he went to look for himself.

"Just bluffing," he remarked, on his return. "I caught her breathing. Tough bitch, though, ain't she?" Paul heard admiration in his voice. He also thought he could detect the slight hollowness that lay at the core of every bluff.

The level of apricot brandy sank by another three inches. Paul tried to think of other things. He thought back to a boat he had once almost brought to the drawing board. A very fast, very lightweight, offshore racer. She would have had two variable dagger keels, a semiplaning hull, and a prau-style outrigger you could shift to either side for balance. In a storm the outrigger could be shipped, and the boat would be as stable as any monohull.

The image of waves and wind meshed with another image. A trip he took, with Nicole, to Lunenburg, Nova Scotia, to look at a client's boat. There was a storm, that trip, as well. They booked a cabin on a night ferry to Yarmouth. He remembered telling the child stories about some of the men who'd sailed these waters as the ship rocked and crashed in the swell. Bjarni Herjolfsen and his fat, double-ended knorr. Fridjof Nansen, who'd tried to drift his old Arctic sealer to the Pole. Joe McMurdo, who'd got closer to the Pole than the Norwegian in a boat one-eighth the size. The idea of the Arctic brought him full circle, to this strange, freezing building and the even stranger woman strung up like a side of mutton below them. He wondered how long the woman could hold out—how long, in Vanzetti's book, her "story" would survive the indignity, the disorientation. How long could he take it, Paul wondered. It must be horrible down there. He searched around the pump for the rope end. "I'm not gonna let this happen," he announced firmly.

"Hey, what," the private investigator said. "Wait. You know she did it. She killed your cousin, man!"

"This won't bring him back."

Vanzetti pleaded with him to wait. It didn't work, in the story, until water got over his nose, he said.

Story? Paul said. Did Vanzetti mean to say his detective story was *fiction?*

Vanzetti ignored him. All they needed was another five minutes. Then they could crank her up. Otherwise they'd have to let her go. It wouldn't work twice.

Besides, Vanzetti whispered urgently, his breath making wisps of steam in the flashlight, they had effectively burned their legal bridges here. The district attorney would have had trouble convicting her before; he would not stand a chance now, once a judge learned she'd been coerced.

"Don't you think," Paul whispered back angrily, "you might have told me that earlier?"

"You knew," Vanzetti retorted. "I told you. If you left it to the cops, nothing would *ever* happen."

Paul shook his head. He wished he'd never gone back to Vanzetti. Wished he were back home, and had never heard of Two-Ton Tina, or Baybarge. Wished Jack was still around and Suzanne was home and Nicole was home as well. Rolling back the film three years. . . .

The woman's voice rose from the trapdoor, far away, hollow.

"Hey."

"Shh," Vanzetti hissed, and gripped Paul's arm.

"Hey!"

"Is ebod—EN-bod—there? I, gaw—you ASSholes. Jergs. Hey, answer me!"

A pause.

"I *know* you're there. I'm freezin'—to death. It's up, goddamn nose. Can't feel my goddamn *forehead* no more. You're drownin' me! I doan know—" (the sound of blowing). "Doan know nothin', god-damnit! Talk to me!" A new tone had crept into her voice. Paul recognized the first cracks of panic.

Another pause, then the voice came again, pleading. "It's so fug-gin'—cooold."

Silence. A minute of it, until her voice came again.

"All right, assholes." The words broke. "All right! You win. Now pull me—the hell up!"

"Goddamnit," Paul whispered. "She'd confess, even if it wasn't true."

Vanzetti said nothing, but felt around for the rope end.

In the absence of an overhead purchase it was all they could do to drag the woman over the lip of the trapdoor without breaking her legs. Paul hoped she would not be so stubborn as to make them repeat the process, because he was not sure it was in their power. The cold was sapping their strength at an impressive rate.

As for the woman, she was trembling uncontrollably, and her face bore an unpleasant striping effect—bloodshot red from neck to nose, and blue-white upward, where the sea had slobbered over her with forty-degree lips. Her mascara had streaked, leaving black smudges around her cheeks. She looked like a wounded raccoon. She twisted her shoulders uncomfortably, where she'd strained muscles trying to keep her air passages above water.

"Talk," Vanzetti commanded, holding the mike close.

"Whaddyawant."

"You killed Jack Briggs."

"Unh."

Vanzetti told her to say it out loud.

Tina told them the tape recordings would be no good as evidence. Vanzetti repeated they did not want to convict Tina; they wanted the guy who hired her. When the woman still kept silent he asked Paul to grab hold of the rope again and Tina blurted out, "Yeah, well, I din' mean to, see? He snuck up on me. I *had* to hit him."

Vanzetti's eyes gleamed in the flashlight's glow.

"Where were you?" Paul still sought confirmation. "When you hit him."

"In the boatyard. The design room, it's called. Where they keep the plans."

"Goddamn," Paul said, more emphatically this time. "You got that on tape?"

She was supposed to find plans for the Twelve-Meters. The woman rationed out the words between bouts of shivering. Whenever she hesitated, Vanzetti took hold of the rope. Specifically, she was supposed to find anything with the name "Hendriks" on it. No, she didn't know why. Yeah, she'd done this kind of work before, when there were problems, the unions busting in, pilfering on the docks, that kind of stuff. No, she didn't know who hired her. No, she repeated, she had no wish to go back down that trapdoor. Just the idea seemed to make her shiver harder. The rush of blood reopening channels to her feet made her grimace. She kept trying to rub her shoes with cuffed hands.

Who asked her, Paul butted in. Who paid her?

"No," Tina muttered.

Paul repeated the question.

He'd kill her, she said.

Vanzetti pulled the rope, subtly. Tina said, "Shit. Of all the fuggin' luck. I lose so much money in Taunton yesterday. Know what I mean? Two hundred fifty lousy bucks on the dogs, down the toobs. Now this has to happen. I din' mean to kill the guy, honest. I din' even know I'd hurt him, not bad anyway, till Charlie tole me, a couple days after. He'll kill me if he finds out I told youse."

Charlie, Vanzetti repeated. Charlie who.

Two-Ton Tina coughed. Her bargaining chips were going fast. "Here's the deal," she offered, quickly. "You give me some of that applejack I kin smell on your breath, I'll tell you. You let me go, after this, I'll tell you. Deal?"

"Deal," Paul said quickly, before Vanzetti could protest.

The detective held the bottle to her lips and she sucked the thick liquid eagerly.

"Charlie Armstrong." She licked her lips. "Same guy as always. Charlie Armstrong, my boss. I always work for him."

"Why?"

" 'Cause he pays me." Tina looked at their shadows in contempt.

"No. Why did he want the plans?"

"How do I know? He tells me, do something. The price is right, I do it."

"Say it."

"Say what."

"How he set it up. Repeat it. How much money. Say his name."

"Two thousand bucks," she repeated dully, "cash. Charlie Armstrong, he paid me. Wanted me to do what I already told youse. He wanted me to find plans. At this boatyard in Maine. So I did."

"Slow down," Paul interrupted. "When was this?"

"I thought you knew all that?" Tina checked their faces, or what she could see of them, suspiciously.

"Humor us," Paul said. "We just want to get the details straight. When did you go up?"

"October," Tina said. "Right before Halloween."

"You checked into the Riverview Motel."

"Yeah. What a dump."

"Dressed as a man."

No answer.

"You scoped out the yard," Paul continued, "you found out the night guard lived in the same motel. So the next night, you held a gun on him, tied him up. Then you broke into the boatyard. Is that how it happened?"

She nodded, warily.

"Say yes."

"Yes."

"What did you take?"

"Computer papers," Tina answered. "Lots of numbers. An' a couple of them computer discs. They all had that guy's name on 'em. Hendriks."

Paul remembered the two test-tank computer discs that were missing when he'd finished Jack's boat. The theft seemed so small and stupid compared to its consequences.

"Go on," Paul encouraged her. "Tell us about Jack. What happened."

"But I already told youse," Tina answered. "That guy was an accident. Swear to god, he jumped me first. I had to pop him one; it was self-defense. Is that all you want? I'm just makin' this up," she added, "'Cause you wuz gonna drown me, down there."

"We'll edit that out," Vanzetti said.

"What I really want," Paul interrupted softly, "is to leave you dangling at the end of that rope till the tide comes all the way in."

He could sense Vanzetti's surprise in the shift of shadows beside him. The bitterness had bubbled from many layers down. He really did want to take this woman and shake her until she screamed for mercy. But her eyes had narrowed to slits and her mouth was slack in the fibers of light, and he knew that it would serve no purpose whatsoever.

They dragged Tina back to her car, keeping a firm hold on the handcuffs chain. They drove back to the parking lot under the bridge, and threw her car keys in the slush. By the time she got herself sorted out, Vanzetti commented, they'd be long gone, holed up in a motel much closer to Boston than New Bedford.

He did not think, on balance, that Two-Ton Tina would go to the police, and Paul had to agree with him on that score.

Which left the coast clear for them to return to New Bedford in the morning and talk to Charlie Armstrong at Baybarge.

Tina's "boss."

C H A P T E R   1 8

The term "tight little operation"—as used in an admiring, male, business sense, with undertones of football and sex—could easily be applied to Baybarge, Incorporated.

There was a tight little cement warehouse on an island in the middle of New Bedford harbor. Steel pipes, buoys, anchors, chain lay neatly disciplined across two-thirds of one acre. A pair of twenty-two-hundred-horsepower marine diesels were covered with nylon tarpaulins. Two huge dredging barges and an ex-Navy tug swung at moorings nearby. A work crew serviced the bucket belt on a dredger with maximum organization and minimum fuss. A long metal barge with two decks of offices lay moored alongside the warehouse dock.

The casualties of tightness lay inside the office barge. No one laughed or talked or played radios. The manager's secretary—a thin girl with an Irish complexion, no breasts, and a heavy bra—jumped at loud noises and told them Mr. Armstrong would be right with them.

Through a wire-meshed window they could see into Armstrong's office. A large porthole gave a view of dredging barges in the anchorage. A collection of antique harpoons and long brass telescopes covered his wall. A large calendar showed a harbor tugboat, yellow with a red funnel, churning past the Statue of Liberty. "VMT—towing into the 90s," the calendar read.

The manager himself was extremely thin, fortyish, balding. He wore glasses so thick they made his face look wider at eye level. A VHF radio set and four telephones, each a different color, were lined up neatly on his desk. Once in a while he would look up from a spreadsheet and pick up one of the phones with a caressing kind of gesture. A loud buzzer would ring and his secretary would jump again.

"I wonder if Tina told him," Paul commented, after they'd waited for twenty minutes.

Vanzetti hefted the cassette player and said, "I don't think so. I think she was really scared of that little creep. Not to mention the cops." He pulled at his moustache until it hurt.

"I can't stand that kind of person." The detective nodded toward the glass. "Little incompetent sonsabitches who carve out their own little fascist states in places like this. So they can take out their inadequacies on everybody else. It's those kinds of people fried my great-uncle."

Paul asked him what he was talking about.

"You know. Bartolomeo Vanzetti," the detective said.

"You mean—"

"Yeah. As in, 'Sacco and.' The anarchists."

Paul looked at him in amazement.

"No kidding," he said. "You never told me."

"I don't exactly advertise it," Vanzetti answered. "Not good for business. People look at you like you grew horns, you tell 'em that. There's plenty people still think he deserved it. But don't worry," he went on, sarcastically, "I don't rob payrolls, or throw bombs. In fact, I'm doin' my best to be cool, right now, and not throw anything."

Paul stood up. The surprise of learning Vanzetti's ancestry had acted as a tonic, cleared his thinking, sharpened options. "He's jerking us around," Paul said with conviction. The excitement of the hunt was still strong in him.

The secretary's eyes grew very big and green. Her yips of protest followed them into Charlie Armstrong's office.

The manager did not get up. He looked at them coldly and informed them they had not made an appointment. Paul gently pushed the secretary out the door while Vanzetti laid the cassette player on Charlie Armstrong's desk. They could hear the girl's voice plainly through the aluminum bulkhead. "It'll mean my jo-o-ob," she wailed.

The manager picked up a blue phone and said, "If you don't get out of here, I'm calling the police."

"Good," Paul told him, sitting down on the hard chair reserved for visitors; he was getting sick of all this beating around the bush.

"We wanted to give you an option," Vanzetti added, "just to be nice, but it might save time to get the cops in at this point."

The blue phone hung in the air. Vanzetti pressed the "play" button on his machine.

As Two-Ton Tina's tones came out of the little box the manager's face stopped.

He recovered immediately and leaned back in his armchair, rolling his eyes, feigning boredom, but he had put the phone down again.

"This is outrageous," Armstrong said when the tape was finished. There was a lack of connection between his eyes and his words and Vanzetti used it like the flaw in a hard stone.

"It's obvious you recognized the voice," Vanzetti said. "It's the bosun on one of your tugs. Tina Costa. 'Two-Ton Tina.' "

"Tina Costa works on the *Bay Jupiter*," Armstrong acknowledged, polishing the red phone with his fingers.

"Why did you want Jack Briggs dead," Vanzetti asked casually.

"This is ridiculous," Armstrong repeated. His eyes flicked back and forth, assessing moves, responses. "Who is this Jack Briggs, anyway," he added. In all his anger the manager was finding it hard to breathe.

They weren't going to play games, the detective replied. Tina would testify. The police would get all the evidence and Charlie would get ten-to-fifteen for murder and conspiracy.

The red phone was very shiny now. The manager shifted his attentions to the black phone, then the white. In short, jerky sentences he told them he was accustomed to blackmail. He used to get pressure all the time from Teamsters. The lies of a couple of hick Down-Easters did not impress him.

He reached into a drawer, pulled out a pocket-size vaporizer and sprayed a quick shot of antihistamine down his throat.

Paul and Vanzetti remained silent, as if they'd rehearsed this scene. Behind Armstrong, the harbor darkened. It was starting to snow again.

"Tina Costa's sick in the head," Armstrong continued, when he had got his breath back. "There been problems with her before; beating up union reps, wrecking longshoremen's cars. Just 'cause they tried to sell berthing privileges. . . ."

Baybarge had covered her so far, Charlie Armstrong said, but if she tried to make these accusations public, he would personally see to it that all the earlier incidents came to light. Tina Costa would never testify in court, he finished, confidently. Not that it mattered.

Paul watched Armstrong's hands while he replied. There was something sensual about the way he fiddled with the touchtone buttons, as if all the nerve endings of his little domain began and ended in these Western Electric telephone sets.

Vanzetti began to splutter, insisting that Armstrong would implicate himself as well as Tina if he tried to threaten her with different charges.

The detective was getting angry again. He tried to tower his short frame in menacing fashion over Armstrong's desk and failed. In any case, Vanzetti added, switching tactics, it was not Armstrong they were after, it was whoever gave him orders.

He switched the cassette player to record, hopefully. The manager made a contemptuous gesture. Paul decided they had erred in thinking they could frighten Armstrong with talk of proof and police and legal paper. Paper, and its manipulation, was what this man lived for. To disorient Armstrong, as they had disoriented Tina, they'd have to hit him somewhere else. Here again, the cheapest tool was violence.

Paul steeled nerves that were unwilling and unused to breaking the shells of people. This was a role, he reminded himself. A bluff with no certain link to the threat implied. He got up suddenly, walked quickly around Armstrong's desk, grabbing the vaporizer as he passed.

He put the canister in his pocket. Then he took down the long brass telescope from above the desk. As Armstrong watched in utter disbelief, he lifted it high like a club and brought it down with great force on the red telephone.

The long handle of the receiver broke in two. The heavy brass smashed through the cradle and crushed the phone's innards. Little square buttons marked "TUV 8" and "DEF 3" popped and clattered. Gaily colored wires sprouted and twisted. Chunks of red Bakelite bounced on the floor or hung on electronic intestine.

Armstrong's eyes bulged. Paul worried they might pop right out of their sockets. He hefted the telescope again. Armstrong cringed. The telescope was dented but otherwise whole. Paul brought it down on the blue phone this time, for symmetry. Through the window he saw the secretary cower and cover her ears with her hands.

Armstrong's face went hollow. He closed his eyes, but could not conquer the fascination. He looked at the broken instruments. He was having trouble breathing again. Paul had to remind himself, looking at Armstrong, that this man had caused Jack to die.

Sounds of sobbing came from next door.

"I'm really sick of this," Paul told Vanzetti. "Let's call the cops."

"Wait," Armstrong whispered.

"Call 'em," Paul repeated, not looking at the manager. "He's jerkin' us around." He swung the telescope again, eyeing the white phone.

A man's voice came from behind the door, bright with distress.

"You OK, Mr. Armstrong? You want we should call the police?"

It was convenient, but amazing, Vanzetti thought, that Armstrong had so destroyed personal initiative in this company that his people needed to ask permission even in situations like this.

"No!" Armstrong yelled at his employee. Sweat stood out in little silver pimples from his forehead. His chest poked in and out of his shirt in an effort to suck in enough air.

"Give me my vaporizer," he pleaded.

"No."

"I can't breathe!"

Paul turned the telescope in his hands, and practiced another swing. Armstrong shouted and recoiled at the same time, almost as if he were surprised at the words that came out, "It was my boss. Not me. You can't do this."

"I was just the go-between," he finished, hoarsely.

"Jesus," Vanzetti said, "Just like the broad."

"What are you talking about, 'my boss,' " Paul asked the manager. "What do you mean."

"You got nothing on me," the manager gasped. His face was gray with the struggle of breathing. Paul fingered the vaporizer in his pocket and looked at Vanzetti nervously.

The private investigator, in turn, asked Armstrong what he meant.

The manager tried to talk and choked, a little, on his own saliva. He swiveled in his desk chair, and pointed desperately at the wall calendar with the red-and-yellow tugboat towing gaily into the next century.

It was too much for Paul, who reached into his pocket and placed the vaporizer on Armstrong's desk.

There were two long hisses as the manager relieved his asthma. His breathing improved immediately. In a quieter voice he continued, "None of this is evidence."

"Who's your boss," Vanzetti countered, stepping over to the calendar. "You mean, he's with this outfit? VMT, Incorporated?

He ripped the calendar off the wall and tossed it to Paul.

"VMT, 15 Battery Place, New York," Paul read. "His boss? VMT owns Baybarge? I don't believe this clown."

Disappointment was swelling inside of Paul. They had gone at this all wrong, right from the start. By playing detective-magazine games they had given away the advantage of surprise. Worse, even Tina had seen their bluff for what it was and told her inquisitors only enough to get them off her back.

What was left of the blue phone made a buzzing sound. The secretary's voice came through the mouthpiece, trying to hold the trembling syllables together long enough to form words.

"New York on line three," she warbled.

The detective looked at Paul and lifted his eyebrows suggestively. Paul made bunting motions with the telescope. Armstrong threw himself forward and gathered the shards of telephone in his arms like a baby. "Get out of here," he shouted. "I'm not telling you a thing more." He looked into the circle of his arms in fascination, as if his "boss" were hiding among the plastic ruins. "I'll deny everything, I'll deny that, too, because none of this is evidence. None of this is evidence. . . ."

"Shit," Vanzetti swore in disgust. "What a worm."

He switched off the tape machine and pocketed it.

"You know we can check this out," he warned. "Your 'boss.' Who owns this dump. State records. It's all public information. And if it don't check out, we'll be back."

They hesitated, but there seemed to be nothing further they could do or say. Finally they left Charlie Armstrong among the ruins of his communications.

On the way out, Vanzetti tried to talk to the secretary, to reassure or apologize, but she backed away from him, against the window, her hands splayed flat with tension, virtually sandwiched between the terror on either side of her.

≈

Paul and Vanzetti drove to Boston immediately after seeing Charlie Armstrong, but there was no current information on Baybarge Inc. at the Massachusetts Secretary of State's Corporations Office on Beacon Hill.

The last record of the company showed it had still been a Massachusetts-registered corporation in 1978. After that, all trace of Baybarge disappeared.

There was no record whatsoever of VMT, Inc.

"If it was bought in '78," Paul said, "by a New York company, they could have reregistered it where the other company was listed."

"New York," Paul stated the obvious.

"New York," Vanzetti agreed.

They got back in the Jeep. There were two twenty-dollar tickets on the windshield, an odd vibration in the drive shaft. Clouds were piling up behind the gold dome of the State House.

They found the Mass. Pike and headed for Albany anyway. Wind whistled through the slits in the Jeep's canopy, and the heater had trouble keeping up. They were tired from the night before. Sleep had been short, the motel mattresses lumpy. But it was less exhausting to follow a trail than to rest with no direction.

The snow started again halfway to the New York border. Paul drove just this side of recklessly. The snowstorm piled up on the dregs of the last. Their headlights made innumerable blue lines of the flakes in their path. By the time they got to Albany the byways were full of buried vehicles and the salt and flash of snowplows. Radio stations narrated long lists of school closings. Church fairs, evening classes, quilting bees, support groups across upstate New York would all be postponed to later dates. All nonessential traffic in Berkshire County was prohibited. State government offices would remain open, but service would be limited.

They got to Washington Street in Albany at 3:50—forty minutes from closing time. Only a skeleton crew was on duty in the building housing the offices of the secretary of state of New York. Paul and

Vanzetti followed directions to the Office of Corporations. There they found ten thousand square feet worth of linoleum lined with bound files in alphabetical order.

In the middle of the room stood eight huge metal coffins that held the index cards on which were recorded the particulars of every duly incorporated company, trust, or foundation currently doing business in the Empire State.

There was no one in the room. A radio sounded thinly, far down the corridor.

Paul clutched the calendar he had taken out of Charlie Armstrong's office and approached the records-coffins.

The file bank holding the first letters of the alphabet was the second to last on the left. They lifted the top and pressed buttons. Long rows of files rotated and swung.

"OK. Baybarge," Vanzetti said, flipping through cards. "BAAF, Inc., Basior Schwartz Meat Products, Inc., Bay Company?"

"Baybarge. One word. B-a-y-b—"

"I know how to spell. Whaddya think I am, some uneducated North End Guinea? It's not here. No, wait. Goddamn. Here it is," Vanzetti said, excitedly. "Baybarge, Inc. Got a pencil?"

The files did not list ownership of the company—only officers, address, date, and articles of incorporation.

The date of incorporation was December 5, 1978. The officers were John Almeida, Treasurer; Brigid Perry, Secretary; Hugh Van Meerwen, President. Treasurer and secretary listed addresses in the New Bedford area. The president lived c/o VMT, Inc., 15 Battery Place, New York, New York.

"OK," Paul said. There was no relief in him, or gratitude to fate or Armstrong. Only an extension of the disappointment, the anger he had felt in the Baybarge office. "So he wasn't lying about that, at any rate."

"Jesus, don't be so negative."

"I just wish," Paul said, "I'd busted *all* his phones, that little creep. I mean, 'my boss.' What the hell is that supposed to mean? It could mean anything. It could mean nothing, and we're on a total wild goose chase."

"Yeah, maybe," Vanzetti replied drily. "But it's the only goose we got at this point."

"Thanks to you."

"What's that supposed to mean?"

"It means that I'm wondering if I did the right thing, going along with your ideas. Bullying information out of people. Maybe I should have let the cops handle it."

"Yeah," Vanzetti shot back, "and where would you be now? You wouldn't know who killed your cousin. You'd be hanging around for months while the cops filled out their triplicate forms and waited for the state people to call up Massachusetts. Just like with Nicole."

"Exactly. Just like Nicole. I hired you to find Nicole, too, and look where that got me."

Vanzetti's eyes hooded. Paul felt the anger in both of them reach out like a black octopus and squeeze.

"You asshole. I busted my fucking balls to find your kid. For the lowest rate. I didn't make money on that case. If that's your attitude, you can give me what you owe me, plus plane fare, and I'm outta here. Both cases. Outta here."

"Fine," Paul said. He could feel his jaw sticking out. He knew he must look like an idiot, with his fists bunched and his eyes narrowed. On top of it all, he knew Vanzetti was right; the detective *had* done all he could for Nicole. He had done a sight more than the police, at any rate.

And, for better or for worse, Vanzetti was his only hope.

Once again.

Paul pinched his nose with his fingers to help drive out the rage.

"I'm sorry," he said wearily. "I didn't mean that. Forget I said it."

"Sure." The private detective's eyes stayed very cold.

"I'm tired. We're both tired. Let's get this over with."

"Sure," Vanzetti said again, but the anger stayed in his movements, and he dragged behind when Paul crossed the room looking for the "V" section.

On paper at least, VMT, Inc., was run on the same kind of troika lines as Baybarge. Its place of business was Room 3100, 15 Battery Place, New York. The treasurer was listed as Brendan Hernon, with an address in Hempstead, Long Island. The president was Hugh Van Meerwen of 145 Hudson Street, New York. The secretary, one L. H. Chapman, could be reached c/o 78th Street Corporation, Room 3100, 15 Battery Place, New York.

"Same address," Paul commented.

"Boy, am I glad you came along. I would never in a million years have ever noticed that."

"I said I was sorry."

"Yeah. I know."

They went over to the "S" file. The secretary of 78th Street Corporation was William Sachs of Englewood Cliffs, New Jersey. The president of 78th Street was a Hugh A. Van Meerwen, 23 East 78th Street, New York. The secretary was L. H. Chapman. Paul closed the looseleaf he had bought to record all this information and looked out the window at the bits of snow that danced and played with the light, and were gone.

"So?" Vanzetti said. "Do you know any of these guys?"

Paul shook his head, tiredly.

"Ashley might. But we're only assuming there's a connection with a Twelve-Meter syndicate. I mean, even if we're right, there's hundreds of people who could be involved."

The PI took out a cigarette. The problem at hand had taken his mind off resentment.

"Except," Vanzetti said, "they're not small fry. Stakes are high."

Paul nodded.

"They got to be officers, big money people. That's the connection. All we need is a list."

Paul nodded again. Still staring at the snow.

"I know a guy," he said finally. "Ashley's godfather. He would know all those people. He's chairman of the New York syndicate. On the yacht club side."

Vanzetti paused in the middle of lighting a match. He looked at Paul curiously over the fizzing sulfur. He lit his cigarette, then said, "You trust this guy?"

Paul looked at the detective.

"These New York guys," Vanzetti explained. "*Social Register*. Old money. They look out for each other. Don't they?"

"I never really thought about it," Paul said. "He doesn't seem the type. Not because killing or stealing is immoral, but because it's stupid. Because it breaks the rules of the game."

"I don't mean he did it."

"I know he's fond of Ashley."

"If there's another way," Vanzetti said, inhaling smoke, "maybe we oughta try that first."

"Why do I get the feeling," Paul said, "you're still fighting an old, old battle?"

"Because the battle ain't over yet," Vanzetti shot back. "Because the enemy lives in yacht clubs. Which is something you oughta remember."

They left the office twenty minutes after official closing time. No one had seen them come in, and no one saw them leave. The radio still played down the hallway. Snow lay an inch deeper on the building's steps. No one had ticketed the Jeep.

≋

The snow let up, temporarily, the next day, but weathermen were tracking a new rank of low-pressure systems from the Northwest, trying to conceal the glee in their voices.

In Manhattan, city workers labored overtime to convert snow into a gluey mixture of ice, water, dirt, and crushed dog excrement in preparation for the next onslaught. Bus drivers took aim and sent sheets of the stuff to soak people lining up at bus stops. Steam leaked from cracks in the slush.

Because of the condition of the streets, at least half the editorial staff of *Yachts* magazine wore sailing boots to work. The bright latex-and-canvas footwear was lined up to dry beside a heater in the reception area. Paul explained what he wanted to the receptionist; Vanzetti looked curiously at the cramped desks, the stacked papers, the video terminals wedged between editors in the working space behind. Posters of sailboats covered the wallboard. The messy, smoky room did not look like the editorial quarters of the most influential boat-racing magazine in the United States.

"Just the back issues," Paul said. "Anything on the America's Cup. The syndicates, specifically."

"Just the back issues," the receptionist repeated, sarcastically. She was blond and young and had large breasts. "I'll need to check with Bill. Have a seat."

They preferred to stand, where it was easier to watch her. Bill came out of a small side office and said, "What's it for?"

Paul explained, adding that he was in the boat business.

"You're not from *Sail*? Or another publication?" Bill had pink pants, a thick beard, and a nervous habit of pulling at it. "We charge in that case. Research fee."

Paul reassured him.

"Sign 'em in," Bill told the receptionist, and pretended to be looking for a petty cash chit in the background so he could hear their names. He waited until the receptionist had shown them to the library. This was an overheated back room lined with shelves of back issues, stacked by month. Then he came in and looked curiously at Paul.

"You're not," he said, "Paul Briggs, the naval architect? Jack Briggs's cousin, the one with the Challenge syndicate?"

Paul nodded. Vanzetti tried not to look impressed by Paul's fame. He pulled out a magazine from the January shelf, checked the table of contents, and yawned.

"Well, you should have said something." Bill stuck out a hand and gave them his last name and title. He was the managing editor. He asked what they were looking for specifically. Vanzetti put away his first copy and reached for another. Paul thought about it briefly and decided there was no need to be secretive. Bill might be able to help.

They were looking into syndicate financing, Paul told him. Specifically, the role played by people named Van Meerwen, Chapman, or Sachs, or anyone associated with them.

Bill smiled in the vaguely condescending way of people who often have more information at their disposal than ordinary mortals.

And told them.

Chapman or Sachs he did not know. But Van Meerwen was one of the oldest names in New York yachting circles.

The father, Bill continued, owned a boat that placed well in the Bermuda race. The son, Hugh Van Meerwen, worked as a winch man in the 1980 America's Cup series. Recently he was chosen to head a liaison committee between the three major East Coast yacht clubs sponsoring America's Cup efforts. The committee was the East Coast America's Cup Coordinating Committee, known by its acronym. Bill pronounced it "Ee-kak." Its purpose was to coordinate fund-raising drives. The chairman of ECACCC was ex officio treasurer of the New York Yacht Club's Cup Committee, and, by extension, the Old Glory syndicate as a whole.

"Van Meerwen." Vanzetti tossed the magazine he was reading across the table. He leaned back in his chair and pulled out a cigarette. "Well, surprise, surprise," he drawled, flicking his lighter.

Paul realized his mouth was hanging open and shut it with a snap. All the wild depression built up from the strain and frustration of the last few days seemed to alchemize into bright colors and excitement.

Bill sat down, casually, and started to ask sharp, polite questions about the Challenge effort. Were they having trouble finding money? Was this why they were researching sponsors?

Paul fended him off absentmindedly. His brain was humming in other directions, making leaps of memory, of projection.

Hugh Van Meerwen. Here was the linchpin, the common denominator to all their evidence.

Gradually the excitement looped back to nervous energy, to worry, as the information was assimilated and the problem of what to do with it came into the foreground.

Bill had gone on to questions about design. Was the Challenge team working on an evolutionary boat like Bruce Archibald at the Old Glory syndicate? Or were they trying something new and radical like the French designers did last time? A bit of both, Paul answered, and went back to his thoughts.

Now that the target was clear, there was an obvious path to pursue in running it down. Paul told himself he would not let the conspiracy theories of a low-rent gumshoe foul up the best connection he had in New York.

He got to his feet, abruptly, and had to make apologies to Bill, who tugged at his beard and said "no problem" and looked hurt nonetheless.

When they got back outside Paul found a pay phone and called Winton's office to set up a meeting.

CHAPTER 19

Bradley Winton liked to schedule meetings over high tea in the tearoom of the Lowell Hotel, on East Sixty-third Street.

He thought the ceremony relaxed his clients, made them forget the distasteful fact that every hour they spent together would be billed at a rate of close to thirty-three dollars per minute.

Certainly the flowered chintz curtains and blue-white china brought visions of a more secure time. The very ritual of choosing teas— China Black, Queen Mary, Earl Grey, Lapsang Souchong, Darjeeling, Ceylon, raspberry—made Paul feel he had stepped, for the time being, into another sort of world, where Brittannia still ruled the waves and different-looking people stayed in the kitchen.

Vanzetti had changed into a nylon suit for the occasion. The suit bulged under his left armpit. It seemed to clash with his attempt to hold the teacup the way Winton did, between thumb and forefinger. He wiped his mouth suspiciously after each sip and tried to hide his cigarette in the palm of his hand. Paul noted with curiosity how this private detective, raised in the streets of Boston, armed with a .38

caliber revolver, fell victim to the environment of the tearoom. He must do all the talking, Paul decided.

Over silver pots of Darjeeling and finger sandwiches he explained to Winton how they had found Jack's murderer. Winton listened with the same bland, faraway expression Paul remembered from the yacht club party. He popped the sandwiches into his mouth as neatly and finally as a frog would snap down a mosquito. Watercress, herb-cheese, ham croissant. Pop, pop, pop. The waiter poured boiling water.

Paul asked Vanzetti for the tape deck. The detective looked around uncomfortably and fitted earphones to the jack so the machine would not disturb other tea drinkers. The waiter brought plates of raisin scones with clotted cream and four different kinds of English pre-serves. Winton put the earphones on his head. He cut his scone diagonally, spread cream over one half, and added raspberry jam. Vanzetti operated the tapes, explaining the first voice was Tina, who had killed Jack, the second, the man who had paid her to do it.

As the tapes unreeled Winton did not change expression once. The waiter cleared the scone dishes and brought them each a plate of tiny strawberry, kiwi, and mandarin tarts.

Pop, pop, pop.

The tape ended.

Winton took the earphones off and placed them on the table. He brushed a crumb absently from his dove-gray suit and smoothed the silver at his temples.

"Well," Paul said, finally.

Winton raised his eyebrows.

"What do you think?"

"What do you expect me to think?" Ashley's godfather flicked the earphones another inch across the snowy linen, away from him. He kept his eyes on the instrument, warily, and recrossed his knees.

"I—"

"I cannot believe any of it," Winton continued. "It's absolutely ludicrous anyone in Van Meerwen's family would condone such a thing. Why, I knew his grandfather. I know Hugh. I know Henry."

The implication was clear; anyone Winton knew could not break the law.

"But you heard the evidence," Paul said.

"Evidence!" Winton put the last tart in his mouth and disposed of it in four quick chews. He looked at Vanzetti with distaste.

"Those tapes," he said. "Those noises and cries. I shudder to think under what circumstances those so-called confessions were obtained. 'My boss told me to do it.' For God's sake, that's not evidence! People would say anything in those straits. And the rest is coincidence."

"True," Paul replied, urgent, low. "But what a coincidence. Tina Costa. The Identikit. It goes on," Paul continued. "Her taking time off that week. The tugboat man's knot. The same car being found only thirty minutes away. The fact she knew Hendriks, the Danish designer. She could never have made that up. You link all those facts, through Armstrong, and hey presto; suddenly, you find the chairman of the major fund-raising organization for America's Cup syndicates at the end of the line. So you got linkage, you got money changing hands. You got motive and opportunity. You're a lawyer," he went on. "What are the odds against this being coincidence? A million to one? Two million?"

"The evidence is circumstantial. It is also inadmissible."

"We knew that," Paul admitted, looking at Vanzetti a little resentfully. "But we weren't sure, at first. We had to find out. We traded in our legal options. For information."

Vanzetti grunted "Yeah," and cleared his throat. "We had to."

"That's probably wise," Winton commented drily, "since the DA would not have a leg to stand on in prosecuting this case."

He lifted a finger without looking up. The waiter glided over, noiseless, to deposit a check facedown on a sterling silver platter.

Paul took in the check. He looked back at Winton.

"That's it?" he asked, incredulously. "You're just going to forget all about this?"

Winton looked bored.

"What kind of a lawyer are you," Paul said, more loudly now. "What kind of a man?"

Vanzetti shifted, as if to free himself for action. Heads were turning at the tables around them. Paul threw his napkin on the table. Winton took his and polished the ends of his mouth.

When Paul spoke again, it was at a lower volume, but anger still prickled in the words.

"You know," he said, "Sal here did not want me to talk to you at all. He said you might be involved. I told him, no. But frankly, now, I'm beginning to wonder. Maybe you *were* involved. Maybe *you* were responsible for the death of Ashley's husband."

Winton checked the bill. He tore off the slip to use for tax deductions. He took cash from a crocodile-skin wallet and dropped it on the platter. "Sixteen eighty," he said, "my share plus tip."

Paul snorted in disgust and dug out his own wallet.

Vanzetti spoke up suddenly.

"God," he said disgustedly, "you people are all the same. You stick together. Maybe you weren't in on this, OK. But you're guilty now for sure. Because you won't help out. That makes you an accomplice now. Even if you weren't one before."

Winton put his wallet back in his breast pocket. He gave Vanzetti the same neutral stare he'd once used as an OSS officer, walking past SS troopers in occupied Toulouse.

Then, with the confidence of those satisfied that any mistake they'd made was entirely due to the shortcomings of others, he changed his mind.

"Guilty by default?" he said. "Guilty by indifference. Perhaps you are right. But even so, you've cooked your own goose. There's nothing I can do for you."

"But all you have to do"—Paul swallowed his surprise and leaned forward—"all we want to do is see these people. Confront them with this. Try to scare them into admitting."

Winton thought about it. He took out the claim check for his coat and flipped it across his knuckles.

"Just arrange an interview?" he said. "Nothing else?"

"Nothing else," Paul reassured him. "I don't think we'd get near them without you."

"Probably not." Winton's eyes blinked. "I thought you wanted me to initiate legal proceedings. Or finance them." He looked at Paul.

"I know about you," he went on. "Ashley has told me. You are a little unstable, I think. You become obsessed with people who have hurt you. You could become annoying, were you to decide I was guilty of this crime. And I have a suspicion Ashley would back you in this.

"So I will do as you ask. Because of Ashley," he finished hastily, "not because of your obsessions. I can get you a meeting with Hugh.

I know Lance Chapman, who does the Van Meerwen legal work. I can convince him it will be in their best interests to see you—and that in itself should prove to you they had nothing to do with this tawdry little affair."

Paul was about to smile, to thank him, but Winton held up a warning hand.

"There is one condition."

Winton leaned back and straightened his suit.

"The condition is this. You see, I know Hugh. I have sailed and drunk wine and played squash with him and his family. I know they are incapable of doing the things you suggest. I know when they are bluffing, I know when they are hiding, and I know when they are telling the truth."

"So?" Vanzetti said. He seemed to have recovered some of his confidence, in taking a point off Winton.

"So I will be there. I will be the judge. I will be the jury. What I say goes. If I decide they are stonewalling, I will tell you. But if I decide they had nothing to do with it, I will expect you to cease and desist in this obsession of yours. Forthwith. No more pursuing them. Or me. Do I make myself clear?"

Paul thought about it.

On the face of it, Winton's request was absurd.

Yet, at the same time, it made a lot of sense, for this was the true conclusion of the course he and Vanzetti first chose in the Pier Tavern in New Bedford: a series of compromises, none of them very earth-shattering, all of them expedient at the time. The compromises had cut away and cut away at the options available until they were left, here, in this alien room of imperial ceremonies, totally dependent on the good faith of a man who could yet turn out to be an enemy.

In any case, he saw no other option.

And he was tired, very tired, of casting about in the dark.

Paul nodded. He watched Vanzetti's jaw drop open in protest as the waiter brought the change.

☷

"It my boss, not me. You can't do this. . . . None of this is evidence. . . ."

The clicks of amateur editing gave way to pure background noise.

The man who was both managing director of Van Meerwen Towing, Inc., and the chairman of ECACCC, took his eyes off the cassette player on his desk.

He swiveled his large leather chair a quarter-turn to the left and looked out over Battery Park. Long purple clouds, their bellies swollen with snow, lowered over New York harbor. The Statue of Liberty hid in a premature belch of white haze. One of the Van Meerwen tugs—you could tell them by their bright yellow superstructures and red funnels—did its best to pull a fuel barge toward Port Elizabeth but made little headway against the weight of clouds, the push of current. Stranded commuters tried to dig cars out with shovels, before the snowplows turned them to scrap. The country sound of strike and fling, strike and fling, floated in countrylike silence to the sixth floor of the old Hansa-Lloyd building. The worst series of blizzards since '78 had turned lower Broadway into a village again.

Hugh Van Meerwen was thirty-two, but he felt about seventy. He was very tired and mightily hung over. Last night he had cohosted a charity ball for four hundred of his most intimate friends and acquaintances. The theme was lycanthropy, the setting was the Sixty-seventh Street Armory, the champagne was Krug. It had been a success, on the whole, Hugh Van Meerwen reflected. Aldo Chapin hot-wired an armored personnel carrier and almost succeeded in driving it up the stairs into the dining hall. Katerina Von Ewig-Halssteif came dressed in the winter pelt of a Siberian timber wolf and very little else. She had shown him just how little under a stack of folding tables in a room full of regimental flags belonging to the Second Brigade Forty-second Infantry of the New York National Guard.

The drugs and conversation were equally pure; none of his friends talked of death and confessions, fire and killers. They raised almost forty thousand dollars—16,427 after expenses and damages, to be apportioned equally among the homeless of Manhattan and the New York Yacht Club's America's Cup syndicate. For sixteen hours, right up to the time he'd had to leave the party to go to work, Hugh Van Meerwen had managed completely to forget the troubling phone call from New Bedford.

He wished the party had never ended.

Lance Chapman waved a finger at him.

Van Meerwen had the impression the finger might have been waving for some time, but Chapman came from a law firm that considered it unseemly to use the spoken word. Speech, in the philosophy of Brookside, Chapman, and MacLeod, was what one resorted to if one had not prepared a brief sufficiently well to settle out of court. It was encouraging that Chapman saw no need to resort to words in this instance. Not that these people, with their ridiculous "confessions," had a prayer of involving him.

The lawyer passed a note over the mahogany desk; he almost had to slide himself across to reach.

Hugh Van Meerwen let him strain, not moving a muscle to shorten the distance between them. He was still peeved at Chapman for allowing this meeting in the first place. He was all the more annoyed because Bradley Winton had gone over his head to convince Chapman this meeting was necessary—old men scratching each other's backs like monkeys. Hugh Van Meerwen caught the faint odor of rose water from this old man's jowls as he picked up the note. "They have no case," the note read. "Do *not* speak unless I ask." Classic Brookside, Chapman advice.

Except that Chapman seemed to be preparing to ignore his own counsel. The lawyer worked his chins several times for practice. His bow tie twitched under the unfamiliar stress.

Van Meerwen checked his cuff links, a gesture betraying unease.

"First of all, that machine." Chapman's words came out in a whisper. He jerked his chin toward the tape recorder. "Please make sure it is not running."

Van Meerwen checked the spools and nodded toward the lawyer, who continued, "This is all, of course, quite preposterous." The words came out in a whisper. Paul Briggs and Sal Vanzetti leaned out of the deep pigskin couch they were seated in to catch their meaning. The lawyer changed the way his legs were crossed, and sixty-six-inches worth of pinstripes realigned themselves.

"Naturally, if you persist in making these outrageous accusations," the lawyer continued, "we would be obliged to take the matter to court. I see an ironclad case for slander, conspiracy—even, based on what we hear from Baybarge—vandalism, intimidation, and extortion." Despite the whisper the words rolled out like expensive stones on velvet.

Vanzetti cleared his throat. "You don't want this to go to court," he warned, gruffly. "Shit's shit; it don't care where it sticks."

The detective's voice was hoarse from too many cigarettes. He still wore a gun under his suit, but the jacket was rumpled and the tie was obviously nylon. He had not regained the composure he'd lost in the Lowell tearoom.

It was this building that did it, Paul realized. Walking into the place, with its solid teak paneling and quiet secretaries, was like desecrating a church. The portraits of ancient paddle-wheel tugboats on the walls spoke of one hundred years of arterial hookup to the heartbeat of commerce. The great clock on the wall ticktocked with the assurance of great credit. The sports trophies for sailing and lacrosse were gold and came from Andover and Dartmouth.

The easy calm of Hugh Van Meerwen was the end product— liquor pressed and distilled from vats of crossbred wealth.

Paul wished Ashley were here. She could have brought Winton into their camp, vaccinated them against all this assurance and power before the meeting.

He glanced over at Winton. The financier's eyes were closed, though his back and neck were very straight. Paul suspected he slept in that posture. For some reason the thought irritated him.

"What I want to know," Paul burst out suddenly, "is none of this legal stuff. Who gives a damn about evidence." He got to his feet and brushed his cowlick back, conscious of how long it had been since he'd had a shower.

Winton opened his eyes. Chapman looked shocked. In his court, outbursts would be bad form; physical movement, contempt. Paul took off his glasses and pointed their frames at Hugh Van Meerwen. A deep, clean hatred for this man flooded him—hatred for his silk ruffled shirt, his striped bow tie, for the fifty-dollar curl in his haircut. Most of all he hated the worn Maine hunting boots on Van Meerwen's feet; few men would have the self-confidence to wear them with white socks, under an eighteen-hundred-dollar silk tuxedo.

"What I want to know," Paul repeated, "is why." He walked over and leaned on the desk, placing his fists between a lacrosse trophy and a picture of Van Meerwen at a winch on the last cup defender. Van Meerwen sat back in his chair, from distaste, not fear. Paul's breath was sour.

"Why did you have to steal the plans. Off the record. Never mind lawyers, the whole rigmarole. *Why?* I mean, the computer numbers looked good, but we weren't the only ones. Why not steal the *Go America* plans? Why not get the *Bretagne*, for chrissake? Why not waste Marcel Morgat, or Plehan? He's the one to beat, he's the one everybody's worried about. So why did you have to get my cousin killed, and why in God's name did you have to burn my yard?"

Paul paused, out of breath, dry of words. His forearms trembled on the desk. This was the moment to space out these men with gutter violence, just as they'd done with Tina, with Armstrong. But there was only one phone on Van Meerwen's desk, and Paul had the distinct impression that the clock would stop—every fluted column and vaulted ceiling in this hallowed building would tremble and collapse on their heads at the crudity of it.

Chapman waved a finger at Van Meerwen.

The younger man straightened his bow tie, fiddled with his cuffs. His face was very pale, Paul thought, but this was the only sign of strain.

Paul pounded his fist on the desk, hard, sensing he was going to lose these men forever.

"Tell me," he almost shouted. "That's all I want to know. Why did you have to do it?"

No answer came from behind the desk, so Paul answered for them.

"It was to disqualify us, right? Like you tried to do to the Australians in '83. You asked Tina to rip off anything with Piet Hendriks's name. You were hoping he was involved in the actual design? A Danish national. You could have kicked us out of the cup with that evidence. Wasn't that the reason? Well, wasn't it?"

He slammed his fist on the desk once more.

Van Meerwen looked like he was wishing he hadn't eaten breakfast. Vanzetti, glancing in Winton's direction, noticed his eyes were open.

"I think this meeting is over," Chapman whispered, staring at Paul's fist. The finger waved again.

Obediently Van Meerwen got to his feet. He turned his back, opened a recess in the paneling and removed a camel-hair overcoat and a squash racket.

Chapman snapped his attaché case shut and continued, "Please believe me when I say that we may take action against you for the injury you have already caused my client. We will certainly take action should you decide to carry on with your ridiculous accusations. Justice will be served." The last four words were spoken with ritual emphasis, like a prayer.

Chapman no longer looked at Paul. He did not look at anyone.

Paul's eyes moved to Winton. "Do something," he urged, "for Ashley's sake." Believing deep inside that he'd been tricked, they'd all been tricked, conned by these men who, in the final analysis, had in common interests so vital they made the accidental killing of an outsider pale by comparison.

Chapman moved for the door, followed by his client.

Paul watched, feeling sick.

Vanzetti had an odd expression of mingled anger and I-told-you-so as he watched Winton.

Ashley's godfather sat very still. His eyes had closed again.

Chapman was about to touch the doorknob with his pale, dry fingers when Winton said, "Just a minute, Lance."

The lawyer froze. Van Meerwen bumped into him. They both turned.

Winton still wore the thick woolen overcoat he had walked in with. He unbuttoned it now, as if just deciding to stay.

"You talk of justice," Winton went on, "its forms and conventions. Certainly these men have flouted them in gathering this information."

"Your point, Bradley?"

"My point, counselor." Winton opened his eyes all the way, smiled at Chapman without looking at him. A conspiracy of bow ties, Paul thought. Everybody wore one except for Vanzetti and himself.

"My point is this. I was expecting shock, outrage, flat denials from both of you. I did not see them. I was expecting anger that you should be accused of such crimes. It did not come. I, too, would like to know. Why?"

"We are not beholden," Chapman began coldly, "to this jury-rigged justice," but Winton interrupted him.

"There is another justice to be served," he said. "It is not as formal or as fair as that of the courts. But in some ways its standards are higher." Winton seemed to sit straighter, if such a thing were possible, and looked at Van Meerwen for the first time. "I am talking about the cup, Hugh. I am talking about the club. I'm talking about the sport of yacht racing and its traditions."

Paul watched Winton intently. He had no idea what the man was getting at. He could tell Vanzetti was confused as well, but they both listened to what was going on because of the way Hugh Van Meerwen reacted to Winton's words.

The managing director of VMT, Inc., walked slowly back to his desk. He held his back very straight. Then he put the squash racket down on the shiny mahogany in front of him.

"Before 1983," Winton continued, "the New York Yacht Club, and by extension the America's Cup, lived by the same time-honored codes we'd always lived by. A man's word, the sense of fair play. Honesty of thought, elegance of action. Values Van Meerwen's family has always treasured, as has my own."

Winton's voice got lower and softer as he got closer to the heart of the argument.

"Then the Australians broke all the rules. They built an illegal keel. They kept it secret. They mounted a slick public relations campaign that made us look like a bunch of flatulent hypocrites to the world outside. It's not stealing the cup that hurt," Winton insisted, "it was destroying the consensus behind it; the sense that this was a sport played among men of honor, not a cutthroat commercial scrum where the only law comes from the gutter; that the biggest and most ruthless should survive. . . ." Winton's voice held great insult.

Chapman looked like a phantom with colic. He waved an entire hand at Bradley Winton. The financier ignored him, continuing his story as if he were sitting in his own drawing room—which, in a sense, he was.

The club's Cup Committee wanted to drop out of cup competition after '83, Winton went on, and again after '87. Both times they changed their minds, for one reason and one reason only: that the values and ideals the New York Yacht Club stood for should not appear to perish from the earth. To that end they brought together two sister yacht clubs, Essex and Marblehead-Athenaeum, to coordinate, not only their fund-raising and research, but also the general philosophy that would guide their campaign.

To head that committee, to coordinate the three clubs, they needed a young, dynamic man with a background of traditional values, Twelve-Meter experience, and financial expertise. Hugh Van Meerwen seemed tailor-made for their requirements. Winton put his hands together, like a priest, then dipped the angle of his joined fingers in the direction of the desk. His voice had dropped so low it was just this side of a croak. Yet no one had any trouble making out the words.

"But given the importance of public relations," Winton said, "the absolutely crucial requirement for the cup coordinator was this; he was to be like Caesar's wife—not only above reproach, but above even the appearance of reproach. And this evidence—" the fingers dipped toward Vanzetti now, then Paul—"these wharf-rat types who seem to know so much about breaking and entering and hitting people on the head; this chain of conspiracy, circumstantial though it is; above all, your lack of anger, your refusal to deny; I'm afraid, Hugh, it paints you with the appearance of impropriety. I'm sorry."

Paul felt surprise hit him deep in the solar plexus, then, slowly, turn to pleasure.

Winton had changed his mind.

Van Meerwen looked at Winton in sheer disbelief. He looked at his lawyer. The lawyer let the silence build and whispered back, "You only give us further grounds for damage, Bradley. Any action against my client will be construed as the consequences of slander in subsequent litigation. We will own these people."

"The yacht club is a private entity, Lance," Winton replied. "As well you know. We do as we please for our own reasons, by our own standards. If we wish to revoke Hugh's membership, it will be with due consideration. If we wish to launch an inquiry, it will be in closed session, for reasons we will not divulge."

"You can't do that," Van Meerwen whispered.

Winton closed his eyes, like a bishop.

Paul's pleasure vanished as quickly as it had come.

"That's it?" he asked incredulously. "This man has, basically, killed another man, he has robbed and committed murder. And who knows what else he was planning. I mean, I take it, you've read his eyes or whatever. And your response to that," (Paul could not keep his voice from breaking) "is, throw him out of the *yacht club*?"

Winton held up his hand, still without opening his eyes.

"Look at him, Paul," he said. "It's not just a yacht club. It's the people he grew up with. It's his neighbors on Nantucket. It's his friends from Andover, from—Dartmouth, is that right? It's family, it's his job, it's sailing, it's squash. Don't you think," Winton asked, "five-to-ten in Sing Sing would be superfluous?"

"Yes, I mean, no." Paul walked over to the window, still torturing his scalp. "I mean, it's not exactly Old Testament stuff, is it? Eye for an eye, a tooth for a tooth?" He walked back toward Winton's seat, then to the window again. "If you could have seen Jack lying there. Blood on his head. It's not 'no more yacht club' for Jack; it's no more anything, no more hugging his wife, no more life!"

Winton held his joined hands to his mouth now.

"It's no longer an Old Testament world," he argued softly. "In the Old Testament world, human relations had to do with blood and wine, excrement and barley. Our world has grown immensely more complex. We live at two, three removes. We have abstractified everything into symbols to deal with the complexity. Symbols of power, symbols of knowledge. The yacht club is a very strong set of symbols. Of sportmanship, honor, position. You cut this man off from those, you punish him as effectively as if you cut off his head or his hands, three thousand years ago."

"Maybe I'm old-fashioned," Paul countered, "but I'd rather see some blood on the fucking decks."

"You lost that option," Winton shot back, "when you decided to play detective on your own."

Hugh Van Meerwen watched the man called Briggs stride back and forth, raging like a maniac. Lance Chapman watched the spectacle with obvious distaste, but Van Meerwen himself was beyond reacting.

He had never dreamed it might come to this. A great black weight had settled in the pit of his stomach and was pressing harder and harder against his bladder. He wanted to urinate. He wanted his father to be alive.

He wanted to ring the number he was supposed to call only in emergencies and scream, "You got me into this! I wasn't thinking! It was your planning that caused this mess. Now it's your responsibility. So get me out!"

Hugh Van Meerwen did nothing. His squash racquet mocked him with its inactivity. He was supposed to play Alec Swann at eleven-thirty, but Alec was a member of the yacht club.

A lot of similar doors would be slamming shut in the next week, the next year.

All of a sudden, Hugh Van Meerwen felt very, very alone.

C H A P T E R   2 0

The man hung up the pay phone very slowly.

That was the end of that, he thought.

It was just as well, in a way. He had made a mistake in dealing with Van Meerwen to begin with.

The man wrapped his coat tighter around him. The harbor wind worried at the phone booth. He looked out, and up, at the building in front of him.

The contractors had started construction only two and a half months ago but already the building seemed to touch the clouds overhead. A crane, towering on its own separate structure beside, looked the size of a toy at that height. The crossed girders diminished with perspective; the shrinking rows of work lamps on every floor reminded him of huge ships seen close up at night.

It was very lucky Hugh Van Meerwen had good legal counsel.

Because Hugh had very little else. Even in prep school as a teenager he was ineffectual. Hugh only got through Andover because his grandfather donated a dormitory.

That's the way the world works, the man thought. The smart slog for scholarships, the rich sit back and wait for the harvest. Power, prestige, women. Hugh Van Meerwen certainly never had a problem finding women.

The man grimaced and pushed the envy firmly from his mind. He had no business thinking about women. They only got in the way. In the way of work, in the way of clear thought, in the way of action. The way his business was going, these days, he would need all the thought and work and action he could get just to stay on his feet.

The man took out his wallet and checked the piece of paper was still there.

That was all he had. A piece of paper with two numbers. The number of a box in Grand Central Station, a phone number for an answering service that probably never saw the man they took messages for.

How to get in touch with the nameless, faceless force that was the ultimate in troubleshooting.

The man rubbed the paper between thumb and forefinger. He liked the feel of it, contrasting the total ordinariness of its smooth fibers and blue ink with the huge power it could unleash.

He remembered the pictures of the fire. One phone call, one trip to the post office, and he'd destroyed half a boatyard five hundred miles away.

He tucked the paper in a pocket behind his credit cards.

He would not use it now.

Let things settle down. Let the yacht club's investigation into Hugh Van Meerwen's conduct grind to a halt, as eventually it must, since Hugh had nothing to gain and everything to lose by talking. Let the Challenge people finish their boat.

The kid would keep them informed. The kid would let them know if there was any problem. Time enough then to fight fire with fire.

The man pocketed his wallet. He took out a pack of cigarettes and lit one, with fingers that were quite steady. He was only smoking a couple a day, medicine for when the money problems got a little out of hand. Easily controllable.

He took a deep drag of the tobacco and unfolded the phone-booth doors. The smells of New Jersey blew in from across the river.

It might feel good to do something concrete again, the man thought.

C H A P T E R   2 1

Paul went straight back to work on his return from New York.

He and Bud Fossett and the Lloyds inspector checked the molds very carefully and found a small discrepancy in the after chain-girth measurement—the measure of volume in the stern part of the hull—due to warping from the fire's heat.

However, this was easily fixed with large clamps and a chain come-along.

Then the Gelcoat was sanded right down, to get rid of any particles of smoke, and reapplied.

This part of the job was Mikey's responsibility. After the Gelcoat came the fiberglass proper, in long sheets of matting.

The matting was made of short filaments of glass, crosswoven in such a way that the matrix of fibers would provide all the strength of its crystalline structure, without the corresponding brittleness, when bonded together by a glue of epoxy resin. The resin also provided flexibility.

To ensure a perfectly even ratio of resin to glass, this type of matting was soaked at the same time it was made with a special resin that would not harden until heat and pressure were applied. Mikey's job consisted of cutting the mats to the perfect proportions; setting the widest and strongest sections of matting along the axes of maximum stress, using a stress chart provided by Paul as a guide; and rolling the matting down until it married with the mold, even in the narrowest and tightest corners. The extra strength imparted by this technique translated into a hull 20 percent stiffer than normal. That stiffness, in turn, meant you could crank 20 percent more tension into sails and rigging, with attendant benefits in tuning and speed.

At this point in the process, what the glass crew called "nooky" would occur. The convex, or "male" part of the mold would be hoisted into the hollow, "female" section and screwed in tight, sandwiching the fiberglass into place between the two molds. The heating wires inside the molds would be switched on, and the combination of resin and glass would bake together, under pressure, in a bond as strong and hard as iron.

Six layers of fiberglass went into the shell of the hull. When the shell was complete, they strengthened it by cutting ribs and stringers of a structural material called "honeycomb core" and laying them at strict intervals along the sides of the boat and down its length.

The honeycomb was made of extremely thin aluminum, cut and folded, concertina-style, into a light, stiff structure. It derived its strength from the stiffness of the fiberglass used to fix it in place, as well as the law of physics that said the strength of a support grew as a cube of its thickness. Honeycomb core was built to be thick. Mikey cut it in such a way as never to offer an angle sharper than thirty degrees against the shell it lay on, thus eliminating a concentration of stress along a single joint. Then he glued the ribs and web-frames into place with further layers of glass matting and resin.

The Lloyds inspector supervised every stage of this process. He tested the quality and thickness of the fiberglass. He sent samples of the glass and resin to the National Bureau of Standards. He measured the size of, and the intervals between, the honeycomb supports. He weighed every ounce of material going into the hull; he even weighed the protective garments of Mikey's crew before and after work, to deduct each drop of resin that splashed onto their clothes. He did this because the America's Cup rules specified a Twelve-Meter of a given size had to weigh a given amount, no more, no less, and because, according to the rules, a contender must conform to Lloyds construction standards, which were tightly linked to the weight and strength of the materials.

There were only two ways to ensure a boat conformed to weight and strength requirements: by supervising construction while the boat was being built or by examining the boat's structure afterward. Unlike an aluminum boat, a fiberglass boat's structure was all of one piece with the hull; therefore the only way to examine it after building was by drilling holes to see what was inside.

Paul provided Joe Cummings with a camera, flash, and unlimited film to record his observations. The inspector's services were costing the syndicate almost eight hundred dollars a day, but it was cheaper than drilling and filling holes in the hull if a rival syndicate complained that this boat did not conform to specification.

They finished the hull proper in the middle of February. One cold, hushed morning the men unbolted and lifted out the male mold. Then, very delicately and slowly, they pried the halves of the female mold apart, like cracking the shell off a hard-boiled egg, revealing the completed hull shining white in the middle. The men whistled and clapped when they saw how smooth and fair it was. Even the Lloyds man was impressed. Paul thought she looked like an upside-down beluga whale. His feeling of accomplishment lasted almost a half hour, until the ten thousand problems of work to come swamped his mind again; until the recurring sense of frustration crowded the rest of his attention and made him pound hard objects with the edge of his hand at odd intervals. He was doing this much less than when he first got back from the showdown with Hugh Van Meerwen, but his hands were still bruised from the abuse.

After that came the polishing stages, when all the magical instruments were put in place and hooked to the hull itself. Huge coffee-grinder winches that looked like bicycle pedals on an axle. These turned the large graphite drums that would reel the sails in tight against the wind. Piston pumps running parasitically off the coffee grinders to suck out any water that might spray aboard and weigh the boat down in a race. Hydraulic rams and pistons to wind tension into mast, sails, and rigging through boom vangs, Cunninghams, headstays, backstays. Three-hundred-thousand-dollars worth of elegantly machined stainless steel, flush with ball bearings, sharp with gears, smooth with Teflon lubricant, all designed to squeeze the last fraction of horsepower from the muscles of men, for the cup rules specified that no artificial power could be used in working the boat.

The rules said nothing about navigation, however. Therefore, like all Twelves, *Challenge* was loaded to the gunwales with megabytes. Most of the high tech was concentrated in the cockpit's navigation station, where a pair of CBM "Challenge" model video terminals stood on a swivel, enclosed by a plastic spray screen. The computer itself was mounted below decks, bang on the center of gravity. It was powered by batteries and hooked up to an array of sensors that tracked wind direction, wind speed, speed over ground and water.

The sensors had their own, small computers in the form of microchips. These automatically corrected readings, averaged and combined them to give vital information on time, distance, and exactly what the wind was doing. Fancy software, in turn, took these data and cut them up, made magnetic loops and circles in the humming gold circuits, and spewed the results back on the screen in the form of what the skipper needed to know to plan his race; roll rate, polar plots, effective speed from waypoint to waypoint. What showed up was information as simple as the course to steer for the best speed in a given situation or as complex as a "wind history," a chart of what the elements had been doing where over the course already sailed, complete with predictions as to what they might do in the future. The computer automatically correlated this input with data from a navigational satellite so the navigator could at all times read everything in relation to the boat's actual position on the water.

The computer was not limited to weather and navigation. Separate programs processed information from pressure-sensitive diodes on keel and hull, digitizing their input into "pictures" that showed how the water was flowing, where drag and turbulence were building up. Another program "read" light-sensitive strips on the sails through a laser camera mounted on the mast and translated these data in much the same way.

Sensibly, the deck layout was planned and supervised by the helmsman, Queegie Hopkins.

Paul's job, at this point, was reduced to checking up on outside technicians, subcontractors hired by Hillman to install and tune the fancy equipment.

The change was pleasant, for a while. He could slow down, spend a little time with Jessica in the mornings. Think of things other than modulus, pitching moment, the Twelve-Meter rule.

Then the comedown hit. He found himself missing the rushing, the impossible deadlines. The lack of direction left him sensitive to lack of direction in other parts of his life.

On the third night of going to bed before 1:00 A.M. he woke up at two with the sheets soaked in sweat and the fire-dream roaring inside his skull.

It was a question of which fear was greater.

He waited until dawn so that light would queer the resonance with the night of Jack's death.

Then he went to the design loft.

He made himself coffee, picked up a pen and some scrap paper and with no preparation or creative foreplay started to draw.

Lines, boat lines. Fantastic hulls that would never see water. He could visualize them, vaguely, magic ghosts in the back of his mind.

His heart pounded like an Olympic hurdler's.

Yet there was nothing magical about marking dots, the carbon and grease of ballpoint ink, on wood fiber. In this very opposition between form and matter, idea and interpretation, the tension and the whittling down, should lie the beauty of his art.

Ignoring his block rather than facing it, Paul put down lines.

Sheer lines, buttock lines. Stems and transoms. Hollow garboards and full. Any which way, different ideas, some connected, some not. A modernized Sharpie, a One-Ton Cup boat, a Trans-Pacific multihull, a planing dinghy.

He sketched for half an hour, at a fast pace, though he knew within the first ten minutes it was hopeless.

As soon as he touched paper the lines skidded off, wrong or uselessly abstract. When he attempted to go to the other extreme, he drew other people's hulls: old, safe, hopelessly stale.

Paul cursed his hands, his tools. The noise of the wind, the temperature of the office, the smudges of the ballpoint.

It was no good, he thought. Either his ideas were off, or his hands had ceased obeying his nerve impulses. There was a line broken, a connection missing. The fear remained, stronger than ever.

He went down to the shop floor to kill time some other way.

≈

Somewhere during this first phase of construction Ashley had stopped sneaking out of the house before Jessica left for school. In fact she'd stopped leaving altogether, except to exercise her Arabs. When Nat was out fishing she took over his couch and watched TV. She became an avid fan of the only soap opera that came in clearly on the Georges Peninsula.

One night Paul came in late, well after his daughter's bedtime. He found Ashley in a cashmere sweater that would have represented a month's wages to Al Prouty, drinking neat bourbon, watching a tape of Jean Prouty's favorite TV show on Nat's video recorder.

"What are you watching?" he asked.

" 'Lives of Love.' "

Paul shook his head. "I never figured you for a soap fan."

She swung around at that. "Why not?"

"I don't know. Public television, I would have thought. Boston Symphony, endangered furry creatures. White people sleeping with natives in obscure corners of the Empire." He threw his bomber jacket on a chair. It slipped off. Ashley got to her feet and picked it up.

"What are you trying to say."

"Nothing. I just thought it was—interesting."

"You don't think I fit in?"

"Christ, Ashley. I didn't say that."

"Yes, you did. And you're right. But I'm here. You know why? Because I've got nowhere else to go. And no one to go with."

"That," said Paul slowly, "is a pretty negative way of describing—whatever we're doing."

She stood very straight, picking at rips in the jacket.

"It is. And it's not. It's what we have in common. Not just Jack, or your family. An affinity for things that are gone. Things that were always missing."

"Speak for yourself," Paul said roughly. He grabbed the jacket and went to throw it in his room.

He came down later and hugged Ashley tight, because in the marshland of emotions inside him the only thing he knew for sure was that he still deeply cared for Ashley, still relied on the basic warmth she provided to fight the cold inside, as well as the cold out.

But Ashley's sense of frustration did not dilute with time. In fact, it got worse. As construction of the boat went into its second phase, Ashley began to lose interest in everything. She grew silent, then morose. Paul wrote it off to cabin fever. Cabin fever was an old Maine-coast affliction that came with the various little deaths of winter; the endless dark nights, the cars that groaned but would not start, the gray, the cold. It usually only took one small blue crocus poking through the snow to weaken the fever's grip. Daylight saving time had the same effect on cabin fever as penicillin had on more conventional infections.

Ashley's cabin fever, however, seemed a particularly bad case. It soon affected all aspects of her life with Paul and Jessica and Nat and Old George. She grew irritable about small things—the level of grime on the kitchen floor, the stack of dishes in the sink. The weather sucked, the driveway was either a skating rink or a pig-wallow. There was never enough cat food for Jacob, though the cat was quite content with the scraps of pizza and ice cream and Pop-Tarts and hamburger everybody fed him at varying hours of the day or night.

Ashley was too fond of Jessica to take out her frustration on the child, and for this Paul was grateful. Nevertheless when Ashley began taking week-long trips to New York, Paul, along with everybody else, breathed a sigh of relief and went about his business with a freedom undreamed of when Ashley's moods controlled the house.

Ashley's trips became longer, more regular.

She was in New York when the deck, which had been molded separately, was attached to the hull.

She called up, a little tipsy, from a Thai restaurant on the Upper West Side the day the twin keels were fitted and bolted into place. She'd never eaten Thai food before, Ashley said. It was a lot better than Vietnamese. The restaurant had holes in the floor, under the tables, so stiff-jointed Americans could pretend they were sitting cross-legged, like Orientals.

She wanted to talk to Jessica. She asked how George and Nat and Jacob were doing. She did not ask any questions about the *Challenge*.

Paul told her anyway. He needed someone to talk to. The keels looked good, he said. They had been beautifully cast by Keelco, in California. They made the boat look like a flying fish, he thought.

That's great, Ashley said.

She came back to French Harbor toward the final phase of construction. She went straight to her house, Jack's house. Paul did not even know she was back until he spotted her the next day, exercising one of the Arabs on a field below the sawmill.

When he got home that night he found she had come to collect

Jacob and take Jessica to Amesboro for an ice-cream sundae. The note she left said she needed time to sort things out. Just her and the cat.

Paul was annoyed she could not take the time to come see him, but the anger brought its own relief; here, at least, were the wages of infatuation; here was some kind of ending to the lack of direction in their relationship.

Catching sight of her on that hillside—hair loose, back straight, wide shoulders wrestling with the reins as her horse took out his neglect on the rider—he had seen her again as separate, a being apart, the skeins of her life no longer tangled with his own.

She came back to his bed five days later, and several times after that. The nights together were wistful rather than sweet. They warmed the body and little else. Behind the inevitable insult, their affair was dying, starved of purpose. When the anger subsided, Paul found he could work better with this knowledge.

☰

One day Ashley drove into the yard and announced she was leaving for New York, for three weeks this time, maybe longer, she wasn't sure. Paul had plenty of spare time to argue with her.

"It's no good, Paul," she said. "I knew it would be a mistake, saying good-bye."

"You've done it, though," Paul replied. "You can't just drive off now."

"It's easier this way."

"It's never easier to leave things hanging. They always come back later. In the dark, usually."

He was standing just inside the gate, freezing his palms on the car door. The gate guard watched them curiously, but the wind bouncing around the yard made eavesdropping impossible. Jacob put two paws on the window and gave his long, deep yowl.

"You're taking him?"

"Of course."

"But he hates New York. It makes him puke."

Ashley shrugged.

"Look," Paul urged. "Take the day. We'll go to Sancastin Pond. No questions, no promises. No talk, even, if you don't want."

"But why," she protested. "I don't see the point."

"Because it never hurts to round things off," Paul said. "Because it doesn't hurt to finish things with a little style."

She looked at him, and the light changed colors in her eyes.

"No questions?"

"No questions."

"I guess I could put everything back a day," she said.

Paul told Ashley to drop off Jacob and meet him at the pond. He picked up his ice-fishing equipment. He bought live minnows at Hallett's store. He got Abbie, at the Diner, to make up some bacon, lettuce, and tomato sandwiches and coffee. Finally he took Bull's iceboat out of his boat house and trailered it over to the pond.

The ice was good, for early March. There had been a week's thaw after the big blizzard. The water refroze afterward, fairly clean in the middle. Since then wind had swept the ice free of all but the biggest drifts and the smallest dustings of snow. It blew well now, maybe twenty knots from the Amesboro side.

He had the iceboat set up by the time her German sports car pulled into the town landing. She wore a thick raccoon coat and a rabbit's fur hat, so she probably had known what he was up to. She shook her head nevertheless and said, "I might have known," as she clambered aboard.

The iceboat was an elegant, sledlike contraption of weathered hardwood and cast iron with a tall mast and long, flexible runners that could be steered from a platform aft. Paul hauled the sail up. The iceboat jerked and shuddered. The sail filled with a bang and they began to move. The runners made a hard "kriss" sound on the ice. Paul aimed for the channel marking the narrowest part of the pond's hourglass shape. He let the sail out, pulled the tiller left. They were going fifteen miles per hour before they were even out of the cove. By the time they'd got any distance from shore they were doing close to twenty-five. The entire skeleton of the craft shuddered and shook as they flew over the rough black ice. Paul did his best to avoid the large drifts. One almost sent them airborne. Snow broke over their iceboat like heavy seas going over a ship's bow.

Paul let her rip through the bottleneck in the pond's center. With a basis for comparison their speed seemed to double, the trees and rocks blurring on either side, the needle wind of their passage making them cry. "Jesus," Ashley yelled, "slow this thing down," but she was laughing as she said it, a laugh stretched with the fear of it and the hardness of the winter light.

Ice fishermen favored the northern end of the pond. They sat in little huts built on runners. Some of them even had tiny cast-iron stoves built in, so they could spend the whole day away from home and the wife and all the pickled staleness that was fermented to bursting point by early March. The men raised pint bottles in silent toast as Paul and Ashley flashed by.

After a few more tacks Paul brought the iceboat into the wind in a clear stretch toward the middle of the north pond. He applied the brakes, let go the sail. He put on his skates and took out a large bit-brace and drilled three wide holes at intervals along the ice. The covering was sixteen inches thick. In the holes, the water looked like black bile.

He baited the lines with live minnows. He dug the tip-ups into the ice. These were little catch-and-lever mechanisms that popped tiny red flags when something pulled at the end of the line. He ran the lines over the catch of the tip-ups.

They huddled under the loose sail, out of the wind, and ate lunch with mittens on. The BLT sandwiches tasted very good, Paul thought; the bacon was full of savory flavors, the tomatoes tasted almost fresh. Mayonnaise and tomato juices dribbled on Ashley's raccoon fur. It was twenty-four degrees Fahrenheit. Shafts of sunshine made the lake gleam like jewels. The trees around looked like lace, but the flatness of the light also gave the snow and ice a rock-solid quality, casting doubt on spring's ability to shift their mass. Clouds coming in from the west, too, looked so heavy it seemed they must settle on the heads of those still basking in the timid sunshine.

"There's something so, sort of, pure about winters here," Ashley said. Excitement had gone from her voice; a certain nostalgia had replaced it. "It's scary, but—I don't know—uplifting? It makes me want to dress up in broadcloth and sing Old Hundred." She offered her cup with two mittened hands and Paul filled it with rum from the flask and steam and coffee from the thermos. He watched her remove a mitten and fish a container of capsules from her coat pocket.

"It's like pure alcohol—pure anything, I guess," Paul said. His eyes were on the pills. "Uplifting, so long as it doesn't kill you."

"I wish," she said, "you wouldn't look at me like that. They're not strong or anything."

He turned his head away.

She flung the bottle of pills from her. The capsules scattered on the ice, dozens of them, shiny red and white. They looked ridiculous, cheerful, like children's marbles agains the black-veined surface.

"I can't take it, Paul," she yelled. "I can't take the goddamn cleanness of it. I made a mistake coming back here. I made a mistake with Jack. Now I see it. You, too. Every minute I spend with you is another mistake."

He scanned around him, but all three tip-ups were still untripped. No fish had scarfed the sleepy minnows finning in the dark below, the hook burning sharp under their dorsals.

"It took me long enough. To see. I can't think down here. In New York my mind is more clear."

She took a handkerchief and wiped her mouth, then poked loose strands back under the rabbit hat. Her eyes shone, but not with tears. She looked at the tree line, unfocused.

"I was so young when I met him," she went on. "He was the first man with any, like, integrity . . . the first one like that I ever cared for, in New York. So different from most of them. He was going to do wonderful things. He was going to do them without screwing people. You know how unusual that is? He was how I remembered my grandfather as being." She chuckled, without humor. "When Jack brought me up here, I thought I had got religion. Jesus Christ," she added, "you caught a fish."

Paul skated over to where the tip-up's little red flag shone against the fractured surface. Without thinking, without responding or deferring to the wriggle and strike of life on the other end, he reeled in the handline, pulling a spray of furiously shaking scales from the safety of the hole.

"A pickerel," he announced, bringing it over to the iceboat. "Maybe a pound." He took the hook out of its mouth and laid the fish on the ice. It flipped twice, then lay immobile, looking wide at the sky, gills sucking at the poison air.

"You're going to eat it," she said, "aren't you."

"They're good," Paul said. "We were lucky to get one so quick."

Ashley looked at him squarely.

"I wasn't going to come back," she said. "I was leaving for good, this morning."

"I know," Paul said.

She got up and scooped the fish with both hands. It jerked out of her grasp, fell on the ice. She retrieved it, holding it firmly but carefully around the middle. Then she walked, very delicately so as not to slip, over to the hole and the sprung tip-up.

She fed the fish, headfirst, into the slushy water. It sank without moving for a second or more. Finally, with a brief flash of tail, it became part of the blackness again.

She came back and kneeled next to Paul on the iceboat's deck.

"I'm not strong enough," she said. "I was brought up with defenses. There's not enough of them around here. There's no movies and concerts to keep me from getting obsessed with myself and my problems. There's no toys to distract me from the woods and the cold. All the way from the North Pole, that cold. I tried my best, and now I know I can't do it.

"I don't care about Jack anymore," she continued. "He's dead. I can't change that. I don't care about his boat. I'm cold to the bones, and I want to go home."

Paul looked across the ice, where a second tip-up had flipped. He hoped the same pickerel had not so soon forgot its lesson of fear and pain to respond instead to the hunger in its gut.

He looked back at Ashley, and felt a sudden fierce pang of missing her. Though she knelt only two feet away, it was as if she was already gone. She'd been gone for a long time, he realized, and tried not to feel sorry for himself.

"Come on," he said. "Help me rescue that other fish, and we'll go back."

"Paul—"

"Forget it," he said, and skated over to the other fishing holes, making wide, graceful sweeps with his blades.

☷

The last work on the *Challenge* was completed in early April. They trucked her down to Newport and launched her in the same week. Paul went with the boat.

Ashley flew up from New York to smash a bottle of Rhode Island sparkling wine on the bow for the TV cameras. Channel 10 translated her into a graceful bird in turquoise and blond plumage.

On the evening news only she, and the elegant silver hull, stood out among the drab Merton wool, the Irish walking hats of guests assembled under the drizzled rooftops of Newport.

She stayed at the reception for less than fifteen minutes, touched Paul's arm with her hand and his mouth with her cheek, and was gone, south, to be with her kind until summer came again.

On the day of the *Challenge*'s first sea trial Paul left the crew house in the south end of Newport and went early to the Williams and Manchester yard, where the boat was being prepared.

He presented his identity card—bar-coded like a supermarket commodity—to a guard who knew perfectly well who he was but pulled the card through an electronic verifier anyway. Then he walked back and forth on the dock across from the big travel lift, watching the crew get the Twelve ready for sea.

It was more like a military operation than a sporting event. Thirty-six men, two semiarticulated trucks, a pickup, three forklifts, a travel lift, a crane, and two vans were required to keep the operation running smoothly. This morning, everything and everybody were working overtime.

The focus of all the effort waited patiently, stirring a little against the shallow, wind-driven chop. The pier she was in had a wire-mesh gate enclosing it. The gate extended from the harbor bottom to five feet above high-tide mark, to protect the secret keels from spying divers. Its mesh was electrified, a painful but not lethal charge, unless you were a fish. The gate smelled constantly from the small fish it electrocuted.

As if this were not enough, a series of green tarpaulins, weighted at the bottom, hung around her waterline like a Victorian petticoat. And the keels themselves were painted in camouflage patterns, to further elude detection.

Once Paul might have laughed at the security overkill. Now he took it for granted, squinting his eyes to picture the hull without its modesty skirt.

The mast towered, impossibly high. Winches and wheels gleamed like jewelry. The hull seemed to taper way too narrowly to carry that pressure of sailcloth. Every line, every curve slotted neatly into the pattern burned in his mind from the days and nights spent revising and recorrecting her plans. He found himself wishing hard. Go, girl. Do Jack proud. Do it for Ashley. For Maine. The fingers on both hands were crossed, like a schoolboy's.

Paul caught himself, embarrassed, and straightened his fingers, wondering what had happened to him that he could get so involved in a style of boat he did not basically agree with. He supposed it was like becoming infatuated with a flashy woman whom you knew was not your type; but her moves were so full of style, and her curves so perfect, that just by breathing she slapped at mediocrity, and made you wish her luck in all her endeavors.

There was something else, too. With Ashley gone, the *Challenge* had become his last link with Jack. This was the last project connecting him with the mind and work of his cousin. When the *Challenge* was gone, Jack would disappear as well, and with Jack would go his old life, the life of Suzanne and Nicole, of long summers and easy sleep.

A limousine drove into the middle of Paul's musings and parked by the sail trailer.

The guard checked a list and saluted. The chauffeur opened the back. Shoop appeared in the full splendor of the outdoors look currently fashionable in New York City. Three-tone sweater, windbreaker pants, Breton fisherman's boots. Munoz, Baldwin, and Hillman followed, all dressed in "Challenge" rain gear.

A second, smaller limousine of European make drove in on the heels of the first. Sam Lightoller emerged in a green loden coat and blinked around in the false confusion he affected. Two men with duffle coats sporting yacht club badges stepped out behind him. Lightoller waved in Paul's direction. Paul nodded back. He had not seen the old man since the fracas at the New York Yacht Club. It seemed like years ago.

Hillman and Queegie Hopkins consulted for a minute. The sun of April found a chink in the clouds to bless the scene with its cheerful impotence. It flashed off Queegie's mirrored sunglasses.

"Let's get this show on the road," Hillman yelled, and waved at Paul to join them.

⚏

The tender dropped the *Challenge* a couple of miles south of the bridge.

The foredeck man slipped the tow line. The boat lost way. Queegie shouted orders. The mastman and sewerman tailed onto the mainsail halyard, the grinders ground, and a sharp flood of ultralight fabric flapped quickly up the mast, rattle-banging in the chill eight-to-ten-knot breeze coming at them from the south.

The foresail—a number two, medium-weight genoa—followed. The skipper nudged the wheel, paying off to port, feeding in 10 percent of port trim tab to give the narrow keels extra lift.

The grinders attacked their winches again, hands blurring. Dacron line spurted off the winch drum as the sheets were hauled in. The sails stopped slatting. They filled, bellied, and tightened. The Twelve-Meter hesitated; then she groaned, leaned, and started to move. The passive pitching of a drifting vessel changed, took on force and rhythm. Instead of waves playing with the hull, the hull carved through the waves, making more waves of its own. Spray crunched and hissed on either side. The wind picked up the spindrift and flung it into their faces, numbing the skin.

The digital speedometers flashed 0.70, 1.28, 1.88. The *Challenge* was sailing.

Queegie took her on a starboard tack right past Fort Wetherill. Paul stood behind him, in the after part of the cockpit with the tactician, Shoop, and Hillman. Munoz sat on the deck by the computer terminals. Lightoller and the men from the sponsoring yacht club had chosen to watch from the tender.

The helmsman snapped nonstop orders. His gloved hands caressed the huge, starboard-side wheel, easily holding the boat close to the wind to see how well the keels worked on this crucial angle of sail. Paul drowned a petty resentment; tradition had it that you gave the designer first crack at the helm. He turned to the computer terminal, flicked the "standby" switch and watched twenty-seven different sets of liquid crystal numbers fade from the deck displays.

Queegie glanced over, a frown on his face.

"Can we get a feel for her, without the numbers?" Paul asked. The skipper shrugged. It was a small concession to make.

They were in the middle of the main channel now. The wind had picked up and the boat was heeling ten, twelve degrees to port. The crew was all clawing fists and craning necks as they played the winches, adjusting the big foresail, the mainsail, and interconnecting rigging for maximum drive power. Paul kept his hands warm and his mind blank and felt the boat lift and rush through the soles of his feet.

He thought she moved well on this angle of sail, pointing as close into the wind as any Twelve he had ever heard of. He leaned over the side, to starboard, and felt a thrill of excitement. There was only flat, lacy, sliding foam where, at this speed, there should have been a swell of green water encroaching on the hull, pulling and sucking just where it started to separate from the tapered stern. He could see the starboard keel, like a bonito's fin, streaking along just under the surface. By Christ, it's working, he thought. Elation fizzed in his bloodstream.

"Hey!" someone shouted, pointing in the direction of Newport.

A small black inflatable, powered by an outboard motor, was skidding across the waves in their direction. As they watched, the craft took station behind and to the north of them. A figure in black oilskins pulled out a video camera and started filming their progress.

Queegie smiled, and raised his hand with the middle finger extended.

"I thought the tender was going to do that," Paul said, curiously.

"They're not ours," Queegie said. "They're the competition. Marblehead, by the look of it."

"And here's the chopper," someone called.

A helicopter was making slow buzzing circles around them, very high up at this point but steadily decreasing altitude.

"That's Old Glory," the helmsman said. "Fuggin' spies. They want to check out our keels. Looks like Bruce Archibald's getting nervous. Well, we won't make it easy for 'em. Ready to tack?"

"Ready," the tactician called and counted down, "four, three, two, one," in a parody of match racing. "Tack," Queegie yelled and spun the wheel to starboard.

The crew leapt smoothly into a ritual of great strength and split-second timing; a precise suite whose expression was curves and tensions and airflow; a disciplined chaos in three parts.

First, as the boat headed into the wind, the starboard trimmer eased off the line, or sheet, holding the genoa jib. He spilled wind from the sail and allowed it to shake and rattle. The port grinder threw himself into his crankshaft, supplying raw power to turn the winch drums. His face froze with effort. As always, the grinders' movements reminded Paul of monkeys thumping their abdomens to the beat of forgotten gods.

Then, the *Challenge* swung round through the eye of the wind. The port trimmer took up the slack on his winch drum. With the help of the foredeck hand he pulled the genoa across to take the wind on the other side of the boat. The main trimmer and grinder went through roughly the same process for the mainsail as the huge boom swung over the cockpit. Loose line coiled over the decks.

Finally, the great hull shuddered, followed through, taking the wind on her port side. The mainsail filled. The genoa drew taut and hard as a dancer's belly.

Queegie let her swing down at a wider angle to the wind than was necessary, to give the boat a chance to pick up speed lost in the tack. The trimmers automatically compensated, letting the sails out, a quarter, half an inch at a time.

"Give 'em some shape," Queegie called.

His order set off another rolling explosion of reflex and tendon. The tactician eased off the backstay, a stainless-steel cable that normally pulled the top of the mast toward the stern of the boat. The mast straightened, taking tension off the sail, the way loosing a bowstring took tension off a bow. Belowdecks, the sewerman stiffened the mast with a hydraulic ram. The mastman eased off on a halyard to let the mainsail come down a few inches. The main trimmer fine-tuned the traveler—where the mainsail sheeted down to the deck—then let out the sheet a fraction. Finally he adjusted the hydraulic controls to let go pressure on outhaul, downhaul, and Cunningham, three purchases that normally stretched the sail against the rigging. The tactician pulled in the leech, or back end of the sail, paradoxically slacking the center.

All of these moves cut tension at different points and caused the mainsail to belly out.

Meanwhile, the crew shifted the purchase points for the genoa, aft, and inboard. The genoa halyard was eased, and the jib took a greater camber in response.

The added curve in the sail induced a greater pressure differential around the airfoil, and the *Challenge* picked up speed. When she was going fast enough for the wind to start splitting off from the rich camber of sail, thus reducing lift and forward motion, Queegie headed back, closer to the wind.

Thereupon his crew reversed everything they had just done, pulling shape back out of both genny and mainsail, flattening them tight against the wind; playing the nineteen hundred square feet of straining Kevlar and stretched aluminum like a huge taut stringed instrument.

The entire process, from the start of the tack to the finish, took less than thirty-five seconds.

Paul looked around him. Queegie's face was set in concentration. Baldwin stared in some awe at the channeled frenzy around him. Shoop was impassive, but his eyes checked everything. Munoz was scratching his chin and looking hard at nothing. His face bore an unhealthy yellow tint.

Queegie told Hillman and Shoop to move farther forward, they were crowding him. The cabin cruiser came close for the benefit of their own video man, filming from the flying bridge.

The inflatable kept station on the other side, filming for rivals.

After half an hour of tacking and beating, Queegie stepped aside and gave Paul the wheel.

Paul held her on course for a few minutes, letting himself get used to the feel of steering.

She felt heavy and momentous, he thought, although he knew this was normal for a Twelve-Meter.

When he tacked her round she came easily into the wind and slipped onto her new course with a minimum of fuss. The twin keels seemed to give her good maneuverability. Her smallish size allowed her to accelerate well. She settled right down to work, squeezing profit from the rigid margins she played on. Paul felt this boat was moving faster than Twelve-Meters had a right to go on this point of sailing.

Now he asked for the instruments. The tactician switched on the computer and the repeaters glowed into life.

08.21, the speed-over-water read. 08.18, 08.11. The navigator punched some buttons on the computer. "Head down three degrees, to 192," he called. "Optimum course for this wind."

Paul checked the compass, nudged the wheel to port and the numbers on the instruments crept up again. 08.20, 08.48, 08.93. "Goddamn," the tactician yelled, "Goddamn!" Very few Twelves could match that speed on a beat under these conditions. In his mind's eye Paul saw wings spread from this boat, pinions golden in the sun; saw her soar before the other challengers, smashing the French boat with strong beats of her Kevlar feathers.

He held her hard on her optimum course for a while, but they were pushing the limits of the channel.

Queegie took over and paid off onto a broad reach. Word of the good numbers spread quickly. The tactician got into a racing mode, peering around for wind shifts. The navigator mixed data into speed profiles in his computer. Excited chatter drifted back from the foredeck. One of the crew pulled out a thermos of hot chocolate and a bagful of soft chocolate-chip cookies. The Old Glory helicopter swung close, and even Queegie waved cheerfully.

The wind picked up again as they came out in the middle of the bay. Now the boat was running with the wind aft and to one side. Paul nibbled at a cookie and gazed at the digital repeaters lining the cockpit. True wind heading, apparent wind heading, apparent wind speed at ten-foot intervals up the mast, for the wind blew harder the higher you went, and the sails must be twisted to match. He was expecting the speed numbers to climb even more, because this was the fastest point of sailing for any boat. In fact they changed quickly at first, the glaring orange bars flipping insanely in decimals of decimals—but then they slowed and stalled, stubbornly, back and forth around 8.97, 9.03 knots, which was faster than when they were heading close to the wind, but not as much faster as it should have been.

Queegie swung her from a beam reach, with the wind on her side, to a broad reach, the wind coming from astern, then back again.

The tactician put more tension on the jackstay to ease the mast's sideways bend.

There was a rip and a ricocheting noise. The four-inch stainless-steel block where the backstay was fastened to the deck broke off, leaving a jagged metal strip in the fiberglass. The fitting zinged into the air, missing Shoop's head by less than a foot, and bounced off a mast spreader sixty feet above. It fell back to deck, narrowly missing the mastman, and swung to and fro on its nickel-alloy cable.

Queegie screamed at the absent boatyard men. The bowman caught the loose cable and made it fast, then went back to his position. No one else said anything. Accidents were bound to happen on a machine whose rigging commonly bore strains of over six thousand pounds per square inch.

Shoop's expression was thoughtful. Paul had the distinct impression the financier did not care for sailing. Paul looked at the wake curving in a series of boiling white Vs that spread from the stern and climbed the following waves, but there was nothing he could pick out in the signs of *Challenge*'s passage that could account for what she was not doing downwind.

"There's something screwy going on here," the navigator remarked. "We should be going faster."

"What the hell's happening, Gary," the tactician asked.

"I don't know," Queegie replied. "Maybe we should have got a real designer to do this boat." Then he heaped abuse on Brian Duffy for letting water get into the hole where the fitting had been.

The crew's high spirits evaporated as they became conscious of the mood around the wheels.

Duffy came aft to plug the hole with a piece of nylon. His face was very white, but he managed a strained smile when Paul helped him glue the patch on. "She sent a letter, this time," he whispered while Queegie was yelling at the trimmers.

"What?"

"Jenny Crooke. His girlfriend." He jerked a thumb at the helm.

"Oh." Paul vaguely remembered—a woman who skippered Trans-Pacific yachts.

"Three weeks ago," Duffy continued. "Told him she had another job, for five months this time. Head boat. Doesn't want to see him. He's been even worse asshole 'n usual."

Paul grunted. He was trying to understand what had changed in the boat's performance and had no time for Duffy's gossip.

Munoz decided he was too cold and asked to be transferred to the tender.

Queegie used the opportunity to call for a mainsail change. Queegie was the East Coast director for South Sails, and believed, with some justification, that the solution to all performance problems lay in rejigging sail designs. He argued, loudly, about the shape of the main with Steve, the tactician, who ran a loft in Marblehead for the Apex Sail Company.

Steve called up a computer model that gave you the shape your sail should assume for maximum speed when you fed in the conditions of wind, course, and sea state.

Shoop interrupted to ask, with uncharacteristic diffidence, if he could try the helm. Queegie obviously wanted to refuse, but he was a professional amateur sailor, and therefore supremely aware of the importance of pleasing sponsors whenever possible. With Shoop at the wheel, they angled off downwind from the tender on a mildly erratic course.

Everyone was careful not to smile or bitch, although the crew had to adjust the sails constantly to correct the inexpert helmsmanship. Queegie growled some advice, and in a surprisingly short time Shoop seemed to get the hang of it. At any rate the course grew less curvy, and Queegie and Steve could get back to arguing over shape and depth and luff profiles, waving at the sky for testimony.

Hillman caught Paul's eye and winked.

"We'll get it right, mate," he said, and gave the thumbs-up sign.

Paul stared at him. He had not thought the syndicate manager capable of feelings that went against the prevailing mood.

Then he leaned dangerously over different parts of the hull, looking for symptoms, in the splurting water, of a disease not borne by air.

He found nothing. The pattern of the boat's wake was standard. A boat would create waves whose length and frequency increased as a direct ratio of the boat's speed. On this angle of sail, the twin keels lay too deep to have any effect on the waves, and they surged along the hull in all the usual places.

The circular rings on the ends of both keels were supposed to add extra lift when the wind was behind them, reducing the boat's effective weight, adding speed. It had worked on the computer models, it had worked in the test tank.

Paul remembered it took weeks, months, of sailing and testing; of changing sails and retuning the rigging; of experimenting with different rudders, ballasts, keels, even, before you could gain a fair appreciation of how fast a full-size Twelve-Meter would go.

Paul ached for Jack's boat to be superlative, to live up to the affection for his cousin still living in his brain circuits.

But as the day wore on the black conviction did not go away. In fact it grew, and metastatized, deep in the gut, in that seat-of-the-pants place where instinct lived and made connections among unconscious data.

It was not the sails, though improvements in the boat's "engines" were bound to help the overall performance.

It was not something you could change by altering the rudder configuration.

The boat felt wrong, had felt wrong from the very beginning. The entire concept was off base. The margins were too narrow. He had been a fool to go along with it.

The *Challenge* was a dog downwind.

The sun was long hidden behind a cloud bank. The inflatable and the chopper had left with it, as if smelling disaster. The wind turned colder, making his eyes water. Leaning against the port trimmer's station, Paul pulled his windbreaker tighter around his body. He was sleeping two nights out of three now but last night was not one of the good ones and the wind sucked warmth from him. He turned to look at the wake again, still hoping against hope.

There was something different in the shape of the wake, in the feel of the boat. The wake was almost straight now, and the *Challenge* responded with all the strength she could muster, pounding along on a beam reach at an indifferent 8.6 or 8.7 knots while Queegie played with the rigging.

Paul realized the change had nothing to do with any basic strengths or flaws, but rather with the hand that held the wheel.

Shoop was learning how to steer.

Paul looked at the financier. The man did not notice him. He was staring at the gray sea horizon and smiling, vaguely, at nothing in particular.

Paul smiled in empathy, despite himself. But the implications of the boat's performance did not leave his mind, and pretty soon his smile dwindled and disappeared as if it had never been.

CHAPTER 23

Halligan's was just far enough away from Thames Street to provide sanctuary from the college kids looking for beach jobs at the end of April.

It lay far enough from Bellevue Avenue to elude the blue-haired matrons looking for a glimpse of Newport socialites behind the mansion shutters. The Nikon-ridden Japanese never found it; even the Twelve-Meter buffs, primed by burgeoning press coverage of the three Twelve-Meter campaigns that, with the advent of spring, now used Newport as a training base, rarely strayed so far from the fern bars, the "nautical" knickknacks, the brick condos of Bannister Wharf.

The street Halligan's stood on was a stranger to renovation chic. It ran at right angles to the waterfront, as if to disassociate itself from the hoopla. Peeling clapboards, telephone poles, fire hydrants were its habitat.

There was a long, brown room that, even at night, seemed always darker than the outside, so customers always left blinking at closing time. Sawdust covered the floor and specials covered a blackboard on the wall. A bar counter ran under fans and poker lights down the entire left side to a pool table at the far end. Sagging partitions, huge air conditioners, jukeboxes broke the other wall.

The bar room smelled of beer and urinals with an odd undertone of garlic. The paneling was real oak, scrolled, cracked, black with age and tobacco smoke. Paul Briggs felt most comfortable here, in the far corner booth that he had come to view as his personal territory.

Five weeks had passed since the first sea trial. Paul had gone back and forth to Maine several times to sign checks, to see Jessica, but the brunt of the interval was spent at Williams and Manchester, supervising surgery on the *Challenge*'s design. Altered sails. The mast stepped forward three inches. Dagger rudder, twin rudders, two new keels (eighteen thousand apiece), the rings replaced with little winglets to kill tip vortex. Alterations made one at a time, so that each change provided a benchmark for the next. They cleaned the bottoms regularly, rotated sails and crews to cancel outside factors. Nothing helped.

As the interventions grew more and more desperate, so Paul spent proportionately more time at this table, drinking ice-cold draft and the spicy hot brandy toddies that were one of Halligan's specialties. Hillman knew to phone here if Paul was needed.

Paul put down the issue of *Yachts* he'd been trying, unsuccessfully, to read. He lifted two fingers.

Sean did not acknowledge him, but finished his crossword entry without haste. He took a bowl of cold, boiled, blue-crab claws from the icebox and placed it on a tray. He added a hammer and two glasses, bringing the lot to Paul's table at a pace well suited to mourning.

Today had been the worst. Today they tried all the best features together: the recut sails, the dagger rudder, the rotating mast, even the old ring keels, which proved faster, or less slow, than the wingtips.

The results were roughly the same. The *Challenge* would compete with any Twelve in the world heading close to the wind on a beat, but when it came to running a course with the wind abeam or astern, she was consistently lousy.

Today, even the trial boat had nipped her twice downwind. The *Valiant*, an unsuccessful contender to defend the cup six years before, had overtaken the revolutionary boat. To add insult to injury, a rank amateur steered the *Valiant* on that last leg. Cy Shoop had exercised his prerogative as money-man to take a spell at the wheel. His grin was visible across the sixty feet of Narragansett Sound separating the boats when he reached the downwind mark ahead of them.

When they got back to the boatyard Shoop disappeared. An hour later, Hillman announced the syndicate was being dissolved.

Paul finished half his beer in one long swallow. He picked up the hammer, laid three crab claws on the heavy pine, and cracked the shells between each joint. The hard, humid crunches punctuated the hard realizations he had made in this bar, with no company but cold beer, Sean Halligan, and a couple of professional drinkers who called Halligan's home.

Crunch.

You could not design a boat by machine. All the computer models in the world, all the test-tank runs would not guarantee how a full-sized Twelve-Meter would perform. The reason lay in the old problem of naval architecture. No one had yet figured out all the variables in a sailing boat's movement through air and water and the foamy interface between. Until they did, there would be chinks in the best software, the most precise tank techniques.

Crunch. Paul was hitting too hard. Brine and bits of crab cartilage splashed onto his eyebrows.

Crunch. The *Challenge* had been a superboat in test conditions, but she had slipped through the chinks.

Crunch. The only sure way to get a fast Twelve-Meter was to spend twenty-five million dollars, obtain all the data on the fastest Twelve-Meters that had gone before, isolate the best features and build five full-size boats in succession, each different in one crucial way from the others. Which was what Conner had done, basically, in '86.

Crunch. In his frustration, Paul had smashed the claws to bits. He picked some of the sweet white flesh from the splinters of carapace and washed it down with beer.

He shoved *Yachts* to one side, so it would not get soaked with crab juice. It slipped to the floor, flopped open to a picture of a bearded man in a green watch cap. Paul recognized his face.

It was Joe McMurdo. One of the only yacht racers Paul truly respected.

McMurdo had won the single-handed Trans-Atlantic race twice, and the Southern Ocean Racing Conference trophy twice. He had also sailed closer to the North Pole than anyone had ever gone in a sailing vessel. Then he retired from the yachting scene. Rumor placed him on St. Lucia, drinking heavily, living with a girl from New Zealand. For no real reason Paul picked up the magazine, scanned the interview. A sense of déjà vu made him read the end.

YACHTS—So we come to the big question. What do you think has changed in yacht racing?

McMURDO—The trouble with racing is what's the trouble with the country. Reality is always that people follow where the majority goes, which is usually where big money says to. But at least there used to be an ideal of individualism, personal ethics, you know what I mean? And that ideal, you found it in a lot of racing people.

YACHTS—But not now?

McMURDO—Not now. Now you no longer even have the ideal. Big money took over and made a new ideal, which is partly business ethics, and partly the Pentagon ethic, and partly born-again fundamentalism, and mostly professional athletics. It's the ethic of belief, instead of the ethic of searching. It's the ideal of being a cog in a machine— sorry?

YACHTS—I was saying, you sound like you've thought a lot about this.

McMURDO—I have. I was saying it's the ideal of giving yourself up to a team. It means working for a large organization that exists only to win. No matter what. It means losing your personhood, becoming totally specialized, a winchman, or helmsman, or whatever. And making, incidentally, a lot more money. It means becoming one dimensional, instead of three dimensional. I'm sick to death of one dimension! I'm sick of people who are only good at one or two things. See, the whole beauty of the sea is that it *is* three dimensions. It's a whole universe, a way of life. You can't be just a winchman, and be a good seaman. You have to also be a good meteorologist, oceanographer, psychologist, astronomer, mechanic, sailmaker, carpenter, naval architect, physician. . . .

YACHTS—What you're saying is, yacht racing has become a professional sport.

McMURDO—No. What I'm saying is, it used to be a way of life. Now it's just another job, another compromise, another part of the corporate rat race. . . .

Paul nodded to himself as he closed the magazine.

McMurdo's words only sharpened his frustration. He had no desire to build a boat the corporate way. Until someone quantified every variable he would rely on his personal instincts in drawing boats, and to hell with the corporate approach. To hell, in fact, with the syndicates and the yacht clubs and the whole Twelve-Meter scene. He was through with compromise boats.

People would, in some measure, hold the *Challenge*'s failure against him, but he could not let that affect his life.

He got up to go to the bathroom.

If the bar was dark, the men's room was darker still. The light did not work. Stumbling around, trying to find the sink to wash crab off his hands, Paul slipped on leaked water and fell on the tiles, cracking his elbow on the sink.

The pain lanced his anger. He found a plumbing fixture with his left hand and tried to pull himself up, but seven beers and the same number of brandies had crippled his sense of balance. He ended up rotating in a crouch, one ankle bent, to crash into the wall again, to collapse on the floor.

The drink, the darkness, the ignominy of his position burst what bubbles of self-respect he had left.

Water dripped in a toilet. A car honked in the street outside.

Paul thought of his father. His old man had died angry. At the end he could not even wait to put pen to paper to rip up the projects he had not yet started. His father used gin as a poison, and the gin was kind to him in the end; it sneaked back up his throat while he was passed out and drowned him as he slept, on dry land.

Sitting in a pool of suspect water, Paul felt the self-pity come back, soft and easy, like a familiar companion who would always pay the tab and listen to your stupidest jokes.

He could construct a whole scenario. The failure of the *Challenge* would taint him with the sour smell of defeat. It would be harder to sell the French Harbor designs. Without the production craft, the family business would go back to storing the boats of summer people and repairing fishing vessels. It would wither, like the rest of the coast. Paul would end up like his grandfather, with a three-day beard, a heavy liquor bill, and a lot of unanswered questions.

Paul used both hands to get back to standing position. He found the sink. He cleaned himself, in the dark, with great care. Then he went back into the bar, carefully keeping despair locked as deep as possible beneath the false hope of brandy.

When he came into the room Paul saw a man was sitting at his booth. He lined up his walk and accelerated, ready to reassert, even in extremis, territorial claims on his favorite seat—but halfway across the floor Paul recognized the shape, the suede jacket, Shoop's way of aiming through his bifocals like a sharpshooter.

Paul rolled into his seat, using momentum to make up for coordination, but the financier was not fooled.

"You're blitzed out of your mind," Shoop remarked in a completely neutral tone as Paul sat down opposite.

Paul shrugged. He knew Shoop never socialized with the hired help unless he needed something. Paul thought about cutting the protocol and asking the man what he wanted, point-blank. But he simply could not muster the energy.

Shoop picked up an intact crab claw, looked for a way to eat it, put it down again. He took out a napkin, rubbed his hands fastidiously.

"I'm ordering food," he announced. "What would you like?"

"Not hungry," Paul muttered and drained his beer.

"You should eat," Shoop said.

"I'm fine," Paul retorted, waving for another round. "I'm drunk, mostly. It's how I want to be, today. Tomorrow, too. Next week, maybe. Food," he waved his hand, airily, "interferes with the process."

Shoop steepled his fingers. He stared through the penumbra at Paul, who matched his gaze, trying to ignore the alcohol hum in his brain.

"I must be going insane," Shoop commented, finally. "I know for a fact that you've spent the last ten days either drunk or recovering? The boat you just finished makes molasses look fast."

"Not upwind." Paul held up what looked like a couple of fingers, but he was sure he had only held up one. "Let's get our inshults—our insults, straight. The *Challenge* beats molasses, upwind.

"Anyway," Paul finished, "it wasn't my fault."

Sean came over with beer and a martini for Shoop. "Specials on the blackboard," he said, reciting them anyway in a thick Pawtucket accent. Pollock chowder with scallions and new potatoes. Herb-and-garlic pogies roasted over vine branches. Pie made of linguica sausage, white Saumur wine and shallots.

Shoop blinked again. He asked for chowder and broiled pogies. He wanted to order the same thing for Paul, but Paul, with liquor sloshing unbuffered in his stomach and the memory of Squidlips's boots coming to mind at the mere mention of the word "pogie," refused vehemently. Shoop ordered sea-clam pie for him, instead.

"Is this the way they always eat in Rhode Island?" he asked rhetorically, after Sean had left.

"Why do you say you're crazy," Paul asked, in a flat tone, to make conversation.

"Because," Shoop said. "It is nuts."

Paul raised his eyebrows.

"Investing three million bucks of my companies' money in a drunken has-been."

"That's me," Paul agreed affably, and raised his glass in a toast. "Mazeltov."

They drank in relative silence until the food arrived. The sea-clam pie consisted of many layers of sweet pastry that somehow managed to contain the meats and juices stuffed inside without losing crispness. The steam from spices and diced clams and savory sausage made Paul salivate like a dog. The pie washed down well with beer. If the soul was sick, the stomach, at least, had needs that were easy to fulfill.

Shoop burped. He licked his fingers clean of the last taste of fresh garlic and olive oil and barbecued fish. Paul grinned sourly.

"I'm quite serious, you know?" the financier said, fishing out a handkerchief.

"About what."

"How much do you think it would cost to design and build the Twelve-Meter you told me about in New York?"

"It's OK," Paul told him, kindly. "Pogies have that effect, the first time. Like Haitian zombie fish. Take two martinis and call me in the morning."

"Answer the question."

Suddenly the thought entered Paul's head that Shoop might not be talking rhetorically to make some fancy point about his losses or investments.

"Let me get this straight. You want to do this *again*? You want to build another Twelve? By yourself, without CBM?"

Shoop looked at him.

Paul tried to narrow the focus of his brain, but even with the steadying effect of food he could not do it unaided. "Brandy," he said. "I need brandy."

"Coffee," Shoop called. "Two. Make 'em strong."

"Brandy," Paul contradicted him. "Cognac, since you're paying."

"No, coffee."

"Spanish coffee," Paul offered, as a compromise. "You really must be nuts," he added, to change the subject. "Haven't you been burned enough? I know it's tax-deductible—"

"I'm not asking for judgments on my mental competence," Shoop snapped. "Answer the question."

Paul felt very thirsty. He could never get the variables straight in this condition. Still, it was important to humor people like Shoop. They might be insane. Worse, they might mean what they said.

"Seven hundred grand," he said, slowly, reluctantly. "But that's bargain basement. Cutting corners on everything. No test tank. No computers. You'd do better playing the state lottery," he said. "It's only fifty million to one, odds."

"When are the first races?"

"Next June. Eleven months, two weeks."

"Could you do it in that time? Get a plausible America's Cup challenger designed and built and sailing?"

Paul shrugged. "You could get a boat. At that price, I don't know how plausible."

Shoop pulled at his chin.

They sat in silence for seven or ten minutes. The Spanish coffees came. Paul drained his swiftly. It was a foolish move. The whipped cream seemed to react badly with the sea clams.

He stifled a belch and loosened his belt under the table.

Shoop sipped, his eyes far away. "Tell me," he said finally, "about the perfect Twelve-Meter. The one with the variable keel?"

The variable keel, Paul warned, would be extra.

How much.

Another two hundred grand. If it worked at all. They would have to bring in outside engineers. No one had ever tried it before.

"What about," Shoop asked, "what about that clause in the Twelve-Meter rules. The one that says, 'no radical innovations'?"

"That's no problem," Paul answered. "The winged keel on *Australia II*, the hydrofoils on the last *Bretagne*—those things stretched the clause so wide, it'll accept just about anything."

Shoop nodded.

"So tell me," he repeated, "about the rest of the boat."

Paul described, roughly, the boat he had mentioned in their first meeting at the CBM building, right after Jack's death. It seemed like a year ago. In the telling the boat seemed to get inside him and bring a microscopic flicker of hope in its structure. Hope diluted the despair a little. It did nothing, however, to help his stomach.

The two men sat still after Paul had finished. Shoop was calculating in his head. Paul already had forgotten what they were talking about and was concentrating increasingly on digestive steady state. His stomach was rumbling with sedition.

"You see," Shoop explained finally, "I didn't buy what Canaday was saying. So I had my research team do a little checking."

A knot of thick, blond-haired men in windbreakers bearing the logo of a rival Twelve-Meter syndicate came in, shouting and scraping chairs and ordering drinks. Paul winced inwardly.

"And I found out," Shoop held up a finger, "the great secret."

"What's that," Paul asked, because he was expected to.

"America's Cup racing," Shoop announced, "is not about charity. It's not even about sports. It's about *profit*." He used his finger to tap on the table, emphasizing his words. "Profits on that ridiculous Frobie. Sales up twelve and three-quarters percent this quarter. Sales on the 'Challenge' mainframe up seven percent. Profits on accessories. Profits on real estate. Canaday bought a half-finished tract development outside La Rochelle when they got into this. 'Cité Challenge,' he calls it. Now it's worth a third more." Shoop brought his hands down to knock the table. "You know the real reason they're quitting?"

Paul shook his head.

"Because they were careless. The computer company they bought copied somebody else's hardware. They got sued. It's going to cost 'em fifteen, twenty million. They should have stuck to jobbing, mail order. But that's neither here nor there. The point is, right now, *they're making a profit out of the America's Cup*. It's returns on advertising and PR; it's invisibles, spin-off, but it's there. What do you think about that?"

Paul swallowed hard. He needed another brandy. Shoop's words, the stress of choice implied, only made the nausea worse.

"I think that's exactly what's wrong with the whole thing," he whispered. "I think that's what happened to the *Challenge*. I think Twelve-Meters are all about profits now. The gimmicks, the top-secret keels, the wind lasers; I think all that is great public relations and it makes good media meat and it sells Frobies and computers and Swiss watches an' it makes for Twelve-Meters that are not boats anymore an' I won't do it."

But the effort of getting out the words put too much pressure on Paul's stomach. Acids rose in open revolt against the twin insults of grease and alcohol. The first heave hit him as he was lurching to his feet. He had his hand over his mouth when he reached the men's room door. He only found the sink by moving so fast that the door was still open, letting in light, when his guts came spewing out.

Paul reappeared ten minutes later. He was very pale and weak. He had a blinding headache. But he felt better, and thought clearer, than before he'd got sick. He walked up to the booth where Shoop still brooded, a large sandy-haired sphinx dominating the ruins of dinner.

Paul did not sit down this time.

"You can do this two ways," he announced. "You can try to make a profit. Cover your bets with a machine boat. Trust computer models and test tanks. Use lots of fancy gadgets, use Boeing and IBM and milk this for all the publicity you can get."

"Or?"

"Or you can do it right. You could maybe have the last America's Cup campaign where people counted a damn. You could let me build a boat that's honest, seaworthy, and pretty, and feels right in the gut. Not a computer machine, like *French Kiss*. Not a floating Lego set. A real boat. You can hire people who are sailors first and prima donnas second. You can ask normal people to take out shares. Local people. People in Maine. You won't win that way, of course, but at least you'll lose with some style."

Shoop thought about it for a minute.

"A people boat?" he said softly. "That, of course, would be the best PR gimmick of all."

"Oh, Jesus H. Christ," Paul groaned, and asked Sean for the bill.

☰

They walked down Bristol Street toward the headquarters house. Paul, weakened by throwing up as well as the depressant effects of alcohol, shivered in the night air. Shoop blinked at the street lights owlishly.

"Gipfel," he said, "a financial service company we took over last spring. I'm trying to raise capital on it, but it's got zero name-recognition. People say, 'Gipfel who?' Needs a hook, something to hang the name on. An advertising gimmick, a PR slogan. 'The Gipfel America's Cup Team.' " Shoop tried the words and liked them.

"What in hell happened to amateurs," Paul complained loudly. "It used to be just love of sailing."

"Don't knock the profits," Shoop said. "What's PR to me gives you an opportunity to crawl back out of the hole you've dug. Get your life back in balance."

"My father never crawled out of it," Paul retorted. "All he asked was to build the kind of boat he could be proud of—"

"And you can't beat that?" Shoop laughed harshly. "You're still paralyzed by that history? All that pretty talk in New York; balance, the rhythm of the sea, et cetera, that was all hot air?"

The words struck echoes in Paul's mind, jangling memories of New York, and Ashley leaning against a mantelpiece, rubbing a Chinese deer.

"I know what I can't do," Paul retorted, angrily, "and I know what I can."

"Then why don't you do it, instead of sitting around pissing and moaning?"

They walked in sandpaper silence until they got to the crew house.

"I'll give you a month," Shoop offered. "I'll pay your rate, plus expenses. You can use my facilities. I've got offices in New York, if you want. You could even use my house in Aspen if you need to get away for a while. See what you come up with. Then we'll talk again."

Paul looked at him.

"I don't get this," he said. "You're not locked into a particular design anymore. There's no particular reason to hire me. You could have any naval architect you please."

Shoop's lips bared.

"Not really," he said. "First, the top ones are all under contract. Also, they're much more expensive.

"Also," he repeated, "I still like your ideas. And last, most importantly, I've learned a vital lesson from the *Challenge*. It ain't the meat, it's the motion."

"That makes your baby want to dance," Paul said automatically. "What are you talking about."

"This is the 1980s?" Shoop continued. "It's not the product that's important, it's the process; it's the selling, not what's being sold. It's *all* PR. We've done Burke tests, focus groups, marketing surveys up to our ears. It's a sure thing. All we have to do is make sure the design is 1,000 percent secret."

"I don't follow."

"It's simple." Shoop spread his arms wide to demonstrate how simple. "We make sure nobody—and I mean *nobody*—knows how the design works out. Good or bad. At the same time we plug the daylights out of the boat in the ad campaign. If everything works right, we'll get enough investors in Gipfel, by the time of the actual races, we'll already have our money back. Don't you see? The boat's irrelevant!"

"I already told you." The anger was still there, but fatigue now made up the greater part of Paul's reaction. "I can't work on that kind of campaign."

"It's your life?" Shoop said simply and lifted his arm. "Goodnight."

A long black car pulled up by the curb. The rear door opened and Shoop got in. The door slammed. Tinted windows shut off all further communication. Paul realized the limousine must have followed them at walking pace all the way from Halligan's. He had noticed nothing.

The armies of Paul's mind had all laid down their weapons except for a small battalion of commandos who ran after the last-chance limo screaming "Wait!"

Paul found himself yelling Shoop's name. Already the car was pulling away from the curb.

He stumbled after it, knocking hard on the rear window.

☲

Paul spent the next couple of days with Shoop and a pair of lawyers, hammering out details of a new contract.

It was a tough document. It called for security around the project on the scale of a Pentagon missile site. It contained wording that allowed Shoop to break the agreement if the least detail of the new Twelve were leaked.

The only concession Paul got out of Shoop was a promise not to force anyone working on the boat to join in the marketing side of things.

But it was better than nothing.

When the contract was signed Paul went back to Maine.

He found French Harbor still groggy from winter. Even in early June, the cool sea kept the temperature below forty at night. People moved with economy, saving their strength. The oak leaves had barely cracked to take advantage of the extra sunshine.

His house smelled. The yard was gloomy. The only work was repair work and Paul had to lay five men off until July.

He tried to start the process. He tried to make some of the preliminary moves on an eventual Twelve-Meter but found he kept shifting his chair around; every corner of the design loft held a presence that watched without blinking.

Maybe it was panic, but Paul thought he would work better somewhere totally different, in a place free of memories.

So Paul swallowed what he'd regained of his pride. He took Jessica out of school early, packed up his tools and the data he needed. He called Shoop, to let him know, and flew to Aspen with his daughter.

CHAPTER 24

For the second time in three years, Paul took the instruments from their case and laid them neatly in a row on the great round table.

The tracing paper lay, terrifying, before him. He had tacked it, flat and ready, to the table. Its absolute blankness implied the possibility of perfection. The possibility of perfection made all men cowards.

Paul looked away at the round room with its spiral staircase and circular windows. The largest window framed a view of Ajax Mountain and the pastel-brick bristle of village stretched at its feet.

Shoop's house was a large stucco ranch house in the Spanish style with arches and courtyards and a round tower. It lay halfway up Red Mountain between a mansion belonging to a movie star and a "Swiss" chalet occupied by a corporate lawyer.

The house had been built for a prince of the Gulf; it featured bullet-proof steel blinds that could be lowered in three seconds to cover the picture windows. Roof and floors were covered in red tiles. There were huge fireplaces and Navajo "rugs." Colorful mobiles hung from the ceilings and stabiles rose to meet them.

The office was in the tower. A Santa Fe decorator had decided that since the tower was round, everything it contained should curve as well. The Japanese lamps, even the mobile suspended from the beams, were organic in shape. The salmon-colored walls heightened the illusion of living inside a seashell.

Only Paul's equipment and the stereo system—racks of compact-disc players, woofers, and tweeters—brought right angles to the scene to relieve the brain's left side and cut the curse of curves with Western measurement.

Now Paul forsook his tools. He got a cup of espresso coffee from the kitchen, brewing it in a copper machine whose size, pipes, and decorations make it look like a fascist monument. He resisted the temptation to put rum in it. He went back to the tower.

He shuffled through a stack of digital discs. They were all opera: Wagner, Puccini, Verdi, Bizet, Mozart. Paul, thinking of the scene where Don Juan sold his soul for an idea he had of beauty, put on Mozart. The overture filled the room with structure, the antithesis of fear. Paul went back to the table.

Luckily, he thought, there was a lot of structure inherent in what he was setting out to do.

☶

Designing a Twelve-Meter from the ground up was a lot more complex than simply correcting someone else's work. Still, it was not pure creativity, unfettered imagination, either.

Rather, it was like opening a series of Chinese boxes.

Each box was a set of restrictions. It contained another box nestled snugly inside. Inside that box lay another set of restrictions, and so forth, until you reached the innermost and tiniest box and found what room was left for true change and free association.

Paul picked up a thick stack of folders in which he had collected all the relevant data.

The first and most general restrictions were set by the laws of physics themselves, the spectrum of forces ruling a sailboat's movement through two different environments at once.

Here was the domain of sail and hull forces. At this level, a Twelve-Meter was nothing more than a floating shape, squeezed like an orange pip between the various pressure differences pushing the sail and keel to the side and forward against the sea's drag.

The second range of limits was imposed by the boat's sailing environment: waves, weather, and the type of race it had to run in them.

An area where heavy winds and stiff seas were common called for one type of boat. A bay of light breezes demanded another. This was a crucial first choice to make, for a heavy-weather boat would fail miserably in light airs, and vice versa.

In much the same way, a small, nimble boat would whip a long, heavy boat on a short racecourse with many twists and turns.

Paul glanced through diagrams of the racecourse designed by the Société de Régates Rochelaises. He looked at printouts of fifty years' worth of wind data gleaned from archives and weather buoys without really seeing them.

The third, the tightest and most arbitrary box of restrictions, was the Twelve-Meter rule.

In its simple form, the rule read:

$$\frac{(L + 2d - F + Vs)}{2.37} = 12$$

What this meant, in English, was if the boat's volume (length factored against concavity under the waterline) and sail area were balanced against its freeboard (the distance between deck and waterline) then divided by a constant and restricted to limits on weight, length, and mast height, the sum should work out to twelve.

This implied, in turn, that a naval architect had to work like a juggler balancing plates on a high wire. He could not increase one variable without subtracting from another, or the entire act would unbalance and eventually collapse.

Thus, if a designer wanted a longer boat, one that would go fast in strong winds, he had to compensate, under the rule, by reducing sail area or taking fullness out of the hull shape.

If he wanted more sail, he had to make the boat shorter or take volume out of the hull. More hollowness (and thus stability) between keel and waterline meant less sail area. And so on.

Once the naval architect had taken all these factors into account, he was free to design what he wanted.

Paul stared out of the round window. Snow still hung at the peaks of the Rockies. It was quite warm outside. The cottonwoods marking the course of Roaring Fork River were dark with summer green.

He looked toward the right, toward the condomiums of Snowmass, where Jessica was spending the day riding at a place called "Moonstar Ranch."

He hoped she was having a good time.

Leporello added up Don Juan's successes. Paul went back to the weather data for La Rochelle.

A weak sea-breeze structure—warm air rising off the European continent, sucking in sea air during the afternoon and evening— conflicted with frequent frontal systems unleashing rain and strong northwesterlies on the Bay of Biscay in general and La Rochelle in particular. The data split right down the middle. Rough seas and frontal winds averaging twenty-three knots were a little more frequent in late spring and early summer. Late spring was when the Doyen-Kruyff Cup race would take place. The first America's Cup trials, to determine who would challenge the French for the America's Cup, would be held immediately afterward, in early summer.

However, the lighter sea breezes, six or seven knots in the mean, dominated slightly toward August, when the actual cup races would be held. The problem thus included a tactical element; should you design a boat for the lighter air of the America's Cup itself, running the risk of never making the finals if the heavy-air boats shut you out in the elimination series? Or should you build a strong-wind boat that might be left standing in the zephyrs of late August?

The nature of the America's Cup course itself might have swung the decision one way or another. But the Société de Régates Rochelaises had opted for the Newport-style course rather than the Fremantle; 24.3 miles around five long legs which, if anything, favored precisely the kind of long, heavy boat that might stall and wallow at this time of year. . . .

Paul had been thinking about the weather of La Rochelle, on and off, since he first decided Shoop was serious about hiring him to design the second Twelve-Meter.

He was convinced the weather and racing environment were too chancy to call.

But he could not put out of his head one stanza of an old rhyme that Jens, the cook on the *Sheba*, had liked to recite when he thought the weather was going to turn.

The rhyme went:

If it's wet from the east from Deal to Calais,
It'll blow like a bitch on the Bay of Biscay.

No matter what the sheaves of neat isobars indicated, Paul thought, the La Rochelle area had earned a reputation for strong wind among seamen.

Paul looked over the figures again. He played Don Juan once more, the side where the Don sold out to Mephistopheles. He wondered what kind of a boat Jean-Louis Plehan and Marcel Morgat were building. He decided the data called for a medium-to-heavy-weather Twelve-Meter. That decision, in turn, generated a fairly rigid set of parameters, and these he jotted down on a notepad.

A longish boat, forty-five feet at the waterline, sixty-six feet on deck. Wide, maybe thirteen feet. Medium-to-heavy displacement, around twenty-six tons. Medium sail area, seventeen hundred square feet plus. A heavy-air boat to all appearances—with one crucial difference.

Paul looked at the pencil he was using for the specs. The tip was trembling gently. A feeling of great porosity pervaded his chest. He went back to the espresso machine.

Mrs. Schultz, the housekeeper, was in the kitchen. She made him a mocha cappuccino with Dutch cocoa sprinkled on top. When he came back he dug out the scrapbook and looked over some of Herreshoff's plates again.

He unfolded his father's yellowed sketches and gazed over those lines as well.

Today, for some reason, the older boats—*Maria, Persephone, Istalena*—looked innocent, even naive. Twelve-Meters were a different game altogether.

Once again, Paul picked up a pencil. He tried to touch it to the paper. Any mark was better than blankness. Blank paper was infinite. Even a dot cut infinity by an endless amount. But he could not bring himself to mark the paper's surface.

Paul hurled the pencil across the office. It hit a mobile, which swung at the impact. His heart was racing, just as it had done when he started work on Jack's design.

The fear was still around.

He went over and picked up the pencil. He put it back on the desk. Then he leaned back in his chair and closed his eyes. It would do no good at all to panic at this stage, he thought. Despair might be called for, but it must not be courted. There was plenty of time for despair to come at its own gentle pace.

There was another good reason to take it easy. He knew from experience that fear existed only by grace of your efforts to kill it. Frontal assaults reinforced its existence, and its power.

Which left trickery. Fooling himself into ignoring it. Pretending it was not there. Forgetting the block. He should be good at that. He'd been practicing forgetting for years. . . .

⅏

In the worst days after Suzanne left he had used many different drugs to trick himself into oblivion: uppers, downers, pot, TV, rum. Anything to fill the holes, anything to avoid the not-Nicole, the not-Suzanne. Even religion.

None of the religions stuck, and few left any trace of substance in his brain. The main exception stemmed from a two-week stay in a Mertonian retreat in the Adirondacks.

It was an enormous, gloomy castle, an old hotel built of limestone. A thousand small bells rang a million silver notes in the wind. At 4:00 A.M. matins, the flagstones numbed his bare feet. The drums of dead Iroquois seemed to fill the hills. A waterfall outside filled the air with the complex thunder of rushing water.

A very young nisei priest in loose clothes told them to listen to the water until the water washed you away and left you an empty space to build on.

Then—the Japanese smiled a little as he said this—start again, from the beginning.

Outside, wind plucked softly at the stones of the tower.

Clouds broke and folded on the crystalline peaks.

Paul picked up his pencil again.

⅏

In the beginning there were perfect curves.

Like this. Without letting himself think he sketched a long shallow arc, for the deck, or sheer line.

Form.

That curve was reflected by a deeper curve beneath: a smooth, gentle slope that would gracefully accept and easily release the molecules of water moving by.

Movement. The bottom of the hull.

The two arcs blended together, smooth, elegantly raked in opposing directions.

Paul's hand drew them in with short, accurate gestures. He was amazed at how easily his fingers moved. It was as if they belonged to someone else, and he could watch them dispassionately, sketching in volumes to buoy the lines against an idea of substance.

Not too abstract.

His fingers moved faster and faster. The lines grew, flowed, blended. They seemed to have taken shape and built up in his brain so there was accumulated pressure and a feeling for space.

The sketch took on depth, and substance.

Long, lean bows, so she would go easy close-hauled, cut well through a chop. A very slow rise from the waterline both fore and aft, so any heeling would dunk the lowest overhang into the water to extend the boat's effective length and therefore her speed. A shorter keel root, to reduce wetted surface, to improve the aspect ratio. A full "bustle," or depth between keel and rudder. More beam, though. This one did not have enough beam.

Paul's hand stopped. His breathing was short and ragged, as if he had been running. He ripped the paper off the table, balled it up and threw it into the round wastebasket. Before he could worry about it he took out another piece of paper and tacked it smooth on the table. . . .

It all came down to instinct. His instinct was buried deep under unresolved absences and inactivity. It would take time to translate that instinct, so all the thousands of variables meshed and flowed and worked together perfectly.

He flipped the Mozart, picked up the pencil and sharpened it, carefully, with a razor.

At least the lines had not skidded into nothing, as they had in his abortive attempt last winter. At least they looked like a Twelve-Meter. At least he could sketch now. That was something.

If he sketched and sketched and kept on sketching, he might get to a point where the constant flow of neurons between hand and ideas zapped the self-consciousness impeding it. Then he could draw exactly what was in his dreams.

Paul began working again.
He had a whole month to get it right.

⚡

He found Mozart did not help to create the perfect lines for his Twelve-Meter. He had to go out and buy more compact discs.

Beethoven was a slight improvement. The Ninth Symphony seemed to help with the shape of the underwater stern, but he tore those drawings up as well. The sketches he did to Bach were better. In fact, he got past the level of sketches with Bach.

One day he put on *St. John's Passion*. He managed to rough out a boat that looked very like what he was looking for. It was only slightly different from the first series of sketches, but there was a little less fullness aft, though she was, in fact, slightly wider in the beam. The same fine bows, but a straighter run to the buttocks (a line running approximately lengthwise at a level between keel and waterline).

The lines seemed to hang together, balance out. Hope exploded inside him. The extent of his elation was a measure of the fear he had eluded. It kicked at his gut with all the power of a mule's hind leg.

He switched to "The Well-Tempered Klavier" for more elaborate work, determining the center of effort, the first calculations. There was an optimum mathematical ratio of width, or beam, to depth, to ensure maximum speed. There was an optimum ratio of volume to length, called the prismatic. He factored both into this hull. His brain raced with equations. His fingers could not punch the calculator fast enough. His pencils seemed to grow blunt as soon as he picked them up.

He was aware of discordant notes in the design, but reasoned he could cancel them out in the juggling necessary to fit it into the Twelve-Meter rule. He made a finished plan.

He started playing with the rule just before dinner one evening.

For this work he had chosen the Mass in B-minor, a Berlin Philharmonic recording. The surging choirs fit in with the fresh spate of confidence inside.

The planimeter showed he was going to have to take volume from the ends if he was to maintain the same sail area. He rubbed out a line on the tracing paper, bent a spline until it described the narrower shape he wanted. He anchored the curved wood with lead ducks and penciled in the new line. Jessica peered over the edge of the spiral staircase, through the circular railing. Paul, totally intent on the lines, his hearing filled with violins, did not notice her until she stood in front of his table.

He stifled an initial irritation. It was dangerous enough squeezing the right shapes from his brain without being interrupted. But she could not know that. She could never know that. He ran his fingers roughly through his hair, grabbing at the lines of normal life—braked his racing thoughts. When he spoke to her his voice was even.

"What is it, Jess."

He had to repeat the question.

"Can you read to me?" she asked finally, playing with her lower lip. A gesture of nervousness. In the new Moonstar sweatshirt and jeans, she looked older and cooler than her years.

"Not now. You know I'm busy. You know I have a lot of work to do."

The kid was looking at him very intently. Paul recognized that stare of blue. When Suzanne used it, it always spelled trouble; deep, pent-up opposition. The set of the mouth reminded him of Lucinda, as well. Jessica came by her stubbornness honestly, from both sides of the family.

"OK, Jessica. What's the problem."

She shrugged. He was going to have to dig it out of her. He could always ship her to Lucinda, he thought.

"Why don't you go read to yourself for a while. We'll go out for supper in a little bit. I'll read to you after."

She shrugged again. Paul felt his lust for the lines he'd been drawing evaporate into anger.

"Damn it!" he burst out. "I can't play with you all the time," he yelled. "Just amuse yourself for another hour, and don't interrupt me again, OK?"

The color drained from her face. She turned and half ran, half slid down the staircase, like a snake with legs, slamming the door at the bottom. Paul shoved his guilt under far deeper, far blacker anxieties. He got up to put another disc on the player. He couldn't find the record he wanted. He threw the stack of them to the floor in frustration and sorted them out on the tiles. When he returned to the table he automatically picked up a pencil, looked down at the plans. The anger had pulled him out of himself, and he saw the lines he was drawing with a fresh eye.

The shape was off. The volumes were off. They were not far wrong, but they didn't have to be. This boat was not balanced right. It was close to what he wanted—but given the delicacy of the equilibrium he sought, it might as well be a garbage scow.

His hope was a bombed-out house in a conquered city. Guilt smoked in the holes disappointment had blown. He walked among the ruins of ideas, Paul saw, leaving his daughter with strangers, or alone.

He threw his pencil across the room, as if it were poison.

Paul found himself running down the spiral staircase with all of Jessica's recklessness and none of her skill. He slipped at the bottom and nearly broke his wrist cushioning the shock. He ignored the pain, got up, and hurried off to look for his daughter.

☙

The next day, Paul decided to take time off.

It was a calculated risk.

The catalyst for the decision lay in the need to please his daughter. However, he was honest enough to admit to a stronger motivation, in that taking a couple of days off might release pressure that was interfering with his work.

So he went hiking with Jessica. He spent a lot of time in the hot tub on the terrace. He took pills so he could sleep.

When the two days were up Jessica went back to Moonstar Ranch and Paul went back to the Twelve-Meter.

He threw out all his old drawings and tacked fresh tracing paper to the table.

He sharpened all his pencils, put away the piles of figures and data.

He put Schumann on the disc player this time. The Fantasie Stücke. He knew it was a good choice when he closed his eyes for a minute and saw colored shapes come and go to the music, behind his eyelids.

He tried to make his mind blank, but the shapes were too strong. He sighed in exasperation and picked up a pencil.

The first two drawings absorbed all his nervousness. They both started off well, then went completely off base. Paul put on Schumann's concerto for piano and orchestra in A-minor and started over.

Piano and strings answered each other in counterpoint, rolling together in arpeggios, parting in andantes. Like the waves a boat made, he thought. Their wavelengths grew by five, six, seven, nine, eleven, and eleven feet with every added knot of speed, from four knots on. A one-to-one ratio rise, peaking at two-to-one; a pause; a pause; and then an even, one-to-one fall.

Maybe, Paul thought, the waves were trying to tell him something. More likely the overdose of hot tubs was addling his brain. He jotted down the progression anyway. He even began to draw on that basis.

Arpeggios and andantes.

℠

When it finally came, it came so easily Paul did not notice it.

He had gone through three or four discs of Schumann and played them all over twice.

For some reason, the music only seemed to get better and better. In between pencils, looking for a spline to get the right curve, he would jump to his feet and conduct. As the pieces grew more and more familiar it seemed he acquired power over them, bringing in cellos, kettledrums, brass sections by the magic of good timing and the sweep of a ruler. Sometimes he would burst in vocally, shouting ta-tum, ta-tum, tum TUM! to underscore just how he wanted the orchestra to play—then go back to the drawing, utterly oblivious to what he'd just done.

He was on the third replay of the A-flat symphony when there came a slow ringing noise on the metal steps of the spiral staircase.

Mrs. Schultz appeared at the opening, her broad face flushed with the effort. "Telephone," she announced. "A woman from Moonstar."

Cold claws grabbed Paul in his chest. "Jessica," he said. "What's happened?"

It was four-thirty, Mrs. Schultz continued, a disapproving tone in her voice. He had forgotten to pick up his daughter.

Paul looked around him to hide his astonishment. Seven hours had passed. He had not noticed the sun swing outside the windows to sneak up on Snowmass Mountain from behind. He checked his watch to make sure. Last of all he looked at the paper before him.

A long, sleek sailing boat lay boldly outlined on the table, in profile and cross-section.

He looked at it with no mercy in his eyes.

The lines stood up to his gaze.

Paul let it go at that. He knew only time would confirm or deny the balance of the boat he had drawn. He might look at the same drawing tomorrow and know it was dross.

He switched off the disc player, carefully locked the sketches in the office safe, and went to fetch Jessica.

The drawing stood up to his gaze the next morning and the day after that.

Paul took it slowly and did not let himself get carried away. He was careful to spend more time with his daughter, even though with the closing of the local schools Mrs. Schultz had found some girls for Jess to play with, so she was active and content, as far as Paul could tell.

Paul suspected that, if the boat were right, it would turn out to be due to paying more attention to his daughter. Not because of some higher morality, but because responding to someone else imposed an economy whose discipline bore fruits in other fields. He knew this belief was at least half superstition, but he did not care. Just as he did not care that he had used a totally irrational parallel with the progression of hull waves to find the proportions he needed. So what. He would have dissected chicken entrails if he thought it might help the boat.

The design survived the alterations it needed to conform to the Twelve-Meter rule. Another three days passed and he could look at the boat he had drawn, in all its angles, and still feel a rush of confidence for the cohesion of it; the way each line curved to meet its logical conclusion and was inevitably reflected by a line curving the other way, diagonally across the hull, in a balance that was just the right side of perfect.

Contentment, not excitement, filled his stomach, and he knew by that the fear was starting to die.

At which point he called Shoop in New York.

"We got something," he told the financier.

Shoop's voice crackled over the phone.

Paul took in the boat, pinned like a butterfly to the table. His eyes caressed her lines, taking time over each detail. The sweet hollowness between keel and waterline, like the curve of a woman between her back and her buttocks. The subtle flattening aft of the beam, in an easy swell that would seduce the water up and past the rudder. The long, lean, bow to cut the waves and counterweight the fore and aft pitching of the hull. The straight, fast buttocks lines, the low overhangs he had salvaged from earlier drawings. The elegant swoop to her deck. And, last but not least, a small keel, like a shark's fin. A keel theoretically too small for this hull; a keel that would flare and curve like the wing of a bird, lift this heavy boat, make her fly in winds she was not designed for.

Something strong stirred within him, like sap rising in an old oak, in the spring.

When Shoop hung up he dialed the number for Moonstar, to tell his daughter they were going home.

C H A P T E R 2 5

It was a different pay phone this time. One of the new kind, a little rectangular cubicle on a pole, a half-receptacle for half-conversations, with a steel counter deliberately slanted so you could rest nothing on its surface.

The man listened to the kid on the other end. The kid said a new "Challenge" group had been formed from the ashes of the old. They had hired Jack Briggs's cousin to create an entirely new Twelve-Meter.

The man covered his shock in silence.

There was no other information, the kid went on. The naval architect had gone to Colorado to work. The new syndicate seemed to be obsessed with security. They had an ex-CIA man working to make sure there were no leaks. He had compartmentalized the whole team; no one on the construction side would be told anything about the sailing, and so on. The kid did not think it worthwhile to keep up the phone calls. Maybe they could scratch their arrangement.

"No," the man told him.

"Why not?"

"Because you can still be of use."

They would keep up their contacts. Same schedule, same payments. Same sword hanging over both their heads.

The man hung up. He walked down the midtown street and turned into the entrance of a club. A liveried doorman pretended to push the revolving doors for him.

He went to the bar. The bartender mixed him a martini without words or money passing between them. When he got the drink, he retired to his usual corner and lit a cigarette.

Men in similar suits passed in and out, under the oil-painted gaze of the men in similar suits who had gone before.

The man finished his drink and his cigarette at the same time. He ordered another martini, lit another Camel. He was up to a pack a day.

It had all been for nothing. The burglary. The killing. The fire. Somehow, that emotional cripple, that cousin of Jack's had managed to stay in the running for the America's Cup. However marginally.

It should not upset him to this extent. The first *Challenge* was a dog downwind. The second, designed from keel to masthead by a man with virtually no Twelve-Meter experience, would probably be even worse.

And the yacht club probe, as predicted, had come up with precisely nothing.

Normally the environment of the clubhouse—with its coded reassurances, its implied message that any group capable of creating not only the notion of sportsmanship but the perfect martini was bound to survive and conquer forever—relaxed the man when he got in this kind of state.

But not tonight.

Tonight the news about Paul Briggs only reminded him of how vulnerable they all were to the real world; the place where lies and deceit could upset the most perfect of games.

It made him angry, sometimes. This complacency, this refusal to grasp facts. Some of his fellow clubmembers had ancestors who went down on the *Titanic* with exactly the same elegant hopelessness they themselves would display when it all came crashing down in flames around their heads.

The man got up and made a signing gesture toward the bar to

put the drinks on his bill. But Artie held up a finger and moved to the end of the counter to speak with him.

"I'm sorry, sir," he whispered. "Can't put you on tab anymore."

"Why not," the man asked, though he knew very well. He checked around the room. A couple of his fellow members were watching, motionless, like dogs catching the first flash of white underbelly.

Artie looked uncomfortable. He coughed. "I'm sure it's an oversight, sir. And when you're paid up, the committee will restore your privileges, it's automatic."

"But I told them." The man kept his voice very level. "I told them I have to stagger the payment this time."

"Yes, sir," Artie said. He'd heard it all before. The man took out his wallet, laid a ten on the counter and walked away without waiting for his change, to prove he was not that hard up. He left the club, headed downtown, smashing his fists together hard, trying to control the anger.

He would show them. In a week or two the Metropolitan Central contract would come through. Eighty grand for thirty seconds on TV; eighty grand to stand there and spout some drivel about how great Met Central was for helping America win back the cup.

And once they did win the cup, he would never have to worry about club dues again.

The man walked blindly for ten or fifteen minutes. He found himself on Forty-eighth Street before he was sure he wanted to go there.

His expensive bearskin coat brought them all out of the doorways. Slim, curved, willing. Heartbreakingly beautiful. Very young, some of them. The deep makeup only emphasized their lack of visible erosion.

Here was the real world, he thought. The place of willing victims.

The memory of another woman, very different but just as self-destructive in her own way as these girls, passed through his mind.

There was a young girl, a child really, with blond hair and long legs. She came up close to him. She wore a short skirt and an even shorter jacket and her teeth chattered over her chewing gum. Still she managed to put a fair measure of enthusiasm into the "Hi, how you doin' tonight" that was all the vice squad allowed them before they got booked for soliciting.

The memory-woman faded.

He talked quietly with the girl in the entrance to a computer supply store.

Then he followed her downtown, trying to keep anger and frustration toward the back of his mind, watching her long legs open and close, open and close, flashing like soft scissors in the darkness before him.

C H A P T E R   2 6

When Paul got back to French Harbor on June 25 he walked into an operation that was totally different from the old syndicate.

The source of this change appeared to be a sleek man in a foreign-cut suit who had taken over Paul's office at the boatyard.

The sleek man's name was Gordon Stone. He reminded Paul very much of a badger. Not so much in the stubborn sense of the comparison, but because of his small, sharp, black eyes, and the stripes of gray in the middle of his layered haircut, and his air of having more important things on his mind than whatever he was talking to you about.

Shoop had sent Stone to take charge of the security aspects of construction and design. He had already negotiated to lease the old Georgeville Clam Company spread on Sandy Cove. He had rented a former Church of the Nazarene meetinghouse and a couple of smaller houses in the same town for the crew. The idea was, the Clam Company would be a lot easier to protect.

Paul exploded when he found this out. They had agreed to find a more secure plant, he told Stone and Hillman, but nowhere was it written he would give up control of the operation to Shoop's private police. He could handle the new plant, he told Shoop's men. He could hire his own people to take care of security.

They were sitting in the design office when Paul threw his scene. Stone said nothing until Paul had finished. Then he looked carefully around the room where Jack had died.

"Your own people haven't done very well so far," he commented in a voice that held absolutely no inflection. It was the kind of voice an alien being with only a theoretical knowledge of English might use for communicating with earth. "You've had three events. Burglary, murder, arson. All unchallenged. If we don't come up with a system that I believe is 100 percent secure, fail-safe, the contract is off."

Paul bitched and moaned. He asked Hillman to intervene. Hillman refused. He called up Shoop. Shoop backed up the sleek man.

They would hire local people, Stone offered, to mollify Paul. He could even put Paul's private detective on salary to run the system Stone set up.

Paul agreed, finally. He had no choice. There was still that mortgage on the yard.

He followed Stone's advice, rented the old aquaculture plant, put John Poole in charge of moving the Twelve-Meter operation to Georgeville, and retreated behind the parameters of design.

ᗰ

Paul's formal OK to shift the Twelve-Meter operations to the clam company allowed Shoop's man to move into high gear. Without fuss, or even appearing to act much faster than anyone else, Stone initiated a storm of activity that engulfed quieter types like Warren Hillman. Little dust-devils of energy spun off the main wind and sparked movement in hitherto undreamed of quarters.

First, Stone and Hillman rehired Queegie Hopkins and what was left of the two Twelve-Meter crews. They set them up in the A-frame, and the meetinghouse.

Once the crew was rehired, Stone got to insulating all aspects of design and construction from the outside world.

He started with the clam company.

The clam-company plant consisted of a cluster of Quonset huts and work sheds on a short, sandy peninsula near Georgeville.

Stone sealed off the entire peninsula with razor wire. He mounted video cameras on telephone poles and covered every square inch of ground with their electronic focus. He made the largest Quonset airtight, put in heat and air-conditioning, welded up most of the doors, and installed electronic locks on the few that remained.

Then, at Paul's suggestion, he brought in Vanzetti.

Vanzetti's moustache was broader, his car faster, his manner more confident, if such a thing were possible. He decided Stone was CIA, and treated him with a strange mixture of respect and mistrust.

To protect the area at night, Vanzetti and Stone devised a system of parallel patrols. Two men on foot would cover the perimeter and the dock, reporting regularly by walkie-talkie. A third man, locked in the office, would monitor the TV and alarm systems and make sure the outside patrol checked in at precise intervals. There would be no other contact between inside and outside.

It was all very efficient, and basically alien to the Down East way of life.

People—mostly French Harbor people—grumbled, bitched to Abbie in the Diner. All of a sudden half the boatyard was working at the clam company. There was traffic on the Georgeville Road. Vic and Abbie's lunch business was down seventy, eighty dollars a day. Hallett's store stayed open until all hours, catering to the Twelve-Meter crowd, and the village kids were starting to hang out in front, late at night, until nine or ten, or even later.

In Georgeville, opinion was much more positive. All of a sudden there were jobs in town. Not many, and certainly not great career opportunities, but Georgeville people weren't fussy. To a village that lost its only source of salaried employment when the aquaculture company folded, back in '77, any job was a good job.

⚞

The new syndicate's wind of change blew beyond security.

Shoop's people took the classic financial structure of a Twelve-Meter syndicate and turned it on its ear.

Most Twelve-Meter campaigns were run principally as nonprofit organizations; charities, in essence, for yachtsmen. The charities were run by yacht clubs or skippers or principal sponsors. Corporations donated money to these charities and in return earned the right to trumpet their association in advertisements.

Shoop's people decided to reverse the emphasis of the money

structure. They would still run the campaign as a nonprofit corporation, soliciting tax-deductible gifts.

However, the main thrust of fund-raising would be directed at getting people to invest in a new investment plan directed at lower- and middle-income wage earners.

The investment plan—no surprises here—would be managed by Gipfel Financial Services.

This was the meat and potatoes of Shoop's earlier commitment to yachting populism. A media blitz heralded the new "Gipfel America's Cup People's Campaign." Full-page ads in major newspapers announced "You Don't Have to Be Gary Watkins to Have a Hand in Bringing the Cup Home." A thirty-second TV spot featured a video clip of the first *Challenge* and called it "A Challenger for the Ordinary Man."

The idea of the people's campaign was simple. One dollar out of every ten invested in a high-interest money-management plan would go toward subsidizing the *Challenge II* effort. In return, the investor would receive a frameable certificate proving his participation, and a proportionate number of shares in Gipfel. The assumption implicit in every ad was, the more people invested, the greater the value of the shares they received, and the greater their eventual return when the company was sold.

And, of course, the more dollars they put in, the more Gipfel could reinvest for itself, in properties with a much higher rate of return than money-management plans.

The financial press screamed foul. "A New Form of Leverage?" the *Wall Street Journal* asked rhetorically. "Sailing on Junk Shares," *Forbes Magazine* howled. But the people Gipfel was trying to reach seldom read these publications, and the Gipfel plan attracted a good number of investors.

≈

Once his initial shock was over, Paul was too busy to notice much, or care how Shoop's men were running the new campaign.

He locked himself, with his draftsmen, in the new design space of the clam company's administration building. When the design process was largely over, he moved into the main Quonset with John Poole and the carpenters and Mikey Richman's glass crew.

Seasons rolled by, did what they were supposed to do, waxed, waned, and faded. Temperatures climbed and dropped, but it was all the same in the working spaces, which had to be kept at an even temperature for the machines and materials. Paul tried to chop out a maximum of time to see Jessica, and this imposed the only structure on his life that was not related to construction deadlines.

Even so, he never saw his daughter as much as he thought she needed. During the summer he told himself he would take her on a vacation after Labor Day, when the design work was complete. After Labor Day, he promised himself a week at Thanksgiving, somewhere warm, before construction began. At Thanksgiving, he swore Christmas, and after Christmas he vowed he would take the girl skiing during February vacations. But the seasons kept changing, and the work kept piling up, and the only trip he took during that entire period was for the boat.

☰

The boat, for its part, went fairly well.

The first indication Paul might have a moderately successful design on his hands came after he had gone through the basic cycle of design, revision, and computer testing on his own, limited computer system.

After two or three cycles the figures looked good, unbelievably so, better than they had been for the first *Challenge*.

Paul did not believe a word of it. "It should be a decent, mid-to-heavy-air boat," he told Shoop, "with maybe a couple surprises from the keel. Nothing spectacular."

When the basic design work was done Shoop sent up engineers, from his "Skunkworks" to work on what the design crew called the "curvy keel."

The Skunkworks was a secret think tank in Arlington, Virginia, owned by one of Shoop's holding companies. It specialized in inventing ideas for weapons systems, then coming up with ways to put the ideas into practice. It worked exclusively for the Pentagon. It made a great deal of money for Shoop.

The engineers looked over Paul's ideas for three days. They claimed there should be no major technical difficulties. A "piece of cake," they called it. They took his drawings back to the Skunkworks and modeled them on a "Cad-Cam" imaging program.

Three weeks later an armed courier delivered a set of specs and a sample of material to French Harbor.

The plan, as modeled by the Skunkworks, called for a keel structure made of titanium alloy, with a long trim tab aft and a rounded flap on the leading edge. The titanium skeleton supported a long lead torpedo at the bottom, to lower the boat's center of gravity.

Inside the structure was a network of valves that injected or sucked hydraulic fluid. The fluid pushed or pulled a matrix of hexagonal cells outside the structure that, in turn, expanded or deflated the skin on either side of the keel.

The skin and the cells both would be made of the material in the sample. This was a synthetic substance almost as strong as steel. It was also flexible as plastic and sleek as cellophane. It was called Permutex.

By pushing the hydraulic cells out on one side of the keel, pulling them flat on the other, and angling the tabs on the sharp ends, you could curve the entire keel. In cross-section, the curve looked a lot like the wing of a bird or an airplane. Most importantly, you could curve it to the left or right (depending on which way the boat was leaning) to impart maximum lift. Because the same hydraulic mechanism was geared to both sides of the keel, an increase in volume on one side meant a decrease on the other. Thus the keel's volume did not change, and the Twelve-Meter rule was not broken.

Paul made only one model of his design, to stay within budget. He had no time to build a working model of the variable keel. Instead, the model had seven different, interchangeable fins to approximate the various configurations of the real thing.

In late September the provisional design for the new keel was approved by Lloyds and the technical committee of the Société de Régates Rochelaises, and Paul altered the computer programs to include all the variables of the changeable fin. Then he sent the data down to be formatted to the gigantic computers of the Skunkworks. He flew down to Arlington with Hillman to be present when the numbers came out.

≈

It was the first time he had seen the Skunkworks. They consisted of a very long, uninteresting metal building surrounded by shaved lawns and two sets of fences. Backlit letters on the wall spelled out "Tetra Systems Inc." Warnings by the gate stated that only authorized people were allowed in and all others would be chewed by attack dogs.

Stone met them at the gate. He had arranged identity cards, with their photos already burned into the plastic. The cards read "Authorized SECRET ONLY" in pink capitals over their names.

Once through the main gate, he avoided the big entrance, heading instead for a small side door with a red light burning over it. He stuck his own ID card in the slot, punched a code and handed a written authorization to the two plainclothes security men who opened the door.

Stone and the two guards led them down uncarpeted corridors with TV cameras at every corner. It was six-thirty in the evening but the corridors were busy. Intense navy lieutenant commanders with glasses and black briefcases bustled in and out. The PA system paged colonels and captains. An endless plate-glass window afforded a view of eight or nine mainframes, arranged in star patterns, each eight feet high and six or seven deep. The machines sat impassively in the cold neon. A small figure in a full space suit loaded and removed tapes.

"Latest model Crays," Stone said over his shoulder. "A half-billion operations a second. We're going over here," he added, pointing out a windowless conference room where three large computer terminals, with corresponding printers and shredders, lorded it over the usual folding tables, water carafes, and waste baskets.

They waited for ten minutes while a team of Air Force officers cleared their operations from the terminals.

"We're sneaking this in," Stone whispered as they waited. "The National Reconnaissance Office bought the entire week of computer time; but then again, since the NRO isn't supposed to exist, there shouldn't be a problem. Right?"

It was the closest Stone had ever come to a joke.

The Air Force team gave up the conference room. A large man with muttonchop whiskers and ballpoint stains on his lips fed in the program, whistling through his teeth.

"The biggest problem was adapting the lines-processing program from the Orion subs to sailboats," he commented as he worked. "What a bitch," he laughed, clicking the terminal keys. "But we added a lot of free analysis on inertia and acceleration. And we built in a new wave-simulation package, got it from some whiz kid at Cal Tech, based on fractal progressions. You wouldn't believe how good that is. We looped the test-tank figures right back into the last cycle. I think you'll like our results."

The screens on all three terminals flashed. Stone ran his ID card through a verifier on the side of the terminals. "I had to get you all cleared for his," he said, looking at Hillman and Paul, "with Pentagon liaison. Hope it's worth it."

As he spoke a schematic of an aircraft appeared on the screen. It looked like a long skateboard, with four very fine wings and detachable engines swept well up and forward. "Trans-atmospheric observation vehicle, H-prop, NRO N-12582," the legend read.

The fat man lunged with incredible speed for his girth. He hit a key and the diagram vanished. When he turned his face was pink from embarrassment.

"You didn't see that," he told them. "Some jerk didn't clear the terminal right. Now I gotta enter that in the log, and somebody's gonna catch hell for it, and it ain't gonna be me, I can tell you."

He punched another sequence of keys, muttering as codes rose and fell on the screen. Then, quite suddenly, a 3-D profile of Paul's Twelve appeared, in bright cobalt lines on a black background.

The hull was sectioned into thousands of different rectangles, or "panels." What the computer did, the fat man announced, was analyze the hydrodynamics of each separate panel for each separate condition of wind and wave, then put it all together into a composite analysis of how the hull would perform as a whole.

"We've already done all the calculations," the fat man said proudly. "We're just feeding in the results slowly, so you can absorb them." Paul realized that by "we," the programmer was referring to the computers. When he said "you," he meant his visitors, and by extension, humanity in general.

The Twelve, still in bright blue, revolved around two separate axes, making complex 3-D shapes as its lines crossed and folded, then disappeared. A mast and sails leaped on the screen and went through the same pirouettes. Then, hull and sails together.

"OK," the fat man said, "pay attention. We're gonna run through different wind speeds, sea states, and apparent wind angles. The green lines show lift. The red ones are coefficients of drag. The numbers will show up underneath. Ready?"

He hit a key.

The new *Challenge* appeared, fully rigged, in the same unearthly blue. She stayed static for five seconds. Then an electronic wind sprang up. A sea of neurons flowed past her hull. Hundreds of thin, wavering green lines mounted around the forward part of her sails and hull. Varying shades of red built up at the after ends.

The boat shifted, jerkily, around 360 degrees. The colors deepened, lightened. The numbers changed. The boat vanished, and reappeared. "Three knots," the fat man said. "Sea state two."

They went through the spectrum of winds. Paul watched the numbers intently, trying to keep himself from growing too unhappy as the optimum speeds went from low to average in light wind.

Trying to keep his heart from pounding as the wind rose and the speeds got better, to where she was consistently picking up 0.07, 0.09, 0.12 knots sometimes from all the Twelve-Meters whose speeds and performance had become the data base of this computer program.

"Good work, Jim," Stone told the programmer, as if the real achievement were the software. Hillman said, "Not too shabby."

The computer winds ran to thirty knots and stopped.

"So that's with the keel flat," the fat man said. "Now we run it through again with the keel curved."

The boats appeared, shifted, vanished. There was little change in the first numbers. At 3.5 knots Paul saw the *Challenge* was still uncompetitive. It would be wiped out by a lighter boat.

At four knots of wind he noticed a quiver in the figures. An extra 0.4 with the breeze aft.

At five knots of wind the improvement applied to windward as well.

At seven knots the *Challenge* was moving faster, across the board, than any boat her size had a right to expect.

"The keel don't help so much over thirteen, fourteen knots," the fat man commented.

"It doesn't matter," Hillman answered. He slapped Paul hard on the back. His usually placid features were split in a grin. Even Stone wore a small, vicarious smile. "It's the lower wind speeds we needed it for." Hillman looked at Paul for confirmation.

"She's competitive," Paul admitted. "But it's only computers."

"What do you mean, 'only computers.' " The fat man smiled, pretending to make a joke of it. "The most powerful imaging tool in the entire free world, and he calls it, 'only computers.' "

"But it's not salt-and-steel," Paul protested. "We had good results last time. It doesn't mean peanuts till you get the real thing.

"I know what's going to happen," Paul continued, pointing at the computer terminals. "Shoop's PR people will take these results and make a big publicity campaign out of it. Oh, they'll keep the details secret but they'll hype it to hell and gone. Then, later, when the boat isn't the incredible superboat the computers thought it was, people will point at me" (Paul's index finger reversed) "and say, 'It's his fault.' "

"Don't be so paranoid," Stone advised. "No one's hyping anything. This project is security classification 'A,' and it's going to stay that way."

≈

Stone was as good as his word.

Occasional reports appeared in the press, but because no journalists succeeded in breaking the screen of secrecy surrounding the *Challenge* effort, they ended up reporting on the secrecy itself. The artwork was always the same: telephoto shots of the clam company, and the first *Challenge*.

In late March a piece appeared in *Starboard Magazine* under Sandy MacLean's byline. The article put the *Challenge* syndicate at the very bottom of the list of potential contenders. "While the almost pathological secretiveness of the *Challenge* team has caused much speculation as to just what it is they are trying to hide," MacLean wrote, "informed sources claim there is precious little fire under all that smoke. Apparently due to budget restrictions, only one model of the secret design was tested, and very few computer simulations were attempted. Observers state that a competitive Twelve-Meter—no matter how fancy her appendages—is highly unlikely to evolve from such a limited program. Some have gone so far as to question the syndicate manager's judgment in retaining Paul Briggs as designer for the new Twelve, given the poor performance of the first Briggs design. Briggs, who finished the first boat after the death of his cousin and partner in the design firm, reportedly has little or no experience in Twelve-Meter work. . . ."

Paul refused to get upset about the piece. But he suspected it was MacLean's article that finally goaded Shoop into action.

Six days after the issue of *Starboard Magazine* hit the newstands, Shoop—who was not supposed to show up until the trials three weeks later—arrived unannounced at the meetinghouse.

C H A P T E R   2 7

It was evening. The old Church of the Nazarene had been converted into a dining hall, recreation center, and headquarters for Warren Hillman and the Twelve-Meter crews.

The crew hung around the main hall, reading, drinking, watching TV. Wives and girlfriends were helping clear the serving trays after dinner. The mood was relaxed, for they had only just come up from winter training down south, and the novelty had yet to wear off.

Shoop arrived with three cases of Doyen-Kruyff champagne, and fifty-odd shoeboxes. He had two cohorts to help him carry everything in. They were tall, gray-haired men in expensive leisure clothes from the sponsoring yacht club in Byram, Connecticut. Paul recognized them from the sail trials of Jack's boat.

Paul was at the meetinghouse to go over scheduling changes with Hillman. He had taken the opportunity to pick up his daughter and give Nat and Squidlips Coggeshall a ride as well. Queegie was training them, under protest, as backup winchmen.

Paul watched as Shoop opened box after box of athletic shoes. The shoes all carried the bright logo Shoop had chosen for his campaign. This was a stylized mountain range, the symbol of Gipfel Financial Services, with a minimalist Twelve-Meter sailing beneath. Hillman loyally handed the shoes around, shouting sizes.

Shoop passed out plastic cups and filled them with Doyen-Kruyff champagne. He stood on a chair, holding his own cup of bubbly.

"I have in my hand," Shoop announced pompously, "a report summarizing the test results—that's model tests and computer tests—of the new design for the *Challenge II*. The boat that is lying at the clam company, only a few miles from here. The boat that is going to be launched at the end of this month. . . .

"The results say"—Shoop paused, coy as a starlet at the Academy Awards—"we have a boat that is better, by a significant percentage, than any other Twelve-Meter afloat today."

He gave a couple of speed figures to prove his point, then held up his cup and sighted over it, toward Paul.

"A toast," he called, "to the best damn designer in America!"

Everyone turned to Paul, as if in doubt. Then they looked back at Shoop.

Squidlips Coggeshall was the first to break the spell. "Yaaah," he roared, let loose a fart, and poured half his champagne between the large, blubbery appendages that had earned him his nickname. The rest went into his beard.

The men from Byram stared at Coggeshall.

By the time the third case of champagne was opened even the professional Twelve-Meter men were letting their hair down. Loud voices and laughter foamed around the meetinghouse. Fifties rock 'n' roll blared fuzzily from a ghetto blaster.

Paul went down to the basement. He had put Jessica to bed in a stack of sails between two weight-lifting machines. The noise of tromping feet and music overhead was deafening, but she slept on with the utter dedication of the young.

Back upstairs he elbowed his way through the crowd. He managed to grab Shoop's elbow and drag him away from the yacht club men.

"What the hell's going on," he said.

Shoop looked at him down the length of his nose.

"A little morale building?" he replied, at length, licking champagne from the side of his mouth. He was featuring the cashmere look tonight—cashmere shirt, sweater, slacks. Suede shoes.

"I thought we agreed. No one on the team had to do any selling."

"And have they?"

"You know what I mean." Paul pointed at a pair of the new boat shoes, with the bright logo and the "Gipfel America's Cup Team" emblazoned in purple on a red racing stripe.

"It's a gift, Paul," Shoop told him. "Don't be a bore."

"All right. Fine." Paul searched for his glasses, to see the financier better, without success. He rubbed his eyes and realized they were still on his nose; the room was getting steamy and body heat was fogging the lenses. "Then what about keeping everything a secret," he continued. "No one was supposed to know what the results of the computer tests were."

"That was the idea," Shoop agreed.

"So why'd you tell 'em?"

"I told them nothing specific," the financier explained, patiently. "I said the results were good, that's all."

"You mentioned two optimum speed numbers," Paul said. "You know these things have a way of getting out. I'll bet you anything you want there'll be a report about it in the next issue of *Sail* or *Starboard*. You could cancel my contract, if I did what you just did."

Shoop smiled, without mirth.

"I told you," he said. "Secrecy sells—"

"Then why—"

Shoop looked at him levelly, before continuing.

"—but it only sells if people think the secret is worth the finding out. It's all salesmanship, Paul. Remember that."

Paul said, "You *wanted* it to get out. I should have known."

Shoop just smiled enigmatically.

"It was that *Starboard Magazine* article, wasn't it," Paul went on, but the sentence was broken by the unguided flight of a champagne cork that narrowly missed Paul's ear.

The party was getting out of hand. Nat sprayed Doyen-Kruyff from a bottle over the heads of the audience. Shoop moved to rescue the yacht club men who were looking, wild-eyed, from side to side, like cornered cattle.

Paul went outside, thinking; it was exactly that kind of "leak" that killed Jack. Word got out that the computer results were good, very good. The next thing you knew, a brick-shaped woman with steel wool in her ears was on the road for French Harbor.

As if on cue, a pair of headlights swung off the Amesboro Road and started up the driveway to the meetinghouse, sending shafts of white-yellow light scanning through the trees.

Paul shivered. Nine months had passed since he started work on the new *Challenge*. Winter was almost over. In ten days, it would be spring. The country was still locked in cold; fresh water was frozen. The car's tires made potato-chip noises on the iced puddles as it rolled to a stop in front of him.

The driver's window rolled down. A voice came from the darkness of the car. It was soft, with a small catch in it, as of doubt or unshed sleep. Its accent was hybrid: a little American, some British. Mostly it conveyed pastel colors, steel drums, and the scent of tamarinds.

Paul stepped to the porch railing. "I didn't hear you."

"Is this the Twelve-Meter place? The *Challenge* team," the voice continued, when he did not answer immediately. "Can't you hear, man?"

A girl's voice. Its lilt seemed vulnerable against the cool wind. The way she said "place," in two syllables—"plee-ess"—was pure Caribbean. But the face behind the voice shone white.

"Oh. Yeah. This is it," Paul answered.

The driver got out. She was small, dressed in jeans, a thick red sweater, boat shoes. A pair of headphones was hooked to a cassette player in one hand. She took a canvas bag from the rear seat and climbed the porch steps. At the top she hesitated, eyeing the door but not approaching, as if thinking access might be denied her, for reasons she could only guess at.

"You looking for someone?" Paul asked.

The porch light caught her face when she turned. Paul's first impression was of disproportionately large eyes, blue eyes whose very lack of pigment would somehow color everything around them. The light molded shadows from strong cheekbones, a well-curved mouth. A face that would react first and worry about how it looked later.

Paul's second thought was, this girl hasn't eaten in a week.

"There might still be some dinner left," he said—and stopped, uncertainly. He had not meant to say that, or anything like it.

"I'm not looking for dinner, thanks," the girl said. "I'm looking for Gary."

"Gary?"

"Yes. Gary Hopkins. The helmsman? This *is* the Twelve-Meter place? There can't be more than one in this town."

"Oh." Paul had only drunk a couple glasses of champagne but his brain was not functioning at peak speed. "You mean Queegie?"

"Yes." In the sheen of light her gaze became completely level, dry, neutral. The night rustled like savannah grass. "Queegie. Would you mind telling him I'm here? Tell him Jenny's here. Jenny Crooke.

"What's the matter," the girl said after a pause. "Did I say something wrong?"

"You're the one," Paul said. "The one in the Trans-Pac."

The girl looked at him. The neutrality in her gaze had doubled.

"Why don't you come in," Paul said, and went to open the door for her, but the girl made no move to follow him. Instead she set her bag down and put her hand out in a stopping gesture. The poise had fled her eyes. They now filled to the brim with warning and alarms.

"Ask him to come out—would you? If it's not too much trouble," she added. "I don't want to walk in on the party," she explained.

"Christ, it's no party," Paul began, but the look she sent made him stop, and after a second he nodded, turned, and retreated inside to look for Queegie.

The dining hall looked like a fraternity house on graduation night. Empty champagne bottles, corks, and plastic cups littered the folding tables. Paul spotted the helmsman at a side table. He was arguing about sails with the tactician. Only the ruffled hair and an untucked shirttail betrayed the fact that Queegie had drunk his share of Doyen-Kruyff that night. The mirrored glasses, the confident tone were always there, drunk or sober. Paul had a sudden, sharp intuition; Queegie might have got along well with Jack. They were both grandstanders, both good enough to get away with it. Paul called from the door. "There's a girl," he jerked his thumb behind him, "at the entrance to see you."

"A girl, Queegie," one of the trimmers took up. Someone else whistled, more out of a general need to celebrate than because of Paul's words. The tight discipline of Team Challenge had broken down with a vengeance.

Queegie went on talking as if Paul and the rest were all part of the woodwork. His voice was loud enough to carry clearly.

"That sail will be no damn good in the Rochelle waves," he stabbed the point with a finger. "It's *too* precise, too sensitive, it'll stall."

Paul repeated his message. Queegie noticed him this time.

"Another one of your Maine-iac critters looking for a job?" he yelled back, making sure Cal and George could hear him. "Or looking for something else, har har." He took off his sunglasses and winked at Steve, who said "heh, heh" loyally.

Paul smiled pleasantly. He was getting used to the helmsman. He was also looking forward to watching Queegie react to the woman who had kept him dangling for a year. "It's a friend of yours. Hard to believe, but that's the way it goes. White, but she's got a Jamaican accent—"

All of a sudden, the room lost noise.

Steve-the-tactician shot an apprehensive look at Queegie.

Blood washed out of Queegie's face, then immediately rushed back in. He pushed off from the bench and strode aggressively toward Paul, braking six inches away from his nose.

"You had to yell it over the whole world, didn't you," he hissed. "Make me look like a fool." His eyes were tight with fury.

Then he elbowed roughly past the designer, through the entrance hallway. There was a rush of cool air. The front door slammed.

Paul shrugged at the tactician. He heard the girl say something, formless words on the porch. He found his respect for Queegie had increased a hundredfold; if the helmsman could attract a woman like that, there had to be more to him than nasty comments and a talent for tacking.

Queegie said, "Oh really?" The girl replied, still too low to hear. Paul was about to close the door, not wanting to eavesdrop, when he heard the hard-soft sound of flesh striking flesh and the thud of something falling on the planks of the porch.

Paul wasn't aware of having moved until he opened the front door and looked out. Queegie's back was to him. Rounded angles of blue jeans lay at his feet. The girl was trying to get up, pulling with one hand on the porch rail while the other clutched her cheek. The helmsman was taut as his own rigging, his hands balled.

The porch light blotched the scene with shadows. Paul could not tell if she were bleeding. Her eyes were shaded so he could not read them either.

"Five whole months, this time," he said. "You had to go for five whole months. Well, I hope you got a whole lot of thinking done. A *whole* lot of thinking."

Her eyes were in the light. Pride and hurt struggled in their depths. She got a knee under her and unfolded against the railing. Queegie brought his hand back.

"Don't, Queegie," Paul said. "That won't help."

The helmsman spun around. What control he'd had was gone. "Keep the fuck out of this, Briggs," he yelled. "This is none of your fucking business. Just get out of here, or I'll break your fucking neck."

Paul stood his ground. The girl said, "I'm OK. Please leave us alone," but he could not move. His own rage rose hot and singing in his ears, and his hands were trembling with the strength of it. Queegie put four fingers on Paul's chest and shoved him toward the door, hard. Paul shoved back, but he was off balance, and the helmsman had at least thirty pounds on him, so the movement knocked Paul further into the door jamb. His glasses slipped off his nose with the shock.

The door swung open. Nat said, "What's going on, chief?" His large frame filled the doorway. The tactician hung behind. Queegie's lips drew back. Light reflected on his milk-commercial teeth.

"I don't believe it," he said. "More shit-kickers. I guess it's just all you do in this place, stick your nose into other people's business."

Paul still said nothing. The girl picked up her bag with one hand. The other covered her cheek, from pain or embarrassment. "Let's get out of here, Gary," she said.

Queegie looked from Paul to Nat to the tactician, as if to memorize the scene.

"Please," the girl said.

"Leave 'em alone, Paul," Steve urged. "They'll figure it out."

She moved toward her car. Queegie said "Shit" and got in the driver's seat. The girl looked at the men on the porch without seeing them and climbed in beside him.

The taillights bounced down the dirt driveway and turned to the left, to disappear in the direction of the A-frame where Queegie slept.

Nat, drawing on his vast inexperience, made some comment about women and the trouble they caused. Paul retrieved his glasses and set them back on his nose. He did not go in immediately, but stood staring into the darkness for a minute, still in the grip of the incident and its resolution.

Then the cold got to him. He shook his head and followed the others inside.

C   H   A   P   T   E   R   2 8

There was a five-piece band playing Charleston tunes in the Model Room of the New York Yacht Club. Lights danced on the miniature brasswork of Krupps, Morgans, Vanderbilts. Waiters staggered under trays loaded with flute glasses of champagne. Streamers in black and gold and silver curled from the minstrel gallery, and Ashley Palmer Briggs was having the time of her life.

She couldn't quite remember what the party was in aid of, or who'd thrown it, but it didn't seem to matter. She had lost Uncle Bradley but had found someone much more interesting. He was a young Swiss-Frenchman with a nose like Charles Boyer's and an accent like Yves Montand's in Z. She had achieved an almost perfect balance between the mellowness of pills and the giddiness of champagne. The bleak dark months in Maine seemed like another lifetime, lived by another person, someone the present Ashley would not particularly like.

The only trouble was, the champagne made her want to pee. She gave Michel a quick kiss on the cheek, told him not to go away, and vanished into the powder room.

The powder room lay up and off the main stairs. It was plush with red velvet and mirrors. A very tall woman sat on a stool by the vanity table, adding lipstick and talking on the phone about how that wretched Eloise had spoiled everything by doing something else totally inconceivable. She had left by the time Ashley came out of the stall.

Now the champagne was making her feel giddy. She tried sitting down, but that only made the dizziness spread. Before she knew it she was back in the stall, vomiting. When she came back out she rinsed her mouth, opened the window and leaned out, seeking fresh air.

City sounds echoed out of the night. Honks, motor noises. No stars were visible through the glare of nearby Times Square. From an invisible window underneath, a man was whispering. She was thinking about Michel, and how to invite him, subtly, to Newport for the following week.

It took a minute for the words drifting from below to sink in. But when they did, it was as if Maine, in all its cold and darkness, had crept back into her stomach.

The man had mentioned French Harbor. She was sure of it.

". . . the whole thing was a mess," the voice continued. "So when you tell me—"

There was a pause, like someone talking on the phone, waiting for an answer.

"I'm not doubting you. If you say—"

Another pause.

"I believe you. So their new boat tests great. So it'll win the Cup. Okay?"

Ashley leaned out of the ladies' room window, looking for another window below her. She seemed to remember there was a men's room right underneath, as there was one just overhead. But the powder room was built on the interior airwell, on the second floor. The flat roof of the bar lay four feet below. The voice came from an odd, triangular shaft, built of stone, sunk vertically into the roof. Yellow light shone at its bottom. The shaft extended maybe seven or eight feet below her window. Ashley thought the shape of the opening must be acoustically perfect—there was no other explanation for the clarity of the sounds coming through.

"But that's exactly why you *will* keep calling me," the whisper came again. There was something familiar in the emphasis that Ashley could not quite define. "Because he *was* killed. Because you *were* part of it."

She was leaning almost beyond her center of gravity. The nausea came back and she withdrew swiftly. She felt cold all over. She looked at herself in the mirror for a second—a very pale, wide-eyed woman in a turquoise evening dress and a lapis necklace—then ran out the door and down the stairs, holding her stomach, looking for the men's room.

She went too far, ending up at the gents' next to the cloakroom. Two men, strangers, came out, discreetly checking their flies. She waited for them to disappear, then peeked in, but there was no one else inside, and no telephone either. She ran back up the stairs, trying to orient herself by where the powder room was, and found a door off the next landing.

She waited outside for a minute then pushed the door. A waiter coming down the stairs called "Miss!" in a shocked voice.

There was no one here, either. Just Victorian-era urinals, a pay phone on the wall, and a narrow window half-open beside it. She fled, past the outraged waiter, around the main staircase to the quartermaster's desk.

The quartermaster, luckily, was one of the old guard. He knew her by name. He made no objection when she asked to see the guest list.

Luckily, also, it was not an America's Cup party, so the list of people with a direct interest in the *Challenge*, and her performance, would be fairly small.

Five people, as a matter of fact. All of whom she knew. Two of whom she did not think were capable of jaywalking, let alone murder.

Three who would probably run over their mothers if they got in the way.

The reaction had caught up with her now. Her stomach was cramped and sweat stood out on her brow. The old quartermaster pulled out a chair from behind the desk and she sat down gratefully.

It was simple, really. First she would call Paul and tell him what she'd found out.

Then she would go to each man, in turn, and say she had heard him on the phone, which was the truth. She would add that she had recognized his voice and seen him leave the men's room; this wasn't the truth, but they could not be sure. She would watch how they reacted, and know who had done it.

Ashley lifted her chin. It wasn't a bad plan, given the amount of champagne she had drunk. She got to her feet, quite steadily, and looked up the alabaster staircase.

Jack would have been proud of her, she thought.

C H A P T E R 2 9

The call from Ashley came in a week after the incident with Queegie.
Paul took the call in his office at the clam company.

He hung up the phone slowly after Ashley had finished, wondering
why her information aroused so little anger in him, or even surprise.

His strongest reaction, in fact, was relief.

Despite all the very good reasons he had made up to avoid going
to the meetinghouse, he would have to tell Hillman about this sometime, and there was no point in putting it off.

Paul got to the crew's headquarters at the end of the evening
wrap-up.

The backup crew was doing calisthenics outside. Paul grinned as
he watched Squidlips and Nat sweat and groan in the fading sunset.
They could not keep up, even with the jumping jacks.

Inside, two sail makers discussed a new computer program that
analyzed stress points in relation to wind speed and direction. Warren
Hillman, Queegie, and the tactician sat with a sports psychologist
Shoop had hired to work out a more scientific training schedule.
The psychologist was plump, short, bearded. He was dressed in a

yellow plaid suit. They discussed motivation peaks, attention plateaus, and psychological domination versus the secret need to fail.

There were two women in the room. One, the wife of a navigator, did crochet and watched TV.

Queegie's girlfriend sat in an armchair in one corner of the long room, her feet up on a coffee table, reading a sailing magazine. She wore dark glasses, but they did not cover the purple bruise on her cheek. She saw Paul but did not acknowledge him.

Paul avoided acknowledging her as well. He figured she was embarrassed for the Queegie incident, and recognizing him, in a sense, meant recognizing her boyfriend's problems.

He got a cup of coffee, peeled Hillman from the encounter group, sat him down by a stained-glass window, and told him what Ashley had said.

"What you're telling me," Hillman said at length, "is that there's someone here calling up other syndicates and giving 'em our secrets?"

"That's what it sounds like." The fact that the conversation included the circumstances of Jack's murder, Paul continued, implied whoever was selling information had been doing so from the start of the first campaign.

"Ashley says she has some kind of a lead on who this guy at the yacht club was," Paul continued, "but she wouldn't tell me who. I get the feeling she wants to do this on her own, without help. Maybe it's her way of making her peace with Jack. Anyhow—what was I saying—it could be anybody. Van Meerwen was coordinating three different yacht clubs, three different syndicates, hundreds of people, it could be anybody on the East Coast who was working with him. . . ."

Paul had trouble getting his words straight. In any case Hillman was not interested in the tie-in with Jack's death. That was over and done with. Hillman lived for the here and now.

"Cy'll be pissed," he said, "even if it suits him, in a way. I'll make a list," he continued, "all the guys who been in since the start. I want to talk to Queegie about this, see if he's got any ideas. You should do the same with your own men. What we do," he continued, "is what I did on the *Excalibur* campaign—we figure out who might have leaked the information, then we give them each different pieces of info, new secrets, and we wait to see which piece leaks out. Sort of like putting dye in the blood, to see where there's a balls-up . . . Paul?"

"What?" Paul drew his eyes back guiltily. "Sorry, I didn't hear you."

Hillman repeated his statement.

"Oh," Paul said, "sure."

"Good." Hillman looked at him with concern. "You sure you're OK?"

"I'm fine," Paul reassured him.

"Taking care of yourself properly, are you? We need you around here, Paul."

Paul repeated he was fine, a little crossly, and Hillman went off to interrupt the psychology seminar.

Paul refilled his coffee. He decided to eat dinner here. He called Jessica, called Mrs. Gilbert, asked her to baby-sit. He was doing a lot better, it was only the second time this week. He found a copy of the *Maine Times* lying around. It obviously had been picked up because it had an article on the Challenge effort with a sidebar on Shoop. "It is widely believed Shoop is using the America's Cup as a platform to sell Gipfel Financial, but so far no one has been willing to meet the price he is asking," the article read. Paul tore out a subscription filler and started making notes of things he had to do in the morning. He had trouble paying attention. After thirty-five minutes he could only think of seven or eight items, though there had to be dozens of things demanding his attention, some of them of great urgency. The curvy keel, for example, was creating a number of problems. There were recurrent glitches in the hydraulics. Also, the French, after initially approving the design, now were worried it might curve more on one side than the other, changing the keel's volume and thus contravening the rule. They wanted more information. Shoop claimed the information was proprietary, which meant Paul had to call Arlington and La Rochelle and brief the lawyers Shoop had retained in Paris. . . . Paul caught himself checking his profile in the window, and smacked the pencil on the table, furiously. There was too much activity in here to concentrate. He would have to go somewhere else for dinner.

Something came between Paul and the light. He looked up, ready to be annoyed. His eyes led over various curves—hips, breasts, neck, mouth—to the insolence of her nose and the royal blue of her eyes.

"Hello," Jenny Crooke said.

Grade-school training ran deep. Paul had got to his feet before he realized how outdated and goofy the gesture was.

The color in her cheeks seemed even deeper at close range. She spoke softly, though there was no one close enough to overhear.

"I never thanked you. For the other night. I mean, nothing would have happened. But it was good of you to be concerned."

"It's OK." Paul waved his hand, deprecatingly, very aware of how stilted he came off. But she wasn't finished.

"You're the naval architect?"

He nodded. He stuck out a hand, still too formal. Her smile was total, her clasp cool. They grinned stupidly at each other.

"I didn't mean to disturb you," she said. "I just—"

"You're not," Paul interrupted her. He grew conscious of a strain in his chest, as if he could not suck enough air. This is ridiculous, he thought. Bring in the first attractive girl and he reacted like a high school sophomore.

"I wanted to say," she went on, "I like your stuff. I worked on a French Harbor 38 for a month. And I saw the *Zulu* in Georgetown once. She was beautiful."

Paul stared at her.

"You've got a reputation," Jenny Crooke explained. "In some circles."

Silence, for a beat or two. To break it Paul said, "You've been on a charter boat, right?"

He got a guarded look in return.

"It's a small group," he told her.

"Which means, you already know why."

Paul shrugged. "I didn't mean to be personal."

"It doesn't matter." She looked at him seriously. After a pause she added, "I had sort of a personal question for you, actually."

He just looked at her. It was not a bad way to pass the time.

"D'you mind if I ask it, then?" she said.

He nodded assent.

"Why don't you do those kinds of boats anymore. I mean, why'd you get into Twelve-Meters?"

He must have looked his confusion.

She shrugged. "It just doesn't seem—after the *Zulu*, the French Harbors, the *Flasher*—it wouldn't be your type."

For some reason, the question rankled him.

"How would you know what is my type of boat, what isn't?"

Her eyes widened a little, then lost warmth, like the sea when clouds passed over the sun. She nodded.

"It's none of my business." She turned aside now. "I'm sure," she continued emptily, "we'll see each other again."

Paul nodded back. He could not think of a single word to say in return. He watched her move lithely back to her seat. He picked up his pencil and his jacket. Then, without glancing once in her direction, he strode out of the meetinghouse.

☷

Paul drove home too fast that night. Unlike Vanzetti, who sped for show, Paul tended to drive too fast when he was nervous or upset.

It did not bother him, he told himself as he drove. He only looked at her occasionally. His vision centers were interested, but that was as far as it went. It could go no further because he barely knew the woman. There was nothing special about her, except maybe the eyes.

If her eyes followed her inside meteorology as the surface of a pond changed to weather, it only meant she was easy to read. If the fragile face evoked protective feelings, it was only a father instinct, misplaced. The only secret in her fragility was whatever self-mortification kept her from eating enough. The only mystery to her trim way of moving was a minimum of physical coordination.

And if her image kept surfacing, unbidden in his mind—if his personal geography, these last few days, tended to include estimates of distance to and from Queegie's place or the meetinghouse—it was only because she affected him as an ideal, no more. An ideal of womanhood. He could deal with her as he dealt with the other icons, the pictures of sloops and schooners.

Nevertheless, in the days that followed Paul took care not to go anywhere near the girl.

He worked late every night, leaving for home well after dark in the illusion night would protect him. So it was with a sense of shock, and doom, that he walked into the guard's office at the clam company on his way home a whole week after last seeing Jenny Crooke, and heard her voice come from behind him. It rose out of an armchair to one side of the bank of humming blue TV sets and infrared meters that was the domain of the night guard.

"Excuse me," she said, "I need a ride to French Harbor. They tell me you go that way."

He swiveled, almost panicked. The eyes hit him like a truck. They were full of doubt and questions. Ridiculous, he told himself.

Bobby was on night shift, again. The guard turned up the TV. The Boston Celtics were playing New York, the score 114 to 112, and he was not interested in psychodramas.

Paul put on his coat and went outside, half hoping she would interpret this as refusal, but she came out with him into the cold.

"What are you doing here."

It was all he could think of to say.

"I'm working in the sail loft."

"I mean—"

"I need to go to Hallett's Store."

He searched, desperately, for reasons why not.

The girl's features were clear, even out here. The clam company was ringed with cameras, and spotlights to illuminate them. The lights turned everything to dead shades, silver and mauve. They glared off the razor wire and the chain-link fences. German dogs moved in the purple shadows and flashlights winked. For the first time Paul understood why people in French Harbor referred to the clam company as "that James Bond place."

"What happened to your car?"

A shrug. "It was hired. I took it back."

"I can get it for you, whatever you need."

"I can get a ride back here." The West Indian accent seemed to come stronger when she was nervous. "If it's any bother . . ."

Paul asked himself why he needed an excuse. He should just refuse to take her. Tell her the truth. I can't take you because you affect my vision centers, and we might crash. I can't take you because I'm afraid I could make a fool of myself with you. Instead he shrugged.

It was only a fifteen-minute drive, and he would not see much of her in the dark.

The real reason she'd asked for a ride, she told him when they were in the Jeep and bumping over the rutted dirt of the clam company access road, the real reason was, she had to get away from all that.

"Uh huh."

"It gets so, sort of, inbred, do you know? Have you got any cigarettes?"

"No."

"Look, man," she said, "it's all right. If it's really that inconvenient, I'll walk."

"It's too cold to walk, you'll freeze to death."

Silence from the passenger's seat, except for involuntary bursts from her lungs when the Jeep went airborne over bumps. He was driving too fast for this road. When he got to the end of the dirt he overaccelerated. The Jeep skidded out on a winter's accumulation of sand on the verge, leaning crazily to one side as it hit clean asphalt, coming level again. In his embarrassment Paul burned rubber to bring the Jeep back to speed. She put on her shades again, as if to block out his driving. Her silence was as much a comment as if she'd commented.

After a couple of minutes had passed the girl explained, "Queegie wouldn't take me."

Paul did not reply. He was concentrating on driving. He knew the maximum speed he could take every corner at. The sooner they got to French Harbor the sooner he could be rid of her and the twisted implications of her presence.

He heard her mutter "Bloody hell" in exasperation. He knew he was overreacting. Overreaction as significant as friendliness. It was to blow this imaginary point that he finally relented, and asked, "So why do you put up with it?"

"It's none of your business."

"Fine." Lack of conversation suited him perfectly, but then she added, "I'm sorry. But it's private. In the same way, I don't ask you what's wrong with you. In your eyes. It's a look. . . ."

"Idle conversation," Paul sighed, "this is supposed to be."

"You started it."

He snorted.

"I'm sorry," she repeated. "Listen, I'm not prying. But I did have another reason for the ride." She stopped. Paul glanced quickly toward her. In the sheen of dashboard lights she was looking straight ahead. Her dark hair curved forward, hiding expression.

"Well?"

"I wanted to ask if I could borrow one of your boats that are in the water. The old sloop. One of the workboats, even. I know it's pushy of me, but—I need to get out. On the ocean. For an hour or two, only. Just a little distance."

"From Queegie?" he could not resist saying.

"From Gary. Yes. From the meetinghouse as well. From the wives. Their endless bloody crochet. From all those macho racing boys and their designer racing gear. From the thousand-dollar sponsor watches, the visions of glory.

"And don't worry," she forestalled his next question, "I can handle boats. I've been skippering for years. I've been racing since I was twenty. I can handle anything. If the boys," she added softly, "if the boys thought a woman was capable of anything besides sewing, I wouldn't be working in the sail loft. I'd be working on your fucking boat."

"It's not a 'fucking boat,' " he objected.

"I'm sorry," she said again. "It's a nice Twelve-Meter." Her tone was carefully neutral.

"What," Paul asked her, "are you trying to do to me?"

"Nothing."

"Look," he said vehemently. "I'm no fan of Twelve-Meters. It's not a secret. I think they're a game, like crosswords or algebra. An equation to solve. But they're still boats. And boats are my job."

"Would you work on a Twelve, though. If you had the choice."

He did not need to think to answer.

"No. I'd much rather work on a round-the-world racer. Or a Maxi. At least they put to sea and hack it or sink, like a boat's supposed to do. Or maybe a no-rules class. Ultralights, multihulls. I'd even prefer those Jumbo-boats the Kiwis raced San Diego with, in eighty-seven, for the America's Cup. Twenty-seven crewmen, ten-story masts; see how you can make the bastard fly. That's exciting, at least."

They were coming into French Harbor now, over the crest of Lookout Hill, past Gilbert's Service Station, past the indiscretion of windows, shining cold with television. The lights of Hallett's store beckoned from up the hill.

"So why don't you."

"There's other problems."

"You should do what you want to do."

"When you get older," Paul told her as he pulled into Hallett's, "you realize you can't always do exactly what you want."

"Really."

"It's called growing up."

"Then what's the point?"

"The point of what?"

"You name it." She was out the door and round the front of the car before he had a chance to react. "Thanks for the lift," she called. She had a straight, pert nose that she held high against the light, walking into Hallett's.

"Shit," Paul growled. He reversed the Jeep, hard, scattering gravel over Hallett's steps, and turned back up the hill, toward home.

To hell with her. He'd been going to tell her she could use the boats if she wanted, but she had not given him time.

Serve her right. Especially after that remark about selling out. He was not going to talk to her again, even if she wanted to, which, given the way he'd treated her tonight, was highly unlikely anyway.

C H A P T E R 3 0

A blond man in a light cotton jacket and lace-up shoes walked downtown across Sixty-sixth Street and glanced casually westward.

There they were. Two large MCI buses, white with yellow, tan, and brown stripes, the red, white, blue of diplomatic plates. Parked one in front of the other by the Franciscan monastery.

The blond man, who had been raised by Franciscan brothers, almost chuckled to himself. That was irony for you, he thought.

He turned right, gently swinging his plastic Gristedes shopping bag, a subtle mark of belonging to the Upper East Side of New York. He walked up the opposite side of Sixty-sixth Street from the buses. When he got to Madison he put on a pair of calfskin gloves. Then he crossed again and walked back down the same street until he was right next to the second bus in line.

There were no cops and only one pedestrian on this side of the street. The bus drivers never stayed with their machines. The blond man stopped and kneeled next to one of the buses to tie his shoelace. Or pretended to, because it was impossible with gloves on.

One last quick look up and down the block.

He rolled the plastic shopping bag over its contents like wrapping. Then, very smoothly and casually, he poked it under the body of the bus until he found one of the support frames.

The object in the shopping bag had two large magnets attached to it. They found the steel and clung, out of sight behind the bodywork.

The blond man got to his feet and walked to Lexington Avenue, then down to Sixtieth Street. No one was following him but he went into Alexander's department store and rode a few escalators to make sure. Finally he took a city bus south, to Forty-seventh Street.

It was while he was on the bus that the beeper in his pocket sounded. He switched it off, mortally embarrassed. He hated it when that happened. People tended to stare.

At Forty-seventh Street he found a public phone and called the answering service that had beeped him. After that he walked to Forty-fifth Street, across from the UN building, and used the phone on the corner to call the number they'd given.

Across the street, diplomats of various nationalities drove in and out, in limousines and buses. A loudspeaker paged Mr. Olateno, of the Nigerian delegation.

In one and a half hours, the two MCI buses would pull up at the curb, and three-quarters of the diplomatic delegation of the Soviet Union would embark for the trip back to their compound on Sixty-seventh Street.

The blond man checked his coat pocket while he punched the buttons. The miniature transmitter was safe and sound, the switch taped shut. When the switch was opened, it would send a signal to a receiver tuned to the same frequency. That receiver was taped to a shaped piece of plastic explosive wrapped in a Gristedes shopping bag. . . .

A voice said, "Yes."

The noise of trucks in the background. Another pay phone.

"Go ahead," the blond man replied.

"This is Mr. Cranston. I dealt with you before—a job in Maine—"

"I know," the blond man said. "Stick to this business."

"I have a job for you." The man on the other end sounded odd, almost unwilling, but most people sounded odd when they talked to the blond man on business.

"Send a package," the blond man told him.

"I wanted to make sure," the voice on the phone said. "There are two jobs. The first has to be done by the end of the month at the latest."

"Where."

"Rhode Island."

The blond man thought about it. "It will cost double."

"Double!"

"Take it or leave it."

A pause on the other end.

"All right."

"Send the package."

"There's something else—"

"Mr.—Cranston, we've done business before, you know the rules. Phones are for emergencies only. Good-bye."

"Wait! It's just—I want the Rhode Island thing to be done very cleanly. I mean, so there's no pain. Do you understand?"

The blond man hung up.

≋

On the other end of the phone connection, Mr. "Cranston" listened to the burr of the dial tone for a good minute.

Movers unloaded office furniture from a truck parked next to the phone booth.

Above his head, a gleaming, new, thirty-five-story office building soared so high it seemed to collect every reflection in the sky to offer it to the city.

The man did not look at the tower or the workmen. He was trying to figure out where he would get the money. Double the money, now.

He'd devoted himself to the America's Cup effort to the exclusion of everything else. He had lined up no new jobs, and now the chickens were coming home to roost. Metropolitan General had used someone else to do their TV spot. He'd already fired half the people in his office as an economy measure.

Now everything truly depended on winning the cup. His company, his reputation, his career. And if anyone got in the way, they would be crushed. It was a matter of survival now. He had no choice.

He must remember that, the man told himself as he hung up the receiver and lit a cigarette.

He left the phone booth and headed crosstown, chain-smoking, toward his overheated office.

He decided that if he sold the Porsche, he would have just enough money to cover the expense of the man he had just talked to.

There would be plenty of time for sports cars once the cup was won, the man thought.

C H A P T E R   3 1

They took the *Challenge II* outside on April 2, with the aluminum cage locked around her secret keel and tarps wrapped all around her aluminum cage. They stepped her mast and tuned her rigging.

Paul's grandfather came back from Florida the day after, tying the demo 38 in her accustomed place behind the *Ettie*. He actually looked fitter than when he left. For some reason, a six-hundred-mile longshore passage that would have exhausted younger men only seemed to recharge Bull's batteries.

Paul caught the occasional glimpse of Jenny Crooke but easily avoided coming into contact.

He saw her once in French Harbor, taking out Coggeshall's lobster boat. Squidlips had leased the *Betty-Anne* to the syndicate as a tender. Paul assumed she had got the sea transport she wanted and had no need of him now.

The realization brought its share of bile. He thought of her more, not less. He heard her voice, with its soft Islands' lilt, in his head as he worked. Still he remained convinced it was only a fascination with physical rhythms, enhanced by the pull of sex.

Whatever the nature of his infatuation, he fought it with military diligence. Queegie's comments grew nastier, then stopped, ominously, altogether, but Paul paid no attention. Steve checked nervously in Paul's direction every time the girl came within sight, but Paul decided it was none of his doing, and none of his responsibility either.

He thought he had it all fairly well under control until one day Warren Hillman called him at the office, and said, without preamble, "One of you has got to do something."

"What are you talking about."

"You or the girl," the manager said, and repeated it for emphasis. "You or the girl. It's getting crazy."

"There's no need," Paul said. "There's nothing between us. I stay away from her in any case." Which was close enough to the truth.

Hillman sighed.

"Come on, mate," he said. "You may be trying—but I've seen you look at her. Everyone has. It's a standing joke around here. You can't keep your eyes off her."

"There's nothing between us," Paul said, without moving his jaw. "And frankly, even if there was, it'd be none of your damn business anyway."

"That's where you're wrong." Steel had formed inside the warm articulation of the salesman. "It's my job to keep this team running and you're messing it up. It doesn't even matter what's true or not true," he continued. "Queegie thinks it's true. That's what matters. There's nothing—and I mean nothing—that will wreck a team like two men fighting over the same woman."

"I don't believe this," Paul said.

"If you could just take a vacation," Hillman went on smoothly. "Work somewhere else for a week or two. Let things settle—"

"I don't believe this," Paul yelled. "I mean, damn it, I live here. I'm busting my ass to make this boat a success, I'm busting my butt to keep this woman with a guy she's worth ten of, a man who beats the *shit* out of her, I saw him do it. If that's not crazy enough, I get a goddamn *athletic* director telling me I'm making their problems worse, and he suggests I *leave*. Not permanently, he says. Well thanks one whole hell of a lot, Warren. But this is my yard. I'll have you know it's *my* town. I belong here. You don't. Gary doesn't, and that girl doesn't. If somebody's leaving, it ain't gonna be me!"

Paul slammed the phone down. He grabbed his jacket and stomped out of the room.

He had to page Jenny Crooke because, for security reasons, he was not allowed in the sail-making area, and he had to arrange to meet her in the guardroom, because she could not come to his office. When she appeared in the guardroom he told her, "Sit down."

"Why?"

"Just sit down."

The guard—one of the new men Vanzetti had hired—stared, fascinated. Paul ignored him. The girl sat on the same armchair she'd used a week ago.

"Warren Hillman says I'm chasing after you," Paul told her. "It's ludicrous. He says I'm making trouble between you and Queegie. That's ridiculous, too. He says I should leave here. Or you should."

She stared up at him. This time her gaze told him little. It was all mirrors reflecting mirrors, glare, false images. He could read nothing there. What a poker player she would make, if she could summon that look at will. He heard himself blustering, "Well, you deal with it. It's none of my damn business. Do you hear me? If you're getting your boyfriend upset, *you* leave." He pointed a finger at her. "*You* do something."

"You were right," he continued through gritted teeth, "I don't particularly love Twelve-Meters, but that is still my boat out there, and I want her—I need her—to do well. And I don't need a woman getting in the goddamn way!"

He left then, slamming the door behind him. He got in his car and drove straight to the boatyard.

✸

It was cold out on Georges Sound. The wind was blowing only twelve to twenty in gusts, but with the water around forty degrees, and the temperature around freezing, the exposure factor for a man in the open was severe.

Paul took the production boat out of the lee of Cully Head under mainsail and large genoa, and steered west to clear Two Ladies Islands.

He would have taken the *Ettie*, but the sloop was slow in winds below twenty knots, and he felt a need for speed and action.

He checked the compass and his watch. When he had sailed long enough at this speed to clear Hen and Chickens Rocks, he headed in a more northerly direction, into the heart of Georges Sound. He let the sails out to the greater wind angle. The FH 38 accelerated. The waves came up from behind and she half-surfed, half-crabbed down their backs.

He did not think much beyond compass courses and dead reckoning. The waves rolled under the sloop's keel and lifted her, taking her for a free ride in a crash of whipped water, before lifting her bow in farewell and rolling out. After forty minutes of this, the effect of their massive green repetition was like some kind of meditation, stoning the brain, breaking connections. The constant rush of wind and water added to the disorientation. The endless lead and lag, action and reaction as he steered the boat and adjusted her sails gave the illusion of blending with the ocean's infinite mindlessness. A semblance of calm snuck back into Paul's mind, the fatalism of a human alone at sea. You did what you could, but above and beyond the precautions you took, the sea did what it would. There was no point fighting forces so far beyond your control.

He heard the crash of the lobster boat's bow wave before he saw it coming up astern. It took no ESP to know the girl's face would be in her wheelhouse window before he spotted her black hair jolly-rogering in the wind.

The *Betty-Anne* came level with his cockpit.

She took off her dark glasses and removed the earpiece of the cassette recorder. She leaned out the window and looked at him for a moment.

"Hillman says *I'm* chasing *you*," she yelled, finally.

"He told me that, too," Paul yelled back. "I bet he says that to everyone he meets."

She smiled and reduced engine revolutions, for the tender was pulling ahead of the sailboat. They sailed in tandem for fifty, one hundred yards.

Paul's calm had vanished, driven away by the strength of feeling the girl's presence aroused. Still the lesson remained. There were some things it was useless to fight. Even if this obsession were only physical, based on images and associations, nevertheless it must run its course before he could be free of it. At sea, you rolled with the punches, or you got knocked down.

With the acceptance came a measure of serenity. He grinned back over the water. She really was tiny, he thought. She looked like a teenager, bracing herself between the overhead tackle, where the trap lines came up, and the wheel. Even at that distance he could see the challenge in her eyes. He came to the decision without knowing it.

"Waquoit," he called, pointing north and east, toward the river inlet.

"Wa-what?"

He shook his head.

"Follow me," he called, and jibed the sloop, hard and deliberately, the boom and sail whipping over his head until the lines brought them up short, smacking her onto a new course toward the loom of forest on his starboard bow.

≈

The Waquoit River was a deep, rocky inlet leading into the Sancastin State Forest.

Local legend had it that an eighteenth-century fisherman, who'd found a cache of gold and been drowned by his greedy mate, sailed his shallop here on a full moon.

Half a mile up the river's length, if you knew your way past the rocks and the tapestry of trap buoys, was a wide pool surrounded by high, half-quarried granite and pines.

Paul dropped the anchor in the pool's center, switched off the sloop's engine, and put fenders over the side. Jenny Crooke brought the *Betty-Anne* close and he took the lines she offered.

When the boats were secured, riding gentle to one anchor in the outgoing tide, he went below to hook up the power. He cleared Bull's duffel bags off the deck and got a fire going in the tiny coal stove against the forward bulkhead. He did this because he did not know what else to do at this stage. When the fire was drawing well he went back up on deck. She was standing in the cockpit, by the wheel. The sun was lower than the rim of trees around them and she hugged herself against the cold.

They looked at each other. She smiled, nervously, and shrugged. He took two steps and hugged her, awkwardly. After a second's hesitation she brought her arms around him and hugged back. He increased the pressure. His cheek—almost of its own will, it seemed—touched hers. She did not respond or withdraw. Her skin was very soft and cool. So were her lips.

Paul's heart was racing like a steam engine up an incline. A steamy feeling built up inside him. When the pressure seemed too much to bear he bent and touched his mouth to hers. The moisture on their lips seemed to conduct electricity between them. She shuddered, as if she'd been shocked. Her lips parted slightly.

After five minutes they went below without a word, following a shooting script written some time before.

The Peeping-Tom colors of sundown peered through the cabin portholes, cutting circles and arcs on her skin as she undressed. Her tan was unbroken; what he thought was sunburn was actually an oaken hue that lay within her skin, blended by the light into a rich orange. A single golden chain glinted at her neck. They came together standing. Her eyes reflected the orange glow and absorbed it. She was so small and light, he could lift her onto the bunk as easily as a pillow. The stove had not had a chance to work and it was cold in the cabin, so he pulled the blankets over them.

They lay on their sides facing each other. A great "now-what" in the air between them. This time, it was she who brought him close. Their legs folded, one of his on one of hers. He pulled himself apart a little, rolled the blankets down, unwilling to miss anything; the gentle sweep of hair against Bull's dingy pillows, the long neck; the small breasts, nipples standing on darker circles, the taut brown belly; the long thighs, smooth as molten glass, and the perfect V between them, valleys within valleys within valleys, like the pool within the cove within the river their boats lay in.

When they joined, it was simple and unplanned, two hands clasping in prayer.

Their stillness changed, acquired rhythm, each rhythm drawing greater rhythms from within itself until it turned into movement. Two wells of water drawing on each other, aquifers pulling in aquifers. The rhythms grew stronger, quicker. Her hands knotted painfully into his spine, and it seemed to Paul that every circle and line he had ever made suddenly melted and fused into every circle and line of her body, as if she was the perfect form he had been seeking to draw all these years, and he had finally managed to achieve it at the single expense of totally and completely dissolving himself in the effort.

The mutual egotism of sex dissipated a little. He looked at her face through the predicted melancholy, and got a sudden strong feeling that she had crept inside him and was looking out at him looking at her inside him. He knew then, without knowing how, that he was in trouble.

Their mingled liquids pooled and cooled beneath them.

The stove crackled and warmed the little cabin.

The portholes went purple, then cobalt, and finally reflected only chinks of fire from the stove.

"How did you know," he asked her, some time later.

"I didn't know," she said. "Warren told me."

"How'd he find out?"

"I guess it was obvious."

"That I'd gone out on the sloop?"

"Oh. No. Your office in French Harbor told me that. I mean, he knew I was falling for you. He warned me, weeks ago."

"I wonder how he knew?"

"He saw me looking at you, mahn. He told me it would wreck the team. He asked me to wait. I said, OK. It was only a matter of time anyway. With Queegie."

"I never saw you looking at me."

"I do what I want with my eyes."

Paul shook his head. "This is nuts," he told her smell and forms and feel, for he could see little in the dark cabin. "I know nothing about you, except that you belong to Queegie."

"I don't 'belong.' "

"OK. But, I mean. You were with him."

"You think I should feel guilty about that?"

"You must feel some kind of—"

She moved, restlessly. "I knew you'd let that interfere," she whispered back. "You're the one with guilt in you. You need to rip it out."

"You don't have guilt? About Quee—about Gary?"

Her hair shook against him.

"None. Where I come from, it's very hot and star apples grow wild in the forests, and people sing all the time, even when they don't have a pot to piss in. Rum is very cheap. No one can afford guilt."

"You know, I don't even know where you come from," he said. "I don't know you at all."

"Some things."

"What?"

"You sense things," she said. "I think your instincts are good, when you don't starve them in your hard Yankee way."

⚬

Later still, she talked about Tobago. Not everyone in Tobago was black, she said. Her family was one of the old English families. The original Tobagan Crooke was well named: a liar, a cheat, a "Gentleman of the Coast." He shipped as mate for Roger Chadwicke, who owned an armed brig and a letter of marque from King William entitling him to capture or sink all enemies of England. Together they plundered ships of every flag on the pretext they could never keep track of who, exactly, England was at war with, in an era when conflicts were common and it took months for news of peace or war to cross the Atlantic. Then, by complete coincidence, a plundering spree on French ships happened to coincide with a period of hostilities between France and Britain, and Chadwicke quickly obtained pardons and grants of land for himself and his crew. The original Crooke settled back to make rum and fornicate and die of syphilis in relative respectability near Canaan.

As a result of all the fornicating, Jenny added, the Crookes were not entirely black, and they were not entirely white. There was African, Spanish, even Mayan blood in their veins. They once owned a small distillery. This might still be in the family had they not been so conscientious about personally testing their own wares. White trash, Caribbean-style, the girl summed up, sharpness in her voice.

They didn't sound like white trash, Paul told her, to keep her talking.

He had not met her father, Jenny said. Her father was a drunk. He caned her regularly when she was growing up. He used bamboo switches. Her mother was too frightened of him to interfere.

Her father threw Jenny out of the house when she was seventeen for sleeping with a man called the Mighty Mongoose.

The Mighty Mongoose was very tall and black. He was a calypso singer with a band called the Mongoose All-Time Adventure Bingo Band. She toured around the lower Caribbean with him, as lover and roadie, for almost eight months, which was a month longer than most of his lovers lasted. When he grew tired of her, she got a job on a charter schooner out of Bridgetown.

Paul held her against him while she talked. His hands were consistently amazed at the contradictions of her body; how soft yet resilient, how solid yet fragile.

He wondered why she was so thin. The thought made Paul conscious of his own stomach. He got up and found a tin of baked beans in the galley. He added molasses, heated the mixture, and brought it to the bunk with a tin mug of rum. Then he called up Camden Marine on the VHF radio. After fifteen minutes of garbled traffic they patched him through to his own number.

Nat's voice was guarded, noncommittal, well aware that the ship-to-shore channel was an open link. Apparently no one had worried. The weather was too fair, and it was obvious the two boats were together. A lot of meaning lay hidden between "obvious" and the other words. Jessica was fine. He would call John Poole.

Paul tuned the radio to the weather channel. The forecast called for light southerly winds, veering westerly.

When Paul got back to the bunk he found Jenny Crooke mostly asleep. He folded himself around her as gently as he could. She stirred and mumbled, "The forecast's wrong. It'll back east in the morning."

"How do you know?" he asked her.

"I just know."

Somewhere around 3:00 A.M. he got up to check the anchor and take a piss. The stars were very bright. The wind was coming out of the east, as she predicted. Luck, he thought. The smells of their mingled bodies wafting off him seemed to blend with the aroma of tide wrack and pines. The feeling in his stomach was very warm.

When he came back, her eyes were open. He was chilled from standing outside, and her body felt hot as coals. They slipped into lovemaking like ducks slipped into a lake—gently, because it was easier than not—and just as easily slipped back into sleep together.

Paul's dreams were colored, fuzzy, full of half-familiar voices, highways with no speed limit, airplanes flying without engines, the rush of wind. The wind component grew louder, climbed to hurricane force. The nature of the sound changed, darkened to the staccato of nightmare, automatic weapons, rifle butts on doors, black machinery pounding past design limits, an electronic man shouting, "Identify yourself, you in the boats, identify yourself," as if that could ever be a reasonable request in the morning, before coffee.

Paul sat bolt upright and cracked his head painfully on the deck-head over the bunk. He fell back on the pillow, swearing.

Light knifed through the portholes and pinned details against background. A pair of blue jeans, crumpled on the deck. A half-eaten plate of beans. A tan neck and a curl of black hair, stirring in the shadows of the bunk beside him.

Jenny woke up, her eyes wide. "Drug search!" she muttered. The world was filled with the clatter of pistons.

Paul got his pants on and opened the hatch to the cockpit. A huge, V-bottomed, white-and-black-and-international-orange machine jinked and hovered over the mast, scrambling air and water into a frenzy of ripples. A Coast Guard chopper, a Goat with radar cone in the nose and a man with a megaphone in the gun door. Paul made telephone motions with his hands, then retreated below, shutting the hatch. He called up the chopper on the Coast Guard working frequency and gave them the names of the boats and their occupants.

"We have a report you were overdue," the radio crackled back. "There's been SAR out since dawn. Don't you people ever file ETAs?"

"I told 'em," Paul answered. "There's been some kind of screw-up. Over."

"You'll get the bill," the Coast Guard pilot warned. "We have to charge you for some of the costs. Lucky for you we've only been up since dawn." He signed off. The noise increased, changed pitch, then slowly, mercifully, diminished, until all that was left was a thin chattering that dwindled across Georges Sound and was gone.

Jenny looked at Paul. He looked back at her. The same thought was in both their minds—Queegie had called the Coast Guard on them—but all she did was grin like an idiot, and all he could do was grin back.

C H A P T E R   3 2

Morning was a movie, with a Hollywood set designer who spared
no expense to ensure spectacular backdrops. Thick chains of violet
clouds from a weak low moving into the area cut off half the sky,
focusing sunshine between their links like the flaps of a klieg lamp,
so that people leaving their houses to chop wood or take kids to
hockey practice felt like they were on stage, spotlit. The air was
clear and cool as spring water. The wind polished smells, sounds,
highlights. Colors rang true. The Eel Pond drawbridge, rising to
admit the sloop and the lobster boat idling behind her, seemed like
a curtain rising.

Paul spotted the man as soon as he was clear of the bridge pilings,
and his heart pounded harder.

He was a little too distant to make out the features. On the other
hand, it was 7:40 A.M. on a Saturday morning in March, and the
yard was closed. The figure did not look like Bull or John Poole or
Old George, the only people likely to have business that day on the
rigging dock. It did look a lot like Queegie Hopkins. Paul took the
sloop into the rigging dock. The figure strode to meet him, planting

itself at the head of the dock. Mirror sunglasses flashed. It was indeed Queegie, standing arms and legs akimbo by the diesel pump, like some doom-laden sheriff in the last scene of a Western.

Paul ignored him, for the moment. He brought the sloop around, bow heading out of the harbor, put the engine in reverse to kill the speed, and let the wind push her gently into the dock. He hung out fenders and ran spring lines from bow and stern. It was close to low tide, and the pilings were high in relation to the water. Queegie came up to the dock's edge, above the sloop, watching across Eel Pond where Jenny Crooke maneuvered the lobster boat to her mooring. His face was white and set. His fists were knotted. Paul felt the guilt Jenny had seen in him stir, fester, and raise fumes. He shut it off, hard. Jenny was right. There were some situations where guilt, and fault, were irrelevant. Though he could still feel sorry for the guy.

"Queegie," Paul began, seriously.

The helmsman looked down, but said nothing. Paul threw bow and stern lines on the dock; Queegie made no move to tie them up. Paul shut off the engine and the electrical system. He took off his glasses and climbed up the ladder. As his head came level with the planking it confronted Queegie's boat shoes, khaki pants, windbreaker, and finally the rugged features of the helmsman. He had taken off his shades. The small blue eyes looked like metal tools, cold and sharp and poised to cut.

"Gary." Jenny Crooke's call came across the water. "I need to talk to you."

Queegie ignored her. He kept his eyes on Paul.

"Let me get the lines, Queegie," Paul said levelly.

"Gary," the girl called.

"You son of a bitch."

Although he was expecting some initial challenge, the helmsman's voice came as a shock: broken, ragged and soft against the wind. Queegie licked his lips. Paul deliberately refrained from doing what he felt like, which was stand sideways and raise his fists in an attitude of war. Violence hung in the air, like a jet with dead engines.

"You goddamn sneaking lying cheating double-crossing wimp asshole son of a bitch asshole."

"I should explain things to you, also—"

"Shut up," Queegie replied. "You *bastard*!" Now his fists opened and closed, spasmodically. He was working himself into a state where controls no longer existed.

"Gary," Jenny shouted again, "wait, please. It had nothing to do with him."

Queegie roared, "Shut up, you *whore*!"

"It has everything to do with me, now," Paul contradicted her. The talking had gone on longer than he expected, and he believed there might be a chance to deal with Queegie on human terms, rather than at the level of rutting goats.

"I'll deal with her later," Queegie muttered, mostly to himself, and hit Paul with great force, at kidney level. Paul doubled over, staggering against the head of the ladder. Queegie backhanded him low, in the face. The helmsman's muscles were strong from hundreds of hours of steering Twelve-Meters and even a reverse blow felt like getting a boulder thrown at his head. Paul overbalanced, sideways and backward, off the ladder. The entire midsection of his body felt numb, but his brain reacted against the constant of gravity and sent his left arm, just in time, to hook around one of the ladder's vertical stanchions. He fell, but only a couple of feet. His body straightened out, agony radiating from spasmed muscles in his side. Scrabbling weakly, he managed to get a purchase with the toes of his boots on the slippery weeds of the rungs.

He hung there, for four or five seconds, while his lungs caught up on air. He could see the wooden rung where his cheek rested spotting scarlet. Queegie's high school ring had laid open his cheek. The sight of his own blood brought anger burbling to the surface.

When Paul had enough air to feed his muscles he took hold of the stanchion with his right hand. Slowly, laboriously, he climbed back to pier level and stood as straight as he could.

Queegie towered before him, in exactly the same attitude, exactly the same expression on his face.

Paul held up a hand and said, thickly, "OK. OK. Maybe I owe you one. I owe you that one. Maybe." He had to wait for more breath. He flexed his right arm a little, in case talking was not what Queegie had in mind. "But from now on," Paul finished, chopping his hand in denial, "that's it. That's enough."

It was meant as a warning, and that was how Queegie took it. The helmsman closed in immediately, fists up. He feinted with his left fist, jabbed at Paul's stomach with his right. Paul moved fast to one side, out of the way of both man and drop. Queegie whirled and lashed out with his right leg in an ersatz karate kick that glanced off Paul's thigh and immediately fouled his pants pocket. It caught there, just long enough for Paul to grab the heel with his left hand, then his right. He twisted the foot, viciously, around Queegie's knee. The helmsman, already off balance, yelled in pain and fell, rolling with the movement to save his joint. He landed heavily on the deck, against one of the gasoline pumps on the side next to the *Ettie*. A crow cawed from high above their heads in the rigging mast.

Paul let go and stood back. He could see a couple of figures hurrying toward them. It looked like his grandfather, and another man behind him. The cavalry was at hand. He touched his face gingerly.

The helmsman pulled himself up the gas hose. One of the figures down the dock shouted. Queegie tested his knee. It worked. He hunkered down and charged. Before Paul had time to readjust his thinking the helmsman had got an arm around Paul's neck and driven him, with the momentum of the rush, against the second gas pump. With his other fist he jabbed short, vicious blows at Paul's side, the same area he had hit earlier. He made hoarse, satisfied grunts every time his fist connected, torn words: "Liar, bastard, li', bas'." One of Paul's arms was jammed against the pump. He wrestled the other around Queegie's throat but the helmsman simply sank his chin close to his neck to prevent Paul getting at his windpipe.

Then Queegie had another idea. He leaned back, pulling Paul's neck forward with the crook of elbow around it, and snapped forward, slamming the back of Paul's head against the gas pump's steel housing. Twice, three times he repeated the maneuver, harder and harder. Every time a yellow lamp flashed in Paul's head, and every time he felt lightness spreading around the pain in his scalp. Mingled with the lightness was a clear understanding that he was going to have to do something drastic now, or lose it entirely. Queegie pulled Paul's head back for the fourth time, to gain swinging room, and again Paul let his head snap back in automatic reaction, but instead of trying to twist away from the impact, Paul brought his forehead sharply forward, as hard as his neck muscles would go, butting the hard bone straight into Queegie's mouth.

Queegie yelled, and pushed away, loosening his hands so he could hold them to his nose and mouth. He took away one hand and looked at his fingers. Blood dripped in lavish red splashes from his nose.

Then a stooped figure in a blue frock coat pushed between the two men, ramming Paul back into the gas pump, causing Queegie to stagger backward a step or two, toward the edge of the pier. Old George's face bobbed behind like a half-shaven moon. Shock, concern, and a kind of grief contorted the features under the soiled captain's hat.

A half-empty liquor bottle fell from Bull's pocket and rolled across the boards.

"Jaysus," Bull shouted angrily. "Look at you. Like a couple of school kids fighting over girls again lookit Christ." His white hair flew in the wind. Anger crackled in his eyes.

George stooped, picked up the bottle, stashed it in his coat.

"Get out of the way, ole man," Queegie said, "I'm gonna kill the little double-crossing son of a bitch." He tried to move toward Paul but Old George took his arm, in an almost sympathetic gesture, and hung on. Queegie tried dragging him closer to Paul but Old George was very heavy and he could be very tenacious when he chose. He dug his fat nose into Queegie's jacket. Bull added a shove, and pushed himself back between the two men, arms horizontal and stiff. "Cut it out," he shouted, "this is not the time." He looked at Paul with an odd expression; anger, apprehension, and sadness all mixed together. "This is not the time," he repeated, an expression Paul wrongly attributed to immediate circumstances of blood and jealousy. "You should go home," he told Queegie levelly.

There was a distinctive splat and a burst of crow guano appeared on the left shoulder of Bull's coat.

Jenny had left the tender at her mooring in the middle of Eel Pond and rowed to the rigging dock. Now she climbed a ladder at the end of the pier. When Queegie saw her he froze. The girl looked at him and shook her head helplessly. Queegie's face scrunched up, like a five-year-old's. His eyes almost disappeared in the folds of his face.

"Damn you, Jenny," he said hoarsely. He ripped his arm, violently, from Old George.

"I need to explain, Gary," she said, once again. "I'll see you at the house."

"Go home, Mr. Hopkins," Bull repeated. "There's no point in staying here."

Queegie ignored him.

"I don't want to see you, whore," he told the girl. "Not at the house. Not anywhere, ever again. Stay away from me. Whatever you do, stay away from me." He looked at Paul, then Bull, as if they were equally responsible.

"Stay the fuck away," he repeated. He looked once, confusedly, around the horizon, as if he could not believe these events could happen in the normal frame of time and space. He took two, three steps backward, looking fixedly at the girl, then wheeled and strode down the dock, toward shore, chin hunkered back in his neck, his back arched forward.

"Shit," Paul sighed, and looked at the blood crusting on his fingers. He felt pity for Queegie. Then he looked up and saw Jenny looking after her lover, her eyes more full of pain than eyes had a right to be, and the sympathy vanished.

"Paul," Bull began.

"Don't," Paul interrupted. "I know. I don't need it."

Old George made his goat sound. Paul glanced up sharply. Tears were running down the guard's face. Instinct sent Paul danger signals, and his chest grew cold with fear. Old George might be simple, but he did not waste tears over fistfights.

Jessica, he thought. His chest locked with fear.

"What's going on." Paul looked at Old George, then at his grandfather for answers. "What are you doing here, anyway," he whispered. "Nat was supposed to tell you. Is Jess—," he swallowed, unable to form the words.

The old man looked behind him all of a sudden, as if afraid he might fall as Paul had just done. He stood very hunched. From behind the pumps Bull dragged out a stool used by the gas attendant on summer holidays. His muscles seemed to drop his bones on the seat, piled anyhow behind the wrinkled skin, all the energy gone.

Without looking at Paul he said, "Jessica's fine. It's Ashley."

"What about Ashley." Paul dropped his hands, damage forgotten. "What the hell's happened!"

Bull still would not look at him. He blinked rapidly against the wind.

"A plane crash." He shook his head, the confusion of an old man to whom youth and death simply did not equate. "She died."

Paul said "No," forcefully. Reality was the words you used to define it, and for a split second he could make his own magic, deny other people's words by the power of his own.

But now Bull, with George as chorus, began relating the details; 3:30 P.M. yesterday, Newport State Airfield, two others in the plane, crash on takeoff; and the words of Ashley's death grew in number and strength until he could no longer deny them existence.

"Someone should go down there," Bull said. "I don't know if her parents know yet."

Paul nodded. He looked at Jenny Crooke where she stood, immobile, at the end of the dock, staring after Queegie, arms hugging herself tight against the wind.

Life on one end of the dock, he thought. Death on the other.

But the only one you could truly rely on lay on the landward side. Death would never disappoint you or stand you up. As it had not stood up Nicole and Jack. Or now, Ashley.

Paul hesitated for a second only. Then he turned his back to the girl and followed Queegie down the dock.

᙮

He got a flight out of Bangor at 10:30, changed in Boston, and arrived in Providence a little after two that afternoon.

At T. F. Greene Airport he rented a car. He headed east, through Providence. The capital of Rhode Island looked like a city rebuilding after a major war. The expressways seemed to turn and bank, narrow and dilate for no apparent reason. The brickwork crumbled, the billboards announced appliance sales.

He turned right down Route 118, crossed the Mount Hope Bridge. The airfield lay off 118 in a broad plate of fields rimmed by trees, minimalls, insurance agencies, car dealers. Access ran down cracked asphalt between chain-link fences, ranch houses, and mobile homes. Paul spotted a shine of metal through a copse to his right and braked instinctively. A Middletown Police patrol car stood across a gate in the chain-link. A compact car with US Government plates was parked after it. A sign on the gate read: "No Admittance, Restricted Area Keep Gate Closed."

A fat, red-headed cop in dark glasses leaned from the patrol car window when Paul got out.

"Read the sign," he said. "You can't go in."

"Is that where the plane crashed?"

"No, they're playing golf in the rough, and I'm here to protect them. What d'you think?"

"My cousin's wife was in that plane," Paul told him. "I just got down from Maine. I have to get through."

The dark glasses precluded human contact. A large, freckled hand pointed down the road.

"Check with the airport people," the cop said. "Maybe they'll let you. I can't." He went back to reading a paper.

There was no other way through the chain-link, Paul saw. When he got to the airport proper he went to the largest building, a broad, white aluminum hangar with the words "Newport Airways" painted on the side. Single- and twin-engine aircraft were tied down against the southwest wind. A young man came out from the "Airport Management" door. There was no room here for the FAA, he told Paul. They were using the old terminal, across the parking lot, for their investigation.

The old airport terminal was an ancient, barnlike structure, painted coral, with a ridiculously tall brick chimney. A round control tower rose on one end, sheathed in corrugated iron, with a circle of glass at the top. The windows were filled with houseplants.

The building's northern end had sagging bay fronts, a flagpole, shards of abandoned runway showing through the grass. The paint was flaked, the grass was wild. A couple of gray-haired men, dressed in work clothes and work boots, beckoned him around to the other side and met him at the entrance.

"Can't use the main door, it's blocked."

"I'm looking for someone who can let me get to the crash site."

"The FBI."

"FAA, I think?"

"Yeah. FBI. Well, come on in."

The terminal had been converted into a maintenance depot. An old, cream fire engine and a fifties-vintage sanding truck occupied half its space. Beside the fire engine, cases with "Federal Aviation Administration—Northeast Regional" stenciled on them lay next to twisted bits of metal Paul decided not to look at.

Old office furniture, lockers, and partitions cut the rest of the building into living quarters. There was a length of linoleum that might once have been a waiting area. Scrap wood burned cheerfully in a huge stone fireplace. The two workmen led him past a wooden booth with a sign reading "Information," to the base of the control tower. There a man in a nylon suit took out forms from an attaché case and lined them up on a slanted counter.

Paul looked curiously around him. The room took up the whole ground level of the tower. Its furniture was World War I surplus. The clock was round, copper, forties functionalism. The meteorological charts on the wall were all pre–Pearl Harbor. There was a chart of U-boat silhouettes by the door. The counter was an old Air Force radio console with the innards ripped out. Obviously this place had been the airport's operations center and was left intact when replaced by the newer building.

The FAA man was thirtyish, balding. He chain-smoked low-tar filters. "I'm going out there right now," he said, "I'll talk to Zelewski. Normally, they don't allow next of kin," he continued, "at least not on the immediate site." He picked up a nylon parka, a wad of forms and left Paul standing at the entrance to the tower.

"Why'd ya come here?" a voice behind him said. "You a reporter?"

Paul turned. The larger of the two workmen was seated in an armchair to one side of a formica table, by the window. He had a square, rugged face and a good head of silver hair under a cap that read "Rhode Island Department of Airports."

The other man was small, strong-chinned, hook-nosed. He dusted off a chair, using today's edition of the *Providence Journal*. "Ukraine Emigres Claim Soviet Bus Bomb," the headline read. He did not succeed in removing the mark of a work boot from the vinyl seat.

"I'm—family," Paul said and sat down, realizing that in fact he was not sure why he had come. There was a vague sense of obligation, nothing of substance. Until this moment, travel had imposed its own ethic on thought, and no goal seemed more important than to buy the ticket, catch the plane, keep moving, always keep moving. Movement denied death, at least temporarily. But now movement had stopped. He realized he felt strange, empty, in shock.

A deep sadness welled back inside him, and it wasn't until this moment that he realized it had gone, or at least diminished, baked out by the warmth of one night with Jenny. Not even a night, a lousy ten hours to give him the illusion of not being alone.

The FAA man came back ten minutes later.

"You can take a quick look, if you want," he called toward Paul. "Zelewski wants to talk to you."

Paul followed him out of the building across the parking lot. The contrast in temperature was painful, for he had got warm by the fire, and the wind was cold.

Down to the end of the runway, past orange markers, rows of landing lights. The grass became a field, cut with old wood fences, rough with scrub and soggy ground. There were trees on the perimeter, ranch houses he had seen from the access road, small boats covered in blue tarps. Neighbors looked curiously from backyards. Their Polaroid cameras clicked and whined. He had no trouble making out the wreckage now.

Two large pieces stuck out among a lot of torn, blackened scrub, uprooted trees, a broken fence. Men stood around the bits of plane, stretching strings or tape measures between them.

From close up it was just possible to recognize the torn and twisted metal as an aircraft. Paul kept the pieces in his peripheral vision as he advanced, fearing surprises. His heart was pounding again. About fifty feet away from the first large chunk he almost stepped on a flap of aluminum, crumpled like tinfoil. Beyond that, a deep score in the earth, surrounded by more metal. Then, maybe nine feet long and the height of a man, what must have been a tail section, for it still bore a recognizable letter "N" and most of a rudder. Cables and structural pieces stuck out anyhow.

From that point on junk of every size littered the ground. Paul had never realized how much equipment went into a six-seat plane. A wheel, still hooked to landing gear. Cables. A ballpoint pen. A seat lay on its side, the green fabric whole, the safety belt unfastened. Paul tried not to visualize Ashley sitting there, terrified, as the ground came up to smash her.

A tall, thin man in a gray ski jacket put away a tape measure and approached Paul. He looked like an Airedale, with his long nose and cropped blond hair. His eyes stuck out. He asked for Paul's driver's license, and seemed satisfied by the fact that his name and town of residence were the same as Ashley's. He said his name was Zelewski. He assumed Paul wanted to know some of the details.

There had been three passengers in the plane, the tall man said. A pilot, Chip Olson, of Jamestown. Mrs. Briggs. A friend of Mrs. Briggs, a Swiss national, Michel de Gretz.

The plane took off at 3:07 P.M., March 28. Yesterday. Full power setting, proper flaps. At around 150 feet the pilot apparently lost control. They had, so far, found only one witness, a nine-year-old boy, who actually saw what happened. However three other persons in neighboring houses claimed they heard a loud report just prior to the sound of the crash.

Whatever the circumstances, the plane apparently stalled, swiveled into a nose-down position, and plummeted. Its airspeed was around eighty-five miles per hour when it hit the ground. It somersaulted, then skidded thirty-two yards, ripping the wings off, breaking the fuselage in two. The left engine caught fire, igniting the fuel tank in the left wing, which accounted for the charred grass. They would have to wait for the autopsy results, Zelewski added, but it looked like all three passengers were killed on impact. At least nobody had burned to death.

Paul looked at the horizon while Zelewski spoke. He wished the FAA man would not talk so loud. He felt he ought to ask questions, act intelligent, check the throttle settings himself, but he simply did not have the energy.

A loud report could mean anything: a backfire, igniting av-gas, a shattering propeller.

Zelewski pulled out a small spiral notebook and a fancy ballpoint. "I bent a couple rules, to let you see this," he said, establishing the basis for exchange. "I'm gonna ask you a couple questions."

The naval architect shrugged, still absorbed in his own thoughts.

"John Briggs," Zelewski said. "Your cousin. Ashley Palmer Briggs was married to him. Died a year ago, January. What happened?"

Paul looked at the investigator, wondering what he was getting at, knowing, in the back of his mind. A little animal wiggled out of somewhere dark.

"He was young," Zelewski commented, "relatively."

He should tell him, Paul thought. Unlikely as it all was, he should mention the phone conversation with Ashley.

But the timing was so wrong. Ashley would hardly have been able to locate, trap, tip off, and be elaborately murdered by some co-conspirator of Van Meerwen's henchman within ten days of overhearing some remarks in a men's room.

And if this *were* more than just accident, then the implications were enormous in weight. Too enormous. He did not have the energy to go through it again. He shut the starting horror back, firmly. An *accident*. Slam.

"What's it got to do with any of this?" Paul indicated the wreckage.

"Procedure." The panacea excuse. The investigator flipped pages in his notebook.

"You're saying what?" Paul thought out loud. The words were out before he could stop them. "There's something funny about this?" He gestured toward the shattered plane again.

Zelewski caught him, sharply. "What do you mean, 'funny'?"

"Forget it." Paul turned away. "Stupid comment."

"Something suspicious? Tampering? Sabotage?" Zelewski's voice hurt Paul's ear. "What made you say that? Something made you say that."

"The 'loud report,' " Paul muttered, wishing he had not brought it up. He could not get the image of that passenger's seat out of his head.

"Do *you* have any reason?" Zelewski said, even more loudly than before, but Paul turned away abruptly and started walking, away from the tail section, away from the passenger's seat. He kept his head down to avoid stepping on any part of the plane.

"You oughta talk," Zelewski yelled after him. Paul kept walking and Zelewski continued, warning him now, "It would be easier to talk to me now, than subpoena you later."

Five steps. Six steps. Paul froze in his tracks. It had nothing to do with Zelewski's words. He had barely heard them.

By dint of detouring around bits of plane he was circling closer to the forward section of fuselage, and there was correspondingly more wreckage in the torn earth at his feet. Slotted longitudinal members, a crumpled propeller blade, a life jacket.

What had caught his attention, bringing the breath up short in his chest, was a small two-tone gleam. Red and white. It could have been anything, color-coded cable, candy wrappers, transistors.

He dropped to his knees and poked at the dead grass until he could see it.

A pill. Two pills. Small gelatin capsules, of the kind Ashley had flung once over the ice on Sancastin Pond because he made nasty remarks about her reliance on them, so many months ago.

Ashley.

The pills brought her back, through the shock, the way nothing else had. He could smell the perfume, see the mocking smile on her fine lips. Could almost hear the endearments and the sarcasm, offered with equal sincerity in that rough voice of hers. A wave of missing her broke over him, sharper than pain.

He picked up one of the pills between thumb and forefinger. Antidote for strong feelings. She and Jenny Crooke were alike in that. Not that he knew the girl at all, but it was something you sensed. Now the image of Jenny replaced that of Jack's wife.

Kneeling in the damp brush where Ashley died, holding the pill in his fingers, Paul knew he should feel shame. The thoughts of Jenny Crooke, the sudden need he had to see her again, felt like the worst kind of betrayal. He prodded his feelings, internally, the way he might have felt a broken arm.

"You'd better come back with us," a voice shouted in his ear.

Paul started. His fingers let go of the pill. The investigator swooped down beside him, like a blue jay, stabbing long fingers into the brush in exactly the same motion a jay would use to dig grubs with its beak. He held the pill up and examined it lengthily, turning it this way and that in the light.

"Downers," he announced, "prescription." His eyes popped at Paul, bird like. "More and more funny aspects to this crash," he remarked, and sniffed. He took out a handkerchief, wrapped the pill in it, put the hankie back in his pocket. He stuck his gold ballpoint in the ground where the pills had lain.

Then Zelewski took out a small plastic bag, the kind used to store leftovers. The baggie held a piece of metal. The metal was crazily contorted, but still you could distinguish telescoping sections, the tip-guard of a small antenna.

"I shouldn't even show you this," Zelewski yelled. The religion of secrecy ran deep in his federal soul. He prodded the antenna. Bits of chrome flaked off the blackened steel.

"Antenna," he continued, "for a small AM receiver and amp. We found some circuitry. The FAA guys think it's like what people use for model planes. Nothing like the radio systems in a normal aircraft."

Paul stared at the baggie. "In the luggage?" he suggested, scraping the words out over his vocal chords. "That guy, de Gretz? He could have been a model freak."

Zelewski stared at Paul, then reached in his pocket again and took out yet another baggie. This one held three or four short lengths of torn, discolored cable, the protective plastic stripped away. The investigator poked them, as well, and his eyes seemed to bulge even further. He looked back at Paul.

"Blown," he said. "Not torn. Not cut or sheared or melted. Blown. These cables led to the control surfaces in the tail section. Once they were severed, the pilot lost control of the aircraft. They never had a chance.

"I'm not allowed," he went on, "to draw conclusions now. But I have enough here, just in my pocket, to justify getting a lot more answers out of you than I been getting."

Paul stared straight ahead, saying nothing.

The sight of the miniature receiver brought back a picture of Fossett, the police chief, and the man from the state arson task force. There had been pieces of model radio in the burned corner of the Twelve-Meter shed, as well.

He looked up at Zelewski, who had put the baggies away and now held his wallet up to Paul's face, open so he could read the gold badge with the profiled eagle and the words embossed around it. "United States Department of Justice, Federal Bureau of Investigation."

The old guys had been right from the first, he thought irrelevantly.

Zelewski was not FAA at all.

C H A P T E R   3 3

When Paul finished talking with Zelewski he called Ashley's parents from the old terminal. A maid with a thick Spanish accent told him they were on their way to Rhode Island. "Que desastre," she said, over and over, and started sniffling.

He called the Newport house and left a message. They had a right to know what was going on, and the FBI man was unlikely to volunteer the information without being prodded.

Paul got back to Green Airport too late to make the last connection in Boston. He spent the night at a motel, and took the first flight out the following morning, getting to Bangor around noon.

After the first taste of spring in Rhode Island, Maine seemed gray and dry of colors. The highways were cracked and hummocked with frost heaves. Paul pushed the Jeep as fast as she would go, driven by a sense of great urgency.

The urgency had something to do with the chance that Ashley had been murdered. It had more to do with the hope of seeing Jenny Crooke before Hillman kicked her out.

The knowledge he might already be too late brought sweat to his armpits. Please, he repeated over and over, wrestling the Jeep around curves it wanted to take straight.

He skidded into the driveway of the A-frame house where Queegie lived only one hour and ten minutes after leaving Bangor.

There was no car in the driveway. No smoke rose from the stovepipe. Paul shook the door. It was locked. No one ever locked doors in houses around here. He looked through the sliders and saw empty cardboard boxes, a heap of discarded newspapers, a note on the table, weighted by a set of keys. No lights, no dirty plates, no coats, no books. Queegie—and Jenny—were gone.

Paul ran back to the Jeep. He drove to the meetinghouse. Panic raged, but he kept it clamped with a brute effort of will, even drew off it for strength. At a certain level of despair, he thought, panic became fuel; it was an old survival mechanism. Otherwise he tried not to think too much.

At this hour the crews were over at the clam company but there was a limo pulled up next to Hillman's sedan in the meetinghouse parking area. Paul burst through the entrance doors and found Shoop and Hillman seated at the farthest table, where the pulpit once had stood. The table was piled high with computer printouts and accounts sheets.

Shoop wore corduroy today, with cowboy boots. Hillman must have known the boss was coming, for he wore a tie under his parka.

The financier pushed his chair back as he followed Paul's approach. He slid his glasses down his nose and folded his arms like a superior court judge. His jaw was knotted tight and his eyes were cold. The body language was eloquent but Paul had no interest in Shoop's moods and messages. He strode up to the table and asked, without preamble, "Where are they? Queegie, Jenny Crooke. What happened to them? There's no one at the A-frame."

Hillman cleared his throat, and glanced nervously at Shoop, who kept looking at Paul.

"Spare me the steely looks, Cy," Paul snapped. "Where are they, Warren."

Shoop said, "Gary Hopkins has quit. He took the tactician, Steve Erickson. Two other crew members. The best of the bunch. Because of you," he continued, "and that—that tramp."

"OK." Paul refused to be drawn. He rocked back and forth on his feet. "We can discuss that later. Where is she? The 'tramp.' "

"We have lost the only professional Twelve-Meter helmsman we can get," Shoop rumbled on. "You have effectively sabotaged this whole effort—"

"*Shut up!*" Paul yelled.

Shoop's teeth clicked. His eyebrows shot skyward. Paul cut him off with a shoulder.

"Warren? Come on!" He slammed the table with his fist. The financier looked at Paul as if he were rabid.

"We understand," Hillman looked at Shoop, "You must be very upset about Ashley."

"Don't make excuses for me," Paul hissed. "If you don't tell me I'll find out at the clam company."

Shoop cleared his throat. Paul pounded the table again. Hillman shrugged, unhappily.

"Slow down, Paul. She went to Amesboro. The bus station."

"With Queegie?"

Hillman shook his head. "She got a ride with one of the cooks."

Paul ran for the doorway. Hillman called his name, and Shoop yelled something, a warning, but the door cut off their voices and Paul was not listening anyway.

The Amesboro bus station was actually a convenience store. It sold greeting cards, frozen vegetables, cigarettes, and newspapers in racks along the front. A small waiting room in back held pinball machines, a phone booth, and an overweight family on plastic seats.

According to the schedule the only bus of the last two hours had left for Bangor at 2:30 P.M. Almost two hours ago. Paul got back in the Jeep. He filled up with gas opposite the police station and headed north again, back where he had just come from, pushing the limits of the vehicle's stability, tapping his fingers nervously on the stick shift, endangering the lives of fast dogs, slow cats, skunks just coming out of hibernation. . . .

The first trickle of rush hour began as he reached the Bangor city limits. Streams of outbound cars hindered his turns. He had trouble finding the bus depot, finally stopping to ask at a pizza parlor. He did not get to the station until quarter to five.

Panic gave way to a sense of complete doom. Too late, he must be too late. He ran through the glass doors to the middle of the waiting area, looking up and down the aisles.

It was a modern travel terminal carved from the brick bulk of an old commercial building; fake tiles, yellow panels, bright lights. Black plastic chairs with coin-operated TV sets attached. She was nowhere to be seen.

Despair grew in Paul's chest. There were only seven or eight people waiting, and no one who even looked like her. He asked at the ticket counter. There was no other waiting room. He checked outside, but nobody was fool enough to wait in the cold. He checked at the ticket counter again. She could have caught a St. Croix bus for Calais, the man said, or a Greyhound for Montreal. Or the city bus to Bangor airport.

It was then Paul realized he had lost her. In a flash of intuition he saw she had gone straight to Bangor International.

From Bangor, she could fly to New York or Boston, change for Miami or Nassau, change again for Trinidad. He could try to catch up to her at the airport, but there were a lot of flights on Monday evenings, and he knew it was a forlorn hope.

Paul turned, slowly, for the door. His muscles drained of nervous energy. He had trouble moving. As he turned he saw a scrap of blue on the floor behind an archway leading to the front of the building. Blue denims. Someone was sitting behind the archway. Someone with boat shoes on his, or her, feet.

Breath catching in his throat, he walked around the archway.

Jenny Crooke sat on her canvas sail bag, listening to her Walkman. Her face realigned itself a little when she saw Paul, but the dark glasses were on and he could not see her eyes.

He stood there for a moment, beating back the shock. His heart pounded, his face was a war zone. His throat was parched. He was so sure she'd be gone. He cleared his throat.

"Where d'you think you're going," he croaked, finally.

A pause.

"South," she said.

"Where, south?"

Another pause.

"St. Thomas. There's a boat I can work on, if I want. Charter schooner. Standing offer."

The PA system hawked. "Greyhound announces the departure of the five-o-five to Boston and New York City. Gate three." She glanced toward the speaker.

"That's your bus? Boston, New York?"

A nod. Paul squatted to her level.

"To catch a plane?"

Another nod.

"Why didn't you just go to the airport?"

"Money." She shrugged; there hadn't been enough.

"Are you leaving because Quee—I mean, because Gary left?"

"No."

"Then why."

"It's obvious I'm not welcome. Everyone blames me for Gary leaving. I seduced you. Painted woman. Old Man Shoop is back. You know," the first shred of feeling showed in her face, "you look really odd, Paul. Are you OK?"

"I'm OK. Go on."

"Gary," she half-smiled. "In typical fashion, he called up the Byram Yacht Club, the commodore. Told them he was quitting because the whole team had come undone. Unprofessional, he said. A hick challenge, he called it. The commodore was quite upset. He was at that party when I came. He got sprayed with champagne."

"That's not why you're leaving."

"They might withdraw their backing. Are you sure you're all right?"

"Jenny, I know why you're leaving."

"No shit, man."

"You're going," Paul told her, spacing his words so he could exert maximum control over what he said and how he said it, "because I turned my back on you. Yesterday morning, on the dock."

Silence. People lined up at one of the gates for the New York bus. She glanced in their direction.

"You're leaving," Paul continued urgently, "because you thought I was shutting you off. Because of Queegie, because of Ashley's dying. You said I was prone to guilt. You figured maybe it had taken over, pushed out what I felt for you. I'm right. You know I am."

The loudspeaker repeated the announcement for the five-o-five to Boston and New York. Jenny drew her legs under her.

"You could have said something, mahn," she muttered. "I know you were shattered by your cousin dying. I understand that. But you could have phoned, at least."

"Listen." Paul leaned forward. "You're right. You're absolutely right. I panicked. I shut off. It's a habit. I've spent three years shutting off because people have left me, one way or another. But I had time to think about it yesterday. When I saw where she died. And I realized I was through with it. Bored with the self-indulgence. I was—I *am*—ready to face things more. You, for example."

The words were suggestive. He reached out, lifted her dark glasses. She did not turn her head, but the eyes behind the lenses were blank as blue-painted walls.

"It's not just you," she said.

"If you leave, we'll never see each other again," Paul replied. "So stay. We'll go to Shoop. He won't quit now, Queegie or no Queegie. There'll be a job."

"Don't harass yourself, man," she told him, getting to her feet. "I can get a job anywhere."

The bus driver came out of gate three, took a final look around, and glanced at his watch.

"Then stay for this reason," Paul urged. His voice was unsteady. "To give us time. To see if we can pull this off. You and me. What am I saying, Jenny. I don't want you to go."

She looked at the gate and hesitated.

"If it doesn't work, it doesn't work," he added. "But if it does—well, hell. Think of how much fun it could be!"

She looked at him. Then she took her headphones off and shook her hair free. "Paul," she said, "how was I to know you gave a damn? How was I to be sure you weren't fooling me? Wanking yourself? Or maybe you just did not have the strength. It takes strength. How was I to know?"

"I'm not making excuses. It's something you have to decide."

"Lahd." She looked away. After a heartbeat she looked back. The blue eyes had cracked a little, Paul saw, like pond ice breaking, the warmer water upwelling through the fault lines, pooling over.

"But it's so much warmer in St. Thomas," she complained. Her movements no longer angled toward gate seven.

A temporary victory.

Paul picked up her bag.

"Wait," she said. "If I go back to French Harbor—and I mean if—it has to be on my own." She saw the confusion in his face and touched his sleeve impulsively. "Things would have to go at their own pace. You know? We can't rush them. That way, if it doesn't work out, the damage is not so bad."

"Sure," Paul said, "what you're saying—"

"What I'm saying is," she told him firmly, "if I came back, I'd need another reason. I'd want to work on the boat. I could live at the A-frame again. I'm sorry to be so hardheaded about it, but I don't like to be tied. I'd need my own job."

"In that case," he urged her, "we better go see Shoop. He thinks we'll never get another skipper, and it's all your fault."

"Rubbish," the girl said calmly. "I could get another skipper tomorrow. One twice as good as Gary."

Paul stared at her. Queegie was one of the top-ten big-boat racing skippers. The rest worked for the other syndicates.

"Who," he asked, finally.

"Joe McMurdo."

Paul laughed, thinking she was kidding.

She frowned at him.

"Joe McMurdo?" Paul said. "He would never do an America's Cup."

"I know him pretty well," she contradicted him, "and I think he would, if I asked him."

She looked at him defiantly. The tilt of her chin suddenly made him think of Ashley. The plane's passenger seat bubbled to the surface of his mind, belt loose, sideways, lonely in the Newport scrub.

"Hell, it's always worth a try," Paul said.

Then he turned and headed for the exit.

He did not check behind him.

He had a feeling she would follow—and besides, he still held her bag.

Joe McMurdo was not quite as enthusiastic as Jenny Crooke had hoped—she had to fly down to St. Lucia to convince him—but he eventually agreed to skipper the second *Challenge* and showed up in French Harbor two days before the new boat was launched.

The first thing he did was pull the crew from their tuning and polishing. Together they took out the earlier, double-keeled boat so McMurdo could start getting a feel for Twelve-Meters.

Paul's first glimpse of him was in a bosun's chair, seventy-five feet up the mast of the old *Challenge*, taking apart the mechanism that locked the sail in place on top of the spar. A wiry forty-five-year-old, with eyes as mild as his beard was outrageous and a habit of not speaking when he had nothing important to say.

He dressed only in green work clothes, a watch cap and sheepskin boots. He spent a lot of time looking through people behind a pipe that was usually dead. Paul soon decided he was just as much a prima donna, in his own way, as Queegie Hopkins had been. This judgment was more emotional than rational. It had a lot to do with distrusting the easy way McMurdo and Jenny Crooke spoke to one another. Paul himself had trouble speaking to Jenny since the day he brought her back from Bangor.

The second *Challenge*—everyone called her *US 93*, after her racing numbers, to distinguish her from the earlier boat—was launched in early April, with a minimum of fuss and champagne. McMurdo took her out for her first sail trial the day after the launch. In accordance with new security rules set up by Vanzetti, both the lobster boat and the yard's workboat sheepdogged her out to sea to keep away intruders.

The trial was not a success. This was the first real-world test of the curvy keel, and the keel proved very temperamental and tricky to handle. Too soft a touch on the three wheels regulating its shape, and nothing happened; the Twelve sailed on as before. However, if you coarsened the adjustments just a little, the keel curved too much, and stalled. Then it felt like the boat was chained to a huge bucket dragging along, under its center of gravity. The beeping of the stall alarm, wired to sensors in the fin's edge, seemed to permeate the morning.

As they wrestled with the keel a light plane dropped out of the clouds and circled repeatedly above them. They noted the registration number. Everyone knew it belonged to one of the rival syndicates. Squidlips showed his buttocks at it. The plane flew on, unimpressed, taking pictures for a good hour.

Finally, with the day drawing to a close, they left the keel in neutral position and sailed her normally, without frills. It was blowing and she settled down well to the breeze, taking the waves confidently and quite fast, as a longer boat should. Then the genoa tore. The sail collapsed overboard and McMurdo radioed for the *Betty-Anne* to tow them back in.

For two days running it blew too hard to sail. When the front had passed through, the wind dropped. As soon as the wind fell, the fog came in. Everyone relaxed, thinking they'd get a break from training, because fog on this coast, like uninvited guests, tended to come for Sunday and stay for the week. However, on the second day of fog McMurdo roused the crews at 6:00 A.M. and told them they were going out.

What about the fog, he was asked.

The fog would stop planes from flying, McMurdo answered. It

would do no harm to keep the other syndicates in the dark when they got the keel to work.

But they had no navigator, no tactician.

Jenny Crooke was the new tactician, McMurdo replied. And Paul Briggs could fill in for the navigator. The rest of the time, they would rely on the lobster boat's radar.

The boats quit the clam company dock a little before nine. Visibility was one hundred yards and dropping. From the shore, the boats seemed to lose substance very quickly, hard molecules of steel, wood, and plastic streaming off in every direction to become part of the soft, gray cloud. You heard the diesels of the workboats, the crackle of the radios, the calls of the crew even, a long time after the boats themselves were lost to sight.

ᴢᴢ

Vanzetti watched the boats disappear from three different angles on the massed TVs of the clam-company security office.

There was a worried set to the private detective's face. He exchanged a few words with the duty guard. Out of habit he checked the monitors again. Then, figuring that what he was supposed to be protecting was out of his hands anyway, he got in his car and drove to the Diner for breakfast.

Vanzetti was getting to be a regular at the Diner. He had driven there from the clam company so often he knew to the second how long it took: 13.7 minutes without fog, traffic, or cops whipping around the unbanked curves at an average speed of 60 MPH.

There was a booth he normally used that he considered "his." Abbie, the waitress, knew him by name and reputation and served the coffee black and sweet without his having to specify.

As to the other customers, while they did not exactly accept the newcomer—this would have taken two lifetimes spent exclusively in the area, one by his parents, the other by himself—they at least were civil. When Vanzetti walked in some of the more ebullient types would occasionally nod in his direction.

The rest simply treated him like a chair, or a square of wallpaper, which was a step or two up from the blank, hostile stares normally reserved for outsiders.

Abbie served the coffee and took his order for a plate of scrambled eggs. Vanzetti watched her move back to the counter. She had a wonderful ass, in his opinion. He liked the way she handled men.

He thought, not for the first time, she would be first-class in bed. He also thought she looked a little pensive today. Maybe the fog had that effect on people. It was probably an instinctive thing, a relic of earlier stages in man's development. The gray stuff suddenly cut your defense perimeter to nothing, providing a whole world for your foes to hide in, and you grew—well, thoughtful as a result.

Maybe that accounted for it, Vanzetti reflected as he sipped his coffee.

Why he'd been getting so nervous about the clam company these last few days.

It was more than Paul's cousin getting wasted. That was a professional job. But if she was killed for what she knew, the motive for violence had died with her.

Vanzetti pulled out the Bangor paper and looked at it without great interest.

He had done everything humanly possible to shield the Twelve-Meter from spies or arsonists or whatever, he told himself. That was what the contract specified.

If there was a hole a mile wide in security outside the plant, it was none of his concern.

The goddamn fog! It rolled beyond the curtains and he cursed it under his breath. He was not used to fog or working in the country; he was not used to silence and trees and land with no people. He had grown up in Boston, and people were his habitat. Almost with nostalgia the detective concentrated on an article about a fire in Augusta. It had been a three-alarm blaze that destroyed three multiple-family dwellings and a Laundromat.

Abbie brought the plate of eggs over. Instead of dropping it on the table, as she usually did, she perched on the bench opposite, leaned forward and said, "Can I talk to you for a minute?"

Vanzetti nodded. He tried not to let his surprise show. All along he'd had a feeling she was hot for him. But some waitresses could convey that impression to every customer.

"It's probably nothing," she continued, whipping her ponytail back. Her eyes were earnest. "I wouldn't even think about it, normally, 'cept I get worried about Paul."

"Paul Briggs," she went on, misreading the disappointment in the detective's face. "It's as if someone's trying to wipe out that family. I mean, Jack. And his wife. I don't know. . . ."

"So," Vanzetti interrupted her, "what did you want to tell me?"

"It's probably nothing."

"Tell me anyway." Vanzetti shook salt on his eggs, scooped up a forkful, waved it magnanimously, but all the while he was thinking, "How does the son of a bitch *do* it?"

"There was a guy in here yesterday," Abbie continued, staring out the window at the fog. "I didn't think nothing of it, then, 'cause he wasn't interested in Paul or the Twelve-Meter boats or the yard or anything."

The detective's features darkened. The bandit's moustache seemed to take up more of his face. Abbie thought he looked a bit dangerous. Not unattractive, just dangerous. She went on, a little uncertainly.

"We get 'em, now an' again. Something about these bays around here. They migrate through 'em or something."

"Who?"

"Oh. The birds. It's a flight path, they call it. For going north in the spring and south in the fall, you know. They like the shore, I guess. Kinda like tourists."

"I don't get it," Vanzetti said. "What's birds got to do with it?"

"That man." The waitress leaned closer now because some of the customers at the counter were shutting up so they could eavesdrop. "He said he was a bird-watcher."

Vic rang the bell hard from the kitchen to signal she had orders backing up. Abbie ran off to tend to her other customers. When she came back she did not sit down but repeated, apologetically, "I guess I'm just being stupid."

"Why," Vanzetti asked her, "did you think he wasn't a bird-watcher?"

She shrugged and wiped her hands on her apron.

"No reason, really. Only, he didn't seem the type, you know? He didn't have a notebook or binoculars, though they coulda been in his car.

"And he wanted to know how to get places," she added. "Cully Head. The Point, 'course everybody wants to go there to see the lighthouse, the estates. . . . And Georges Spit. I mean, there used to be a house there, years ago, but the swimming's a lot better farther up the cove. Not that you'd want to swim in April." She laughed.

"What cove," Vanzetti asked.

"Sandy Cove. Where the clam company is. You know."

"Abbie," the detective asked, more urgently, "where is this place. Georges Spit?"

"Why, at the mouth," the waitress replied, a little hesitantly. "The mouth of Sandy Cove." The security man looked twice as sinister as he did earlier. "Where it goes into the sound."

Vanzetti pushed away his plate and got to his feet. His heart was beating faster. Abbie was right, it was probably nothing, but his cop instinct had woken up and was yelling loudly to the contrary.

"How do you get there."

"But you haven't finished your eggs!"

Dead silence in the Diner, as customers observed a man who wasn't a fireman acting like one, with no fire whistle having blown or anything.

"Just tell me," Vanzetti repeated, very calmly, "how to get to Georges Spit."

Abbie told him.

≋

Joe McMurdo got the keel to work about forty-five minutes after they hoisted the sails.

Part of it was because the wind was lighter, the boat's speed was lower, and therefore the keel could take a deeper camber without peeling the water right off its curve and stalling.

Partly, it was because McMurdo was getting the hang of the mechanism.

The skipper relied entirely on Paul to tell him where he was going and what course to steer. Jenny Crooke told him what the wind was doing and called for sail changes.

McMurdo himself stared through the mist, his feet braced apart, his hands lightly touching the four different wheels he had to play with.

There were, as on all Twelve-Meters, two identical sets of wheels on each side.

On this Twelve, the largest wheel controlled the rudder. Behind that were three smaller wheels. One controlled the angle of the short trim tab on the keel's forward end, the second regulated the curve of the keel itself. The third angled the after trim tab.

At first the boat stalled, constantly, just like last time. Each time they stalled, McMurdo would flatten the keel and call for another tack. The stall alarm would stop beeping, the slap of waves grow louder. Again he would try to feed in just enough curve to enhance the lift of the hull.

His fingers were everywhere at once, touching, caressing the controls. He seemed to listen to the way the boat moved and alter his own feedback accordingly, sensitive as a violinist who knew every note of the music, every tone and burr of the instrument he was trying to play.

Paul was too busy trying to figure out where they were through the multiple course changes to get very depressed over the keel's failure to perform.

Just as he was too busy to worry about how his affair with Jenny Crooke seemed to have stalled as finally and inexplicably as the keel.

She still slept at the A-frame, so he had not seen her nights. And since McMurdo had co-opted her as replacement for Steve, he barely saw her in daylight either.

They'd had lunch together once. When he tried to ask her what was wrong, she told him there was nothing wrong, she only wanted to go slow. When he'd asked her, significantly, how long she'd known Joe McMurdo, she remarked, "If it's virgins you want, mahn, hang around the fourth form." If she needed to take her time about this, Paul had decided, that was fine. He had an America's Cup challenger to prepare and that left little leisure for games.

On the twenty-second tack, McMurdo hit on just the right sequence of tab and curve, and the hull suddenly came alive. It seemed to surge through the water like a motor had suddenly kicked in. You could sense the sudden lift, see it translate into a tiny change in the ratio between wind and the rate at which water passed along the side of the hull.

A weight Paul barely realized was there dropped off his shoulders.

He threw himself backward from the computer and screeched joyously.

"Goddamn!" he yelled, "I can feel it! *It works*! I *love* you, baby," he told the boat.

Jenny turned around in surprise, then grinned. McMurdo said nothing but the ghost of a smile touched his face. Paul, his earlier jealousy forgotten, hugged the girl so hard her ribs cracked. She kept her back stiff but he didn't care. The crew examined the boat's wake and spoke words of cautious optimism. Then McMurdo called for another tack and they pushed hope aside in the routine of frenzy.

An hour, and many tacks later, they set the spinnaker, and found out the spinnaker boom was defective.

They learned this the hard way. The boom was set and the great hollow sail was drawing. The blue mountain logo of Gipfel Financial Services loomed across its outside surface, symbolizing the geological power of money. The mastman—a blond-haired twenty-year-old named Dennis, noticed the piston fitting that hooked one of the sail's lower corners to the end of the boom had not shut properly. He took a risk and shinnied out along the pole to close it, edging out far above the water, away from the port bow of the boat where it dipped and crunched into the cold Atlantic waves.

The kid was large, close to two hundred pounds. The torque of his body as he clung to the boom caused the fitting to twist. It slipped out of the sail. The end of the boom dropped. When the topping lift arrested its fall, Dennis's grip slipped, and he fell into the water.

The spinnaker flew out of control. The foredeck man yelled, "Man overboard!" Panic crawled in his voice because in fog this thick, in water this cold, a swimmer could easily drown before he was located and rescued. McMurdo automatically jibed the boat around. One of the grinders threw a life buoy at the kid's face as it disappeared astern, white against the gray mist and the grayer waters. Paul grabbed the VHF and radioed for the tender to pick him up. The *Betty-Anne* was a little astern of them, tracking them on radar. John Poole, at the wheel, had no trouble locating the mastman. He came right up in their wake and only just avoided running him over. He threw the boat in reverse and fished him out.

Dennis insisted on going back to the Twelve-Meter. His job was to sail, he said, flush with a new optimism born of their keel working. But McMurdo, chastened by the incident in a way Queegie never would have been, decided the fog was getting too thick for safety and turned the Twelve-Meter for home.

"I think this might do well," he commented to Paul as they sailed quietly northeast on a broad reach.

"What."

"The keel."

Paul grunted politely. He was punching out satellite coordinates on the computer to give them a course back to the mouth of Sandy Cove, plus an estimated time of arrival for the landfall, and he could not respond without losing track of where he was in the process.

"By the way," McMurdo added.

"Yeah."

"Jenny and me."

Paul said nothing, but he had the course, and the ETA was about to show up on the screen and now he could devote every atom of his attention to what the skipper was saying.

"Once, a long time ago," McMurdo said, "we were on a ketch. It was a delivery, north, through the Windward Passage."

"I'm not sure I follow," Paul said, putting a bored tone in his voice on general principles.

"Just listen," McMurdo told him. "Anyway, we ran out of wind one night, and a fishing boat full of Bahamians came up. We thought they were in trouble. Instead, we were. They had machetes and rifles. They took over our boat."

Paul glanced up, but the skipper had his back turned into the wind, both hands cupped around his pipe, trying, for the sixth or seventh time this sail, to get the dottle lit.

Jenny stood rigid behind him, pretending she had not heard a word.

"They rounded us up in the cockpit," McMurdo continued. "I think they were going to shoot us, dump us over the side. All except Jenny. We didn't know what had happened to her. Then she popped out of the forward hatch with the pump Winchester and put a charge of buckshot in their captain's ass."

"Yeah," Paul repeated.

"What I'm trying to say, is, OK. We had a fling once. It didn't work out. But we've been through stuff together that made us very, very close. That's all. I thought you might want to know."

McMurdo had got his pipe lit now. He was pulling fiercely at the stem, looking like a bearded combustion engine.

Paul double-checked his courses.

It gave him time to assess McMurdo's words, as well as the helium feeling that came into his own stomach when he heard them.

There was nothing between Jenny and McMurdo. Knowing that brought out the other big question Paul had been asking himself about the helmsman.

"I been meaning to ask you," Paul said.

More smoke.

"What made you change your mind."

"About what."

"About racing Twelve-Meters. I thought you gave it up. It was too one dimensional, or something. I read an article."

The skipper did not seem fazed. In fact he almost smiled around his pipe stem.

"I needed the money," he said. "To build another boat.

"A school boat," he continued. "So I can teach kids you don't have to be a millionaire jerk to enjoy sailing, enjoy the ocean. I figure, if this does well, I can do some promotion, some ads maybe, get the bucks.

"Plus," he added, "I got to admit, I missed it." He waved his hand around, at the Twelve-Meter, the fog. "Match racing. It may be one dimensional, but it's exciting as hell. And it sure beats sitting on your ass ashore, drinking the distillery dry."

The *Betty-Anne* materialized out of the fog on the exact minute Paul predicted they would be off the cove's mouth. They turned into the wind and let down the sails. John Poole took the Twelve-Meter in tow. The crew gathered around the after cockpit, stamping to keep their feet warm against the damp. The mastman who had fallen overboard wore two extra, borrowed sweaters but was still shivering. Paul loaned him his bomber jacket which, though the leather was rent, had a real sheepskin lining and was very warm.

Jenny Crooke avoided both Paul and the skipper and sat way aft, by the backstays, her face turned into the wind as they entered the mouth of Sandy Cove.

C   H   A   P   T   E   R   3   5

The man waited patiently in a stand of bayberry bushes at the tip of Georges Spit, looking across water toward the west.

He had arranged this hide well. He had rested a bundle of spruce branches between a stump and a nearby tree to sit on. Comfort, he believed, was very important on long stakeouts.

The bayberry was old enough to have thick branches at shoulder level, providing him with both camouflage and a place to rest his rifle when the time came.

It was chilly and very damp in the fog, but he was dressed in layers, two pairs of socks, thermal underwear, corduroys, and a light, waterproof windbreaker from a mail-order firm. The jacket, ironically enough, featured a silhouette of a Twelve-Meter on both shoulders. A blue forage cap covered his short blond hair.

The man reached between his feet, unfolded a poncho, and checked the two rifles rolled inside.

They were identical, M 1903-A4s, Korean War versions of the classic Springfield that was in turn nothing but a Mauser knockoff.

Modified for sniper service, .30 caliber, with Weaver sights. Old, but reliable and above all, very ordinary.

The bolt was on safety, a round up the spout. The metal cold but dry.

The man put one of the rifles across his knees. He did not need to keep it so handy, but the weight felt good, like having a friend in his lap.

Once again he took out the snapshot of the target and checked the main features; tags, he liked to call them, easy to recognize and aim at when the time came. Brown hair. Glasses. Habitually wore one of those old-fashioned flight jackets like you saw in dogfight movies.

Finally he took out a thermos of hot tomato soup. As he sipped, he looked out through the fog again.

The fog was inconvenient. They had scrubbed the trial yesterday because of it. He came out here at 5:00 A.M. on the off chance it would lift, and they caught him flat-footed; he had not expected them to sail by while it was thick and by the time he got his rifle ready they had already moved out to sea, shades within shades within shadows, the men indistinguishable from each other at that distance.

But despite it all, the hit man decided, the fog could be his friend. It would hide his position when he took out the target and conceal his retreat when the job was done.

In the fog, in these woods, it felt like there was nothing around him but dead and empty space.

Empty space beat people. He did not care for people. It was people who screwed you up, every time.

He picked up the rifle, and, resting it on the bayberry branch, traversed across the grayness, for practice.

≋

Vanzetti found the car half-buried in a patch of poison ivy three-quarters of the way up the dirt road leading to Georges Spit.

There was nothing out of the ordinary about the car. It was a late-model Japanese subcompact, two door, royal blue, no accessories besides an AM radio. No rental numbers, no dump or bumper stickers.

Maine tags. The galvanized bolts holding them in place were very shiny.

Vanzetti cursed himself quietly. Abbie's directions had been anything but perfect, and he'd got lost twice on the way.

The problem was, the car was *too* damn normal. The perfect, forgettable transport. The only odd thing about it was the total lack of any oddness. There wasn't even anything on the front seat. Nothing. Not even a candy wrapper.

And it faced outward. It had been backed into its hiding place, ready for a fast getaway.

Vanzetti left his sports car just down the track from the compact, square in the middle, to block its retreat. He checked his revolver was loaded, and put it back in its holster without snapping the restraining strap back on. He pulled up his jacket collar, to hide the white of his neck. Then he started jogging up the trail.

He came to the end of the track in less than two minutes, huffing mightily, for he was unused to this kind of exercise.

The cove lay in front of him, blending into the fog that still lay thick on the peninsula. The shoreline stretched on either side— toward the head of the cove and the clam company on his right, toward the end of Georges Spit, presumably, on his left.

Boulders, kelp, and driftwood near the water. Bushes, jack pine, scrub oak after that.

He noticed a speck of white, very bright in the dun fog and dead grass. A patch of white flowers.

Snowdrops. The name came unexpectedly to his mind. His mother had liked them. Spring was coming to the northland, he thought, irrelevantly.

There were too many rocks around to take footprints. Vanzetti moved to his left, instinctively keeping close to the bushes as he advanced toward the mouth of the cove. His city shoes were filling with sand and bits of salt hay. He was practically walking on tiptoe to avoid making any sound. His breath still came fast, but not so harsh that he missed the first thrum of diesels pulsing from the water ahead and to his right.

He checked his watch.

11:40. Way too early, but the boats were coming back in. The fog had got the better of them as well.

"Oh, *damn*," Vanzetti muttered to himself. He looked up and down the shoreline, but saw nothing, no trace of human presence whatsoever, if you excluded the odd bits of sea-borne litter on the high-tide mark.

Maybe it *was* only a bird-watcher, he thought. They had weird habits, to suit their quarry. But surely no nature lover, however eccentric, would bother looking for birds in a *fog?*

Vanzetti pulled out his revolver and put his thumb on the safety. Its heft felt good in his hand. He had to get to the mouth of the cove, for that was the narrowest part of the waterway, according to Abbie, and therefore the point where boats came closest to shore. If he could not find the man in time, at least he could warn the crew on the boats.

Vanzetti headed down the shore again, running as fast as he knew how. The salt hay crunched at every pounding step, and once in a while he hit a piece of driftwood, and it cracked.

The hit man was focusing so hard on the boat sounds coming across the water he almost missed the crack of breaking wood to his right.

Reluctantly, he lifted his eye from the eyepiece. All three boats were in plain sight now, cruising slowly, one after the other, ahead and to his left. They looked so much like ducks in a shooting gallery, he had to keep himself from chuckling.

The target was there, right in the center of the cross hairs. The bomber jacket was unmistakable among the bright, nautical foul-weather gear. Just another fifty yards to make sure. Then a light, two-pound pressure on the trigger, and the guy was history.

Wood broke once more, louder now.

People, the man thought. The rage flowed, sudden, sullen. Someone taking his damn pet for a walk. Or a real bird-watcher. Screwing him up again. He would have to put off the job until tomorrow. He rose, slowly, to peer over the tangle of bush.

That was no bird-watcher. Adrenaline spurted into the man's system, setting off well-polished alarms. He sank back in his hideout.

Opposition. Someone who knew he was here. The figure was running hell for leather through the fog, with something in his right hand, lifted at an eighty-degree angle, cop style. A piece. One of the security men, most likely.

The hit man was a professional. He considered his options, decided he had two.

He could abort the hit now, forever, ditch the rifles, and make his way out. The rifles could not be traced. He would be fifteen thousand dollars poorer, but that was a least-risk option.

Or hit the target now, and hit the security man also, if he got too close.

Even if he aborted the hit, the man thought, they could get him for attempted, and conspiracy.

He made his decision quickly, as he had been taught. He would hit now, get it over with. Might as well be hung for a sheep as for a lamb. He picked up the rifle, rested it on the bayberry branch, and sighted so the cross hairs lay square on the front of the bomber jacket. No time to check the other "tags." There was only one bomber jacket, anyway. He squeezed the trigger, very gently, with the front part of his right index finger, leading very slightly to compensate for the movement of the boat.

⚹

Dennis fell as *US 93* came through the entrance of Sandy Cove.

He fell backward, to port, when the boat was rolling in that direction. He slid down the side of the middle cockpit, to a sitting position. His chin nodded against his chest.

Everyone was feeling good about the trial. The boat seemed fast. No one linked Dennis's movement with the muffled crack that had sounded out of the fog, four or five seconds ago. No one noticed the faint dark haze that settled on the deck, to port, behind Dennis's back.

"Yo, Dennis is tired," the main grinder said.

"Must have been the dip," the port trimmer replied, winking.

"Seriously," Jenny said, "you OK? Dennis?"

"Aw, he's just foolin'."

"Yo, Dennis!"

"It wasn't that cold, man!"

There were four or five people in the after half of the cockpit, next to the mastman. McMurdo was looking over the bow, toward the *Betty-Anne*, keeping the tow line straight. The others were looking down at Dennis in silence as the first wash of dark liquid seeped from around his legs and began to cover the cockpit deck. In the flat light of fog it seemed more chocolate-colored than red.

"Jesus," Paul burst out suddenly, "he's really hurt." He bent over to look closer at the mastman, but one of the trimmers was faster.

"Dennis!" the trimmer said urgently. "Come on, man." He touched him gently, with almost the same gesture Paul had used on Jack, a year and a half ago now. "What the hell happened?"

"Don't move him," someone else advised. "If he hurt his back."

"He's bleeding real bad."

"Oh God. Oh God."

"Everybody get down," McMurdo yelled suddenly, "get down on deck! You," he told one of the crewmen, "take the helm. But stay down." He practically hit the man to get him to stoop.

Paul, kneeling to one side of the trimmer, held Dennis's shoulders up. Jenny had a finger on the side of his throat. Her face was more pale than Paul had ever seen it. She was shaking her head.

The trimmer had a hand on each side of the mastman's head.

Joe McMurdo undid Paul's bomber jacket. Against the dark of the sweaters underneath he could just make out a small patch of frayed threads forming the center of a circle of wetness. He felt behind Dennis's back and went very still. "I told you people to get *down!*" he roared, his face still turned toward the mastman. "You, too," he yelled at the man who was steering. "Just keep the rudder midships. That's right."

McMurdo brought his hand out now. It was dripping red.

"That sound." Paul made the connection. "Oh, Jesus." He stilled an urge to gag, turned around in a crouch.

"Paul—"

"I'm getting the radio." Paul unclipped the VHF. He radioed John Poole, told him to stay under cover, someone was taking potshots. He called up the clam-company guards on the port frequency and told them what had happened. He asked them to call the police. He changed position, getting up on one knee because he was cramped and because his knees were trembling from shock.

Then, still on one knee, he peered over the coaming.

The water moved by, limpid, unchanged. They were well into the cove now. The trees and rocks of the shore were mirrored upside down on its silver surface. The dark green of pines, the tin tracery of oak, the russet beach grass, the cetacean gray of granite; over and above it all, the fog, sucking colors from everything.

No movement, no sign of man marred the silence.

Two of the crew had lain Dennis down now and were trying cardiopulmonary resuscitation on his chest and mouth. Panic stretched their faces. McMurdo told them it was useless, but they were doing it for themselves as much as for their shipmate and they kept at it, regularly counting out the rhythms of life. One, two, three. Thump, blow. Four, five, six. Thump, blow. The crewman doing the artificial respiration had blood smeared on his face.

Paul looked at Dennis. The kid's features had the classic look of disturbed sleep. Here, again, the obscenity of violent death lay in the contrast. Where a couple of hundred seconds ago had been enthusiasm, eagerness, a skinful of memories, hopes, lusts, there was now nothing whatsoever. Who in the name of God would want to hurt a kid like that, Paul thought—and remembered the bomber jacket.

"Oh, no," he muttered.

"What?"

"They were aiming for me."

"What are you talking about."

"The jacket," Paul explained. "I always wear that jacket. Oh, shit. Oh, hell." The realization seemed to take the force out of him. He leaned sideways against the computer's spray shield and closed his eyes to block some of the shock. An arm got in his way, however, locking around his neck hard enough to hurt.

He opened his eyes in surprise.

"Don't," the girl said. Her eyes were hard, almost fierce. "Stop it."

"Jesus. Jenny." He did not push her arms away.

"Stop it," she repeated.

"Stop what." Though he knew what she was thinking.

"It's not your fault," she said. "When are you going to understand, you can't take responsibility for everything?"

Paul shook his head, slowly, and said, "I know that. But this isn't the time."

He looked once more at Dennis's face. One of the crewmen was making awkward, glottal sounds as he struggled not to cry. The tears came flooding anyway, channeled through the folds of a face that was screwed up like a child's. It was Brian, Brian Duffy, the kid Queegie had chastised in front of Paul in Newport. So long ago now.

Paul thought he had never seen so much misery in one man's face before. It made his own seem small by comparison. He allowed himself one last surge of remorse and sorrow.

Then he turned his thoughts to the living.

"I've got to do something."

"That's better," the girl said. "Damn it. That's better!"

"No," Paul said, "you don't understand. First Ashley, now this. I've got to get these people out of the way of all this."

"Get 'em to France." McMurdo's voice came at his ear.

"What?"

"You owe it to them."

The skipper was getting to his feet now. "Steady," he told the helmsman. "We're out of range, I think."

Paul got to his feet, in turn. The *Betty-Anne* was slowing down. The clam-company dock loomed out of the fog. Warren Hillman and two guards stood at the end. Warren's face looked white, even at that distance.

The two crewmen still counted out CPR on Dennis.

One, two, three. Thump. Blow.

Four, five, six. Thump. Blow.

"Why did you say that," Paul asked McMurdo.

"Because someone's out to get you or this syndicate. It doesn't matter which, at this point. And you don't know who it is. You don't know how he'll come at you next."

"And how would going to France solve that problem?"

"Because you'll put him off balance," McMurdo said urgently. "Whoever he is. It'll be strange territory, but it will be strange for him also. As long as you move fast," the skipper added, then bent to help the men who were clustering around Dennis, getting ready to lift his body to the dock.

≋

When the shot had sounded Vanzetti was too far away to spot the sniper, so he'd continued his panicked rush down the shoreline.

When he got level with the boat he thought the sniper had missed, because nothing was happening in the cockpit.

Daring to hope, he turned off the shoreline, into the woods, and stopped to look, listen, and sniff the wind like a dog.

He saw nothing, heard nothing. The soft wind stirred branches. It mixed fog into the matrix of trees, bushes, and ground cover.

Shit, the detective thought. What if it was a hunter, out looking for ducks. He had never thought of that. If it was a hunter, he, or his dog, would show themselves soon, searching for the bird they had killed, or else walking to the car in defeat.

The detective traversed slowly along the riprap, looking for signs of passage. Now he almost hoped for something to justify his panic. He would look like such a fool otherwise. Not just to himself, but to the waitress as well.

A shout came from across the water. It could have been a boat command, routine, except for the note of fear behind the voice.

Something glinted dully in the moss to his right.

It was long and smooth in a way nature did not care to match. He caught the shape of a stock. Above that, half hidden among the roots of a bush, a black tube.

A telescopic sight. Of no use whatsoever for ducks.

Vanzetti pushed his way through the undergrowth, caution forgotten. His breath felt locked in his chest. He dropped to his knees by the rifle.

A Springfield, by the look of it. The M 1903 conversion. A sniper's rifle. A killer's gun.

Now he wished, fervently, it had been a hunter. He wondered, without much hope, if it was Paul the sniper was aiming for. Decided it must be.

There was a leaning arrangement of branches where the sniper had sat. Bright scars of broken wood where he cleared a field of fire. A brighter glint of brass in the moss to one side, next to another little patch of snowdrops. Vanzetti picked the metal from the moss.

It was a cartridge, .30 caliber, spent. Vanzetti sniffed it, holding the shell carefully at both ends, though he knew, deep down, whoever had done this hit would not leave fingerprints on his tools.

Just as he knew that whoever pulled the trigger on that rifle had not missed.

Shit, Vanzetti thought. Paul Briggs had trusted him. And now he had let him down.

A sound came from behind the detective.

Vanzetti wheeled, rising as he turned, but the slug was moving even as he was and it hit him just below and to one side of his right ear and night was instantaneous.

The detective fell heavily and lay still. His right hand, still clutching the cartridge, flopped in the middle of the cluster of small white flowers, crushing them.

The fragrance of snowdrops rose in the woodland. It mingled briefly with the scent of gunpowder, and was gone.

C H A P T E R   3 6

The late sun of May lingered over the coast of France. It injected streaks of pink and orange into the patient waves rolling into the Bay of Biscay from the north and west. It teased the old town of La Rochelle with light, but in the growing cuts and tunnels where the sun could not reach, the shadows seemed twice as dark.

One of those cuts included a short, cobbled alley that led from the Rue Saint Nicolas to the waterfront of the old city.

An arch cut across the alley. Beyond the arch, on the left looking seaward, a "Bar Américain" leaked electricity into the evening.

The alley's end afforded a sliced view of the old harbor, silhouetted against the last rays of sunset; the deep basin, where one of the French Twelve-Meters was currently on display; beyond that, a lighthouse, winking mainly for tourists these days; and behind the lighthouse, almost in line from this angle, the two ancient towers that once guarded the approaches to the citadel.

In the corner of the alley farthest from the harbor, Paul Briggs and Warren Hillman stood, watching, skulking.

From their vantage point they could see Brian Duffy, the starboard trimmer for *US 93*, say something to the bartender in the Bar Américain and reach for his hip pocket.

Behind Hillman and Paul Briggs, a man in a cheap blue suit lounged in the intersecting street, keeping a cigarette alive.

"So what do you think?" Warren Hillman asked Paul.

"I think," Paul replied slowly, "La Rochelle has got to be one of the nicest towns I've ever been in."

Hillman looked at him in mild exasperation.

"I suppose it's jet lag," Hillman commented. "You've only been here what—two days?"

Paul nodded.

He was one of the last to come over. Even the *Challenge II* and her trial horse got here before he did, on a Panamanian freighter to Le Havre, and then by special truck convoy, south, to La Rochelle.

He'd insisted on hanging around while Vanzetti went through the first in a series of operations that were supposed to reconstruct the left side of his face. . . .

Paul shook his head. He did not want to think about the last month. He had come here to do, not think, and this was the first step in their plan of action.

"What happens now?" he asked Hillman.

"Well." The manager stuck his face shyly around the stone buttress of the house they were hiding behind. "Normally he'll down a quick shot here. Then he'll roam around the harbor a bit, probably have a beer at one of the cafés on the quay, the Marine, probably. Then he'll go up to the road on top of the ramparts and brood. Then he'll go up the Tour de la Lanterne"—Hillman crushed and broke the French vowels—"the Lantern Tower, and brood some more. Then he'll go back to the hotel for dinner. And after that, it's bedtime for Duffy. He's been doing this for three weeks, as I said."

"And he doesn't talk with anyone? Leave a note anywhere even?"

Hillman shrugged. "I only followed him two, three times. I didn't check everything he touched. If he's the spy—"

"What do you mean, 'if,' " Paul interrupted. "You told me you were sure."

"Well, it's true. He must be. Remember how I gave the crewmen different bits of information? Told 'em not to tell anyone, even each other? I told him"—he jerked his chin toward the bar—"we were going to put the double keels from the old boat on the new boat.

And what do you know, two weeks ago, we find an article in *Yachts*. Rumor has it the *Challenge* is going back to a double keel. . . . But none of the other hints I dropped ever came out."

"As far as you know."

"As far as I know. But assuming it's Duffy, he's either very tricky indeed, or he's only contacting them when he's got an important bit of news."

"Well, in that case," Paul began, but Hillman suddenly signaled for quiet.

Brian Duffy came out of the Bar Américain. He had on bright red shorts, boat shoes, and a *Challenge II* windbreaker. His blond hair shone in the bar lights. He turned left, immediately, toward the old harbor and onto the waterfront.

Paul and Hillman followed him onto the quays, and the man in the blue polyester suit followed them, quite openly.

It was easy to shadow someone on the quays. This was the nexus of a seaside town already gearing up for the world's biggest boat-racing event, and there were a lot of people wandering slowly around the harbor, taking advantage of the sun's afterglow and the gentle temperatures of April in southwest France.

They followed the quays around the harbor.

The old harbor of La Rochelle must have been designed, consciously or no, with an overarching aesthetic in mind. It lay in a rough semicircle around two basins that ran to the sea through a narrow channel between the two huge towers at the harbor mouth.

The tower on the left, looking outward, was tall, built of many smaller towers sort of fused together. The one on the right was squat and round. Between them, at this time of year, they focused the light from the sunset so it would perfectly illuminate the old houses running around the harbor proper, turning their stone the color of wildflower honey.

The quays themselves were long, wide, cobbled, lined with the masts of yachts and fishing boats on one side, with plane trees and cafés on the other. At this hour, the water was starting to take on necklaces of light from the cafés and the windows above them, draping them around the greater necklace of the town's waterfront. A quarter-moon, wrestling out of a cloud bank over the Atlantic, seemed almost superfluous in terms of decoration.

For some reason, as he dodged slowly in and out of a crowd of

Belgian tourists, Paul got a sudden, overwhelming desire to paint this scene—incorporate, between all the colors and forms, the sensual pleasure that came out of the very cobblestones around here, the feeling that time was far better spent pleasing the senses than fine-tuning keel, rigging, and masts.

"There he goes," Hillman said, darting like a frightened minnow behind a large sign. The sign advertised "Menu Touristique 'La Marine' 67 Francs Toutes Charges Comprises."

The café had a very long terrace, full of wicker chairs under a blue canopy. The decor inside was fake nautical, full of brass and made-in-Taiwan telescopes that reminded Paul, uncomfortably, of Charlie Armstrong and Baybarge.

"The Marine. What did I tell you. Oh, hell," Hillman groaned, looking back the way they had come. "I thought you told him to piss off."

Paul turned as well.

The man in the blue suit stood beside a rack of postcards in a tourist shop next door, pretending to look through shots of Twelve-Meters, towers, and bikinis.

"I told him not to come," Paul sighed. "My French isn't so hot. In fact, it isn't. And he don't speak English. I suppose I should be grateful, though. I didn't know Stone cared."

"Don't get sentimental," Hillman told him, checking over the café sign to see what Duffy was doing. "Right now he doesn't want any more bad publicity. So you've got a bodyguard."

"Can't *you* tell him to shove off? I mean, look at him—he might as well be carrying a button saying, 'I'm following these guys.' "

"My French isn't much better—hullo, what's he doing now."

Apparently the Marine did not appeal to Brian Duffy this evening. He'd wandered aimlessly inside, among the booths and waiters and, just as aimlessly, out again.

"Looking for someone?" Paul suggested, but Hillman shook his head.

"He often does this. If not here, somewhere else. He'll probably go to the ramparts now—just watch."

"I hope so," Paul said doubtfully.

He was supposed to meet Jenny Crooke at a restaurant in town in about fifty minutes. He had not seen the girl, to all intents and purposes, in over a month. He wanted very badly to talk to her.

Sure enough, Duffy turned the northern corner of the tidal basin and headed for the squat, round tower. He did not look back once, which was lucky, because while Paul and Hillman tried to hug the side of the wide street, and act like tourists, the bodyguard did not bother with such niceties and walked stolidly twenty paces behind them, ignoring their glares and shooing gestures.

They passed a group of Blousons Noirs, French bikers in black spandex and chains, acting tough on 300-cc Japanese dirt bikes for the benefit of lycée girls under the plane trees. Past a man with a homemade telescope, selling glimpses of the mountains of the moon for a franc. Past an old length of chain, set on stone pillars, its massive links forged to look like bones.

"The Protestants used that chain to close the harbor when the King attacked." Hillman had been reading up on local history and was eager to share his knowledge. No one else on the Challenge team was interested. "Rabelais claims they tied the giant, Pantagruel, to his cradle with that chain. That's how big he was. . . ."

They followed the sailor as he skirted the tower's base and climbed a set of steps leading to the massive wall beside it.

The last sunset worshipers had left the ramparts. The only lighting besides the moon was provided by four scrolled iron lanterns spaced at longish intervals. Thus there was plenty of darkness to shroud Paul and Hillman as they loitered in Duffy's path.

The ramparts were very tall and wide. In medieval style, where defense was indistinguishable from normal living, they provided an outside wall for the burghers' houses leaning against it. There was even a narrow cobbled street on top of the ramparts, with cafés and front doors and steps.

On the other side of the street, to seaward, was a raised sentry path, and the usual massive, toothy crenellations. Brian Duffy walked slowly down the path toward a third tower, this one much taller than the pair protecting the harbor. From a thick base it narrowed through two balconies to a long octagonal spire, fretted with carvings and gargoyles and topped by the large stone lantern that gave the tower its name.

Duffy followed the road as it curved around the tower, then disappeared into the entrance.

"This is where it gets tricky," Hillman said. "It's probably best just to watch from here."

"But what does he do?"

"He just goes up to the high balcony. And looks out to sea. Like some bloody romantic poet or something.

"I mean, you've got to admit, the tower's romantic as hell, isn't it?" Hillman continued, enthusiastically. "They locked up some revolutionaries here after the Restoration. They carved their initials in one of the cells. Secret society, they were, Carbonari, antiroyalist. Took 'em up to Paris and shot 'em."

Far above their heads, Paul caught a glimpse of blond hair moving around the top balcony. Suddenly he felt sick to death of the whole aimless sneakiness of what they were doing.

"That son of a bitch," he told Warren, "that son of a bitch helped kill Ashley. And Jack. And Dennis. I'm going up there," he continued.

"But what will you do?"

"I'm not sure. Just keep that goddamn bodyguard from following me, will you?"

They both looked behind them, where the man in the blue polyester suit lounged against the wall, smoking yet another cigarette.

"He'll see you," Hillman objected, "for certain. There'll be no one up there at this time. They only just opened it nights, for the cup."

"Maybe there is someone else. Maybe he hid, last time, until you left. Didn't you ever see *Vertigo?*"

Paul did not argue further, in any case, but made his way around the tower and through the entrance. The steps were endless, circular. The stone felt massive. When he got to the top he stepped cautiously onto the balcony.

The darkness and salt wind were more pushy up here. The town lay behind him. Across the tidal flats, to the south, Paul could see the lights and breakwaters of Les Minimes, the huge yachting harbor with its spanking new Twelve-Meter center where the *Challenge II*, *US 93*, was berthed, under heavy guard like all the Twelves. But Duffy was nowhere in sight.

Paul edged cautiously around the balcony, one step, two steps— and went still.

Brian Duffy was leaning far over the parapet, resting most of his weight on his elbows. He was gazing, as Hillman predicted, out into the Atlantic.

In the treachery of moonlight his face seemed strange. Paul remembered the agony suffusing that face when the mastman was shot. He moved backward, now. If Duffy were the spy, the agony was normal, and just.

Then he stepped out, resolutely, toward the parapet. He walked around its curve until Duffy was in plain sight once more. He could hear Hillman hissing in the background, but called out anyway, to the crewman.

"Brian."

The man jumped, a dangerous reaction in those circumstances. He shot out a large hand and grabbed the stone railing to help his balance.

"What," Duffy said. "Who is it. Key—ella?" His voice was rough and cracked a little.

"It's Paul Briggs. I want to talk to you, Brian."

The sailor stared. The whites of his eyes gleamed orange in the backwash of light from the lantern above their heads.

"Paul," he whispered. "Paul Briggs."

"Yes."

"What do you want."

"What do you think."

"So you know. Don't you. You know," Duffy whispered.

"That's right," Paul agreed. "We know. We know everything." Wishing this were true.

"Who's that with you. Is that Warren?"

"Yes. We need to discuss things."

"No," Duffy almost shouted the word. Even in the low glow of the lantern, Paul could see the hand tensing on rough stone. "You'll just tell the police. I won't go to jail. 'Specially not here. I can't."

"You're a spy, mate," Hillman told him. "Jail's where you belong."

Paul gripped Hillman's shoulder. This was getting them nowhere.

"Brian," he began again, and stopped short.

As they talked, the crewman had shifted more and more weight from his legs to his arms. Now he lifted the legs entirely, and pivoted on his buttocks to straddle the parapet, with one hand bracing him behind. It was a neat, athletic maneuver, made foolhardy only by the fact that it was executed on a ledge ninety feet above very hard cement.

"I've been thinking about it," Duffy said calmly. "If I do it right, I won't feel much. Just like getting knocked on the head."

Paul could think of nothing to say. The manager, too, was silent.

"I didn't mean to do it," Duffy said. "I only agreed 'cause of Queegie. He was such an asshole to me. To everybody. I thought, if I gave information to one of the other syndicates, it would only hurt *him*." His voice changed upward. "Who's that behind you?"

"Oh, shit," Hillman groaned.

Paul did not bother turning around.

"It's the bodyguard," he told Duffy. "Shoop's given me a body-guard. You know."

Duffy was silent.

"Go on," Paul said, "tell us. Tell us what happened."

There was a pause. When Duffy went on his voice was still high, and it had got tighter. "Well, I only called him once. Everything screwed up. Real fast. There was that break-in, at your office. Your cousin was killed. And they said I was involved now. I wanted to get out right then—you've got no idea how much. But they said they'd tell the police."

"Who's they?" Paul asked him, hardly daring to breathe.

"But I don't *know*!" Duffy burst out. "That's the living bitch of it. I never knew! It was like someone in the dark, out there." He looked down, to his left, and drew back, visibly repelled. It was his own broken body he saw, lying on the pavement below.

"What do you mean, you don't know. You gave the info to some-one. Someone paid you. Right?"

"I got cash, in an envelope," Duffy replied miserably. "I didn't want it, but what could I do? I had a number to call. And it was a guy in a bar, in Newport," he continued, anticipating the next question. "I was bitching about Queegie. I was pretty tanked, and he got me talking. I never saw him before, or since. He gave me a number. Said if I ever wanted to help another syndicate, to give a call to this number."

Paul asked what the man looked like, but the description, vague to begin with, rang no bells.

"You're lying," Hillman told the crewman. "After all the team's been through. And your own mate was killed. Murdered! And you're still too scared to tell us. You're nothing but a bloody coward!" he finished, viciously.

But Duffy was not lying, Paul knew. The agony in his voice matched the lines twisting in his face. Duffy was a kid, twenty-five years old but still a kid, and he was lost in waters way over his head, and he saw only one way out at this point. Paul caught the slight, testing shift of his buttocks, and said, "NO! WAIT!"

"Brian," he continued, "please. We don't think you're lying. There's a way out of this. Besides jail. Besides the cops."

Duffy had frozen. His gaze turned downward again.

"That's the wrong way, Brian," Paul continued, urgently, trying very hard to get his thoughts in order, "you'd really have to get it just right. It's only ninety feet. More likely, you'll just be paralyzed. A vegetable. In a wheelchair. Think of it. They'll have to spoon-feed you. Fifty years of bedpans. Brian, listen to me!"

"I am listening." The words came as part of the wind.

Behind him, Paul heard the bodyguard say something in French. Hillman replied in a low voice. The word "police" was repeated twice. Paul hoped Duffy could not make out what they said.

"You can help us," Paul continued, as gently as he could. "You can feed information to that number you have. You can help us trap the guy who killed Dennis. In return, we'll forget about this. We'll forget all about it. You're not the one we want."

"Oh, let him jump," Hillman advised, and Paul wheeled around fiercely and said "Shut *up!*"

"I give you my word," he told the crewman. "I give you my word." He could think of nothing else to say.

For a long minute, Brian Duffy looked at the long parking lot below him, with cars the size of small candies, and the lonely estuary behind.

Then a couple of lines in his face relaxed. A strand of something less than despair showed in the spaces between.

"I'll do anything," he said simply—and jumped, lightly, grace-fully, back onto the balcony.

C H A P T E R   3 7

The restaurant turned out to be only a five-minute walk from the tower with the lamp, but even so Paul showed up twenty minutes late.

It was called Les Quatre Sergents, and appeared to be an old art deco greenhouse. Inside, long vines writhed around green-painted ironwork and frosted glass. White parasols protected diners from the ornate lily-shaped lights. A stone fountain played on delicate mosaic.

Jenny Crooke sat at a table under a palm, attended by a sycophancy of waiters.

"Sorry," Paul said, trying to find the chair the maître d' was pulling out for him.

"It's OK."

The smile was wide and calm, but although she was not wearing her shades, her eyes were unreadable. The way they'd been, more or less, since Bangor.

"You look great," Paul told her. He meant it. She'd got a good tan from sailing on top of her skin's natural pigment, and it made the blue of her eyes very vivid. Also, for the first time since he'd met her, she wore a dress. It was a bright, violet-blue frock with a loose purple sweater on top. It made her look even smaller, more fragile.

She wore a thin silver ring on a meaningless finger. Paul wondered who had given it to her and swallowed the thought back down.

Briefly, he explained why he was late.

She listened hard. The eyes got colder than Arctic blizzards when he referred to Brian Duffy.

"Couldn't you," she commented when he'd finished, "couldn't you simply get the number he calls and have the police look it up?"

It might have been possible, Paul told her, in the States. But the new number was local. The French cops would have nothing to do with crimes committed back home. They had made this plain to Warren Hillman.

In any case, Brian Duffy was sure his contact always used public phones. You could tell by the street sounds, he said.

"Wouldn't it be safer," she asked carefully, "to wait for Stone? He's supposed to show up, isn't he? He seems, I don't know, used to this sort of thing?"

Paul shook his head. He felt his jaw go hard.

"I'm gonna do this," he told her. "It's too important to me to let someone else screw up. It's too important to screw up, period."

She seemed a little startled by his tone.

Duffy was going to ask for a meeting, this time, Paul said. He would claim to have physical evidence so important it had to be delivered personally. The plan for a new keel, perhaps. They had not decided. They would use the entire team, surround the rendez-vous. When the contact showed up, they would trap him.

She listened politely, but Paul sensed her thoughts were else-where.

She ate well. This dinner had been set up weeks ago, since before Jenny left with the rest of the sailing team, and both felt some need to do justice to that sort of planning. Grilled eel with garlic, Perigord goose braised in cognac and stuffed with chestnuts, goat cheese. Dry white Graves, a pushy red Bordeaux. The wine loosened their tongues but not their minds. The food had so much character and quality it made the great pockets of vacuum in their conversation that much more obvious.

Over dessert, Paul asked her, once again, what had come between them since their night in the Waquoit River, and how to be rid of it.

Once again, she put him off, with closed looks and phrases that meant little.

Yet she did not object when Paul offered to accompany her home. He did not need to use his excuse, that he had to check the Twelve-Meter, only ten minutes' walk from her house.

This was no pretext, in any case. Since *US 93* was launched, Paul had got into the habit of checking the boat every night before leaving for home and bed. It was a routine that had little security value, but it helped him sleep a little better.

Mercifully, the bodyguard was nowhere in sight when they left the restaurant. They found a cab at the taxi-stand. She was staying in a house that belonged to the father of a Frenchwoman she had sailed with in the Miami-Kingston race.

The house was on the outskirts of La Rochelle, in Vieux Minimes, right next to the yachting center. It was actually a small, whitewashed cottage with different levels of red-tiled roof, a stone patio, and a walled garden full of perfumed plants.

Paul sat on the patio and watched clouds blot the stars. The wind was starting to blow, and it was getting cooler. A front was coming in, Paul thought, with some satisfaction; they would need more of the same when racing began. Jenny came out with an oil lamp, two wool blankets to put on their knees, and a frankly filthy bottle that, by its shape, had to be Bordeaux.

"From the cellar," she commented, and shrugged. "I'll replace it before I go."

There were so many cobwebs the label was unreadable. Paul used the corkscrew she offered and poured them each a glass. In the kerosene light the liquid looked like arterial blood. Paul pushed the association out of his mind. When his tongue touched the liquid it almost recoiled. The wine tasted so deep, it had so many different textures that his taste buds could not cope with the complexity, at first.

The second taste was easier. He sipped cautiously. Soon, it became far easier to drink than not.

"Jaysus," Paul said softly, "that's some wine."

"It *is* good." She sounded surprised. "Have another glass." She gestured hospitably.

The wine was also very powerful, Paul realized, after his first glass. It made the Bordeaux they'd drunk at the restaurant seem like red piss by comparison. Paul did not know he was getting loaded until he suddenly got a feeling like he was lord of this particular part of the world, omnipotent, with courage and strength enough to take on all comers, all enemies, all sly and perverse opponents of truth, justice, and the free passage of shipping.

Jenny may have been feeling somewhat the same. At any rate she suddenly blurted out, "Look.

"That time, in Maine," she went on. "It was wonderful. I felt things. I don't know. Things I hadn't felt in ages. Too long. It was like spring, after a long winter up north. Landfall, after a long, boring passage. Nice . . ."

Paul held the glass to his lips, rigid, his tongue half-awash in the ruby richness. He did not want to move, to risk disturbing this mood. Over a month, she'd been holding it in.

The wind rustled in the leaves of the acacias. Even in the lamplight he could barely make out her profile, the sheen of her skin, her dress.

"But then—you shut off," she continued. "That's really OK, you know. It wasn't your fault.

"Still, it reminded me. We both have long histories. Well, I can't speak for you. All I really hear is rumors. You're old enough, you're bound to have a history, of course. And I've been through too many places and people for my age. Too many affairs, broken. One way or the other.

"And suddenly," she went on, "on that dock, I saw. I had no right to just jump out of one and into another. On the same dock, so to speak. There you both were, Christmas Past and Christmas Present. No matter how good it felt, I had no right. . . . And, Lahd, it felt good, you know."

Paul took his tongue out, making absolutely sure he did not spill any of the wine on it.

"You had no right to give up, though," he countered. "And no right to shut yourself in. Not permanently."

"But you do it."

"Not with you."

"I asked you once," she contradicted him. "What that was in you, in your eyes. I suppose it was a leading question. Still. You refused to reply, mahn. That said something."

From the vantage point of omnipotence, all confessions should seem small. All except this one, perhaps.

The words came, regardless.

"All right," Paul said, though she'd demanded nothing. He poured himself another glass of wine. Restraints were gone, controls were loose, he might as well take advantage of it and get good and shit-faced.

"You heard about my daughter, right?" he began. "My daughter who was lost. You must have."

The shape of her hair swung a little.

"You see, Suzanne asked me once if it was OK to let her walk to the bus. Suzanne was from Chicago, it seemed—funny, to her. And I said, 'Of course it's safe. All the kids do it. This is French Harbor,' I said, 'nothing ever happens in French Harbor. . . .' "

"But you couldn't have known." She responded to the stress in his tone.

"No," Paul agreed, "I couldn't have known."

"What about your wife?" the girl asked. "Why did she leave?"

"She was right to go," Paul told her. "She had no life left. Every detail of that house hurt. She spent a whole year bursting into tears. Do you know how exhausting that is? I couldn't even have milk in the house because they printed pictures of missing children on the back of the cartons. Even when we went away somewhere, my face, Jess's face— Anyway. It was too strong.

"So one day," Paul continued, "I came home, and she wasn't there. She'd left Jess with the neighbors, said she was going shopping. She took nothing but a little traveling bag, some clothes. She left everything. I guess that was the point. She never even told her brother."

"And that was when you got those scars."

Paul looked at her.

"I asked around, mahn. They told me. You were trying to kill yourself."

"That's not true," Paul protested. "I was driving too fast."

"What's the difference."

Paul snorted. Across the table, candlelight caught Jenny's eyes.

"There's more," she said. "There has to be. I mean, what happened was bad. As bad as it could be. But four years, Paul! Four years is a long time. You should have come out of it."

"You can't know."

"There was something beyond that. Wasn't there."

"I'm not the wind, Jenny. You can't read me like cat's-paws or white squalls."

Silence crept between them. To cut it Paul said softly, "It's no big deal. I have problems with my work. I never seem to do boats as well as I remember my father doing. All my life I was brought up with his drawings. People praising his boats. How fine the *Maria* was. Him and Herreshoff. They were like gods. I didn't want to be a naval architect at first. The competition was too fierce."

It had come very easily, for all it was bottled up so long.

She leaned forward.

"But that's crazy. Your designs are beautiful. They all have something special. Even *US 93*."

"I'm not saying it's rational. It's just a feeling. But if other junk piles on top—"

She touched his hand with hers. It was a movement void of conceit.

A spot in Paul's chest grew warm. The warmth spread deeper and further than the glow of alcohol.

"I think," Paul said, "I could stand having you around more." He added hastily, "I'm not trying to rush things. But it's the truth."

She got up, came behind him, and twined her arms around his neck. Her cheek felt like warm goose down against his own.

"Look," she said again. "I am here. I really am. And I meant what I said. I only want to take it slowly. Just let the history settle. Paul—there's someone watching us!"

She had looked up, over the wall, where a shadow moved near a streetlight, and back toward the house.

Paul got to his feet, swaying slightly in the wash of wine. He tiptoed to the wall until he could see around the angle of the house.

The man in the blue polyester suit lounged calmly against the opposite house, smoking a cigarette. When he saw Paul he lifted a hand in a comradely gesture.

Paul sighed and waved back. He realized his heart was pounding. The memory of a bullet that came from nowhere was not so easily repressed.

"It's the goddamn bodyguard," he said. "The one Shoop hired. How am I supposed to get away from history with him dogging me every step I take?"

"That's not what I meant, you twit," she said. "I was talking about the people. . . . How's Vanzetti?" she went on, more seriously.

The detective was doing fairly well, Paul told her. He was living to get out of the hospital and track down and damage the man who had shot him. It was this which had kept him alive.

How was Paul's daughter, she asked.

Jessica wanted to come over for the races. Paul was newly aware that exposing her to a little risk might be less cruel than excluding her from his life. He had promised to let her come, if no problems surfaced in the meantime.

"I hope she comes," Jenny said suddenly, "I'd like to get to know her."

She had sat down again, and was staring into the depths of her wine glass, so he could not read her eyes, but he thought, on balance, it was the most hopeful thing he'd heard all night, and upended the bottle over his own glass to celebrate.

As he turned it over, he noticed that spilled drops had dissolved some of the dust, and he could now read the label.

"Goddamn," he exclaimed, and started to laugh.

"What are you chortling about," she said.

"You said you would replace this?"

"So I did. What's so funny?"

"Only that I have a feeling it's gonna cost you something like two or three hundred bucks. Even I've heard of this one. Nineteen forty-two, no less." He whistled.

She took the bottle from him and read the label.

"It was worth it," she said simply.

"I'll drink to that," Paul answered, and did.

C H A P T E R 3 8

Over the next four days Paul and Hillman between them concocted a bait to lure the man who had hired Brian Duffy as a spy.

They created a bait so intricate in its details, so succulent in its secrecy, they were sure it would bring Duffy's contact panting as soon as he heard about it.

The bait was a fake, a large-scale plan of the wetted-surface area—the underwater hull—of *US 93*.

It looked like the real boat—with two crucial differences. Whereas the real Twelve-Meter had a fairly conventional alignment of fin keel and rudder, this decoy Twelve had two long, thin keels, ending in long, narrow wings.

Also, the schematic showed a hull covered in a very tight, very thin skin, entirely made up of long blisters of Permutex, separated by membranes and filled with a light oil.

The idea was based on a similar feature occurring naturally in dolphins; a thin layer of fluid between two outer skins that apparently retarded turbulence, enabling the animals to achieve speeds of forty knots or more.

It was an old idea that no one, including the Office of Naval Research, had yet succeeded in putting into practice.

Notes in the margins of the plan implied the new keels and skin would be used for the first time in the Doyen-Kruyff race, one month away.

Sitting in a locked hotel room he had set up as a design office, Paul almost tricked himself into believing the blister-skin idea could work. The main problem, apart from the weight factor, would be getting the tiny membranes between the blisters to flex without distorting. He thought if the idea intrigued him, it might pass muster with whomever was blackmailing Brian Duffy for information.

Duffy had a simple, rigid schedule for making his calls: Tuesdays and Thursdays at 3:00 P.M. Paul and Hillman showed Duffy the forgery and coached him on what to say.

On the first contact day they listened in as Duffy placed the call through the hotel's switchboard.

The phone rang three times, with the loud double burr of the French system. On the fourth ring someone picked up the receiver.

"Oui?" The tone was abrupt, the accent not French. He pronounced the word like "Wee."

"It's me. Duffy."

A grunt.

Duffy looked around nervously. He was using the guest phone in the lobby. From behind the reception desk, Paul and Hillman, sweating a little from nerves as well as the proximity of the kitchens, gave him the thumbs-up.

The receptionist had retreated to the bar with Michel, the bodyguard. Michel was ordering his midafternoon pastis.

"Listen," Duffy told the man on the other end, "I've got something. Something really big."

"Yes. Go ahead."

The connection was mediocre, but even above and around its hollow static Paul could glean little from the voice. It was educated, North American, male. Apart from that, it was not high, not low, not hoarse or particularly mellifluous. Exceptionally average. But Paul could still hate it with force and purity.

Hillman caught Paul's eye, shook his head. The voice lit no circuits in his head either.

"But I have to see you, this time. It's important."

"Unacceptable. Out of the question."

"It could change everything," Duffy told him, anxiously.

"So what is it?"

The crewman looked around, for permission and encouragement. Hillman nodded at him.

"A plan of a new keel," Duffy almost whispered. "A new skin for the hull. They left the office unlocked. They haven't used 'em yet. They're going to put 'em on for the D-K Cup. I photocopied it."

There was a pause.

"Call me Thursday. Same time," the voice said, and hung up.

"Shit," Duffy muttered and slammed down the receiver.

"Shit is right, mate," Hillman agreed with him.

"He's being cagey," Paul added. "He'll go for it Thursday."

"But what if he asks me to leave it someplace or mail it or something?"

"Then we'll mail it," Paul said, "and see who starts complaining about the improvements. They're not legal, you see," Paul explained, unable to restrain a smile at his own cleverness; "if you look at 'em real carefully you can see, they throw off the measurements."

But they never got a chance to use Paul's fake.

On Thursday, Duffy's contact told him, flat out, he was not interested. There was too much risk involved in physical evidence. "Get me something I can use," he advised his spy.

Duffy nearly panicked, over the phone. He seemed to think Hillman would turn him over to the French cops if the ruse failed. Luckily the man on the other side hung up before he could betray this strange anxiety.

But the days passed, and the weeks, and there were no attempts on Paul's life, or anyone else's. It looked like McMurdo's advice was sound, and the killer had not followed them onto French territory. Anger and fear retreated into the background.

Paul called Lucinda and told her it would be OK to bring Jessica for the challengers' series.

Once again the frenzy of routine, the routine of frenzy took over, spiked now with the drumbeats, growing louder and louder, of approaching competition. Once again the sheer lack of proportion between work and time to do it squeezed out the luxury of plots and subterfuge.

⚒

The date of the first race drew nearer.

When Paul was not locked in the office he was out on *US 93*. The navigator McMurdo wanted could not make it before the actual America's Cup series, and Paul was filling in.

The hours passed in the salt, sun, and crashing water of the "Mer," or bay, of Perthuis were perfect antidote for the blackness of the last few weeks in Maine.

The work was brutal, even for Paul, whose job as navigator consisted mainly of tapping at the computer, working out courses, lay-lines, and performance curves.

But this was a different kind of sailing from the lonely tune-ups in Newport or Georges Sound.

For one thing, they were on display out here. The racing zone was constantly ringed by press boats and spectator yachts. The yachts came in all sizes, from tiny outboards and day sailers to pocket ocean liners owned or hired by sponsors of the different Twelves. Their wakes crosshatched the Mer de Perthuis, complicating the wave patterns of the Atlantic. The sky was filled with light planes, helicopters, and dirigibles hired by newspapers and TV crews.

Another big difference was the competition. Fourteen challenging syndicates this year. The usual countries had sent competitors, but now there were also entries from West Germany, Japan, and Brazil to compete with the Italians, Swedes, British, Australians, New Zealanders, Americans, and Canadians. Not to mention the defending French. Most of the syndicates had at least one trial boat. The New York Yacht Club had three. The Compudyne syndicate from San Jose, California, had four, separate new boats.

In all, there were thirty-three Twelve-Meters out on the half-protected bay off La Rochelle. On a good day, their colors made the blue ocean look like a painting by an abstract artist. Blue hulls, red hulls, aquamarine and ebony and tangerine, yellow and white and silver and gold. Hulls with stripes and one with sparkles. Sails with logos and cartoons, stars and planets, rainbows, geometric designs. Crewmen in designer gear. On everything, every hull, sail, and article of clothing, a company name, for the whole idea behind the Doyen-Kruyff Cup was to provide a medium for advertising before the actual series started and obvious displays were banned under the International Yacht Racing Union rules.

When the wind blew, and the swells started in from the northwest, it looked like a medieval joust taken to water. The elegant, sharp hulls cut the waves like deadly weapons. The bright sails were pennants, stiff with defiance, gay with bravado, wearing the symbols of the corporate damsels whose honor was at stake among these sandy islands and green breakers. Toyota, Siemens, Compudyne, Gipfel. The whole feeling was one of war, long minutes of tense idleness punctuated by seconds of muscle-ripping, brain-stretching panic when the Twelves clashed. Then the huge pressure translated straight into the men, and above and beyond the good-natured taunts was a deadly intent, a sense of quest that Gawain might have recognized for its strength, if not its sacred purpose.

In this quest the Holy Grail was a plate silver cup, ugly as hell, that had been worth only 105 British pounds when it was made and now represented an industry worth over five billion dollars.

Paul became addicted to the long hours offshore. His lips acquired a permanent base coat of zinc, his face got deeply tanned. The sun drugged him, the motion of the sea crept into his sleep. He was sleeping six, seven, sometimes eight hours at a stretch now, and he seldom dreamed. When he did, the dream was full of the tension of racing. The presence of Jenny lay in the background, like a balm, for that was part of the seduction of the hours at sea, easy: structured interaction with this woman. Interaction in a privileged place, to boot, for Jenny's understanding of life and people seemed largely based on her affinity for wind and water.

Sometimes that affinity almost smacked of the mystical. She had a "nose for wind" that went far beyond what was usually meant by the term, far beyond the facts. The facts consisted of clouds, wave patterns, the warming effect of the sun, the structure of frontal systems. She knew all these things, as did any good racer, but still she consistently could predict wind shifts, or changes in wind strength, long before McMurdo or the machines or anything else could. Time after time she would say something like, "Lift in fifteen minutes," meaning the wind was going to shift to an angle that made it easier to reach the buoy they were aiming for. The wind might be steady, no indication whatsoever of a change, but nine times out of ten it would shift in the direction she'd predicted. "It's a gift, I guess," she would say, with an expression that conveyed she had long ago got sick of trying to explain it.

Paul did not press her.

In this matter, as in more personal things, he was willing to let time provide the answers.

For now, simple proximity was enough.

ᵚ

Two weeks before the Doyen-Kruyff Cup, Hillman and McMurdo took a long, hard look at the most dangerous of the competition. These included France's *Bretagne* and *Gauloise*, Japan's *Nippon Sword*, San Jose's *Go America*, Marblehead-Corinthian's *Boola-Boola* and New York's *Old Glory*. The Challenge men went out in the tender and filmed the workouts, but mostly they looked at how these boats did in the informal skirmishes on Perthuis Bay.

They decided that while *US 93* still looked as good as the best the other syndicates had to offer, nevertheless they could not afford to sit still while everyone around them was carving up hulls, redesigning keels, changing rudders, masts, bustles and blaming it on them.

So Paul went back to the drawing board.

He designed, and helped build, a small high-aspect-ratio rudder, or canard, to put under the bow, and fined down the after trim tab of the keel to compensate.

This helped a little with maneuverability, but seemed to detract from the keel's performance, so it was scrapped.

He tried adding tiny winglets to the torpedo at the keel's bottom. The winglets would create opposing vortices to cancel out turbulence arising from the sudden drop-off in lifting forces at the keel's tip.

This speeded them up, very marginally, in winds over ten knots. He would have liked to fatten the boat's middle a touch, slim down the bustle by a hair. However, with a fiberglass boat the expense was prohibitive, and Hillman refused to authorize the changes.

Finally they gave up on the hull and concentrated on improving the sails.

One of Shoop's aerodynamics wizards was in charge of this side of the campaign. He had already tested a new Permutex-based sailcloth that was smoother, lighter, and denser than the usual Kevlar-Mylar laminate.

McMurdo and the aerodynamics wizard watched endless films and sensor graphs of what the practice sails were doing. They sketched out new patterns: a headsail with vents, a spinnaker shaped like a competition parachute. Then they redrew the sails in three dimensions on the computer. A second program cut up the new designs into shapes that would distribute the stress of wind in optimum fashion around the airfoil. The computer then dumped this information directly into an automatic cold-wheel cutting machine that split the dense fabric into perfectly geometric panels. These were then sewn, like jigsaw pieces, into whole sails.

They went out and tested the new sails and filmed the tests. Then they went through the whole process again. And again. And again . . .

The crew was the other factor subject to fine-tuning, for Hillman believed that tuning minds was as important as tuning bodies. He hired an attitudinal therapist, from England, whose job was to give the crew seminars three times a week for as long as they were racing.

Paul went to the first seminar. The therapist told them they were going to be part of a new family, cohesive, united against the world outside. That family was The Team. The blocks, the fears that hindered them—the blocks that made them change a genoa in twenty seconds instead of eighteen—were products of laziness and procrastination. Anything could be accomplished as long as they did not put off their duties until tomorrow. He, and other members of The Team, would support them in their new life. Together they would win. Winning was all.

McMurdo left within five minutes. Jenny Crooke went with him. One of the crew went to the bathroom and found the door locked. He was told he must put it off. "Concentrate on your goals, not your bodily needs," the therapist advised him. "What are you going to do if you're turning a winch and your muscles tell you to stop?" The therapist added that, while the seminars were paid for, they could join a month-long retreat in the fall for only fifteen hundred dollars apiece.

Paul had no need to go to the bathroom during the first seminar. However, he knew fear. He saw the therapist did not know the meaning of the term and refused to go back. So did Squidlips, who was a Maine fisherman and therefore congenitally incapable of joining anything. The crewman with the weak bladder complained to Hillman.

But the rest of the crew seemed to find a positive mental attitude in the therapy sessions. Paul could hear them, three times a week, at the end of the seminar, shouting "WE WILL WIN!" and "KILL! KILL! KILL!" from the dining room of the little hotel.

Jenny told him they were lucky, in relative terms. The Compu-dyne syndicate, she said, had hired a sports guru. *They* had to med-itate, every morning, for two hours, before breakfast, before drinking a cup of coffee even.

☆

May drew to a close. The D-K Cup, and the beginning of the America's Cup series, were no longer distant goals but immediate, nerve-racking realities. People began streaming into La Rochelle, building up in bars and cafés along the quays of the old harbor. The SNCF ran special TGVs, orange high-speed trains from Paris. TV networks filmed prerace teasers from the Twelve-Meter center. Sponsoring corporations flooded the town with booths and give-aways. Four different crews made music videos at the new TV studio at the Palais des Arts. Hotels throughout La Rochelle started hoisting "Complet" signs. The CBM Corporation, running hard to pay legal bills, sold their "Cité Challenge" condo complex at a handsome profit. J. Harmon Canaday stopped by on his way to pass papers, to see Shoop. In green golfing shorts and dark glasses, he looked more like a turtle than ever.

Shoop was not around. He and Stone were in Zurich, closing a deal no one outside the Pentagon was supposed to know about.

However, no deal could have kept Shoop away from the official opening of the Twelve-Meter season on June 3. He showed up six hours before the gala ball that marked the beginning of the first race week.

Two days later the *International Herald Tribune* featured a shot of the ball that included Shoop, an Italian count, a British peer, and a Nobel prize winner. Through the grains of the wire-service picture you could spot the financier grinning as widely as he was able. Gone were the fine calculations, the cost/benefit, the doubts. Shoop had got what he was after.

Paul did not make the ball. He was in his workshop that day, running through different options for reballasting the boat in ac-cordance with weather trends. He was deep into the work, hunched over the drafting table, isolated in neon, when someone spoke from the doorway.

"I coulda been anybody."

It took a second or two, but the Boston nasal, the tough-guy intonation finally won out over the sheer unlikelihood of their presence. Paul swiveled on his workstool and stared at the intruder.

"Relax," Sal Vanzetti reassured him, "I'm a friend."

"I don't believe it." Paul walked over slowly. On impulse he grabbed the detective around the shoulders. "What are you doing here?" He could feel a ridiculous grin spreading over his face.

"Same thing. Looking for the guy killed Dennis."

"I mean—" Paul glanced at Vanzetti's head. A swathe of short hair and stitch marks showed where the assassin's bullet had scored. The detective was thin from his stay in the hospital. But his moustache was just as fierce, and his eyes as sardonic. Paul felt an unexpected rush of affection for the man.

"Last time I saw you, they had little plastic tubes up your nose and wrist and everything else, and they were watching your heart on an oscilloscope."

"Yeah." Vanzetti grinned, and Paul knew from the grin he truly was better. "I'm too nasty to kill. So Stone hired me back. Full-time. I'm in charge now. And it looks like you need me," he continued, his voice suddenly serious. "Why'd you get rid of the bodyguard?"

Paul looked offended.

"Michel? No way. He's down in the bar. He's got the bottles of pastis under permanent surveillance. Ain't no one gonna get into one of those bottles without him knowing about it."

Vanzetti gave him a look. The humor was gone, and the eyes were grim. He made a note on a spiral-bound pad. "I'm gonna have to do something about that. You should never go out without someone watching your back."

Paul looked at him thoughtfully.

"In that case," he said, "you should do it for the crew as a whole. As we know, if I'm at risk, they're at risk. Though I don't think there's a problem, anyway."

"We can't let our guard down," Vanzetti replied, flatly, and asked if there had been any incidents.

"That's what I'm saying," Paul told him. "There's been no problems at all. Although," he added, "we have been playing with our pet spy."

Paul told him about Brian Duffy.

What happened after, Vanzetti asked.

"Well, nothing. We've been so busy—"

"You simply left it at that?" Vanzetti looked even grimmer.

"Yeah."

"Wish you'd leave this stuff to the professionals, 'stead of playing cowboys," the detective told him. "You ain't equipped to deal with it."

"Well, the pros were out of town," Paul shot back.

"You could have called Stone."

"We didn't do so bad."

Vanzetti was silent. Paul watched the detective, fighting the illusion that if Vanzetti was here, they must all be back in Maine, back in time, back when Ashley was alive.

After a while he continued, more evenly, "I suppose we could have gone on with it. But there's really been no time. And frankly, we sort of shot our bolt with that. I mean, this is the America's Cup. If they don't want a secret keel, what the hell do they want?"

Vanzetti was not amused.

" 'Something we can use.' " He pondered the quote for a moment. "I guess the most practical thing would be information that would win a race for them. Tactics?"

Paul shook his head.

"Too vague. Skippers make general plans sometimes, but they modify it according to what happens. The wind, what the other boat does. Although—" the idea hit him casually, but it seemed to pick up weight as he considered it—"I suppose there might be a middle ground. . . ."

Vanzetti slicked his moustache down with two fingers.

"I mean something in the design, some fault." Paul was thinking aloud. "Something you could exploit in itself, in a particular move.

"Of course," he rapped his head with his knuckles, "It's so obvious, why din' I think of it?"

"What," Vanzetti asked, imperturbably.

"We just combine the two ideas," Paul said. "Tactics and design. Duffy tells him the keel's got a weak spot. We could say, if the boat has to point up or head down too suddenly, it stalls. I won't go into it, but what that means is, before the water was flowing smoothly over the keel—next it gets all turbulent and confused and the boat almost stops in the water. You get it?"

"No," Vanzetti replied. "But you're the scientist. I'm just a dumb cop."

"It doesn't matter. Duffy tells that to Mr. X. Then, in the race, we see if somebody tries to force us into that kind of maneuver for no reason. It's something a skipper would do. Once he found out we were vulnerable, it would give him a huge edge. It could work," Paul smacked his fist into his palm, "it could goddamn work!"

"Let's hope it does," Vanzetti said, "because I didn't come here to wait for things to happen."

He checked his left armpit, a subtle gesture.

"It's too damn quiet around here," Vanzetti added, and straightened his jacket so the gun would not show.

CHAPTER 39

The night before the Doyen-Kruyff Cup brought clear weather.

In the sail lofts of the various syndicates, all over town, exhausted technicians rubbed gritty eyes, split the last seams, made the last splice, packed the last genoa for the race.

Alarms jangled in the crews' quarters.

In the cafés along Avenue de Gaulle, workmen discussed "Les Douzes" with proprietary interest over black espressos and balloon glasses of local brandy. They predicted, with the expertise of insiders, how the French boats would do.

Joe McMurdo rounded up his first-line crew and took them on a two-mile run as an appetizer, with calisthenics the main course, and showers as dessert.

Guru Sri Pramit finished a two-hour meditation on victory and blessed the fruits the Compudyne crew would eat for breakfast.

A TWA jumbo jet carrying Lucinda and Jessica Briggs in economy class, and Bradley Winton in first, landed at Roissy Airport in Paris.

Paul switched on the down-link lock on the weatherfax, the weather imaging machine that had been hooked up in his office. The data, traced out in photos, isobars, and superimposed sine curves of wind changes, came from a navy satellite orbiting overhead.

The black box allowing him to unscramble the satellite transmissions came, as usual, from Stone.

In the hotel dining room, Warren Hillman looked down the table of faces and marveled once again at the many disguises people used to hide the fact they were nervous.

Some ate more heartily than usual. Many pecked at nothing. Most of them had been preparing for two years for the showdown that began this day. They chewed gum, made bad jokes, drank too much coffee.

Warren started the briefing. He did not beat around the bush or work to spare the stomach acid, the jangled nerves.

"This is war, gentlemen," he began. "This is total war. I know we're not starting the series proper," he continued, "but the D-K results determine who races who in the first heats. Whoever does well will get a chance to beat up the best of the competition, right at the start. Whoever does well should get a shitload of sponsor money. So I don't need to tell you, no one out there will be 'sandbagging.' No one will be pulling any punches. I expect you gentlemen to knock the bastards DEAD!"

Paul got up next. Editorializing was not the navigator's job, so he merely summarized the data from the weatherfax and the French weather station on Avenue des Tamarins. They had a weak occluded front coming in, but probably not until the later stages of the race, midafternoon at the earliest. Before that, northwesterly winds, variable to light, backing later on. Force two to four. Not a big day for heavy boats.

McMurdo got up. "We're as ready as we'll ever be," he told them. "We could use another three months' training, but considering somebody's been trying to sabotage us, somebody's actually killed one of us, I think we've all done pretty well. Let's do this one for Dennis," McMurdo suggested.

"And Ashley," Paul put in.

"Number two genny, light air main," McMurdo added, and that ended the briefing.

The race did not start until the afternoon, but the practice was for the Twelve-Meters to get out as early as possible to warm up. In deference to this custom, the president of Doyen-Kruyff Champagne S.A. had scheduled a brief outdoors ceremony at 9:00 A.M., on the balcony of the Société de Régates Rochelaises, in the middle of the yachting harbor. The ceremony included speeches by the president, the prefect of Charentes Maritime, the mayor of La Rochelle, the commodore of the yacht club and, last but not least, the minister for youth and sports, come down specially from Paris to offer the official blessing of the Republic in general and the Giscardien wing of the RPR party in particular to this racing series for the prestigious Doyen-Kruyff Cup and the even more prestigious America's Cup of which France had the honor to be, for the first time, the defender.

The speeches took up the better part of forty minutes. At the end, the band played the "Marseillaise." TV cameras from French, British, American, German, and Japanese networks panned across the yacht harbor. A French navy-patrol craft fired a round of blanks.

All over the Twelve-Meter basin different teams unleashed their pent-up energy. Lines flew. Tenders roared into movement. As per plan, the French Twelve-Meters, the *Gauloise* and the *Bretagne*, were the first to leave. The two hulls, one powder blue, one black, both with tall silver spars, shone in the sunlight as they passed the yacht club jetty, the outer jetties, the Richelieu light tower, and headed out to sea.

US 93 was tenth in line. By the time they got to the America's Cup buoy, five miles southwest of Richelieu light, the Mer de Perthuis had blossomed with the fine, cupped petals of Twelve-Meter sails.

The sun was very powerful. It bounced off the million facets of ocean and lanced into their eyes like blue spears. They all wore dark glasses but within an hour their eyes would be red and smarting from the light as well as the salt spray.

They hoisted sail and practiced tacking up and down the course, still trying to shave fractions of seconds off the time it took the crew to shift sails from side to side and shape them to the wind. Paul and Jenny worked together over the computer. They checked the batteries, booted programs, filed information on what the wind was doing now, where they were sailing. Every fifteen minutes they received bursts of data, by radio, from the tender as well as from the satellite overhead. The data went into the computer, giving it the weather picture for the Bay of Biscay in general and the Twelve-

Meter course in particular. The military cameras were that accurate.

The sailing programs automatically matched sails to wind, and the crew changed the jib accordingly.

There was no time for spare thoughts or chatter. There should have been no time for nerves, either; but anxiety found every crack in their actions, and painted it with adrenaline.

꩜

When the first flags went up at 12:30 P.M. everyone's heart rate went up several counts with them.

The Twelve-Meters began to converge. The starting line lay between the America's Cup buoy and the SRR committee boat, a half-mile northeast of it. The minutes ticked by, and the great wind machines did their level best to avoid hitting each other as they hissed along at four or five knots, smashing spray like chipped diamonds into the eleven-knot breeze.

Jenny spotted them first. A line of small, sheeplike clouds near the horizon. The occlusion was coming in on time. It should be making itself felt in two, three hours. She punched this into the computer, then resumed watching the wind, the sun, the waves.

With ten minutes to go until starting time the Twelve-Meters began timing their tacks, getting into a rhythm that would bring them back to the starting line at the precise second the gun went off. Jenny stood close to McMurdo now, both of them keeping track of the other Twelves. Paul stayed glued to the computer. The machine tracked their current position and the position of the starting line, using satellite coordinates.

At the five-minute mark Paul began giving course, time, and the number of tacks to the starting line at fifteen-second intervals.

McMurdo stood at the upper wheel, balancing easily against the movement of the boat, calling commands in a voice so low he sometimes had to repeat them. It was his way of dealing with stage fright.

The rhythms and patterns of the other boats began to mesh as their scope for choice ticked away with the clock. They surged back and forth, tacking up and down the line, running downwind, tacking up again. The slower boats tried to cover the faster boats. Space was at a premium. The confusion of wind and crashing spray and shouts and madly squealing winches and acres of straining sail and materials pushed to the point of rupture in your own boat were multiplied by thirteen and thrown back at you on a rapidly shrinking grid of seconds.

"To hell with the Vanderbilt," McMurdo called suddenly, with two minutes and twenty-seven seconds left to go.

The Vanderbilt was a classic tactic named after a former New York Yacht Club commodore. It consisted of tacking away from the line for, say, ten seconds, then heading back when you had exactly ten seconds to go, so as to get to the line the second the race started.

"Do the 'rabbit hole' instead?" the girl asked.

McMurdo nodded.

Quietly, so no one on the other boats could overhear, Jenny told the crew what they wanted.

They were reaching north now, crossing the starting line, which was legal as long as they came back to the other side before the gun. Jenny asked Paul for the exact time it would take to turn around, run over the line, then head up and cross it again just as the starting gun sounded.

Paul worked furiously. On top of course, time, and true windspeed, he had to factor in the push of tidal current—slight but southerly—and the speed the *Challenge* would make running over and back and over the starting line again. He found he could use almost the same course in both directions, and let the current do the work of pushing them back to the legal side of the line. Then, when the gun went off, they would be parallel to the line, and need only head up to cross it.

One minute, forty seconds. They were well out of the fleet now. The advantage of this tactic was, since they were upwind of the fleet, they had clean air in their sails, undisturbed by other boats. The danger was, the other boats might not give them room to maneuver when they tried to sneak back onto the legal side of the line.

Paul counted down the seconds to the tack. At one minute thirty-eight seconds McMurdo spun the wheel. *US 93*, nimble on her small keel, twisted around and charged for the windward end of the line.

Forty-five seconds. Thirty seconds. Their course converged now with that of the other Twelves. The sails of the fleet seemed to stretch without a chink, enormous, the flank of hulls and wake apparently unbreakable. And yet McMurdo would have to find room between them and the line, and do it without getting in their way; for they were downwind of him, and therefore, by the laws of racing, *he* had to give way to *them*.

Kiwi Pride and *Bretagne* were ahead, followed by *Nippon Sword*, *Old Glory*, *Go America*, *Brittannia*, and *Boola-Boola*. Paul kept track of their range and bearing with a hand-held compass.

Fifteen seconds to the gun. They were level with *Old Glory* and spoiling her air but it still seemed to Paul they could never find room to slip between the other boats.

Ten seconds. The bowman called the distance to the starting line in meters. "Thirty-five," he yelled. "Thirty. Twenty-five." McMurdo suddenly said "Gotcha!" and pointed at the *Nippon Sword*.

The current was pushing the Japanese boat a little bit south of the starting line, opening a small gap between her and the *Bretagne*.

At eight seconds to the gun McMurdo squeezed the *Challenge II*, *US 93*, between the Japanese and the imaginary line stretching southwest to northeast across the water. The Japanese luffed up slightly, hoping to force *US 93* back over the line so she would have to circle around and cross the line again before officially beginning the race.

But it was too late. The two boats ran side by side, the silver glass of *US 93* only seven or eight feet from the red aluminum of the Japanese boat. The Japanese skipper bowed slightly and said something that sounded like "Bouta no ketsu" to McMurdo, who smiled back. Warren Hillman's voice crackled over the VHF. "Signing off, chaps," he said. "Break a leg."

There was a puff of smoke, followed by a "Boom" from the committee boat.

US 93 crossed the line three seconds later, well ahead of the *Nippon Sword* and a boat's length astern of *Bretagne* and *Kiwi Pride*.

The race for the America's Cup had begun.

≋

The fleet moved off the line in a pack, following the leaders. The first leg of the course lay almost directly upwind, to a buoy 5.2 miles away. There was only one way to get there—tack back and forth, zigzag at an angle to the wind, until you got high enough to round the mark.

There were two things to watch out for in this endeavor. The first was other boats, who could force you to change course if they had right of way, or make you go slower by "stealing" your air, getting between you and the wind. The second was wind shifts, which immediately changed the direction and number of zigzags you had to make to get where you were going.

The fleet followed the *Bretagne* and the *Kiwi*, which were running almost neck and neck. The French and New Zealand boats "covered" in classic fashion, tacking away from each other for a while, then simultaneously turning to cross paths, with the New Zealander always slightly ahead of the French boat. Once the Frenchman tried to "slam-dunk" the *Kiwi*, tacking back in the same direction as the New Zealander immediately after crossing his stern; but Plehan had not built up enough speed and the New Zealander simply steered his boat a little lower, and faster, getting out of the Frenchman's dirty air, forcing Plehan to tack once more and seek to beat him at the next encounter.

The fleet progressed in their wake, taking each other's wind in turns, stitching a sharp double helix of tacks up the left, or westerly side of the course, for the wind was a little to that side of the course line.

Paul looked up from his computer, and astern. His heart leaped with excitement.

Two Twelve-Meters surged only twenty feet behind them. Two more ran within eighty feet astern of them. Another five were jammed into the same space behind those. Paul had never in his life seen so much grace of movement, beauty of form, tension of material, power of elements crammed in such quantities in so small an area. Their colors painted the world, suffused both sea and sky.

"Gawd," Paul muttered to himself, "they're really beautiful."

The words rang in his head.

"I don't believe it," he told Jenny, "I'm starting to like these boats."

She was busy watching the competition and did not answer at first, so he thought she had not heard. Then she said, "Never thought I'd hear you admit it."

"They're not my favorite," Paul added cautiously.

"Of course not."

"Will you two quit mumbling, you're making me nervous," McMurdo yelled.

They quit. Paul thanked his stars, silently, he had lived to see his boat in its glory. Then he bent back to the computer.

The crew worked beautifully. McMurdo played the keel and rudder with great skill, feeding in just the right amount of curve for every different speed, enough to lift the keel like a bird's wing, not enough to roll the water and make it stall. The water-flow graph on the computer spiked green, showing near-optimum lift over keel and hull. The airflow data allowed them to finesse the genoa to a perfect contour for each wind angle. Tack by tack, inch by inch, they crept up on the black Twelve-Meter with the white lilies and stripes of Brittany gleaming on her counter. They got close enough to put their own bow just upwind of the *Bretagne*'s wheel, to see the lines of worry on Jean-Louis Plehans's forehead, and hear him shouting, urgently, toward men working in the middle cockpit.

"There's something wrong with their backstay," McMurdo said. "I had a feeling this was too easy."

A couple hundred meters from the windward mark, Plehan tacked his boat, hard and viciously, right into their path. They were overtaking the French boat at the time, which meant the *Bretagne* had the right-of-way. Even McMurdo and his tactician, who were expecting a tack, were caught by surprise, and had to crash the boat hard to starboard, to avoid Plehan.

Jenny looked at McMurdo.

McMurdo glanced at Paul.

"Was I supposed to stall her, then?"

Paul said, "I don't know."

The story Brian Duffy fed his contact was simple. *US 93*'s curvy keel worked well (the story went) as long as the skipper made no crash maneuvers. If he had to do an emergency turn, the keel would stall, because the flow of water broke over its curve on a violent turn, and there was not enough time to turn the boat and flatten the keel at the same time.

It was plausible enough to be true.

Duffy's contact seemed interested. They made a policy decision following his phone call. If another boat made a move that had no other purpose than to take advantage of such a weak point they would play along and stall the keel, give her too much curve and slow way down. Once. This would buy time, until they found out who, in the other boat, suggested that particular tactic.

But Jean-Louis Plehan? Paul shook his head, full of doubt. The man on the telephone was American or Canadian. He had worked with Hugh Van Meerwen, in the States.

"If you ask me," the girl said, "that's just Jean-Louis. He's a bastard match racer."

McMurdo nodded agreement.

Paul said, "I think so too."

McMurdo shaped the keel for the new course and speed. The crew trimmed the sails, and they pounded after the French boat.

⅏

They rounded the upwind mark in roughly the same position, right behind *Bretagne*. *Kiwi Pride*, however, had increased her lead to sixty yards. "Look at those bloody Kiwis go," Jenny Crooke said in exasperation.

Behind them, *Old Glory*, *British Dragon*, and *Go America* trod hard on the heels of the Japanese, turning to their sterns to the wind almost as a group.

Spinnakers bloomed in Kevlar balloons. The foredeck became the center of every boat as crews juggled their great hollow sails. The *Challenge*'s new parachute spinnaker looked like a huge Permu-cloth pastry in the sun.

"Wind's going to head," Jenny announced out of the blue. "It's gonna fight with the land breeze for a while, screw around forty-five minutes, maybe an hour, we'll need light sails. Then it'll back northerly."

Paul checked the wind history program.

"This says steadily increasing, 326 degrees—northerly. A little lee off the Île de Re."

"I'll bet you. A hundred bucks."

"You're on."

"With that header," Jenny continued, "we could go up the east side of the course."

"OK," McMurdo said, after a moment.

Paul shook his head. If the wind stayed westerly, the east side would be the wrong side, way downwind from the mark.

"You better be right, kid," he murmured, "or we're gonna get nailed."

"Don't harass yourself, mahn," Jenny replied calmly.

They dropped the spinnaker as they came around the starting mark again. The wind had diminished somewhat. Paul used the Lidar—a hand-held laser that "read" dust motes in the air as far as five miles away—but he could detect no shifts in direction back up the course. If anything, the wind seemed to be veering more to the west and weakening slightly.

McMurdo did not seem to think Paul's data important. He headed for the east side of the course and kept going when the rest of the fleet tacked back.

The TV chase boats stayed with the fleet.

Only the *Bluenose*, a Canadian Twelve, followed them.

The constant background of other people's wake, tackle, winches, shouts, slowly faded and died.

"Sure is lonely out here," the main trimmer commented.

Jenny gave McMurdo the best course to steer for maximum speed. They sailed lower, at a greater angle to the wind; not as direct in terms of distance, but faster in terms of speed and time.

Paul fed the helmsman minutes and seconds to layline, the first tack on which they could make the upwind mark without any further zigzags.

The tide changed below them, unseen, unfelt.

Bluenose was a hundred yards behind, but the lack of close-up competition fooled no one. They tacked furiously back and forth, working just as hard as if there were another boat beside them disputing the same sea space. McMurdo played incessantly with the wheels, scalloping a path that would ease him up the gentler, down the steeper slopes of the swells. Men wrestled spasmodically with winches and lines. Paul checked again with the Lidar. He found that, 1.3 miles up the course, the wind was backing northerly.

"Header," he said, "in twenty-two minutes."

"A hundred bucks, you owe me," the girl said and grinned in delight.

"Kiwis are in trouble," the port trimmer called.

Everyone looked toward the other side of the course, where the New Zealand boat, shrunken by distance, had come into the wind, sails flapping uselessly.

"Their steering's gone," Paul said, trying to quell his fierce pleasure. It looked like the leader was out of the running, but it was a hell of a way to beat a good rival.

"Suits us just fine." McMurdo voiced what nobody wanted to say aloud.

Nineteen minutes later the digital readouts confirmed the northerly shift. McMurdo, to the east of the buoy, could now steer a faster, easier course toward his target.

When, half an hour later, they ran down the layline, they found they were virtually level with the *Bretagne*. They rounded the mark right on the French Twelve's quarter.

The *Bluenose* was now stepping on the heels of *Old Glory*. *Nippon Sword* and *Boola-Boola* battled it out for fifth place.

Kiwi Pride had withdrawn and was limping, in a circle, waiting for her tender.

The wind jinked around, died, rose again. The grinders sweated as they pounded the winch handles, raising blisters even through protective gloves. Squidlips's huge beard was soaked in perspiration. He roared in protest as he turned his half of the winch handle, but his massive muscles, conditioned by years of pulling lobster traps in conditions more brutal than these, worked smoother than anyone else's.

They stayed level with the French boat, even gained a few feet at one point, taking over first place by a third of a boat's length. Across the fifty or sixty feet of water separating the two Twelve-Meters, Jean-Louis Plehan watched them without smiling.

A half-mile from the downwind mark, the masthead lock on *US 93*'s genoa slipped, and the big sail fell ten inches. It sagged, and trembled as air spilled out.

"Goddamnit," McMurdo yelled, "when are we ever gonna get those cranes right?"

They tried jerking the sail lock back into place with the halyard. Finally McMurdo had the mastman hoisted aloft in a bosun's chair.

For the first time in an hour they saw the stern of the *Bretagne* as she powered ahead of them.

They became aware of the bow wave of the New York Yacht Club boat slurping greedily behind.

When they finally reached the downwind mark, the *Bretagne* was two hundred feet ahead, and *Old Glory*'s bow was almost level with *US 93*'s cockpit.

They dumped the spinnaker downwind, to save time. It was a tricky maneuver. The foredeck crew, perfectly coordinated, made it look easy. However the sagging genoa meant they could not head up as close to the wind as they had before. *Old Glory* slipped to windward of them. She came with them, this time, as McMurdo headed for the western side of the course. She crept up, inexorably, and started to pass.

Seventy-five feet in the air, clinging to the masthead as it dipped and swung in tangled circles ten feet in diameter, the foredeck man found a pin had sheared in the locking mechanism. He jammed the spike of his rigging knife in the hole where the pin had been. This reset the catch, making the lock operable again, but he had to leave his knife in position.

They took the opportunity to change the genny, for the clouds were almost upon them and the wind was starting to freshen.

Spirits lifted, with the repair accomplished. Men worked past the threshold of pain. The boat heeled more. Green water began spraying over the bows, sluicing the men on the foredeck. *US 93* crept back up, tack for tack, until she was almost level with the *Old Glory* again, and a little to windward this time.

Halfway down one tacking leg, for no reason whatsoever, *Old Glory* luffed up. Her sharp, blue bow scythed around to the right, aiming for the silver flanks of her rival.

"Shit!" McMurdo exclaimed, and spun the wheel hard a-starboard for the second time that day. Gear shook and rattled as the boom crashed overhead. Men leaped to catch up, trim the sheets for this new tack.

"Is that it?" Jenny said.

Paul was not looking at the menacing bow of the New York boat, even as it threatened the vitals of his own. He was looking over at Ted Collins. The *Old Glory*'s helmsman was not watching the imminent collision, either. He was watching McMurdo, and there was a look to his face that said he knew something was about to happen, and was only wondering when.

"Stall her!" Paul told the helmsman, softly.

But McMurdo barely had time to get out of *Old Glory*'s way, let alone play with the keel. The blue hull hissed close to the *Challenge*'s. McMurdo was spinning the wheel as fast as he could but it was not enough to escape the path *Old Glory* had chosen. The wake from the two boats became confused, sucking the two hulls even closer together. Paul stared, almost frozen, at a genoa trimmer four feet away from him. The trimmer had a silver filling in one of his eye-teeth. Ted Collins kept looking at McMurdo. His expression was not as confident as before, but still he did not alter course. Now the rudder was hard over. McMurdo threw the three wheels controlling the keel and tabs all the way to the right.

The stall alarm beeped shrilly. Red spikes flared on a corner of the computer screen.

US 93 virtually braked.

Ted Collins concentrated on steering again.

The New York Yacht Club boat shot ahead, missing their port bow by two and a half feet.

"Son of a bitch," Paul muttered.

"Give me the course again," McMurdo snapped as he spun the keel controls back into position, and headed into the blue yacht's wake. He aimed to leeward of them this time, the right-of-way position.

"It's a good job we stalled," Jenny commented, "or they'd have hit us for certain." She squirted fresh water in her eyes from a plastic bottle, to rinse them free of salt.

"They'd have protested, too," McMurdo agreed. "Ted Collins would protest the tobacco in my pipe, if he thought it would help."

The crewmen muttered back and forth. Anger sharpened the earlier high of getting the genoa fixed. "We'll get you, my pretty," the sewerman yelled in the general direction of Ted Collins. "And your little dog, too," the foredeck man completed the quote.

The crew, with the exception of Duffy, had known nothing of the deception.

US 93 seemed to lunge after the New York boat, borne on the righteous indignation of her people.

Paul continued sucking information from the computer, but in the back of his mind he was hearing voices.

Vanzetti's voice.

"Surprise, surprise," the detective had drawled when the magazine editor told him Hugh Van Meerwen belonged to the New York Yacht Club's Twelve-Meter committee.

"There was someone else in on it." Ashley's voice, after hearing someone talking about Jack—*In the men's room of the New York Yacht Club.*

It was so obvious, Paul thought. Van Meerwen's connection with the three other East Coast clubs had clouded the issue. But the other person behind this—the other man, who had killed Ashley, and Jack, and tried to ruin Paul and his yard—must belong to the New York syndicate.

US 93 liked these stronger airs. She clawed her way up the course like a shining glass machine, and rounded the upwind mark only five seconds after the New York boat.

The last leg of the course was different. Instead of going straight downwind, as before, the boats had to round a wing mark much farther to the west, before heading back for the finish line. With a good fifteen knots of breeze coming out of the north-northwest now, this translated into a broad reach, the wind almost behind, and a beam reach, where wind came on their side.

The trick keel was not much use with the wind astern, but this did not seem to matter.

US 93 passed downwind of *Old Glory* two-thirds of the way to the western buoy.

The rigging knife started working its way out of the crane mechanism five minutes later. The mastman pointed it out to McMurdo. Men looked up in apprehension. They were so near to the finish.

"Don't worry about it," McMurdo yelled at the crew. "Keep at it, we're doing fine, we've only got another ten minutes, hang in there!"

Working like madmen, pounding plastic, steel, and nylon until heads spun and muscles screamed for release, they fought their way back to within four seconds of the black-hulled Breton.

The rigging knife fell out another half-inch when they slammed into a particularly large wave. It hung, precariously, held by friction only.

But it held just long enough. The guns went off and the flags went up and they crossed the line a mere heartbeat after the French boat.

In this race, coming in second was virtually as good as winning.

Nobody said anything after the gun went off. There was too much work yet to be done to justify the complacency of words.

But the hope, the sudden, blinding discovery that they might have a real shot at winning back the America's Cup was almost palpable in the cockpit of *US 93* as she shed her sails and took a line aboard for the tow home.

CHAPTER 40

Hillman, Vanzetti, and Paul Briggs stood in rented evening dress in a corner of the Salle du Clone and watched the stuffy Doyen-Kruyff reception fill up with people to the point where it reached critical mass and turned into a party.

The Salle du Clone—known to Anglophones here as "Clone Hall"—stood at one end of the croissant-shaped arc of breakwaters, slips, yachting services, condos, and convention centers that formed Les Minimes.

It was designed with the combination of minimalism, color, and concrete that marked modern French architecture.

There was a broad lower floor with shops along one side. Stairs led to a large reception area with a balcony, tan curtains, cork walls. Vast areas of tinted window shaded the setting sun. It felt a little like being on the inside of a huge pair of dark glasses.

They watched the president of Doyen-Kruyff Champagne bestow a hug and a golden champagne cup two feet high on Jean-Louis Plehan.

Twenty TV cameras zoomed and panned. Strobes flashed. The fifteen hundred or two thousand people on both levels clapped. Corks popped. Doyen-Kruyff flowed like soda water. Vanzetti said, "I think only Joe and Jenny should ask. They can talk shop. Keep the crew out of it. You should stay out of it, too."

Vanzetti looked a lot healthier than when he first arrived. The sun and good food had rounded and browned him. He looked very Italian, Paul thought, as he sloped off to find the skipper and the tactician.

Paul hoped he would not find them together. The old jealousy was faded, but not quite dead. He got some champagne and went out on the outside balcony. He looked east over the central jetty, to the Twelve-Meter basin. He could just pick out *US 93*'s pen, comfortably close to two mobile homes full of riot policemen protecting the Twelve-Meter center.

To the left, and behind the sail lofts and outboard dealerships, he could make out the towers of La Rochelle.

Somewhere behind those ancient fortifications his daughter lay, sleeping off her first jet lag under the dubious aegis of Michel and the far more effective guard of her grandmother.

The champagne tasted good. Paul went back inside to get another glass. He felt exhausted, drained, and scoured by salt, sun, tension.

But underneath this deadness the anger still burned. It was a slow burn, it had been going a long time, it was mostly coals by now; but coals could be as hot as flames, and more reliable.

When the sun was down and the sky safely purple he went back inside.

From the sidelines, then the indoor balcony, he watched Mc-Murdo and Jenny move through the crowd, buttonholing crewmembers from *Old Glory*.

They would be joking, wryly mentioning how the New York boat almost tricked them, acting very casual. Hey, how'd you know we would stall if you did that? Who came up with that idea, anyway? Great idea—great. We Yanks have to pull together, right? Sure . . .

The New Yorkers would be suspicious, but Jenny and McMurdo were looking for information so unlikely, so innocuous that they'd have their guard up in all the wrong places.

Paul thought McMurdo and Jenny worked well as a team. But three or four minutes later she caught sight of him and flashed him a smile of such brilliance it burned right through the intervening fug, penetrated his doubts, and warmed his chest as he stood.

Then he lost her again in the turbulent crowd.

Recognition surfaced, now and again.

Alastair MacAndrew, the *Kiwi* skipper, looking grimly through the minister for sports and youth.

Squidlips Coggeshall, drinking straight from the neck of a bottle of Doyen-Kruyff, talking to a woman in a dress like a red waterwheel and a face that had made it even as far as the screen of the Odeon Cinema, in Amesboro.

Cy Shoop, expounding classics to Lord Kilburn of the British Petroleum syndicate.

Bradley Winton, discussing constipation or related matters with someone from the Bank of New Zealand.

The sight of Winton brought old suspicions back to life, just like coals growing wisps of real fire.

Winton, Paul thought. Ashley's godfather. A friend of her parents. He'd always seemed fond of her.

And yet he was the one who had steered them away from Hugh Van Meerwen. He was the one who insisted they not prosecute. He had thrown Van Meerwen out of the yacht club instead: and Paul, like a fool, had accepted this at face value, not understanding that Winton might be sacrificing a sheep—if you could call it sacrifice— to divert attention from the wolves around.

If he had killed Ashley—Paul's fists clenched so hard his nails dug into his skin.

Winton laughed at something the banker said, at least Paul assumed it was a laugh, the way his lips cracked open a centimeter or so and his head shook up and down briefly.

Paul turned away, to get more champagne, to subvert the rage inside him.

⁊⁊

Five glasses of champagne later, Jenny struggled out of the crush and complex noise of the crowd downstairs.

Paul watched her intently as she found McMurdo. Vanzetti materialized out of nowhere. All three of them came looking for him on the balcony.

Jenny Crooke put her arm around his.

"Well?" Vanzetti said.

"Well, what?" Paul interrupted.

"Don't we want to hear what they found?"

"I already know," Paul told him thickly.

Vanzetti glanced at him, without curiosity. "Go on," he told McMurdo.

"Five of 'em," McMurdo began, in his quiet voice, "couldn't get 'em to say anything. Two of 'em said, they thought it was at a breakfast briefing. They were talking about the competition. Someone apparently mentioned *US 93* had a weak point."

Vanzetti leaned forward.

"One said he thought it must have been the skipper. The other one said no."

"It was Winton, right?" Paul burst out, unable to bear the suspense any longer.

McMurdo's eyes were blank.

"Who?"

"Bradley Winton. He runs their committee."

McMurdo pulled out his pipe, checked the bowl, decided there was enough tobacco left there to smoke.

"No. He said it was the designer."

"Their designer? Naval architect? You mean, Archibald? Bruce Archibald?"

"I guess," McMurdo said, lighting a match. "I didn't want to push too hard. . . ."

Now their heads swiveled toward Jenny, who was wearing her shades again and could not be reached. Finally she shrugged and said, "Me, I only got one to talk. My charms are failing, I guess. But yeah." She looked at Paul.

"Yeah, what?"

"It was a breakfast briefing."

"For chrissake—"

"Bruce Archibald," she told him, levelly. "Sounds like professional jealousy, wouldn't you say, mahn?"

Paul's expression hardened.

"Or the other kind. But either way, I bet he's just the hatchet man, like Van Meerwen was. I know Winton's behind this."

"Maybe," Vanzetti said. "Maybe it's the whole friggin' committee. Still, at this point, Archibald is the one we go after."

"He's here, incidentally," McMurdo put in. "The guy I was talking to pointed him out." He pointed the stem of his pipe down at the crowd, but could not find his target. "He's down there somewhere."

"Then I'll go talk to him." Paul lurched off, propelled by revenge, his anger enhanced by the millions of little bubbles from the champagne he had drunk, but Vanzetti put a strong hand on his shoulder and said, "Wait."

"What are you going to say," he asked when Paul turned around.

"I don't know. Whatever."

"Thought so," the detective said. "You could screw everything."

"He killed people," Paul replied hotly. "What else do I have to say to him. The son of a bitch! I tell him we're onto him, finally, and he'll head for the hills, and we go tell the cops." It didn't sound very good, even to Paul, but the idea of caution and delay felt worse.

Vanzetti had his eyes closed. He said "No," and kept repeating "No" until Paul stopped talking.

"Now listen to me, man," he continued. "I got an idea." He led Paul farther down the balcony, away from a knot of German sailors that had formed at one end to sing Bierhaus songs.

"This is what we do," he began.

Paul located Archibald on the ground floor, behind a large ice sculpture of a Twelve-Meter next to the podium.

He was talking to the designer of one of the Italian Twelves. Paul waited until their conversation flagged, then asked, politely, if he could speak in private with Archibald.

The Italian made off in the direction of a champagne-laden waitress.

Archibald looked at Paul. He held a cigarette in his right hand. He took a slow sip of the martini in his left. His manner was cool, amused. He had the same slight curl to his lips, the same military posture. The neat air, the glasses, the blazer with the yacht club burgee were all unchanged. Paul wanted to punch him, repeatedly, on the mouth.

But Vanzetti had drilled him well. Paul simply clenched his fists and said, as levelly as he possibly could, as clearly as he possibly could through the haze of champagne, "I have some important, private matters to discuss with you. I wonder if we could arrange a meeting."

"Certainly," Archibald replied, taking out a pack of Camels and replacing the smoked-out butt with a fresh one.

Paul did his best not to let his jaw drop. Even Vanzetti had not expected Archibald to agree so readily. There were plans—B, C, and D—ranging from hints of evidence to threats of legal action. All bluff, of course, and all wasted. Paul hid his confusion behind excessive politeness.

"Uh, we have a lay week ahead," he said, "until the first match race."

"That's when we wipe you all over Perthuis."

"Maybe." Paul was not going to be drawn. "Which day would suit you?"

Bruce Archibald took a drag of smoke. His eyes were very hard to read. An artery, or a nerve-fried muscle, pulsed between tendons in his neck.

"Well, how about tomorrow?" Archibald suggested. "It's not very convenient," he added, "I'm supposed to make a trip—but I'm worried, if I put you off longer, you'll throw that glass of champagne at me. And that," Archibald finished, "would be a waste of good wine."

Paul stared at him.

Archibald took a sip of his martini.

"Oh nine hundred be all right?" He added, "Outside the SRR? Fine, then. See you tomorrow."

And he turned, and was swallowed by a crowd of blue blazers and straw hats that had clotted around Lord Kilburn.

Paul gazed after him, bemused.

Then he went to find another glass of champagne, or preferably a whole bottle, so his hands would not be idle nor his stomach empty of drink when he walked around Les Minimes to check on his boat.

≈

Vanzetti fitted Paul with a miniature recording device before he was due to meet Bruce Archibald.

The recording device was the size of a matchbox, thin as an average watch. It recorded on a spool of wire the size of a postage stamp and had two microphones disguised as buttons whose wires were led through the very fabric of Paul's shirt.

"Stone," Vanzetti explained. "Got it off a pal in Naval Intelligence. No jokes, please."

"What happens if I get searched? They could still find it."

"Not by feel," Vanzetti contradicted him. "Keep it in your hip pocket. If it looks like they're going to do a serious search, wedge it between the cheeks of your butt. If they look there, you got problems no tape recorder will solve."

"But you'll be right behind me, in that case," Paul said. "No jokes."

"I'll be right behind you," the detective reassured him.

Archibald was ten minutes late for the meeting.

Paul hung around the entrance of the yacht club building, sheltered from the slight drizzle, watching the Twelve-Meter crews in the Bassin Marillac start their daily work routine.

Archibald pulled up behind the wheel of a gun metal Mercedes. The yacht club's naval architect looked very fresh and dapper. He wore a turtleneck and designer jeans, an Old Glory windbreaker, an Old Glory baseball cap, an Old Glory watch. His smile was exactly the same.

"Where we going," Paul asked, as Archibald took a right past the massed condominiums and into an area of warehouses and undeveloped tracts between the sea and the railroad tracks.

"I couldn't put off this trip," Archibald replied. "Professional courtesy, and all that. But I thought you might as well come along. We can talk on the way."

"To where," Paul replied.

"The Penhoet shipyards, in Saint-Nazaire."

"But that's—two hours from here," Paul protested, and resisted an impulse to turn around and check if Vanzetti was following in one of the rent-a-cars, as planned.

"Not the way we're going," the designer replied, turning right again into a warehouse complex with a sign that read "Old Glory—America's Cup—New York Yacht Club—ENTRÉE INTERDITE." A security guard waved them through. Trailers marked "sails," "spars," "hydraulics" filled one side of the courtyard. A sound of lathes came from inside one of the warehouses. A small helicopter, all glass bubble, turbine, and fretwork tail, squatted on skids over a bull's-eye in the center.

Archibald pointed at the chopper.

"We'll be back by lunchtime," he promised, and went to find the pilot.

≋

Ten minutes later they were flying at twenty-five hundred feet, under low cloud cover, following the Atlantic coast north to the Loire estuary.

From this height it was easy to see the remains of the great dike Louis XIII and Richelieu built across La Rochelle harbor to keep the British out and the Protestants in.

Three-quarters of the town had died in that siege. It was one of Hillman's historical tidbits. But the sixteenth century was far from Paul's mind.

He thought there was no way Vanzetti could follow him now, or even know where he was going.

La Rochelle faded beneath them. The coastline softened, from sand to marsh, then hardened back into cliffs.

Paul's head was jangling a little; the effects of Doyen-Kruyff, no doubt, compounded by the incredible rattling, shaking, pounding decibels of the chopper. But he felt no fear, or nervousness even.

Hatred was easier to control when it was narrowly focused.

Paul checked the miniature tape recorder, hiding the movement behind his windbreaker.

The muddy estuary of the Loire river stained the horizon. Closer up you could distinguish the great arc of a suspension bridge. Huddled on one side lay the sullied brick of a northern industrial city.

They landed at the airport only twenty-eight minutes after leaving the Old Glory compound and took a cab into town.

Saint-Nazaire had been bombed into oblivion during the war, because of the dockyards, because of a massive underground U-boat base the Germans built. As a result, it was all modern cement and brick, dingy Marshall Plan architecture, uninteresting and insignificant beside the shipyards that were its reason for being.

A large, portly man in an old-fashioned three-piece suit greeted Bruce Archibald at the security gates near the inner harbor. His name was Pierre Desbarres. He was a chief naval architect for the Chantiers de l'Atlantique. He was happy to show the yards to any colleague of Marcel Morgat. He was doubly pleased, he said, to meet the designers of the American Twelves that had done so well in the opening race yesterday. Even if they had not quite managed to beat Morgat's boat, eh?

He showed them up to his office in the design section. He served them coffee and shots of Calvados.

The office overlooked the inner basin. The windows were pimpled with drizzle. Through the rain Paul could see the black, regimented water of the old dockyards of Penhoet. Railroad tracks, gantries, and warehouses lined the slips. On the far side of the basin lay the humped subpens, with their underground tunnel to the river. The pens were so massively built by Hitler's Todt Organization that all the bombs of the RAF, all the demolition charges of postwar engineers had not succeeded in leveling them. Now you could take a guided tour of the U-boat slips for thirty-five francs.

After the coffee Desbarres walked them through the design section, then down to the river side of the dockyard.

This was where the great ships had been built. The *Normandie*, the *France*, the battleship *Jean Bart*. Desbarres spoke with pride. He himself had worked on the *France*.

Massive dry docks towered ten, eleven stories high. Great machine shops lay silent under the rain. Rows of gigantic cranes stooped hopelessly over empty slipways.

Desbarres found a small staff car and drove them around. Men climbed scaffolding after a coffee break.

The yards had too much capacity now, the Frenchman said, sadly. The only work was a frigate, for the navy, and a hundred-thousand-ton ore carrier for the Japanese. This yard, which was able to build two ocean liners the size of the *Normandie* at a go, was reduced to taking apart an old Greek liner for the value of her scrap. He gestured at a great, rusting hull tied up to the dock they drove on. The name "SS Artemis" was written on her bows.

Shipping was sick, he complained. Everywhere, it was the same. Too many ships, too little cargo.

A loudspeaker squawked Desbarres's name. He told them to look around, if they wanted, and went into a turbine shop in search of a phone.

"I was hoping," Paul told Archibald, "we could find some time to talk."

"Of course," Archibald replied, politely. "Why don't we walk around, like he said. That way, we won't be disturbed."

They ambled down the quay, between the straddled legs of cranes. Archibald lit a cigarette. Men were taking apart the liner's sun deck. In the slipway next door, behind the turbine shop, two enormous automatic welders crackled violently as they put the ore carrier together out of smoke and blue fire.

Paul, pretending to rearrange his thoughts, fiddled in his hip pocket and set the tape recorder going. Belatedly, he realized there was way too much noise, from the welder, the electric cranes, to record anything.

"Let's check this out," Paul suggested, and beckoned toward a gangplank leading to a door in the liner's side.

Archibald shrugged. Paul stepped onto the gangplank and climbed onto the old ship without checking if he would follow.

Inside, emergency lighting fenced darkness in strange corners. Trollies piled with portable generators and electric torches filled the companionways. Some of the normal fixtures had been stripped, but the walnut paneling, the teak decks, the sculpted glass remained. She must have been one of the fancier ones, in her younger days, Paul thought. He headed up the stairs, two decks, three decks, until he found a door marked "Private—Officers Only." The door led past the captain's day cabin, the radio shack, to the bridge, and daylight.

Two-thirds of the liner's wheelhouse was intact. The brass on the binnacle was still shiny, the engine room telegraph pointed at "STOP ENGINES." A red fire lamp glowed beside a red fire ax by the chart room, on the starboard side.

The port side, however, opened on thin air, where the bridge wing and part of the wheelhouse itself had been cut out so a crane could lift material straight out of an electric pump room eight decks below.

The steel where the bridge ended was jagged and burned. The hole running vertically into the ship looked like a fatal wound.

"What," Bruce Archibald said, "did you want to talk to me about."

Paul moved carefully. The deck was wet with rainwater, and quite slippery. He stepped back from the edge of the hole, his hand in his hip pocket.

Archibald stood next to a large arc welder on wheels, looking modern against the ancient brass voice pipes, the Royal Navy gray. The artery beat against the rim of his turtleneck.

The questions Paul had to ask were like an abscess that had built up beyond bearing. They came out with no subtlety or restraint.

"Who is behind you," Paul asked Archibald.

The yacht club designer looked behind him, feigning surprise. "No one."

"Cut it out," Paul replied. "You know what I'm talking about. The spying. The attacks on my people. The boy who was killed. The arson. Ashley. Jack." He reeled them off at high speed.

Always the same, that smile, those eyes, pale behind the glasses. No change. Something cold touched Paul's spine.

"Shit," he said miserably, and turned away to look through the windows at the soaring suspension bridge, the estuary, and the line of sea beyond.

The sea. The one thing you could rely on to stay level.

Archibald said, "What are you talking about."

Paul kept his back to the man and his denials. He noticed the paint was coming off a life ring hooked beside the voice pipe to the crow's nest. Underneath the flaking "Artemis" you could make out another name, faded but still legible.

"R.M.S. Arcadia—Southampton."

A Cunarder. She *had* been one of the fancy ones. The thought floated, oily, pleasurable, on the great pool of Paul's unhappiness.

"Give me your jacket."

"Excuse me?"

Paul turned. The designer had his hand extended casually, as if it were his party and Paul had just come through the door. He flicked the butt of his cigarette over the port side of the bridge.

"Please," Archibald said.

In his astonishment, Paul complied. Archibald felt through the pockets, then dropped the windbreaker to the deck.

"What are you doing."

"Just checking. I meant what I said," the yacht club man continued. "There's no one behind me. I had your cousin killed. I ran this thing, right from the start."

C H A P T E R 41

Bruce Archibald's voice had not changed, Paul realized. Nor had his intonation, except for a hint of protest, of wounded pride perhaps? in the way he spoke his *I*s.

Paul's mouth was hanging open. He shut it with a snap.

Archibald brushed dust from his turtleneck, brushing off the deaths he'd referred to as well, with one backhand sweep.

"There were accidents, of course," he continued. "I seem to be surrounded by idiots. As a matter of fact, they were all accidents, except one. I'm a better naval architect than a conspirator, I guess. But I'm improving, I'm improving, give me credit. . . ."

It was the lack of transition, Paul realized. The total lack of barrier between normal talk and what he was saying now. The way his smile had not shifted or dimmed, not once. The conviction spread, slow but strong.

He had been wrong. Dead wrong. Winton had nothing to do with this. The killer, the man who caused the killing, was standing in front of him, on this ruined wheelhouse one hundred feet above the Loire estuary.

Bruce Archibald.

"I'm talking about Ashley," he said.

And now Archibald's eyes began to deepen, collecting water.

"It's such a joke. The only one I meant to have die, was the one I didn't want to die. You see, Paul"—Archibald tried familiarity—I *really* liked her."

"I—" Paul's voice came in a croak, he had to clear his throat before talking again. "I don't understand."

It was the truth.

"Yes. You see, it's lonely downtown. Where my office is. The business district, it empties after five. Where I live, in Greenwich, is all families. . . . For years," he continued, "I had nothing but my work. My SORC boats, my Admiral's Cup boats, my Twelves. You know how it is. And then she came along."

The water in Archibald's eyes swelled, tightened, became a tear that hung, restrained only by capillary action, on the rim of Archibald's left eyelid. Paul watched it grow, as if it symbolized what had happened to this man's brain, and what could befall it in the future.

"She was so pretty," Archibald said. "She was so—right. Like when you know a boat's just right? Above and beyond the righting moments, the B/T ratios? Fast, elegant, well balanced?"

Paul nodded. He knew. If Archibald were sick, what did that understanding make him?

"We were going to get married. Oh, I hadn't asked her yet. But it was understood. We were perfect, together. . . ."

Archibald's voice hardened.

"And then, *he* came along. At a party. With his big smile and his rustic charm. Jack Briggs."

Paul had never heard anyone pack so much venom into a name before. He watched as a second tear came to blend with and fatten the first. The drop trembled, translucent. It seemed to defy logic, that it should grow, and grow, and still not fall.

The yacht club man did not wipe the tear away. But for the first time his smirk faded, a little.

"Jack Briggs," he repeated. "She married him. She got him the cup work. I couldn't believe it. . . . She sold me down the river, down the river."

Archibald shook his head.

"It was the worst thing that ever happened to me. But I lived with it. And then, I heard he was cheating. Some Scandinavian engineer was helping him design it. The *Challenge*. I asked Van Meerwen to get evidence. It was illegal, of course; but so was what Briggs was doing. I wasn't sorry he got killed. He was a cheat."

"You're wrong."

The lip curled back.

"Am I? Then you took over the same boat. You broke the rules, as well. We heard about the VPP results. How it looked good. But the Dane was doing the work, the whole time. He must have. You had no experience. . . . Because of the—accident, we couldn't use the evidence Hugh got. So the next time, I hired a pro."

"And he tried to burn my yard down," Paul added, hoping the mikes were picking all this up.

Archibald, somehow nodded and shook his head at the same time. Still the single tear did not fall from its perch.

"But you wouldn't take the hint. You got nosy. You lied, you blackmailed, just like Jack Briggs. You even *slept with her*!"

Archibald was trembling, all of a sudden. His fists were knotted like roots.

The spasm passed very quickly. His voice melded itself to the story he was telling.

"You found out about Hugh Van Meerwen," he went on. "Then, she found out about me. Ashley did. She had no proof, of course."

"So you killed her?" Paul said, encouragingly.

Archibald looked sad again.

"You don't understand. She came to me. I was so happy to see her. I thought, with Jack Briggs out of the way, she wanted to see me again. Don't you get it? It would have made it all worthwhile.

"But you had corrupted her, by then. Both of you. She tried to trick me, too. She said she knew all about it. She gave me a week to tell the cops. I couldn't believe it. I was so upset. She told me you knew. I didn't want to. But I had no choice."

Archibald reached into his breast pocket. He removed and opened his wallet. He pulled out a worn three-by-five glossy and showed it to Paul.

A group of people stood frozen amid rococo columns and ship models. The model room at the New York Yacht Club. Ashley was making a face at the photographer, and Bruce Archibald was smiling at Ashley. Her dress looked familiar. Paul realized, with a mental start, it must have been the party where MacLean and Archibald had taunted him, almost two years ago.

"You killed her," Paul repeated, for the machine.

"I sent the packages," Archibald agreed.

"What?"

"Yes," Paul's colleague replied. "That's how it works. A friend of mine runs a construction company. They deal with bad problems that way. He told me. There's an answering service, and a post office box, in Grand Central Station. You send a photo, and any other information you have on the person. Fifteen thousand dollars in "C" notes. He does it within six months, or your money back. You can't stop him, once you send it. He's very good."

"The arson," Paul said. "The plane."

"Yes. Poor girl." Archibald glanced at the photo again. "But it was better that way. She didn't suffer. I told him to make sure. I didn't say anything about you, though."

The tear had disappeared, Paul realized. He had not seen it fall. Perhaps it simply evaporated on his eyelid. Slowly, theatrically, Archibald ripped the photograph in two, four, eight pieces, and flung them over the side of the bridge.

"You're really crazy, you know," Paul told him.

"What do you know about it," Archibald retorted. There was high color in his cheeks now. "How would you like it it you'd gambled everything on one project—your reputation, your business, even mortgaged your house—and some crummy hick like Jack Briggs got a foreigner to design a boat that might be better than yours? You wouldn't understand, you're like him. You think breaking the rules is fine. But that's not what the America's Cup is about. That's not the way *we* do things."

"Jesus," Paul said, "the bullshit never ends. I mean you people are so completely full of crap." Paul felt the old frustration rock him. "You people never had to break the rules because you *made* the rules. From the start. Like you used to allow only one challenging boat, it had to cross the Atlantic on its own bottom, so it had to be built heavy. But you, the New York Yacht Club, got to choose from a slew of boats, you could even change boats during the series, and all your boats were lighter and faster because they didn't have to cross the ocean. You got to check out their plans, but they couldn't see yours. It's always been like that."

"It was a game for gentlemen," Archibald hissed. "You wouldn't understand. The terms were agreed."

Paul ignored him.

"Then, you get complacent," Paul said, "and somebody beats you at your own game. And *as soon* as that happens, the 'rules' go out the window, and you start spying, stealing, lying. And now, killing. It's typical of your whole goddamn background, all the prep-school boys whining for the good ole days of Fisk and Gould when there was one law for the yacht club people and another for the rest of us. . . ."

Archibald's face got even redder. His breath came in bursts.

"It's got nothing to do with it." He spat the words at Paul on a rising pitch. "You're just ducking the issue. Which is, *I am* better than Jack, and you, and I did not cheat to do it!" He almost screamed the last phrase.

Paul looked at Archibald in horror. He had a sudden, sickening flash; he was looking at himself, how things might have been. There, but for the grace of fate, went Paul Briggs, crippled by loss, paralyzed by fear, hobbled by old jealousy.

And it was this man, and his greater insanity, who had set off the explosions that blasted him out of it.

"You need help," Paul told him, speaking softer. "Medical help."

"You don't know what you're talking about," Archibald repeated, and the lip curled again.

"I can make you get help," Paul continued, "I've recorded everything you said." He took the little machine from his hip pocket, as far as he could go without snapping the wires.

Archibald's lip curled further. The tic in his neck was quite prominent now.

"Big deal. I'll simply say you did your usual lying and cheating and tricking. I know all about your lousy tape recorders. Hugh told me."

It felt so dirty, Paul thought. The complexity of the dysfunction in this man's mind did not increase his anger. It did not cause pity either, so much as revulsion. And a sense of waste. Through the bridge windows he sought the sea with his eyes. The calm, the broad cleanness of it. The voice pipe reflected a movement, rounded in the brass. He turned to face Archibald again, and this saved him, as the flat of a broad red fire ax swung toward Paul's head.

Paul recoiled violently. The ax hissed by less than an inch from his temple. He found himself one pace or less from the end of the bridge, where it fell off into eight-decks worth of nothing.

Archibald stood by the wheel, hefting the ax. He must have moved very fast, to grab the ax off the bulkhead and sneak back so quickly and silently.

"Let's see if I can finish what the pros could not," Archibald whispered, and stepped toward Paul.

Behind Paul was death. To the right, his escape was blocked by the metal mass of the arc welder. Paul dodged and ran behind the engine-room telegraph, to a door leading to the starboard bridge wing. The door was locked. Glancing outside, Paul saw why. The wing had been cut away two feet short of the wheelhouse enclosure.

Archibald followed his progress, moving so as to keep between Paul and the only other way out, the door to the captain's day cabin and the companionway.

A box of distress flares hung next to the locked door. Paul kicked it open, with the vague idea of firing a flare pistol at his opponent, but the box was empty.

Archibald moved around the wheel and the telegraph, still blocking his escape.

Movement was dangerous. Staying still, more so.

Paul ran back the way he had come, keeping the engine-room telegraph between him and Archibald. His foot slipped on the wet deck and he almost skidded to the brink. He saved himself by falling on one hip, letting his leg brake him. He jumped back up and got behind the arc welder, only just in front of Archibald's fire ax, which clanged into the metal housing, six inches from where Paul had just stood.

Paul tried to move the welder. It was very heavy. It had dials and controls on the side Paul stood on, and three big red switches.

Archibald raised the ax again. He held it angled, for some reason, pointing the flat of it at Paul's head.

Paul twisted all three switches at once. The machine hummed into life. Dials flickered. A brass handle at the end of a long pink cable spat blue sparks. Paul reeled in the cable, picked up the handle. Grabbing it clumsily with both hands, he jabbed the sparking end in Archibald's direction.

"Get off," he yelled, "get the hell away!"

Archibald ignored him. "What I'm going to do," he explained, only a little breathlessly, "is knock you out. Not cut you. Then, hop! Overboard. It'll look like—a tragic accident. Too bad. What a shame. The Fall of the House of Briggs."

He lifted the ax high again. Paul tried to touch him with the head of the welder, but the handle was too short and he had to jump back before making contact to avoid Archibald's swing.

But Archibald had underreached, in reaction to the jab. The ax handle bounced off a corner of the welder and was deflected. It hit the coils of cable lying on the floor and cut off a chunk of pink insulation. Paul, acting on instinct, looped his end of the cable over the ax handle as the yacht club man tried to lift it again. Now he grasped both ends of the loop, dragging the ax toward him. The head of the welder spat and fizzed as it dangled from the cable's end.

There was nothing wrong with Archibald's reflexes, or his fighting instinct. He immediately let go of the ax handle and charged, angling his small height to achieve maximum impact, arms stiff into Paul's chest.

Paul's arms were still tangled in the electric cable. His attention was distracted by the sparks, as well as the scarred portion of the cable, which was beginning to brown and melt. When Archibald hit him he could not avoid going backward.

To stay on his feet would have meant swinging on the lever of his body toward the void. So he threw the cable away, as far as he could, and dropped to his knees while Archibald's momentum carried them toward the edge of the bridge. He slid on the moisture, and his toes found emptiness.

Every muscle in Paul's body seized up. He went completely rigid, fighting the slide with inertia, and stopped with both shins grinding on the edge of the severed deck, his toes smarting with the idea of vacuum.

Bruce Archibald smiled. He pulled back three steps, yanked the ax out of the tangle of cable and swung it, viciously single-minded, toward Paul's face.

Paul ducked. Now his knees, too, slid out from under him. He was flat on his belly. Everything up to his thighs hung over the cut-off deck. His breath came in short, painful bursts. He saw the ax rise again, and rolled quickly over on his back—but the deck had been cut jagged, at an angle, and he found himself with actually less ground beneath his back than he'd had under his stomach.

For the first time his center of gravity was more off the ship than on it. He was slipping, gently, over the lip of the deck. Only the rub of his clothes on the steel held him back. The little tape recorder in his hip pocket caught on the edge of metal, holding him for a second; then it slipped out. His heart slammed in great thuds. His mind refused point-blank to consider the fact that he was going to die. He sent both arms shooting out like pistons. They grasped for any purchase. The fingers of his left hand knocked painfully on the steel of the welder casing.

Just as the small of his back passed the point of no return he found the edge of one of the legs of the welder and arrested his fall with the tips of three rigid, hooked fingers.

Above him, upside down from where he lay, Archibald grinned. He bent, and put down the ax.

Paul watched his enemy, what he could see of him at any rate. He squirmed helplessly. His fingers were already sending signals of pain, panic, possible disaster. They were literally all that kept him from falling over the rim, eight decks down into that dark dank rusting hole to his death. He tried wriggling himself back toward the welder, but the same clothes that had slowed his slide toward the hole earlier hindered his progress away from it now.

Archibald reappeared in his field of vision. He reeled in the cable, and the brass handle of the welder. It was still spitting and letting off fire. He picked it up carefully, so it would not make contact with the metal deck. He poked it at Paul's fingers, a hint of what was to come.

Paul knew it was over. An arc welder ran on enough voltage to fry him in normal circumstances. Here, lying on a wet metal deck, he had no hope of surviving. The shock would roast every neuron in his body. Then, if his fingers did not lock around the leg of the welder, his jerking corpse would fall eight decks and break against the bilges of the old Cunarder.

The knowledge brought a negative of itself, a film of the images of living, faces of the people he lived with in the most basic sense; Jessica and Jenny, Bull and Lucinda.

Above him, Bruce Archibald raised the welding nozzle, ready to strike. He automatically coiled some of the cable, the way a sailor would.

His fingers touched the tear the fire ax had made in the cable.

Electricity leaped through Archibald's body. His feet grounded on the wet deck.

From Paul's point of view, the sardonic smile stretched, deepened. Abnormally wide, it seemed to encompass his whole being until, like the Cheshire Cat, there was nothing left of Archibald beside that insane smirk.

The yacht club architect began bowing backward. Then his muscles galvanized, jerked shut. He pitched forward.

Still holding onto the arc of cable, he appeared to make a little jump. He rolled stiffly, and disappeared, with virtually no sound, over the torn rim of the bridge.

Paul's back crawled. A tingling sensation pervaded his body as the voltage flowed into the deck and was grounded by the bulk of ship.

The cable was slithering by maybe three inches from his head, but Paul had no time to worry about any further electrical problems. His breath was coming in great sobs, his hands were sweating, even his fingers were sweating. The perspiration made his purchase on the welder that much more tenuous. He squirmed harder, risking that purchase nevertheless, for he had only another ten seconds at the most before his fingers gave up.

The cable went taut, then slack.

Methodically he worked the folds of sweater clear of the rim, tearing the fibers as they caught on the cut steel. It went all right for an inch, two inches. Then the belt stuck.

A deep, resonant clang sounded in the bowels of the hull. Then silence.

But that first inch had been crucial. It now allowed Paul to get a fourth finger around the leg of the welder, which in turn allowed him to squirm harder, even rock back and forth a little, and get over the obstacle of the belt.

Once the belt was hiked past the rim, he could slide his buttocks over. Finally his center of gravity rested, once more, on the solid side of the deck.

Every muscle in his body trembled violently from fatigue and shock.

A shout rang from deep, deep beneath the deck.

Someone had found Bruce Archibald.

᙮

Blue lights. The two-tone blasts of police and ambulance. The utter horror and guilt of Pierre Desbarres, who had allowed his colleagues to go off on their own.

But there were advantages to wearing a label. Naval architects had an ex officio right to walk around ships. Naval architects under the escort of the vice-president in charge of design, with an introduction from Marcel Morgat himself, were people of "standing," who would not be swayed by the base motivations of ordinary mortals.

Or so the inspector of the local gendarmerie seemed to feel. By the time he got there, Paul had repeated the story six or seven times—to the welders who found Archibald, to the wrecking crew foreman, to Desbarres. Each time he gave them the simple facts of the case.

They had switched on the welder. Bruce Archibald wanted to demonstrate how it worked. He touched a fault in the cable. The jolt from the current flipped him over the deck, into the hole leading to the pump room.

Paul omitted everything else. It seemed so much simpler that way. He had even put the fire ax back on its hanger on the bulkhead, so there would be no awkward questions.

Each time Paul told the story he was subjected to an angry lecture about not touching equipment that belonged to other people. The anger was based mainly on apprehension about what the next man up the totem pole might say. Only the inspector gave him sympathy. But he kept Paul at his side until a preliminary autopsy was performed later that afternoon.

Death had come to Archibald by cardiac arrest due to electrocution and/or massive cerebral trauma, the hospital told the inspector.

Paul signed a statement, and he was free to go.

By then it was well into the evening and Paul would not have cared if he stayed or left.

He did not care about the stiff, reproving looks he got from two New York Yacht Club people who came up to take charge of the naval architect's remains.

He did not care about the puzzled, almost awed expression on Sal Vanzetti's face when he came to pick Paul up.

He did not even care about the killer Archibald claimed was looking for him. It seemed obvious the contract would be annulled by the death of the man who ordered it. Assuming he worked abroad at all. Assuming Archibald was telling the truth. These were too many assumptions to make for someone as tired as he was.

When he got back to the hotel he fell asleep on the bed without even taking his shoes off.

C H A P T E R 4 2

The television screen showed two Twelve-Meters, one blue, one silver, dueling in the great green swells off the Île de Re.

The two boats looked like weapons in the hands of master swordsmen. Their long, sharp bows split the water cleanly. Two complex white curls rolled and folded off each slice. They tacked and whirled, feinted and jibed with the grace and speed of samurai.

The TV editors juggled camera angles: helicopter shots, close-ups from the air, close-ups from the sea.

One of the close-ups showed *Challenge*'s crew losing the genoa as the port winch suddenly stripped its gears.

There was an onboard camera on *Old Glory* that featured the New Yorkers in full, salty, sweaty action.

But the last shot before the announcer came back on showed the silver boat crossing the finish line half a boat's length in front of *Old Glory* to win the the first series of challengers' eliminations for the America's Cup.

The Le Plaisance café erupted in a chorus of quiet cheers. Joe McMurdo called for another round of Kronenbourg. Most of the other syndicates believed in a monastic, super athlete style of life. No booze, plenty of sit-ups, steak and steroids, but not McMurdo. Drinking, in moderation, was part of sailing, McMurdo believed.

Paul smiled as he watched the *Challenge* crew try to kill their excitement, hoarding luck for the forty-odd races still to come. They *were* real sailors, after all, he thought; superstitious like the rest of their tribe.

"It's been one hell of a couple o' weeks," Warren Hillman commented across the table.

Paul nodded, thinking of Archibald, and how impossibly low it started.

Jessica's head nodded against Paul's shoulder, reminding him of how little sleep he'd had, despite the fatigue that peaked at Penhoet. He'd wanted nothing but rest, at that point.

Instead, he'd had to confront the normal hassles of reballasting, changing the rig, McMurdo getting almost as crotchety as Queegie used to as he pushed to get the boat ready for the first elimination series. Twenty-hour days, broken only by catnaps.

Yet, somehow, even the little sleep he had got over that period seemed to relax him more than the twelve hours of tossing and turning he'd occasionally managed in Maine. There were no dreams, for one thing. There were no more financial problems, either; as predicted, winning the challengers' side of the D-K Cup had opened the taps of sponsor money.

The news that came yesterday, about the police arresting an American national with a concealed handgun not far from the Twelve-Meter center, was just icing on the cake.

Somehow, all the messy loose ends of the last two goddawful years were trying themselves up.

Paul looked around the bar, feeling absurdly pleased with himself.

Nat was trying to ask the bartender, in a mixture of GI pidgin and sixth-grade French, if they ever showed a program called "M*A*S*H" on TV over here.

"Mache?" the bartender said, and chewed suggestively.

Vanzetti was knocking back cognac and sweet-talking a French girl in the corner. Michel, the polyester-clad guard, was passed out at the next table, a victim of anise.

Lucinda sat proudly in a plastic chair, exuding the almost palpable faith of which mothers knew the secret. The recriminations about Ashley, never spoken, were behind her. To Lucinda, the cup was already won. Her aura did not even fade when Squidlips, spotting a group of Compudyne sailors, showed his buttocks in their direction from the middle of the veranda.

Jenny Crooke got up from the table she shared with the new navigator and his wife. She slipped through the knots of people very easily, double-clutching her hips and stomach the way only women could, in and out of the crowd. She wore jeans, a T-shirt, and flip-flops, and her hair was braided up. No shades, tonight. Her eyes seemed very big and warm in the open.

"You going to check on the boat?" she asked, dropping into the seat beside Paul and Jessica. The offer was implied. Paul told her yes.

Paul's daughter woke up. She looked at Jenny. Her eyes were very level and serious.

Paul carried her over to Lucinda and said, "I'll be right back."

"He always says that," Jessica told her grandmother.

"I mean it, this time."

"Promise?" Jessica insisted.

"Jess," Paul told her seriously, "you know I'll always be back. And after this is over I'll try not to be away so much. I'll do my best, anyway. That's a promise, too," Paul told the girl. Then he went out into the fragrant night.

The Plaisance was right on the Avenue du Quai Marillac, just south of the Twelve-Meter area. There were three other cafés right next to it. They had been adopted, respectively, by the British, the Germans, and the Swedes.

Paul and Jenny walked, very close to each other, elbows touching often, listening to men talking in different languages about the same things.

They were completely oblivious to the shape that slipped out of one of the bars and followed, casually, thirty paces behind.

The night was half overcast, a good ten-to-fifteen-knot southwesterly wind, but between the clouds the stars were very bright.

"I like your daughter," Jenny Crooke said. "She's smart. She refuses to accept me on faith."

"She will," Paul said, hopefully. "Accept you, I mean."

"I think so, too," the girl replied.

Paul stopped, put his hands on her shoulders, and kissed her, hard. Her mouth was soft yet strong in response.

When they got back to walking Jenny said, without bothering to introduce the subject, "It really feels a lot easier now. It's as if you used to be stooping, mahn, I don't know, bent under this bloody great weight. And now, suddenly, the weight's not there anymore."

"Yeah," Paul said. "I remembered how to draw boats again. And I guess you might have had something to do with it, too."

At the gate of the restricted area they showed their passes to two CRS guards. The guards could not smile, though they'd seen Paul almost every night for the last month. They wore jackboots, and submachine guns strapped to their shoulders.

A patrol boat of the French navy showed lights where it was moored at the entrance to the Twelve-Meter pens. It had sonar and hydrophones to listen for divers. Notices on the breakwater warned that swimmers or divers trying funny business would have under-water stun grenades dropped in their vicinity. No one, so far, had tried any funny business.

The *Challenge* pen lay third from the far, northern end of the jetty wall. Paul and Jenny walked slowly down the quayside, thighs touch-ing, talking about the different boats. When they got to the series of floats the Twelve was moored to, Paul lifted Jenny to the deck the way he had first lifted her on the bunk of the FH 38. Then he jumped aboard himself, taking care not to break an ankle on a box full of disassembled winch parts someone had stashed in the cockpit, ready to repair in the morning.

⚓

The sound of feet landing on the deck was very loud to the man sitting on sail bags in the *Challenge*'s sewer.

One pair of feet, probably male by the weight. Walking aft now. Talking. There was someone with him, on the dock probably. That might pose a problem, but it was unlikely.

Every night the naval architect checked his boat. He always checked below decks, in the sewer. He always checked alone.

The second man was probably on the next boat, and would most likely go about his business.

If he did not, if he wondered why Paul Briggs did not come back out of the *Challenge* and came to investigate—well, that would make two, for the price of one. "Mr. Cranston" was getting a real bargain, the man thought, a mite resentfully.

The man took out his pistol. He checked it by feel, making sure the magazine was full, a round in the barrel, safety off. Silencer screwed tight.

All in all, he would be glad to get rid of this job. It had been one of the messiest of his career. Hitting the wrong man, wounding security was not his style. Just as squatting for hours inside the close, dark hull of a racing yacht was not his style, either.

He'd done worse, of course. Once he'd staked out a suspected VC commissar by lying prone in a rice paddy for a whole night.

But it was better, far better, in the open

The hatch cover scraped. The man moved silently behind one of the thick fiberglass ribs of the yacht. He'd checked it out beforehand. If he lay against the skin of the hull itself, bracing his feet on one of the hydraulic pipes that led to the mast, he would be completely invisible from forward when Briggs lowered himself, the way he always did, into the starboard hatchway.

♒

Paul lowered himself into the starboard hatchway and found the switch for the battery-powered lamp that illuminated the sewer.

The long, cavernous hull of the Twelve-Meter stretched before him. Two sail bags lay stacked neatly to each side, in the bow section. In the other direction, converging with distance and darkness, you could see the thick honeycomb ribs supporting the hull; the mast, and its ram mechanism; the mess of hydraulic accumulators and pipes leading from the keel, rudder, and pumps to winches on deck.

To another man it might seem a tunnel of confusion. To Paul, it was familiar as his own face, and twice as normal.

A stranger entered all this familiarity. A man dressed in jeans, running shoes, and a team sweater bearing one of the plastic photo ID cards that identified America's Cup crewmembers.

A man with neat features, maybe a little small for the middle-weight body attached to it. Blond hair, dark eyes. Not fat, not skinny. A very unremarkable man, except for his gloved hands and the ugly black snout of the silenced automatic he held in one of them.

So the police had got the wrong man, was Paul's first thought.

His second thought was, I am going to die now.

There was no calm clarity that came with the knowledge. None of the fatalism of Arctic explorers succumbing to the endless cold. Not even the flash of faces he'd seen on the bridge of the old

Cunarder. Just a silent scream of protest because he'd promised Jessica he'd be back.

The last thought was, Jenny would wonder what happened to him, and come down to look. He'd left her sitting by the wheel, looking at the harbor, but she wouldn't sit there forever. He had to do something to prevent her from getting hurt, before the finger in the plastic glove pulled the trigger through.

Paul started to raise his hands, hoping to slam the hatch down, or at least switch off the light but as soon as he started to move the arm stiffened, the gun came up to the level of Paul's eyes and the man shook his head.

Paul froze. He knew he was going to die but his body hadn't got the message.

There was one other way.

"Who—" Paul's throat froze up, just as it had on the ex-Arcadia. The words came out in a low croak: "Who the hell are you."

"Shut up."

The voice was American.

"Why are you—"

"I told you to shut up." The finger tightened, the trigger actually moved, and Paul's body tensed, waiting for the shock of an ounce of lead tearing through his chest at 550 feet per second.

"Move backward." The voice stayed in the whisper range, carried almost no inflection. The man shook his gun a little, to encourage him. He moved toward Paul, his arm still stiff, his whole being, it seemed, condensed along the line of the pistol sights.

Paul moved backward. He had to feel his way, in an ever-increasing half-crouch, stepping over sail bags as the bow narrowed to a point, thinking the killer probably planned to leave his body way forward, hidden under some of the sails, where it would not be found until the morning.

Then he stopped, realizing the farther he moved, the less his voice was going to carry when he shouted.

And he had to shout. Jenny was up there somewhere. He had to yell loud, the words fast, the tone conveying the mortal danger she stood in.

The man gestured again. He had stopped just short of the open hatchway, short of the glare of the lamp. He was a good fifteen feet away now, not the easiest range for accuracy with a silenced pistol, but the preference for cover was instinctive.

Paul filled his lungs. And yelled.

"Jenny, *run*—"

When the sound came the man took two quick steps forward, to make sure, and pulled the trigger just as a defective, forty-five-pound, high-carbon steel winch drum came crashing through the open hatch on his head and neck.

The bullet hit a moving target. In the very act of yelling Paul had thrown himself sideways. He felt a violent tug on his left arm. He bounced off the hull surface and landed on the squishy, slippery surface of the sail bags.

Immediately he pushed himself off, but his left arm had pins and needles all over it and he succeeded only in rolling back to the other side of the hull. His whole body waited for the next bullets, the quick pain, the spreading numbness. Nothing came.

He rolled to his feet, eyes staring aft as if he would be able to see the lead flying through the air in his direction. But there were no more bullets; only huddled, low movement.

His brain sorted out the patterns.

The stranger was on his knees, shaking his head repeatedly. One of the winch drums rolled, inexplicably, next to his feet. His left arm groped for something—the pistol. With his right arm he was trying to fend off a lithe, squirming force that was tearing into his shoulders and back like a tornado, its breath coming in gasps.

Jenny Crooke. Her feet got a purchase on the deck and pushed hard. The killer lost his balance and toppled onto his left side. His right hand came up as he fell. It held the pistol in an awkward grip. There was a hollow bang above their heads.

Paul shouted again and threw himself convulsively in their direction. But he was too far away, and the numbness in his arm hindered his stretch. He thudded down short of the killer and tried scrambling to his feet, but slipped on something wet and fell again, on his stomach. His eyes locked helplessly as the man stood up, readjusted his grip on the pistol and brought it around to bear on Jenny. She too was mesmerized by the black barrel. She punched and kicked at waist level, struggling desperately to get the man off balance again. Her eyes shone white.

Then something large and dark dropped out of the hatchway, obscuring the light. The shape hit the deck in perfect knees-bent posture. Someone holding a squat revolver with two hands. Black eyes glittered furiously over a bandit's moustache.

"FREEZE, MOTHERFUCKER!" Vanzetti screamed.

The killer turned. Without hesitating he aimed the pistol away from Jenny toward this new intrusion.

There was a tremendous boom, magnified tenfold in the close confines of the hull. Smoke gushed from Vanzetti's pistol.

The man was pushed backward, as if by a hydraulic ram. He doubled over. His gun dropped to the deck. Then he toppled, slowly, onto a sail bag. He lay on one side, breathing harshly.

"You bastard," Vanzetti whispered, staring at the killer. He licked dry lips. "I *knew* you wouldn't let yourself get picked up on the street."

But Paul could hear nothing through the ringing in his ears.

In any case he was no longer paying attention to Vanzetti. He had eyes only for Jenny Crooke, who was crawling toward him over the prone body of the killer. Panic ran riot in her face until she saw him move. She scrambled to her feet and threw herself in Paul's direction, the black braid flying in her wake. Even in the poor glow of the sewer lamp, her eyes spoke of things that were the antithesis of fear and loss and the shame of their combining.

Things really were looking up, Paul thought.

He braced himself to catch her.